RITA Award–winning author
Barbara Metzger
rings in the yuletide with . . .

Father Christmas

AND

Christmas Wishes

Together for the first time in one volume!

**Praise for the romances
of Barbara Metzger**

"Witty [and] certain to entertain."
—*Publishers Weekly* (starred review)

"Delightful [and] fun."—Under the Covers

"Metzger's prose absolutely tickles the funny
bone."—*Los Angeles Daily News*

"Barbara Metzger's voice is always fresh! With wit
and inimitable style, she dares to go beyond the
cliché to create uniquely Metzger stories."
—*The Literary Times*

"The creative genius of Barbara Metzger utterly
enchants."—*Romantic Times*

"One of the freshest voices in the Regency
genre."—*Rave Reviews*

Father Christmas
AND
Christmas Wishes

Barbara Metzger

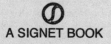
A SIGNET BOOK

SIGNET
Published by New American Library, a division of
Penguin Group (USA) Inc., 375 Hudson Street,
New York, New York 10014, U.S.A.
Penguin Books Ltd, 80 Strand,
London WC2R 0RL, England
Penguin Books Australia Ltd, 250 Camberwell Road,
Camberwell, Victoria 3124, Australia
Penguin Books Canada Ltd, 10 Alcorn Avenue,
Toronto, Ontario, Canada M4V 3B2
Penguin Books (NZ), cnr Airborne and Rosedale Roads,
Albany, Auckland 1310, New Zealand

Penguin Books Ltd, Registered Offices:
80 Strand, London WC2R 0RL, England

Published by Signet, an imprint of New American Library, a division of Penguin Group (USA) Inc. *Father Christmas* and *Christmas Wishes* were originally published in separate editions by Ballantine Books, a division of Random House, Inc.

First Signet Printing (Double Edition), November 2004
10 9 8 7 6 5 4 3 2 1

Dedicated to Peace on Earth,
Goodwill to All Mankind.
Soon.

Author's Note

To err is human, to forgive divine.
To make corrections is . . . not permitted.

Authors love having their books reprinted. New readers, new sales, and new opportunities to make an old book better. Unfortunately, the economic constraints of publishing the double volumes are such that no changes are possible in order to keep the price such a bargain for readers. I am, therefore, begging your forgiveness for the mistakes, misprints, and muddled titles of nobility.

I hope the errors do not ruin your pleasure in the stories, and I hope I know better now than to make the same mistake again. New ones, maybe.

With best wishes,
Barbara Metzger

Father Christmas

Chapter One

The Duke of Ware needed an heir. Like a schoolyard taunt, the gruesome refrain floated in his mind, bobbing to the surface on a current of brandy. Usually a temperate man, His Grace was just a shade on the go. It was going to take more than a shade to get him to go to Almack's.

"Hell and blast!" Leland Warrington, fifth and at this point possibly last Duke of Ware, consulted his watch again. Ten o'clock, and everyone knew Almack's patronesses barred its doors at eleven. Not even London's premiere *parti*, wealth, title, and looks notwithstanding, could gain admittance after the witching hour. "Blasted witches," Ware cursed once more, slamming his glass down on the table that stood so conveniently near his so-comfortable leather armchair at White's. "Damnation."

His companion snapped up straighter in his facing seat. "What's that? The wine gone off?" The Honorable Crosby Fanshaw sipped cautiously at his own drink. "Seems fine to me." He called for another bottle.

Fondly known as Crow for his anything-but-somber style of dress, the baronet was a studied contrast to his longtime friend. The duke was the one wearing the stark black and white of Weston's finest evening wear, spread over broad shoulders and well-muscled thighs, while Crow

1

Fanshaw's spindly frame was draped in magenta pantaloons, saffron waistcoat, lime green wasp-waisted coat. The duke looked away. Fanshaw would never get into Almack's in that outfit. Then again, Fanshaw didn't need to get into Almack's.

"No, it's not the wine, Crow. It's a wife. I need one."

The baronet slipped one manicured finger under his elaborate neckcloth to loosen the noose conjured up by the very thought of matrimony. He shuddered. "Devilish things, wives."

"I'll drink to that," Ware said, and did. "But I need one nevertheless if I'm to beget the next duke."

"Ah." Crow nodded sagely, careful not to disturb his pomaded curls. "Noblesse oblige and all that. The sacred duty of the peerage: to beget more little aristocratic blue bloods to carry on the name. I thank heaven m'brother holds the title. Let Virgil worry about the succession and estates."

"With you as heir, he'd need to." Crow Fanshaw wouldn't know a mangel-wurzel from manure, and they both knew it.

The baronet didn't take offense. "What, ruin m'boots in dirt? M'valet would give notice, then where would I be? 'Sides, Virgil's managing to fill his nursery nicely, two boys and a girl. Then there are m'sister's parcel of brats if he needs extras. I'm safe." He raised his glass in a toast. "Condolences, old friend."

Ware frowned, lowering thick dark brows over his hazel eyes. Easy for Crow to laugh, his very soul wasn't engraved with the Ware family motto: *Semper servimus.* We serve forever. Forever, dash it, the duke unnecessarily reminded himself. His heritage, everything he was born and bred to be and to believe, demanded an heir. Posterity demanded it, all those acres and people dependent upon him demanded it, Aunt Eudora demanded it! God, King, and Country, that's what the Wares served, she insisted. Well, Leland made his donations to the church, he took his tedious seat in Parliament, and he served as a diplomat when the Foreign Office needed him. That was not enough. The

Bible said be fruitful and multiply, quoted his childless aunt. The King, bless his mad soul, needed more loyal peers to advise and direct his outrageous progeny. And the entire country, according to Eudora Warrington, would go to rack and ruin without a bunch of little Warringtons trained to manage Ware's vast estates and investments. At the very least, her annuity might be in danger.

Leland checked his watch again. Ten-ten. He felt as if he were going to the tooth-drawer, dreading the moment yet wishing it were over. "What time do you have, Crow?"

Crosby fumbled at the various chains crisscrossing his narrow chest. "I say, you must have an important appointment, the way you keep eyeing your timepiece. Which is it, that new red-haired dancer at the opera or the dashing widow you had up in your phaeton yesterday?" While the duke sat glaring, Fanshaw pulled out his quizzing glass, then a seal with his family crest before finally retrieving his watch fob. "Fifteen minutes past the hour."

Ware groaned. "Almack's" was all he could manage to say. It was enough.

Fanshaw dropped his watch and grabbed up the looking glass by its gem-studded handle, tangling ribbons and chains as he surveyed his friend for signs of dementia. "I thought you said Almack's."

"I did. I told you, I need an heir."

"But Almack's, Lee? Gads, you must be dicked in the nob. Castaway, that's it." He pushed the bottle out of the duke's reach.

"Not nearly enough," His Grace replied, pulling the decanter back and refilling his glass. "I promised Aunt Eudora I'd look over the latest crop of dewy-eyed debs."

Crosby downed a glass in commiseration. "I understand about the heir and all, but there must be an easier way, by Jupiter. I mean, m'brother's girl is making her come-out this year. She's got spots. And her friends giggle. Think on it, man, they are, what? Seventeen? Eighteen? And you're thirty-one!"

"Thirty-two," His Grace growled, "as my aunt keeps reminding me."

"Even worse. What in the world do you have in common with one of those empty-headed infants?"

"What do I have in common with that redhead from the opera? She's only eighteen, and the only problem you have with that is she's in my bed, not yours."

"But she's a ladybird! You don't have to talk to them, not like a wife!"

The duke stood as if to go. "Trust me, I don't intend to have anything more to do with this female I'll marry than it takes to get me a son."

"If a son is all you want, why don't you just adopt one? Be easier in the long run, more comfortable, too. M'sister's got a surplus. I'm sure she'd be glad to get rid of one or two, the way she's always trying to pawn them off on m'mother so she can go to some house party or other."

The duke ignored his friend's suggestion that the next Duke of Ware be anything less than a Warrington, but he did sit down. "That's another thing: No son of mine is going to be raised up by nannies and tutors and underpaid schoolmasters."

"Why not? That's the way we were brought up, and we didn't turn out half bad, did we?"

Leland picked a bit of imaginary fluff off his superfine sleeve. Not half bad? Not half good, either, he reflected. Crow was an amiable fribble, while he himself was a libertine, a pleasure-seeker, an ornament of society. Oh, he was a conscientious landowner, for a mostly absentee landlord, and he did manage to appear at the House for important votes. Otherwise his own entertainment—women, gaming, sporting—was his primary goal. There was nothing of value in his life. He intended to do better by his son. "I mean to be a good father to the boy, a guide, a teacher, a friend."

"A Bedlamite, that's what. Try being a friend to some runny-nosed brat with scraped knees and a pocketful of worms." Crosby shivered. "I know just the ticket to cure you of such bubble-brained notions: Why don't you come down to Fanshaw Hall with me for the holidays? Virgil'd be happy to have you for the cards and hunting, and m'sister-in-law would be in alt to have such a nonpareil as houseguest. That niece who's being fired off this season will be there, so you can see how hopeless young chits are, all airs and affectations one minute, tears and tantrums the next. Why, if you can get Rosalie to talk of anything but gewgaws and gossip, I'll eat my hat. Best of all, m'sister will be at the Hall with her nursery brood. No, best of all is if the entire horde gets the mumps and stays home. But, 'struth, you'd change your tune about this fatherhood gammon if you just spent a day with the little savages."

Ware smiled. "I don't mean to insult your family, but your sister's ill-behaved brats only prove my point that this whole child-rearing thing could be improved upon with a little careful study."

"Trust me, Lee, infants ain't like those new farming machines you can read up on. Come down and see. At least I can promise you a good wine cellar at the Hall."

The duke shook his head. "Thank you, Crow, but I have to refuse. You see, I really am tired of spending the holidays with other people's families."

"What I see is you've been bitten bad by this new bug of yours. Carrying on the line. Littering the countryside with butterstamps. Next thing you know, you'll be pushing a pram instead of racing a phaeton. I'll miss you, Lee." He flicked a lacy handkerchief from his sleeve and dabbed at his eyes while the duke grinned at the performance. Fanshaw's next words changed that grin into so fierce a scowl that a lesser man, or a less loyal friend, would have been tempted to bolt: "Don't mean to be indelicate, but you know getting leg-shackled isn't any guarantee of getting heirs."

"Of course I know that, blast it! I ought to, I've already been married." The duke finished his drink. "Twice." He tossed back another glassful to emphasize the point. "And all for nothing."

Fanshaw wasn't one to let a friend drink alone, even if his words were getting slurred and his thoughts muddled. He refilled his own glass. Twice. "Not for nothing. Got a handsome dowry both times."

"Which I didn't need," His Grace muttered into his drink.

"And got the matchmaking mamas off your back until you learned to depress their ambitions with one of your famous setdowns."

"Which if I'd learned earlier, I wouldn't be in this hobble today."

The duke's first marriage had been a love match: He was in love with the season's reigning Toast, Carissa was in love with his wealth and title. Her mother made sure he never saw past the Diamond's beauty to the cold, rock-hard shrew beneath who didn't want to be his wife, she wanted to be a duchess. There wasn't one extravagance she didn't indulge, not one risqué pleasure she didn't gratify, not one mad romp she didn't join. Until she broke her beautiful neck in a curricle race.

Ware's second marriage was one of convenience, except that it wasn't. He carefully selected a quiet, retiring sort of girl whose pale loveliness was as different from Carissa's flamboyance as night from day. *Her* noble parents had managed to conceal, while they were dickering over the settlements, that Lady Floris was a sickly child, that her waiflike appeal had more to do with a weak constitution than any gentle beauty. Floris was content to stay in the shadows after their wedding, until she became a shadow. Then she faded away altogether. Ware was twice a widower, never a father. To his knowledge, he'd never even sired a bastard on one of his mistresses, but he didn't want to think about the implications of that.

"What time do you have?"

Crosby peered owl-eyed at his watch, blinked, then turned it right side up. "Ten-thirty. Time for another drink."

6

He raised his glass, spilling only a drop on the froth of lace at his shirt-sleeve. "To your bride."

Leland couldn't do it. The wine would turn to vinegar on his tongue. Instead, he proposed a toast of his own. "To my cousin Tony, the bastard to blame for this whole deuced coil."

Crosby drank, but reflected, "If he was a bastard, then it wouldn't have mattered if the nodcock went and got himself killed. He couldn't have been your heir anyway."

His Grace waved that aside with one elegant if unsteady hand. "Tony was a true Warrington all right, my father's only brother's only son. My heir. So *he* got to go fight against Boney when the War Office turned me down."

"Protective of their dukes, those chaps."

"And *he* got to be a hero, the lucky clunch."

"Uh, not to be overparticular, but live heroes are lucky, dead ones ain't."

Leland went on as though his friend hadn't spoken: "And he was a fertile hero to boot. Old Tony didn't have to worry about shuffling off this mortal coil without a trace. He left twins, twin boys, no less, the bounder, and he didn't even have a title to bequeath them or an acre of land!"

"Twin boys, you say? Tony's get? There's your answer, Lee, not some flibbertigibbet young miss. Go gather the sprigs and have the raising of 'em your way if that's what you want to do. With any luck they'll be out of nappies and you can send 'em off to school as soon as you get tired of 'em. Should take about a month, I'd guess."

Ware frowned. "I can't go snabble my cousin's sons, Crow. Tony's widow just brought them back to her parents' house from the Peninsula."

Fanshaw thought on it a minute, chewing his lower lip. "Then marry that chit, I say. You get your heirs with Warrington blood, your brats to try to make into proper English gentlemen, and a proven breeder into the bargain. 'Sides, she can't be an antidote; Tony Warrington had taste."

7

The duke merely looked down his slightly aquiline nose and stood up to leave. "She's a local vicar's daughter."

"Good enough to be Mrs. Major Warrington, eh, but not the Duchess of Ware?" The baronet nodded, not noticing that his starched shirtpoints disarranged his artful curls. "Then you'd best toddle off to King Street, where the *ton* displays its merchandise. Unless . . ."

Ware turned back like a drowning man hearing the splash of a tossed rope. "Unless . . . ?"

"Unless you ask the widow for just one of the bantlings. She might just go for it. I mean, how many men are going to take on a wife with *two* tokens of her dead husband's devotion to support? There's not much space in any vicarage I know of, and you said yourself Tony didn't leave much behind for them to live on. 'Sides, you can appeal to her sense of fairness. She has two sons and you have none."

Leland removed the bottle and glass from his friend's vicinity on his way out of the room. "You have definitely had too much to drink, my tulip. Your wits have gone begging for dry land."

And the Duke of Ware still needed an heir.

Heaving breasts, fluttering eyelashes, gushing simpers, blushing whimpers—and those were the hopeful mamas. The daughters were worse. Aunt Eudora could ice-skate in Hades before her nephew returned to Almack's.

Ware had thought he'd observe the crop of debutantes from a discreet, unobtrusive distance. Sally Jersey thought differently. With pointed fingernails fastened to his wrist like the talons of a raptor, she dragged her quarry from brazen belle to arrogant heiress to wilting wallflower. At the end of each painful, endless dance, when he had, perforce, to return his partner to her chaperone, there was *la* Jersey waiting in prey with the next willing sacrificial virgin.

The Duke of Ware needed some air.

He told the porter at the door he was going to blow a

cloud, but he didn't care if the fellow let him back in or not. Leland didn't smoke. He never had, but he thought he might take it up now. Perhaps the foul odor, yellowed fingers, and stained teeth could discourage some of these harpies, but he doubted it.

Despite the damp chill in the air, the duke was not alone on the outer steps of the marriage mart. At first all he could see in the gloomy night was the glow from a sulphurous cigar. Then another, younger gentleman stepped out of the fog.

"Is that you, Ware? Here at Almack's? I cannot believe it," exclaimed Nigel, the scion of the House of Ellerby which, according to rumors, was more than a tad dilapidated. Hence the young baron's appearance at Almack's, Leland concluded. "Dash it, I wish I'd been in on the bet." Which propensity to gamble likely accounted for the Ellerbys' crumbling coffers.

"Bet? What bet?"

"The one that got you to Almack's, Duke. By Zeus, it must have been a famous wager! Who challenged you? How long must you stay before you can collect? How much—"

"There was no wager," Ware quietly inserted into the youth's enthusiastic litany.

The cigar dropped from Ellerby's fingers. His mouth fell open. "No wager? You mean . . . ?"

"I came on my own. As a favor to my aunt, if you must know."

Ellerby added two plus two and, to the duke's surprise, came up with the correct, dismaying answer. "B'gad, wait till the sharks smell fresh blood in the water." He jerked his head, weak chin and all, toward the stately portals behind them.

Leland grimaced. "Too late, they've already got the scent."

"Lud, there will be females swooning in your arms and chits falling off horses on your doorstep. I'd get out of town if I were you. Then again, word gets out you're in the market for a new bride, you won't be safe anywhere. With all those holiday house parties coming up, you'll be showered with invitations."

The duke could only agree. That was the way of the world.

"Please, Your Grace," Ellerby whined, "don't accept Lady Carstaire's invite. I'll be seated below the salt if you accept."

No slowtop either, Leland nodded toward the closed doors. "Tell me which one is Miss Carstaire, so I can sidestep the introduction."

"She's the one in puce tulle with mouse brown sausage curls and a squint." At Ware's look of disbelief, the lordling added, "And ten thousand pounds a year."

"I think I can manage not to succumb to the lady's charms," Ware commented dryly, then had to listen to the coxcomb's gratitude.

"And I'll give you fair warning, Duke, if you do accept for any of those house parties, lock your door and never go anywhere alone. The misses and their mamas will be quicker to yell 'compromise' than you can say 'Jack Rabbit.' "

Leland gravely thanked Lord Ellerby for the advice, hoping the baron wasn't such an expert on compromising situations from trying to nab a rich wife the cad's way. Fortune-hunting was bad enough. He wished him good luck with Miss Carstaire, but declined Ellerby's suggestion that they return inside together. His Grace had had enough. And no, he assured the baron, he was not going to accept any of the holiday invitations. The Duke of Ware was going to spend Christmas right where he belonged, at Ware Hold in Warefield, Warwickshire, with his own family: one elderly aunt, two infant cousins.

Before going to bed that night, Leland had another brandy to ease the headache he already had. He sat down to write his agent in Warefield to notify the household of his plans, then he started to write to Tony's widow, inviting her to the castle. Before he got too far past the salutation, however, Crow Fanshaw's final, foxed suggestion kept echoing in his mind: The Duke of Ware should get a fair share.

Chapter Two

"Of all the outrageous, high-handed, arrogant—"

Vicar Beckwith cleared his throat. "That is enough, Graceanne."

"No, Papa, it is not nearly enough! That . . . that bounder thinks he can simply appear in Warefield village and claim Willy! What am I, then, his liege vassal from the feudal days, that some dirty-dish duke can demand my firstborn son? By Heaven, I am not!"

"I said that is enough, Graceanne," the vicar firmly declared. "I shall not have blasphemy at the dinner table, nor such disrespect for your betters poured into Prudence's innocent ears."

Better? Graceanne fumed, but she looked across the table to where her younger sister sat. Pru's blond head was deferentially lowered, but not enough that Graceanne couldn't see the smirk on her lips or the malicious gleam in her eye. If there was innocence at this table, the overcooked capon they were about to eat held more of it than seventeen-year-old Prudence.

When Graceanne would have continued to argue—indeed, she was so angry she would have thrown crockery had she still been in Portugal—her mother begged, "Please, dear, my nerves." Mrs. Beckwith, in her Bath chair at the other end of the sparsely filled table, dabbed at her forehead with a wisp of cloth.

Graceanne subsided, and addressed herself to decapitating a boiled parsnip. She had to choke back her ire when her father smoothed out the embossed page of Ware's letter—a letter she couldn't help but notice was addressed to herself, Mrs. Anthony Warrington—and stated, "His Grace's claim to Wellesley is not entirely out of bounds, daughter. I'll have to think on it."

Graceanne put down her knife and fork. She loathed parsnips and the capon tasted like sawdust. As calmly as she could, choking on the urge to scream, she said, "There is nothing to think about, Papa. Wellesley—Willy—is my son the same as Leslie. I shall never let anyone else have the raising of either of them, duke or not."

"You are being overhasty and emotional, daughter." The vicar managed to express his disapproval around a mouthful of green beans. Then again, the vicar never had trouble expressing his disapproval. "And selfish. Think of the advantages young Wellesley would have."

Graceanne knew her father was thinking of the advantages *he* would gain by letting Ware have Willy: the gratitude of a wealthy patron, and one less little boy creating noise and mess and expense in his frugal household. Furthermore, she suspected her father considered the identical twins to be freaks of nature, somehow unholy. He'd be relieved to have the taint of the diabolical removed from his hearth.

Beckwith was warming to his theme: "I shouldn't have to remind you that what I can provide on a parson's income can never come close to what Ware can offer. Think of Wellesley's education, the career opportunities, the chance to better himself in the world."

"The chance to become a care-for-naught wastrel like his noble benefactor? An opportunity to become a libertine? Or perhaps you think three-year-old Willy needs lessons in arrogance? Is that what you want for your grandson?"

Beckwith paid her objections as much notice as he would

have the capon's protests over being eaten. "I am certain that on reflection you wouldn't wish to hold the boy back with your foolish prejudices and idle gossip. Think how much further our limited resources could stretch in Leslie's direction if the duke takes over Wellesley's upbringing. Yes, a proper mother would set aside her own whims for the best interests of her child."

"Whims? Why, I—"

"Cook tells me that May Turner is ailing, Graceanne dear," Mrs. Beckwith interrupted in quavering tones. "Perhaps you would go visit her this afternoon? I would, naturally, but . . ."

"Of course, Mother." Graceanne returned to pushing the parsnips around on her dish, despite her father's glower. At least her twenty-three years, motherhood, and widowed status gave her the privilege of leaving food on her plate. Heaven knew she had to fight for every other right. But her children? No one could steal them from her.

"I agree with Papa, Grace," Prudence was saying although no one had asked her opinion. "I think you should at least consider the duke's offer to take Willy. After all, it's not as if you'll never see him again. He'll be just next door at Ware Hold. You can visit anytime."

"And take my little sister to cheer him up, especially when the duke is in residence, or happens to have guests? In particular, young bachelor guests who are well-to-pass?" Graceanne couldn't keep the sarcasm from her voice; Prudence had never had an unselfish motive yet. Willy's well-being was so far from being Pru's major consideration that the little baggage had managed to misplace both twins just last week when she found a handsome Irishman to flirt with. Graceanne couldn't blame her entirely, since Warefield was practically devoid of both personable young men and lively entertainments the vicar deemed suitable for his offspring. Graceanne wished she might brighten the younger girl's life, sure that would sweeten her disposition, but not at Willy's expense.

"What's so wrong with wanting to visit at the castle?"

Pru wanted to know. "Why, His Grace might even invite us to stay so Willy doesn't get homesick."

Graceanne had to smile at the thought of Willy being consoled by the doting aunt who threatened him with her hairbrush just the previous day for laying jam-sticky fingers on her muslin gown. Graceanne stopped smiling when her father told Prudence to stop her foolish air-dreaming. He'd never allow her to put one foot over Ware's threshold when the duke had his rakish friends visiting, nor let her stay overnight there no matter how many widowed sisters chaperoned. "Never."

"Your reputation, dear," Mrs. Beckwith murmured, hoping to avoid another angry outburst as Prudence pursed her lips. She should have looked at her other daughter.

"What do you mean, Pru cannot stay there?" Graceanne raged. "Ware's company is fit for your grandson but not your daughter? If her good name cannot survive the rakehell's very presence, how can poor little Willy's moral character?"

"Quiet!" Mr. Beckwith thundered back. "I will not have this brangling at my dinner table. Apologize to your mother, Graceanne, and strive to show more respect for your elders. The discussion is finished."

"I am sorry, Mother, I did not mean to overset your nerves. Shall I wheel you into the parlor until tea is brought? Perhaps Pru will play for us. You know how that always soothes you."

Mrs. Beckwith managed to doze off by the fireplace despite Prudence thumping out her discontent on the pianoforte. Graceanne took up her knitting, colorful scarves and mittens for the needy parish children, including her own.

Too short a while later Prudence swiveled on her stool and snarled, "It is not fair," low enough to let her mother go on sleeping. "I never get to go anywhere or do anything!"

"But Pru, you're only seventeen." Graceanne tried to be sympathetic.

"All the other girls get to go to the assemblies and parties. Lucy Maxton is already engaged, and she's no older than I am! Now the most dashing gentleman in the whole county is coming for the holidays, and I'll barely get to meet him if Papa has his way. They say Ware is a regular out-and-outer."

Graceanne looked up from her knitting. "I daresay a dashing out-and-outer is not what careful parents seek for their young daughters." She scowled at the mittens in her lap. "But you will get to meet him nevertheless. He's bound to call, the maw worm."

"And I suppose you'll give him a regular bear-garden jawing," Pru said with a giggle. "I hope I'm around to hear it, although I don't know how you'll dare. I mean, a real duke, Gracie."

"He's just a man, Pru, even if he is more pigheaded and obnoxious than most."

"Nevertheless, I admire your courage. You even stand up to Papa. I remember when he didn't want you to marry Tony, but you insisted on having the man you loved. It was the most romantical thing I ever heard. Why, all the time you were gone I dreamed of a handsome soldier coming to steal me away."

"Papa gave in because he is dependent on Tony's cousin Ware for his living," Graceanne pointed out. "Besides, my marriage wasn't all romance. Portugal was awful, and Tony was always miles away in danger."

"Still, you had your grand passion despite Papa." She sighed and went back to plunking at the keys. "He won't even let me invite Liam to tea."

"Mr. Hallorahan is Irish, Pru. You know Papa won't approve."

"But that's so unreasonable! Why, Papa calls Liam a jumped-up groom just because he's helping Squire set up a stable. Papa won't even listen when I tell him that Liam's father owns one of the finest racehorse breeding farms in all of Ireland."

"Pru, racehorses are for gambling, and you know Papa doesn't approve of that any more than he does of heretics."

16

"Liam isn't a heretic!" Prudence insisted. "Besides, Papa doesn't approve of anything! Did you know that ours is the only house in the whole village without a single Christmas decoration? The vicarage! We're like,the cobbler's children going barefoot. Even the poorest cottage has a sprig of holly on the door!"

"Papa says that's a pagan tradition to ward off evil, and has nothing to do with the real Christmas celebration, no more than wassailing does or wishing on a Christmas pudding."

"Oh, I know all that," Prudence complained. "Yule logs are from Roman Saturnalia, and mistletoe is just an excuse for loose morals," she recited in her father's stentorian tones.

Neither girl heard their father's approach over their laughter until he slammed his hand down on the side table. "I shall have respect in this house!" he shouted, startling his wife awake to ask if it was teatime yet.

"Yes, Papa." Prudence jumped up and bobbed a hasty curtsy. "I'll go help Cook with the tray."

And "Yes, Papa," Graceanne murmured. "I'll go check on the boys."

"Yes, Papa." How many times in her life had Graceanne said those same two words, tiny words that yet robbed her of her opinions, her desires, her very selfhood?

She stood in her sons' bedroom, the tiny room under the eaves next to the servants' quarters, where the children's play couldn't disturb the vicar or his delicate wife. The boys were tumbled together on their mattress like puppies, flushed with sleep, their dark curls still damp from their bath. Even asleep in their identical nightshirts with her identical embroidery on both collars, Graceanne could tell them apart. No one else in the household could. No one else in the household had made an effort to try in the three months they'd been back from the Peninsula. Mrs. Beckwith was too sickly, Pru was too self-absorbed, the servants were too overworked, and the vicar thought they were an abomination. Graceanne thought they were the most beautiful things she had ever seen. Sometimes just looking at them brought tears to her eyes and made her throat close, they were so perfect. If she never got to see a heavenly angel, she could rest content. If she never had another blessing in life, Willy and Leslie were enough. They were hers. Never, ever, would she say "Yes, Papa" and let him take them away.

Graceanne'd had her one other moment of rebellion almost six years before, when she was seventeen, Pru's age, when she met Tony. She'd threatened to run off with him if her father did not give them his permission to marry. She always suspected the vicar relented more to gain the ducal connection than for fear of losing her. Then again, she'd come to suspect that she'd insisted so hard more to get out of the house and into the world than for love of Anthony Warrington. Oh, Tony was charming and so handsome in his new scarlet regimentals, so full of life and dreams for after he defeated Napoleon. How could any inexperienced, overprotected girl not fall in love? The fact that he was shipping out in six weeks only added to the high drama of the forbidden romance.

The banns were read, Reverend Beckwith performed the ceremony, and Mama cried. Pru was adorable as bridesmaid, and the nonesuch duke himself stood as his cousin's best man. The entire village turned out to witness little Miss Beckwith's grand match.

The rosy glow faded quickly when Tony's orders came before he'd had time to arrange Graceanne's passage to the Peninsula. She couldn't sail safely with the troop ships, couldn't travel properly by herself, and couldn't arrive officially at headquarters at all, in fact, until Tony got permission from his commanding officer, who was known to dislike officers' wives. They distracted his men, he believed. The younger and prettier, the more distraction.

So Tony left his new bride with his sickly mother in a small rented house outside Cheltenham, where the ailing woman could partake of the waters. Graceanne never lost the niggling doubt that Tony'd married her for just that reason, to provide company for his febrile mother so he could traipse off to war with a clear conscience. She spent a year in that dreary locale of antiquated invalids, the unpaid companion to a dying woman. Mrs. Warrington's worsening condition kept Graceanne even more isolated than she'd been in Warefield, where at least she had parish duties and her little sister. Tony's letters were sporadic, his homeward leaves always postponed. He did manage to return to England for the funeral. With no excuse to leave her behind, and no one to leave her with, Tony finally agreed to take Graceanne with him when he returned to the Peninsula.

This time he placed her in the care of the British ambassador's wife in Portugal, miles from his front-line position. Sometimes days or weeks away, Graceanne couldn't dampen his enthusiasm for battle with her fretting.

He did like to show her off to his fellow officers, though, and he did visit her between engagements when he could. Graceanne provided hot baths, good food, had clean clothes whenever he arrived. After a day or two Tony would kiss her forehead and call her the best wife an officer could have, before he departed. He was undoubtedly fond of her, but Tony loved the war. He thrived on danger, laughed at the risks, reveled in the companionship of his fellow officers and his loyal troops. Graceanne hated everything about the war: the dirt, the heat, the wounded men passing through, the friends made and lost so quickly. She hated the confines of the headquarters, the rigid, narrow society of officers' wives. Mostly she hated the endless, encompassing fear for her reckless husband. She almost came to hate Tony for the chances he took.

Then she had the twins, and nothing else mattered so much. Her world was the nursery, not the battlefield. And Tony was even prouder of his young wife.

Then suddenly he was gone—they brought her his scarlet jacket and his sword for his sons—and she and the twins were bundled aboard the next ship and conveyed, willy-nilly, to the Warefield vicarage. No one asked her, no one gave her a choice. Now she was home in Warefield village, Warwick, back to being her father's obedient daughter, her mother's dutiful companion. But she was still Willy and Leslie's mother, and that would never change. She'd flee to America with the boys before she let some imperious nobleman put a decadent hand on either of their heads.

Of course she might have trouble booking passage with the few coins she'd managed to squirrel away from the pittance doled out by her father. She and her sons were living on his charity, the frugal vicar never ceased to point out, and Graceanne naturally believed that to be true. No one had ever discussed money with her, but she assumed her settlements to be negligible since her dowry was nonexistent. Tony used to pat her hand and tell her not to bother her pretty head about such dreary topics. The vicar told her what money she might be entitled to barely covered expenses, with a little bit put aside for the children's education.

So Graceanne never asked for money for herself. She made her own mourning clothes out of the sturdiest black material so they'd last longer, and she did without all the fripperies other females her age took for granted. The widow also tried to pay back in service what her father so reluctantly expended. She made fair copies of the vicar's sermons, writing half of them. She took over her mother's parish duties, the poor, the sick, the Sunday school classes, and the ladies' committees. Graceanne even made an effort at teaching Prudence prudence. She was also trying to manage the understaffed and underfinanced household.

Meanwhile, she was learning to manage her difficult father. There always seemed to be enough money for the vicar's own comfort and scholarly interests, so Graceanne practiced a subtle form of extortion.

She'd have more time to help him, Graceanne explained, if she could hire the twins a reliable nursemaid. Why, she might even be able to start cataloguing his precious collection of religious books. And just think, with more careful attention than Pru's wandering gaze, the boys might never get into his library again to practice their drawing on his latest sermon. As for the new pony cart Graceanne wanted, Heaven knew she could accomplish her errands among the parishioners and in the village so much more quickly than she could on foot. She could deliver six jars of soup to the shut-ins, stop at the butcher's, collect the mail, make sure the Rigg brothers knew about the change in choir practice, and still be home to help Cook prepare luncheon. And, the pièce de résistance, she could take the jabbering, mischievous little monkey children with her. She got the cart. And money for pencils and paper so the boys wouldn't use his, and pennies for treats so they wouldn't get underfoot in the kitchen so often, in Cook's way. Of course the boys had to be dressed warmly, coming from the hotter Peninsula climate. Their grandfather wouldn't want them catching infectious diseases, would he? Doctors were so expensive.

The only thing Graceanne hadn't been able to cajole out of the nipcheese cleric was money for Christmas. Unlike Pru, she knew better than to come between the vicar and his firmest beliefs. So she was knitting mittens and staying up late baking gingerbread men and taking the holly garlands off the pony cart before they reached the stable. They'd have Christmas one way or another. She'd manage, just like she was managing her father. And as for that dreadful duke, she'd manage his high and mighty lordship at Ware Hold, too!

Chapter Three

The Duke of Ware hated to play the fool. That was why he rarely overindulged. Spirits too often made a man forget his manners or his morals, loosened the connection between his brain and his tongue until Bacchus alone knew what drivel he might spew. Which was why, that morning after Almack's, when His Grace awoke with his head on the desktop in his library and the taste and feel of a desiccated hedgehog in his mouth, his first action was to reach for that addlepated letter he'd penned to Tony's widow the night before. Actually, his first action was to dismiss the footman who opened the drapes to let in the sunlight that pierced his aching head like an arrow dipped in particularly nasty poison, the kind of poison that made a fellow wish he'd die, and quickly.

His second action was to gulp at the hot coffee the obliging footman had brought, so Leland hired him back. The coffee restored too little of his equilibrium and too much of his memory—Almack's, Ellerby's warnings, Crow's corkbrained scheme to ask his cousin's widow for one of her twin sons, and how Fanshaw's idea didn't seem so caperwitted by three in the morning and three sheets to the wind. No one needed a matched set of boys, he'd reasoned. Carriage horses, yes. Dueling pistols, yes. Boys, no. By

George, he'd actually written that fustian in his note, Ware recalled. *That* was when he reached for the blasted letter.

The problem with being a well-paying employer who was fair as well as demanding was that one's loyal staff tended to be efficient. They anticipated one's every need and desire. Hence the hot coffee. Thence the letter. Seeing a folded, sealed, sanded, and franked letter on His Grace's desk, one of the duke's devoted retainers immediately sent the missive on its way.

Ware had made a prime ass of himself this time.

He intended to apologize while he was at Ware Hold in Warwick, of course. It rankled, naturally, having to excuse his ungentlemanly conduct to a country nobody, but the female was his cousin's widow, after all. He intended to make amends by raising her allowance or some such. What he didn't intend was to be confronted with a raging harridan within hours of his arrival at the family seat.

Tony's widow stormed through the massive doors of the ancient castle like an avenging Fury, ugly black cloak gusting behind her in the gale of her fierce stride when she caught sight of her victim crossing the Great Hall. "You!" she shouted in a voice of doom that echoed in the high-ceilinged room, stunning the duke, his butler, three footmen, and a housemaid. One of the suits of armor rattled, Leland swore.

The Gorgon—or Graceanne, for he finally recognized his cousin's wife—advanced on Ware. A gentleman didn't run from danger, Leland had to remind himself, especially not in front of his servants. So he dismissed the servants. That was a tactical error, for it seemed Mrs. Warrington had been restraining herself until she had him alone. Valkyries had their standards, too. Now she lit into him, starting with un-feeling and inhumane, pausing only slightly for toplofty and despotic before the descent to rakehell and roué. She didn't quite accuse him of being a child molester, but he could see it dangling on the tip of her tongue. She'd already judged him guilty, and was most likely only biding her time before she grabbed up one of the medieval battle-axes from the wall to perform the execution.

While Mrs. Warrington was roundly cursing him in English, Spanish, Portuguese, and cockney navvy—the passage home must have been an interesting one, he figured—Leland took the time to observe Tony's bride. Bride, hah! He remembered a sweet young innocent, soft-spoken, dewy-eyed, as lovely and gentle as her name. He remembered thinking Tony was a lucky man. He still was; he didn't have to face this termagant anymore. Besides turning into a fishwife, Graceanne had grown thinner, darker-skinned from the Spanish sun, and even less fashionable. Her widow's weeds were a shapeless sack and her hair was scraped back in a straggly bun under a black mobcap his lowest scullery maid wouldn't be caught dead in. And her nose was red from the cold outside. A tiny drip of moisture hung from its end. She was magnificent.

Ware's mouth quirked up at the corners, which nearly sent Graceanne into apoplexy. "That's it, laugh. 'Tis all a great joke to you, that you might destroy whole families! 'I'd like to try my hand at child-raising,' " she quoted from that unfortunate letter. Leland winced, but before he could offer excuses, she was off again on her rant: "Why couldn't you stick to trying your hand at oil painting or poetry like the other idle, useless dilettantes of your class? To think that Tony died to preserve your way of life, when the French might have had the right idea after all!"

With her bosom heaving to keep pace with her tirade, Graceanne wasn't thin all over, Ware could tell. In fact, child-bearing had brought out more than rabid maternal instincts. With the proper dressing . . .

"You may win my father to your way of thinking," Graceanne was shouting, "and you may have your dissolute friend the Regent plead your case. You may spend every last groat of your wealth buying the law. For all I know, even God is on your side or He'd never put you here to torment me. But it does not matter! I swear by everything I hold sacred, you shall never take my sons away from me!"

Ware meant to offer his abject apologies then, truly he did. Instead, he heard himself make another kind of offer entirely. "Since you won't let me take the boy, my dear, perhaps you'd be willing to come with him? There's a vacant cottage at one of the tenant farms. You'd have every comfort those same groats can provide. I can be very generous."

"You can be damned!"

Lud, somehow he'd forgotten she was a vicar's daughter, not a town-bronzed worldly widow. Which just went to prove that a born fool could make an ass out of himself without alcoholic assistance.

Graceanne had gone absolutely rigid, her mouth opening and closing with no sound issuing forth. Most likely she couldn't think of any words foul enough for him. Before she did, Leland closed her mouth in the most convenient—for him—way possible. He'd been wanting to taste those rosy lips for an age. Now he had an excuse. Not a good excuse, admittedly, but one that was just loud enough to drown out his conscience.

He thought her lips would be warm from the fire of her anger, but they were as cold as the wintry day outside. And they were stiff, as unyielding as an icicle. All in all, not a promising embrace. But she smelled of lilacs, and enough of her hair had come unpinned from that spinsterish bun for him to see its honeyed gold color. He was satisfied.

Leland released her and stepped back, waiting for the slap. He deserved it, had earned it, would suffer it like a man. The slap never came. Instead, the thick heel of one serviceable, no-nonsense, unfashionable boot came down on his pump-clad toes with the accompanying command to "Go find a woman with morals as low as yours, if you can."

And then, while the duke was hopping on one foot, one serviceable, no-nonsense, and extremely unfashionable knee landed between his legs. "And go get your own children, if you can."

Gads, he'd forgotten she was a soldier's wife, too.

25

* * *

Of all the imbecilic, hen-witted things to do, Graceanne chided herself as she took up the reins of the pony cart. Calling on a single gentleman alone in his home—of course he thought she was a lightskirt! Then kicking him. How could she have been such a ninnyhammer?

There she'd been thinking how clever she was, to bribe Jem, Ware Hold's gatekeeper, to send one of his boys to her at the vicarage as soon as Ware arrived. She was going to get to the duke before her father could come to an arrangement with him, the way he did with her marriage settlements. She was going to give His Grace time to change from his travel clothes, refresh himself, perhaps have a bite to eat. Then she could approach him for a rational, mature conversation about his cockleheaded notion of stealing her son.

Instead, when she drove her cart through the formal gardens past the ornamental lake where the castle's moat used to be, and up to the front door, where the portcullis once protected against invaders, two grooms ran to hold her pony, as if poor Posy were a mettlesome destrier. A third groom came to hand her down, a procedure so unprecedented, Graceanne nearly tumbled them both to the ground. Then the massive front door opened long before she could reach for the knocker, and a bewigged butler bowed to her. Two footmen in liveried splendor silently posed at either side of the doorway, like bookends. Behind them the Great Hall was brighter than the December day outside, with more candles burning at two o'clock in the afternoon than the vicarage used in a winter month. Graceanne blinked. Two paces into the hall brought her dripping nose the aroma of mince pies cooking, even though the kitchen had to be miles away. One more step, and a welcoming warmth touched her frozen cheeks from roaring fires at both ends of the cavernous room, in hearths large enough to incinerate Sherwood Forest. And no one sat there. Both mantels held huge arrangements of holly and ivy and tinsel stars, while the imposing stairwell's carved banister and every wall in the place was decorated with swags of evergreens and red ribbons. And according to Jem's boy, only the duke, one man, had come to celebrate Christmas here.

There he was, walking across an Aubusson carpet so beautiful it could have hung on a wall. He was immaculate, elegant even in his informal wear that still bespoke the finest tailoring and a valet's fastidious attention. Tony would have called him top-drawer, bang up to the mark. Graceanne's mind called him greedy.

He had everything, His Grace of Ware. All she had was her sons.

So she kicked him.

To do violent bodily harm to another human being was outrageous, underbred, sinful. To kick a man who had such influence and control over one's life was worse. It was foolish beyond permission. Graceanne wished she could kick herself for being such a gudgeon. Instead, she drummed her feet on the pony cart's floorboard. Posy snorted in disgust. "Me, too," Graceanne agreed.

Why, the duke could see Papa removed from his living, frail Mrs. Beckwith thrown out into the cold, beautiful Prudence sold into white slavery, the entire family transported to Botany Bay. He could do anything, the all-powerful Duke of Ware, once he managed to stand up again.

He would hate her forever now.

How could she have been so indelicate? Such a want of conduct, Mama would be ashamed of her. Tony would be ashamed of her. No, Graceanne decided, clucking to Posy to pick up her speed from shuffle to amble, Tony would not be ashamed at all. He'd be proud of her ability to defend herself from unwelcome advances. He'd been the one to teach her, after all. Tony had worried about the rough soldiers, the Spanish peasants, the French Army. He should have worried about his own cousin.

Graceanne's indignation turned from her own idiocy to the duke's infamy. Obviously his reputation as a rake was well earned, the blackguard. Then again, she reflected honestly, it was easy to see how Ware would be very, very

27

good at his chosen path to perdition. Susceptible women—not that she was one of them, of course; she was just being objective—would find his laughing hazel eyes and well-shaped mouth attractive. His dark curls just begged to be tousled, and the slightly hawkish nose only added character to an otherwise classically handsome face.

Ware wasn't as handsome as Tony, she thought loyally. But Tony's good looks were more boyish. Leland had the tiny lines and wrinkles of a mature man, plus an air of dignity and assurance quicksilver Tony never managed to attain. He was broader and taller than her husband, too, which was not necessarily a mark in Ware's favor, for his embrace made her feel overpowered, intimidated, and weak. She did have to admit that His Grace made a good figure, even compared to the young officers in prime physical condition she was used to. Yes, Graceanne could see where some goosish women might succumb to the duke's appeal if they didn't mind being cast in the shade.

Even at their wedding Tony teased that the best man was more splendid than the groom. Heavens, the elegant duke was more splendid than the bride! All the village girls ogled him and the matrons sighed. There was just something imposing about Ware, commanding, confident . . . lordly. Except for the last time she'd seen him, whimpering on the floor.

Graceanne pulled her cloak more tightly about her. Never had she missed Tony more or felt so defenseless—not precisely defenseless, obviously—but vulnerable in her position as a woman. Not just physically, either. Women couldn't handle money or attend university; they couldn't hold decent positions or offices of power. If they visited a man alone, they were considered no better than they ought to be, and the one area that ought to be guaranteed safe, their nursery, wasn't.

No one would ever threaten to take a man's children away from him. No one would dare, even if he mistreated them. Why, her father often recommended from his pulpit beating the wickedness out of children, and the men in the congregation always nodded. He even threatened to practice his preachings on Willy and Les if they ever laid another grubby hand on his books. They'd only been looking for pictures.

This last thought reminded Graceanne that the Macgruder sisters had promised to order some picture books for her for Christmas. She ought to check, especially since having errands in the village was her excuse for going out this afternoon. Vicar Beckwith had been told that Cook needed some special herbs and spices, as if that would improve the woman's abominable culinary skills. At the low wages he offered, it was astounding Cook could boil water for tea. But Papa had optimistically agreed and had given Graceanne a few shillings to accomplish a miracle. Graceanne roused Posy into a half-trot so they might reach the village before nightfall.

The village was full of talk of the duke. Did Mrs. Warrington notice if the standards were flying yet over the Hold, signaling his arrival? Had she heard if he was bringing a party with him? The village could use the custom.

At the little lending library, the elder Miss Macgruder was positive he was bringing a bride home for Christmas. So romantic. The younger Miss Macgruder believed it was a band of like-thinking libertines he'd invited, for an orgy. The grocer's wife declared she heard Ware was looking for a wife; her husband said he was locking up their daughters. No one wanted to talk about choir practice or the Sunday school's Nativity play.

Even more depressed, Graceanne headed Posy back the way they had come. On the homeward trip she had to pass the hill from which Ware Hold commanded the surrounding countryside. It looked dark and forbidding, just like the old fortress it was, with its crenellated towers and arrow slots instead of windows. From this direction Graceanne couldn't see the lake or the gardens or the modern addition that had been built out of the torn-down curtain wall. All she saw

29

was an impregnable stronghold that had been there forever. She'd be lucky not to land in the dungeons.

Graceanne entered the vicarage through the kitchen, after seeing to Posy. Cook was asleep in the corner, a half-empty bottle of cooking wine in her hand. Meg, the village girl who acted as nursery maid, was up to her eyebrows in flour.

"The master ordered me to help Cook this afternoon, ma'am. We're to make something special for tea. Vicar says as how His Grace is sure to visit and we're to be prepared."

If they were to be prepared, Graceanne thought, they'd bar the windows and doors and borrow Squire's hunting rifles. Out loud she said, "I'm certain you're doing your best. Are the boys with my sister?"

"Oh, no, ma'am. Miss Prudence was that excited the duke was coming to call, she had to go ask her friend Lucy what she should wear. But don't fret yourself, I set the nippers to help make some Christmas decorations. Just for the nursery, you know, where the reverend can't mind. I taught the darlings to make paper chains." Meg wiped her nose on the back of her hand before going back to her kneading. "I found that colored paper and the glue you were using to make the costumes for the pageant. And some bits of feathers and that glittery paint you used on the angel's wings."

Graceanne clutched the side of the table. "You left three-year-old boys alone with that stuff?"

"Don't you go worrying, ma'am, I took the scissors away."

Chapter Four

$\mathcal{I}$t took Graceanne two days to clean up the nursery, hallway, and servants' bedrooms from her darlings' handiwork.

It took Ware two days to recover from her. Since the constable, the magistrate, and the home guard didn't storm the little vicarage to arrest her, at least Graceanne knew she hadn't killed him. The *on-dit* in the village of Warefield was that His Grace was recovering from his latest London revels; that he was suffering from the French pox, and who could wonder why; that he'd been wounded by highwaymen on his journey north.

Graceanne offered no opinions on the gossip. She did snap at Prudence that all the idle chatter was a waste of time that could be better spent rehearsing the Christmas pageant or preparing the fancy teacakes their father suddenly insisted upon. The rebuke was enough to send Prudence fleeing the kitchen in a flood of tears, straight to Lucy's house to try out new hairstyles. Discounting Cook and Meg, this left Graceanne alone to assemble baskets of foodstuffs for the poor, make Christmas treats for the children, and bake for a guest who never arrived.

Meg's muffins were fed to the chickens—no one in the parish was *that* poor—and the maid was sternly admon-

31

ished to keep a closer eye on the twins. Graceanne wanted Meg to keep the boys presentable at all times in case their regal relation came to inspect.

"I'm nobbut a maid, Mrs. Warrington, ma'am, not a magician."

"Try."

She went back to work, making sugarplums and macaroons, honeyed ginger nuts and marzipan angels. Graceanne also turned out small mince pies, which were supposed to bring luck. Lots and lots of small mince pies. With enough luck, or enough mince pies, perhaps the duke would never come at all.

He came on the third day, looking far more elegant than Graceanne recalled, and totally out of place in the shabby parlor. He brought pineapples from the Hold's forcing houses for her mother and a leather-bound volume of sermons for her father. They invited him to tea, of course.

Of course he accepted. There was no hope he wouldn't, the perverse man, not with Graceanne laboring in the kitchen, her hair damp with perspiration, her fustiest gown spotted and stained. For spite, before she went to change, she piled Cook's scones on a plate with the tea service instead of her own fresh raspberry tarts.

Upstairs in her shabby bedroom, glancing in the small mirror, Graceanne decided a different dress wasn't going to help matters. She also needed a bath, a hairwash, and a nap to get rid of the dark shadows under her eyes put there by worry over the dastard's machinations. More crucial than her vanity, however, was keeping the scoundrel away from her father. Besides, her other gowns might be cleaner, but they were all black, and not a one of them was any more attractive than the sacklike garment she wore. Graceanne hurriedly scrubbed her hands and face in the washbasin's lukewarm water, swiped at the telltale cooking debris on her skirts, and shoved her stringy hair under a voluminous black cap.

She raced down the stairs, then paused outside the parlor

door to catch her breath. Heaven forfend the repulsive rake think she was hurrying to see him!

The duke was sitting at ease on the threadbare sofa, looking like he'd just stepped out of Bond Street. His snowy neckcloth was a marvel of starched perfection, his charcoal pantaloons hadn't the slightest hint of a crease, and his mirror-shined boots reflected every worn spot on the carpet. Ware looked to her jaundiced eyes like a tailor's dummy, someone who had never worked a day in his life.

Sitting next to the parasitic paragon was Prudence. The minx had no business taking tea with the company, much less sharing the narrow couch with an established libertine. Prudence was all pink muslin, lace ribbons, and blond ringlets—and rouged cheeks, unless Graceanne missed her guess. The little hoyden was sitting much too close to Ware, hanging on his every word, looking up at him through thicker, darker eyelashes than she'd possessed that very morning. No matter what commonplace the duke uttered, Pru's tinkling laugh chimed out and her dimples flashed. Graceanne looked for her mother's frowning reprimand at Pru's coming manners, but instead she saw a new lace cap on Mrs. Beckwith, rouged cheeks, and fluttering eyelashes. Goodness, no wonder he expected every female to fall at his feet! Thanking Heaven she was made of sterner stuff, Graceanne pursed her lips and stepped into the room.

There she was at last, hanging in the doorway like an untrained footman. Leland had been wondering how many more of the little sister's blatant lures he could shrug off before he uttered a crushing setdown. The baggage was an adorable bit of fluff, bachelor fare if he ever saw it, not that he was in the market for an unfledged bird of paradise. Even if Miss Prudence weren't a vicar's daughter, he'd always preferred his flirts to have some experience of the world. Virgins were the very devil. She'd make some man a cozy armful, though, if they didn't marry her off soon. Too bad Miss Prudence had been too young that summer

Tony spent in Warwick; she'd be a great deal easier to turn up sweet than the prickly female Tony did marry.

Mrs. Warrington was already pokering up as she came into the room, and he hadn't even said hello. Leland sighed. He knew he owed the starchy woman an apology, perhaps two or three. He also knew she hated and distrusted him, perhaps with cause. The curst widow wasn't going to make this easy for him. He sighed again as he stood and made his bow, then accepted the hand she offered, but cautiously kept his distance.

"I never offered my proper condolences, Cousin," he said, trying not to wince at the sight of another awful gown and hideous cap. "I am sure you must miss Tony, especially at this holiday season. He was a fine man, a good soldier, a wonderful friend."

The vicar interrupted over her murmured expression of gratitude. "Yes, yes, but as you say, this is the season of joy, no time to mourn." Leland couldn't spot a single token of the season, much less of joy, in the dreary room, but he returned to his seat after the widow quietly excused herself to go help Cook with tea.

Prudence immediately took up the conversation: "And it is a special season of celebration for Warefield, with Your Grace in residence after so long. Shall you be making a lengthy stay? If so, perhaps you'd consider holding a ball at the castle. My friend Lucy says her sister remembers when there were parties all the time at Ware Hold."

"That is enough, Prudence. His Grace did not come to be importuned with your girlish nonsense," the vicar scolded. Then, "Have you had a chance to look over my report about the church steps, Duke? I'm sure you'll see I was correct about the dry rot."

Leland let the small talk flow around him with an occasional nod or a noncommittal comment. He could make social chitchat in his sleep. Meanwhile, whilst the object of his call made herself scarce, he looked around again. No, there were no ornaments, not even a sprig of holly. The furnishings were sparse and worn, the drapery faded, the wallpaper peeling. There were no servants to speak of, and he was the only one to come to Mrs. Warrington's assistance when she returned with the heavy tray. There was meager fare for refreshment, scones that were as hard as rocks and tasted as appetizing, and poor quality tea. Leland noticed how Mrs. Beckwith was quick to turn a cup so the chipped handle didn't show. Her clothes and Prudence's were more fashionable than the widow's, but decidedly village-made and of inferior materials.

Ware knew to a shilling what the vicar earned. Despite his reputation as a man-about-town, the duke was cognizant of every detail of his country holdings, too. His domain was decidedly not populated with impoverished preachers. Reverend Beckwith was not spending his generous stipend on his family, that was clear. Perhaps the man gambled or had another secret vice. But why the devil was Tony's widow pretending poverty? There she sat, like the colorless little mouse he knew she wasn't, humbly knitting in the corner. He couldn't imagine what kind of game they all were playing, unless it was a scheme to get more money out of him. They'd catch cold at that!

"I'll send my head carpenter to inspect the church steps," he offered while taking a bank draft out of his pocket. "Meantime I did bring my annual donation to the poor box. 'Tis the season to give, after all. You must be a charitable man yourself, Reverend." That was a fairly broad hint to find out where all the money went, and wide of the mark at that.

"To a point, Your Grace," Beckwith answered. "My daughter makes gloves and mittens for the needy, as you can see. And no one goes hungry. We send baskets around at Christmas and Easter."

"From the poor box money, Papa," Graceanne said from her corner. "His Grace should know where his offering goes." And where Beckwith's didn't. So the mouse still had teeth after all, and she wasn't protecting Beckwith's cheese. Curious.

"To be sure, to be sure. After that, I believe God helps

those who help themselves." This pronouncement must have sounded harsh for a man of the cloth even to Beckwith, for he changed the subject instantly. "But come, Duke, perhaps you'd like to see my collection."

"I'm sure His Lordship has more important things to do, Papa. We mustn't delay him." Graceanne was determined to keep the two men apart. Her father was just as bent on having a private talk with the nobleman.

"This will take but a moment. A man of His Grace's discernment will surely be interested in the historical significance."

Ware looked around the room. Mrs. Beckwith was smiling vaguely, Prudence was pouting, and Mrs. Warrington was mangling her wools into a regular mare's nest. Why in blazes was she frowning at him again? He didn't want to appear toplofty as she'd accused, so said he could spare some time, to the vicar's satisfaction.

Beckwith led him down the hall and through a locked door, the first locked door Ware had ever seen in a parsonage, even in London's stews when he made his charity calls. If a minister doesn't have faith in humankind, he wondered, who will?

Catching his guest's bemusement over the keys, Beckwith explained, "The imps of Satan are everywhere."

Lud, Leland thought, the fellow was always a religious fanatic, but now a page or two of Beckwith's prayerbook was missing.

But the man did know his Bibles. Beckwith's collection of religious texts was extensive. Some volumes were ancient, most were valuable. The duke wouldn't want to read many of them, but he could recognize their worth. There was even an illuminated manuscript, in another locked cabinet, that he'd be proud to have in his own library of rare editions. No wonder the household was on short rations if Beckwith was as compulsive a collector as the accumulation of books indicated. If that was how the cleric chose to spend his money, Ware had no complaints as long as the man got the locals baptized and buried. And as long as

Tony's children weren't on bread and water to support the man's hobby. He cut short the vicar's lecture.

"Perhaps I can see the children now?" he asked after they'd returned to the parlor. He might have announced he had smallpox, the way Mrs. Warrington lost what little color she had and everyone else found something better to do. Mrs. Beckwith announced the knickknacks needed washing before the holidays, so she filled her lap with china shepherdesses before being wheeled out of the room. The reverend recalled his Christmas sermon needed polishing. Oddly, he took with him a pewter mug, a bowl of nuts, and a carved wood tobacco humidor. He also took two framed miniatures from a piecrust table. "My parents" was all he said.

Even Prudence was willing to peel herself from Ware's side. "If you are going to entertain the little beasts in the parlor, I'll go memorize my lines for the Nativity. You are coming, aren't you, Your Grace? I am Mary again this year." She tossed her curls for effect. "Of course I am too old for the children's play, but Papa insists that if we are going to have the pageant in church on Christmas Eve, it must be dignified. He wants no little girls who giggle and get tongue-tied, so I volunteered."

"And I'm sure you'll be everything saintly and demure." Actually, Leland was sure the little tart would be thrilled to be treading the boards, even in church.

Before she left, Prudence put her magazines and her mother's workbasket on the mantel, and the lid down on the pianoforte. She took two needlepoint pillows with her, saying, "I'll ask Meg to bring them down now."

Leland thought they were all as queer as Dick's hatband, especially when Mrs. Warrington, whom he thought was the only sane one of the bunch, moved the fireplace screen. Then she started putting out the few candles and lifting an oil lamp to the already crowded mantelpiece. She moved the screen again, wedging it in the hearth. At least she finally had some color in her cheeks, he noted admiringly, even if it was from blushing at the peculiarities of this household. Or exertion, as she moved the blasted screen again. At least the rosy tinge wasn't from the rouge pot.

All of Graceanne's improved color fled her face, though, when Prudence returned a moment later. The younger girl curtsied uncertainly to Ware, then whispered in her sister's ear. He could hear Mrs. Warrington gasp, then whisper back, "But when I told them I wanted everything neat for the company, I didn't mean the nursery fireplace!"

Chapter Five

$\mathcal{D}$ash it, Ware thought. Before this no woman had ever been afraid to be alone with him. The way the widow was clenching her fists, he wouldn't be surprised if she picked up the poker the next time she dithered at the fireplace. She was even more attics-to-let than the rest of her family if she thought he'd make improper advances after her previous response. He cleared his throat. "Mrs. Warrington, I owe you an—"

My stars, Graceanne fretted, Ware was going to think they were all lunatics! Heaven knew what Papa had said, but the duke was angry after he'd gone to see the collection. She could tell by the way his lips thinned. Graceanne also noticed how he unobtrusively observed the lack of amenities in the house—and now the lack of courtesy! And, oh, dear, she still hadn't had the opportunity to beg his pardon for her own shocking behavior. With his thick brows already lowered in a frown, he was most likely wondering how soon the court papers could be drawn up giving him custody of Willy. "Your Grace, please forgive— Oh, excuse me."

"Pardon. No, ladies first."

Graceanne licked her lips before starting again. "Your Grace, I cannot tell you how ashamed I am of my dreadful words and actions when I called at your home. I am so sorry to have—"

Before she could say precisely what she was sorry to have done, Ware held up his hand. He knew what *he* was sorry she'd done. "Please, say no more. I also owe you an abject apology."

"In your—"

"You were provoked. I have no excuse for my own less than noble conduct."

"But I—"

"Shall we call it quits? Do you think we have eaten equal amounts of humble pie?"

Graceanne stopped wringing her hands. "Not very palatable, is it, Your Grace?"

He muttered, "Even worse than the scones at tea," which finally brought a smile to her face, which so enhanced her appearance that Leland was reminded why he'd made his dishonorable proposal in the first place. He smiled back. "Do you think we might start over?"

Graceanne had to remind *herself* that one could "smile and smile, and still be a villain." She nodded anyway, and Ware was just speculating that he could win her over after all, when a disheveled serving girl came in without knocking. Her grayish uniform was wet and rumpled, and she had a wriggling, blanket-wrapped bundle in her arms.

"Here's the first 'un, ma'am. I figure he wouldn't stay clean long enough for me to dress t'other without someone watching." She dumped a child in Mrs. Warrington's lap and tromped out.

"Hello, my cherub," Graceanne said, peeling away the blanket and kissing damp curls. "I'd like you to make your bow to His Grace, the way we practiced."

The little fellow did, looking up at Leland with hazel eyes that matched his own. "If you're His Grace," he chirped, "whose grace is Mama?"

Graceanne blushed. They obviously hadn't practiced enough. "My Grace is part of my name, sweetheart. The duke's grace is his address, part of his title."

The boy lowered his brow in concentration, a habit that somehow looked familiar to Leland. Perhaps Tony . . .

"My papa was a major," the sprout solemnly announced.

Leland squatted down to the child's level, and just as seriously agreed, "That's a very proud title."

Tony's son patted the duke's arm. "Don't worry, maybe someday you'll be a major, too. I'm going to be a major in this many years." He held up two chubby hands and spread his fingers out twice.

"Are you?" Ware asked, sitting back down in his chair, having found squatting to be deuced uncomfortable. "Wouldn't you rather be a duke and live in a big house and—"

"That's enough," Graceanne said, scooping the boy into her lap. He climbed down immediately and began inspecting the tassels on Ware's boots. Graceanne watched him with a worried look, but continued: "Stop filling his head with such flummery. He will never be a duke."

"He might be. You cannot know for sure. What if I fell off my horse tomorrow? Granted, it would be a first, but I could be struck by lightning. One never knows. Besides being a true Warrington, the boy has all the makings of a duke. He is confident, intelligent—"

"And he's not your heir. This is your namesake, Leslie, the second-born twin by ten minutes. Wellesley, Sir Arthur's godson, is the elder. Willy is the quiet one."

Embarrassed, the duke looked down, to find one tassel unraveled and the other missing altogether. "The deuces! Uh, pardon, dexterous, isn't he?"

With his eyes on his brand-new boots, Leland missed Graceanne's grab for Leslie, who disappeared under the sofa. She gathered up the gold cord instead, to see if she could reconstruct the shredded tassel. Silly affectations anyway, she thought, wondering how much they would cost to replace. But she mustn't let a petty expense distract her from the point she had to make: "Even Willy is only so temporarily in line for the succession that I cannot understand why you insist on calling him your heir. Surely at

41

your age you intend to remarry and have any number of sons. Therefore— Oh, dear, I shouldn't give him my watch to play with."

Leslie had climbed over the back of the sofa and was standing next to the duke, examining his diamond stickpin. To distract the boy so he could continue his conversation with the mother, Leland unhooked the watch from its fob chain. He tried to defend his ignorance. "I thought children liked watches."

"That's infants, Your Grace. They like the ticking. Older children tend to be . . . oh, my." She'd have to sell her wedding ring to repay the duke for this day's work if he didn't leave soon.

Ware put the pieces of his grandfather's ticker back in his pocket and watched the child, who was *not* his heir, thank goodness, try to climb the window curtains. Amazed at the widow's apparent nonchalance as she plucked her son from certain disaster, he tried to explain. His Grace of Ware was not used to justifying his behavior to anyone, least of all to a scheming widow in a harum-scarum household. He did feel he owed some excuse for that bacon-brained letter he'd sent, though. "I was married twice, Mrs. Warrington, with no issue either time."

"But your wives died early, Tony told me. That's just bad luck. Your next wife might have twins. I've heard such things run in families."

Leland got up to fetch Leslie, who was now trying to stand on his head atop the pianoforte stool. With his back to the widow, he said, "I never fathered progeny outside the marriage bed, either."

"You mean you can't? With your reputation as one of London's greatest rakes?" Graceanne clapped her hand over her mouth when she realized how very improper this conversation was becoming. "I'm sorry, Your Grace."

What, she was sorry he was impotent or sorry she'd been so indelicate? He'd show her impotent! "I didn't say I was incapable of the act," he snarled, "just that the outcome has not been productive. Perhaps you'd like me to demonstrate?"

Graceanne was saved by Meg from having to make some kind of reply. "Here's the other 'un. Do you want me to clean the ashes or mop the floor before the bathwater seeps through the ceiling?"

Ware missed Mrs. Warrington's answer, watching how Leslie took his brother's hand and led him to the guest. Leland was prepared for twins, but this was uncanny. They were the same boy!

He looked up at the widow, who clucked her tongue, used to this reaction. "They are just twins, my lord, not two-headed pigs in a freak show."

Leslie was making the introductions: "He's Papa's cousin, Willy, and Mama says we're to call him His Grace."

The duke could see now that they were not the same people at all. Willy made his bow, but with his eyes cast down, then he went right back to his mother's skirts.

His brother told him, "Don't worry, Willy. He's only a duke."

"Why don't you call me Cousin Leland? Or Lee, if you prefer. That goes for you, too, ma'am, if I might be permitted to call you Cousin Graceanne."

She nodded. "Cousin Leland."

"Cou-lee!" Willy pronounced, still from the safety of his mother's side.

"No, that's a dog," Leland told him. "A collie. A sheepherder. You know, woof-woof." Willy clapped his hands, dropped to all fours, and started barking and woofing around the room, Leslie hard on his heels.

Willy was the quiet one?

Graceanne called them to order. "Boys! We have company."

Leslie wanted to know if that meant they could have the good cakes, not Cook's scones. Graceanne saw the duke's raised eyebrows and looked away. Willy, meanwhile, had changed his chant to a singsong "collie cake" at the top of his lungs.

"Can we, Mama, can we? Meg didn't give us anything to eat all day!"

"Collie cake, collie cake, collie cake."

Graceanne turned helplessly to the duke. "May I leave them with you for a moment? There is no one else to send to the kitchen."

The duke hadn't managed to eat half of one of Cook's stone scones. "Of course. I'd like to see the 'good' cake myself."

Graceanne chewed her lip uncertainly, but she left to prepare a respectable tea this time.

When she returned with a well-filled tray, Cousin Leland's neckcloth was limp, his superfine coat was awry and missing a button, and his carefully combed curls looked like a sparrow had made a nest there. He had a slightly dazed look. "They have a bit of energy, what?"

"It's the cold weather," she explained as she put the tray down atop the pianoforte, well out of her darlings' reach. "They do not get enough exercise." She spread a ragged tablecloth on the floor and began to lay out heavy crockery dishes and sturdy mugs of milk. "Here, sweethearts, your favorite raspberry tarts. And I brought you each a gingerbread man, if you'll promise to be very good while Cousin Leland and I have our tea."

The duke was relieved to see she was setting only two places on the floor. He was also relieved to see she was placing another raspberry tart on a pretty porcelain plate. They were his favorites, too. He got up to assist her, and tried to straighten his cravat while her back was turned. "They seem to do fine in here."

"Yes, but today is special. Usually they have to play upstairs so they don't disturb Papa's studies or Mama's rest. There's not nearly as much room to run and jump." Graceanne realized she was giving him more ammunition to find the vicarage inadequate, so she hurried on: "But we

44

do get outdoors most days. Just now there is less time, what with the preparations for Christmas and all."

Leland could not help looking about him. Christmas might be months away rather than less than a week, judging from the dearth of decorations. "Your preparations must be behind times indeed."

Graceanne's hand shook slightly as she poured the tea. "Yes, well, ah, I meant teaching the village children their parts for the Nativity pageant and rehearsing the choir. One lump or two, Your Grace?"

"One. And I thought it was to be 'cousin.'"

"Cousin." She handed over his cup and plate, then took her own seat after righting one spilled mug of milk.

Leland sat again, too, taking a bite of a truly excellent raspberry tart. "Delicious," he announced. "Your cook must be as temperamental as my French chef. Some days ambrosia, the next day offal. The only reason I put up with him is his way with pastry."

Inordinately pleased, Graceanne confessed that she was responsible for the better fare. "I learned in Portugal, when there was not much else to do. Unfortunately my baking for the holidays has also taken time away from the boys. Mince pies, sugarplums . . ."

"I remember helping to stir the Christmas pudding as a boy, making my wish. Have you and the children done that yet?"

Graceanne stirred her tea. "I'm afraid Papa would not permit such a thing," she said in a voice filled with frustration. "I see you have noticed Papa is very strict in his notions of celebration." She frowned at the bare walls, the cheerless arrangement of faded silk flowers. "He is very devout, you must know, and resents the incursion of pagan superstitions into the religious observation. Since many of the Christmas traditions are holdovers from the Druids' winter solstice rites, Papa has tried to avoid all those trappings."

"And all the lovely aspects that make Christmas such a pleasure, especially for a child," he said under his breath, but Graceanne heard. She privately agreed, but loyalty demanded she defend her father.

"But we do have a Nativity pageant and the choir will sing carols."

"Reverend Beckwith must know he'd have no audience at all to listen to his sermons if he forbade those."

"The congregation members respect my father's piety in church," she said. And then they went home to uphold all the old traditions, but she didn't tell him that. The Christmas pudding for wishes, the Yule log for luck in the new year, the holly and ivy to ward off evil, the mistletoe for fertility. Good heavens, did he know . . . ? She hurried on: "And you mustn't think the boys are missing out on all the anticipation and celebration. We've been decorating the nursery"—may he never learn how—"and both twins have small parts in the play." Mostly because she could not leave them home when she held rehearsals; His Grace needn't know that either, just that her sons were not being deprived. "And of course they will have special treats and a few little gifts." She nodded toward her knitting basket and the mittens sticking out the top.

The boys were getting mittens for Christmas? His tenants' children did better! Yet the twins did not look downtrodden or underprivileged. They were certainly healthy and spirited little tykes, obviously doted upon by their mother. They were handsome to boot, if he had to say so himself who shouldn't, seeing how the lads were the spit and image of himself at their age. Of course he and Tony were often mistaken for brothers instead of cousins, so alike were they in appearance. Nothing could be more alike than these two peas in a pod, he marveled again, watching Leslie and Willy playing at soldiers or whatever with their gingerbread men cookie figures.

He couldn't understand a word of their game, no matter how he listened, although the gibberish seemed to make sense to them.

As if reading his thoughts, Graceanne told him they'd jabbered like this long before they learned to speak the

King's English. "In fact, I despaired they'd ever communicate with anyone else. And yes, they understand each other perfectly."

"And they seem to share so equally." He wrinkled his aristocratic nose when the twins traded half-eaten cookies. "I thought little boys were more possessive than badgers."

Graceanne laughed. "They don't always get along this well, but if one falls, the other cries. They've always been like that. Willy lets Leslie take his toys, but Leslie gives Willy the bigger piece of cake."

She studied the leaves left in her teacup, wishing she could read the future there. Her future was now. With a deep breath Graceanne said, "It would be cruel to separate them, Your Grace. Cousin."

He sighed. "And you. I can see that. Please do forgive my thoughtlessness, that letter, even the suggestion of taking Willy away. Please understand I was feeling desperate. I truly do want sons of my own."

"Then you won't . . . ?"

Hope was shining in the widow's blue eyes. Leland hated to dim that light, but he had to tell her. "Willy—Wellesley—is still my heir, no matter what your wishes, or his, or mine. He'll need to know about the lands and people, to learn the responsibilities facing him, the same way I did."

Graceanne looked at Willy, his face smeared with raspberry jam. "If you can teach him to use a napkin, that should be enough for now."

The duke didn't smile. "For now."

Graceanne understood the door was still open, the threat was still left hanging, but she'd won some time today. "Come, boys, we must let His Grace go about his business."

"G'bye, Collie," they giggled in unison, tumbling out of the room after giving him a quick, unexpected double hug.

The duke brushed crumbs off his pantaloons. Graceanne dabbed ineffectively with her napkin at the raspberry smears on his once-pristine shirtfront. Her cheeks grew pinker than the stains when she realized what she was doing. "H-habit, Your Grace."

"They like me" was all he said, in wonder. Then he asked if he could call another time.

Graceanne couldn't have heard right. "Excuse me, Cousin?"

"I asked if I might come by again, to spend time with the boys."

Graceanne let her napkin flutter to the floor. Goodness, not even Tony had ever wanted to spend time with the boys.

Chapter Six

𝓗is heirs were slap up to the mark. The duke's valet was packing to return to London, but the boys were marvelous. They might be a trifle overexuberant, but high spirits were not to be despised. Ware had always hated those miniature wax dummies his friends trotted out for inspection to be dutifully admired—the ladies always cooed—then placed back on their shelves. What was there to admire in a child with no conversation, no imagination, no sparkle? Neatness? Neatness mattered in a valet—who might be persuaded to stay on with a raise in salary; the fellow did have a way with boots—not in a little boy. Besides, high spirits were natural in Tony's sons. Eton and Oxford could tame any unruliness, Ware complacently decided, ignoring the fact that no amount of rigid school discipline had checked Tony's wilder starts. Warrington had been his mother's despair until he married and became some other female's worry. Aunt Claire had been ecstatic when Tony chose a quiet girl from a strict upbringing. Tony's marriage hadn't given his hey-go-mad cousin any better sense of responsibility, but it had given the duke his heir and a spare! Leland raised a brandy nightcap to the fallen hero. "You were a credit to the Warrington name," he toasted. "Your sons are all a man could ask for to succeed him." And his

49

wife wasn't half bad either, but Ware didn't say that aloud, just in case Tony could hear him. The old castle had ghosts enough.

Graceanne was a puzzle the duke pondered long after snuffing out his bedside candle. In the dark he could visualize her eyes, her face, her form, and be stirred by the images his mind conjured up. Hell, a ghost would be stirred by *those* images. Then he pictured those horrific black sacks that covered the widow from head to toe. They were enough to dampen any man's ardor, even one who hadn't had a woman since leaving London and wouldn't have one while he was resident in the family pile. No true gentleman fouled his own nest, and the Duke of Ware had never been one to tup serving wenches at the local tavern. He required a little more refinement in his convenients. Which brought him back to the vicar's daughter.

There was something deuced havey-cavey about the female. Her fortune wasn't on her back, that was for certain, nor, to judge from the state of the vicarage, was it going to lighten her family's burdens. Even the children she obviously adored were being shortchanged with mittens for Christmas. And she was doing her own baking. So what the devil was she doing with the money?

The duke fell asleep determined to uncover the widow's secrets. And her hair, her shoulders, her ankles . . .

To that end, and others the duke chose not to examine more closely, he arose the next morning, paid his valet's extortion demands, and drove to the manse.

Miss Prudence almost threw herself into his arms when she saw the rig he was driving. "Oh, Your Grace, I've never ridden in a sporting vehicle! Why, Lucy will be green with envy. Her beau only drives a gig."

She almost threw herself on the ground when he said he'd come to take her sister out instead. "I've promised the boys, you see, and cannot disappoint them, no matter how I might wish it otherwise."

When Pru flounced out of the room, Graceanne put down her account books and turned on him. "What is this

Banbury tale of promising the twins a ride? You did no such thing, thank goodness, or they'd have slept in their overcoats to be ready."

Ware's smile was so charming she couldn't be angry, especially not when he shrugged his broad shoulders and confessed, "I came to offer you and the boys a ride, and I didn't want to have to tool some silly chit around the countryside instead. A promise to them was the only polite excuse I could think of. Will you come? You did say the children needed more exercise."

They did, and the account books never balanced anyway. Besides, she was secretly delighted that Ware wasn't falling all over Prudence like every other male in the neighborhood. It was a long-overdue boost to her sorely tried vanity that this exquisite in fawn breeches and caped riding coat preferred her, Graceanne's, company to that of her beautiful younger sister. Of course Ware needed to have her if he was to have the boys, but so what? A mother's pride was gratified, too. With her father's strictures ringing in her ears, she accepted. When she'd told the vicar there was to be no more talk of the duke taking Willy to raise, he'd been disappointed. When she mentioned Ware's request to call again, he'd grown angry.

"You're to have nothing to do with the man, do you hear me? He's a rake. Why does he want to visit children? Mark me, daughter, if he doesn't want Wellesley, it's you he's after. And I won't have any Jezebel living under my roof."

All in all, Graceanne thought she was being very daring—until she saw the curricle outside. "It's too high. It cannot be safe. The horses are too highly strung and they'll go too fast and the boys will fall out. I'm sorry, but—"

Ware's eyes crinkled at the corners. "I wouldn't have expected Tony's wife to be so lily-livered. But come, ma'am, you're insulting both my driving skills and the manners of Castor and Pollux. Perfect gentlemen, I assure you."

The twins were already being introduced to the matched bays by His Grace's tiger. She did have to admit the horses seemed remarkably even-mannered for high-bred cattle.

Any animals that stood still to have their noses patted first by Leslie in the groom's arms, while Willy hopped up and down, calling "Horsie, horsie," were not likely to spook under the duke's capable hands.

"But the seat is so far from the ground!"

"That's what makes the ride so exciting! But I assure you neither lad will come to grief. I have it all planned out. You'll hang on tight to one on your lap, and the other will sit wedged between us. John Groom will keep his hand on the boy's shoulder from his perch behind."

Graceanne was not convinced. Willy and Leslie were still shouting and jumping about, dangerously close to the horses' hooves, she thought, but the groom did seem to have his eyes on them, and a calming hand on the horses. "I fear the children will not sit still well enough."

"Of course they will. You're not babies, are you?" Ware called over to the boys. "Babies wriggle and scream too much and upset the horses, so they cannot go for curricle rides. That's the rule."

Willy held up three fingers to prove he was far beyond infancy; Les tried to tell the duke he was old enough to shave.

"There, are you satisfied now?"

She'd have to be. She'd need a crowbar to separate the twins from those horses, else. She nodded, which earned her a warm smile from Ware.

"Good. They're boys, not hothouse orchids. You'll have to let them grow up someday, you know."

"Surely not until they can dress themselves!" she pleaded.

The boys had been having one of their private conversations, and now Leslie approached the duke and tugged on his sleeve. "Collie, Willy wants to ride the horsie."

"Oh, only Willy?" Leland teased. He stooped down to their level. "I'm sorry, lads, but Castor and Pollux are carriage horses. They're not used to being ridden."

Leslie and Willy were not used to being denied. They

52

went to their mother. Les stuck out his lower lip and Willy stamped his foot. "Want to ride the horsies!"

"But Cousin Leland has explained, darlings, it wouldn't be safe. You know that Posy doesn't like you on her back."

"But these horsies are twins! John said so!" Both children started to cry.

Graceanne was wishing the wretched duke, his carriage, and horses to perdition. The duke, however, commanded, "Stop that nonsense," in a voice that had Meg in the upstairs window stop mooning over John below. The bawling ceased. "I thought you told me you weren't babies? It's too bad I can make promises only to real gentlemen, not infants, for I would have promised to bring a riding horse next time if you behaved today."

Noses were wiped, eyes dried, and the boys clambered over the wheels and into the curricle.

"And you were worried they would fall?" the duke asked as he helped Graceanne onto the bench. "They're as agile as squirrels!"

The argument over which twin got to sit alone was instantly quelled by Leland's masterful decision that Willy would have first choice because he was the elder, and then Leslie would get the center seat on the way back.

As he walked around the carriage to the other side, Leland told John Groom that he felt like Solomon. His bubble of pride burst when the tiger grinned and wondered, if he was so wise, how come Master Wellesley was sitting on Mrs. Warrington's lap?

"How the deuce can you tell that's Willy?" the duke asked, confounded. He hadn't seen a mark different, and he'd been looking.

" 'E's the quiet one. Sticks by 'is ma more."

"Then what in blazes was all that argle-bargle about?"

" 'E had to prove 'e weren't a baby, now, didn't 'e?"

The widow just smiled. Leland didn't find that smile quite as appealing as some of the others he'd fought harder to win.

Graceanne finally relaxed under the carriage robe when

she saw how competently the duke tooled the ribbons. He was careful of ruts, watchful for small animals near the hedgerows, and kept the pair to an even, moderate pace. Assured that John Groom was keeping one strong hand on Leslie's shoulder, she soon eased her death grip on Willy and the railing. The boys were too enthralled to be troublesome. They looked so happy, she couldn't hold back a sigh.

"Are you cold?" Leland asked, looking over briefly.

"No, I just couldn't help wishing ..."

"Wishing ... ?" he prompted her. " 'Tis the season for that, after all."

"No, I was just being goosish, wishing I could give the boys ponies of their own when they are old enough."

She could give them a stable of their own if she wanted, he knew. And Warrington boys belonged on horses as soon as they could walk. Then again, what did a female know about such things? She was like to make a mull of it. Astounding himself with such fiercely protective emotions, he offered, "I'll see to it when the time is right." Which would be as soon as he and John could find the perfect mounts, but no need to worry a fussbudget mother yet. Then, gads, he mused to himself, if she beamed like that for a couple of ponies, imagine what she'd do for a pair of diamond earbobs.

There was something about his smile, and Greeks bearing gifts, that made Graceanne distrust his offer. She became downright panicky when the curricle turned off the road to the village and headed toward Ware Hold on its hill.

"I thought we were going to the village, Your Grace. That is, perhaps we should turn back now. Willy, are you chilled?"

Ware turned and grinned, feathering the corner between the Hold's gates. "What, did you want to show off for your friends in town like Prudence? I thought to take the boys back to the Hold to see the decorations."

"No, no, that wouldn't be at all the thing." She couldn't

quite come out and say she feared for her virtue, but some of that worry must have shown on her face.

"You're not a green girl, Cousin, who's never let out alone."

"But I still have to mind my reputation." His reputation was what she minded most. "Small-town gossip is not a comfortable thing. And the vicar's daughters . . ."

"But my aunt Eudora is up from London. There cannot be the tiniest tidbit for the scandalbroth. She wants to meet Tony's boys. Will you come?"

Graceanne felt that she'd been outflanked again, but she nodded.

Going through the enormous doors of the castle, past the bewigged and bowing butler, the boys were dumbstruck for once. Graceanne kept tight hold on two little hands as two heads swiveled from the rigid footmen to the armored knights to the weapon-filled walls. Graceanne's head swiveled, too, from the irreplaceable Dynasty bowls to the framed miniatures to the collection of carved jade horses. "I don't think this is a good idea, Your Grace."

"Nonsense." Leland turned to the right-hand liveried sentry and assigned him to escort the children to the kitchens. "This is Master Wellesley, and Master Leslie, or vice versa. They would appreciate some hot chocolate and one of Henri's pastries, I'm sure."

The footman gulped. "Me, Your Grace?"

"Unless you wish to imitate an andiron for the rest of your life."

Graceanne reluctantly transferred the boys' hands to the servant's immaculate gloves. "Be good, darlings, and don't touch anything."

"Not even the pretty horsies?"

"On second thought," Ware decided, turning to the other footman, "you go along, too. After they've eaten, I'm sure there is a ball or something in the old nursery."

Before the children were halfway across the vast cavern of the hall, a small, gray-haired woman dressed in the latest style approached, tapping her cane. "So there you are, Ware. I've been waiting an age. Had my tea without you."

Leland made the introductions to his aunt, Lady Eudora Warrington.

"Remember the gel from the wedding. Your father still such a starched-up prig?" Before Graceanne could think of an answer to such a question, the old lady fired off another: "D'you gamble, missy?"

"Why, no, ma'am. My father—"

"Just what I thought, he is. I cannot abide niminy-piminy females, Ware, even if they are good breeders. Told you so. Now I'll have to go trounce my maid again. Already owes me two years' salary."

Scarlet-faced, Graceanne still had to ask, "But I thought you wanted to see Tony's children?"

Aunt Eudora pointed her cane to where the footmen were leading the boys away. "See 'em, don't I? Got the Warrington look, at least. Now you can go put 'em in the icehouse or whatever, take 'em out when they're eighteen or so and fit for society." With that she tapped her way across the carpet and disappeared through an arched doorway.

Her head still spinning, Graceanne permitted herself to be led down a hall and into a library five times the size of the Misses Macgruders' bookshop. The duke seated her on a leather armchair near the blazing fire and said, "Tea will be along shortly."

"But no chaperone." It was a statement, not a question. Oh, Papa was right, she never should have come. The duke was resting one arm on the mantel, looking so confident and at ease and attractive that she was tempted to throw one of his priceless Sevres vases at him. And there she'd been worried about the boys!

Leland laughed and gestured toward the door. "See? It's open, all very proper. You're safe, I promise."

"But you've lied to me before. Twice now, I believe. Once about promising the boys a curricle ride and once about your aunt."

"No, she did want to get a look at the twins, I swear. But please, Mrs. Warr—Cousin Graceanne, I did want to speak to you, away from the parsonage."

She folded her hands in her lap as primly as a schoolmistress. "Yes, Your Grace?"

"I . . . that is, what have . . . um, are you sure you don't gamble?"

"Of course not, Your Grace. My father would never have permitted such behavior. While I was with the army, the wives led very circumspect lives. There were no polite gaming parlors, if that's what you are thinking. Naturally the officers indulged. If you are afraid I'll chouse your aunt Eudora out of her pin money, you are far off the mark."

"No, no." But he sounded relieved nevertheless, adding to Graceanne's confusion. He ran his hand through his hair. "Confound it all, there is no delicate way of putting this."

Graceanne was certain now that another slip on the shoulder was in the offing. First he wanted to make sure she wasn't expensive to keep. She jumped to her feet. "No, there is no polite way to ask a lady if she will—"

Just then a mighty crash came from somewhere down the hall, followed by minor noises, slamming doors.

"Oh, dear, I knew we shouldn't have—"

The butler entered with the tea tray and two footmen to help serve. Leland merely raised an eyebrow. The butler bowed and said, "I believe Monsieur Henri has just tendered his resignation, Your Grace. Will that be all?"

Graceanne couldn't make a scene, not with two footmen standing at attention in case the sugar bowl was emptied. She couldn't leap up and run away from this makebait philanderer or toss his extravagant, ostentatious repast in his lap. So she sat and drank her tea and ate his pastries and made small talk about their favorite Christmas carols. And she seethed.

Then came the unmistakable sound of glass shattering. Graceanne's teacup fell from her hand. Thank goodness it was empty, and the carpet so thick the delicate Wedgwood only bounced. Besides, the footman almost caught it before it hit the floor.

The butler returned. And bowed. "Not one of the stained glass panels, Your Grace. Will that be all?"

Chapter Seven

$\mathcal{G}$raceanne was on her feet. "Please, Your Grace, I must leave."

"No, no. Milsom will handle everything. He always does." The duke blocked her way to the door before she could bolt like a nervous filly. "I haven't yet had a chance to ask you—"

"Please, it will only embarrass us both."

"Then you *do* know what I'm talking about."

"Yes, to my eternal shame."

"Ah-ha, so I was right! You *have* done something underhanded with the money!"

"The money?" If he'd said he wanted her opinion on the Corn Laws, Graceanne couldn't have been more surprised. She sat back down. "What money?"

"It's a little late to play the innocent, Mrs. Warrington." He took up his position in front of the mantel, then started pacing. "Or did you think I was such a here-and-thereian, I'd never ask where the money was going?" He didn't wait for Graceanne's answer, which was just as well, for she didn't have one. "I've been racking my brain to think what it could be. Clothes? Jewelry?" He gave her one disdainful look in passing. "Not likely. I've seen your Posy, so it's not fast horses. You say you don't gamble, and I believe you."

"Am I supposed to be thankful for that?" Graceanne murmured into his tirade, her head rotating from side to side with his long strides.

"So I asked myself, what could it be? Is she paying off some terrible debt? Buying Consols for her old age? Keeping a lover?"

"Your Grace!"

He came to a halt in front of her, glowering down. "So tell me, what in the blazes are you doing with Tony's money?"

"Oh, *that* money!" Graceanne sighed in relief. "You must know I didn't have any dowry to speak of, just a pittance from Mama's family. The settlements, therefore, were negligible. Papa says my widow's jointure barely covers the cost of what the twins break—that is, what they breakfast on."

"Cut line, ma'am, I know to the shilling what your portion is. I ought to, my man of business helped draw up the marriage papers. What I am talking about, if you wish to play the game to its conclusion, is Tony's money. The money I hold as trustee and whose interest I deposit at your bank monthly, having started the account with a substantial sum. The money that is supposed to ensure Tony's children a happy, healthy childhood and his widow security. The money, in short, that is withdrawn and never spent!"

"I . . . I never knew Tony had any money. He never spoke to me about it. We never wanted for anything, but neither did we live grandly. I thought his army pay . . ."

"The army pays chicken feed. Of course Tony had money of his own; his grandfather was a duke. There was no property, since they lived at Ware House in London, but a tidy competence. How do you think Tony bought his commission?"

Graceanne stared at her fingers. "I thought you must have purchased it for him." She shook her head. "And his mother lived in a rented house."

Now it was Leland's turn to study the Turkey carpet he

had almost worn out. "Aunt Eudora moved into Ware House" was all he said. It was enough.

Graceanne was so silent for a moment, obviously think-ing, that Leland could hear a clock ticking, and feet pound-ing down a hall somewhere. Many feet. He let her think. Then he handed over his handkerchief. Damn and blast, he never meant to make her cry. It wasn't as though he was going to have her clapped in irons, either, especially if what he now suspected was true. He started pacing again.

Graceanne dabbed at the tears that trickled down her cheeks and snuffled into the fine linen. "Thank you," she said automatically, staring at a private hell so intensely that she didn't hear the shouts in the hall. Many shouts.

At last she spoke: "That's why he didn't want me to spend time in your company. He didn't care about my good reputation, or your bad one. He just didn't want us to con-verse. It's his collection, of course. I've heard that some men get like that over gambling, where they will lie and cheat their own families to support their wagering. He told me there wasn't enough money to bother about, that he would handle everything for me the way he always did, that women had no head for business anyway. My own fa-ther. The temptation must have been too great."

"That's not much of an excuse. If temptation is too great for a man of the cloth, how are we poor mortals expected to manage? Right now I am tempted to go wring your fa-ther's scrawny neck! To think of you acting the servant in his home so he can purchase moldy old books makes my blood boil. I've half a mind to have him hauled before the magistrate." His pacing grew more rapid.

"You mustn't, please. My mother is of a nervous dispo-sition. That would kill her."

"Then what would you have me do? I cannot just plant him a facer, a man his age, and I certainly cannot issue a challenge to a cleric. Of course, I have it in my power to see he's not a clergyman in my district anymore."

"Please, the church is his life. He really is a devout

man." Graceanne sniffled again, which did not ease the duke's anger one whit.

"Except for greed, deceit, and dishonor, to say nothing of being the starched-up prig Aunt Eudora called him. You cannot intend to let him get away with this."

"Exactly how much . . . ? That is, how tempted was he?" Graceanne wanted to know.

Leland paused long enough in his pacing to listen to the dying commotion in the hall, which she seemed not to hear, thank goodness. Then he named a sum that had the widow gasping. Graceanne knew the value of things from doing the household accounts; this was far beyond any computations she'd handled.

"Why, that's a king's ransom!"

"Not quite," he said dryly. "It wouldn't even pay Prinny's debts for a month. But that's the capital, of course, which should stay intact so the children have a legacy when they reach their majority. Unless Willy is duke by then, in which case only Leslie inherits. Meanwhile, the interest and earnings on investments should be enough for living expenses and incidentals. That's decent living, mind you, befitting a gentleman's sons, no more scrimping and cheese-paring. I had always intended to pay the boys' schooling"—he hadn't thought of it till then, but he should have—"so you needn't count that in your figuring. Nor the ponies."

"Oh, my." She'd never been fonder of Tony than at that moment, nor of His Grace! With a radiant smile, she said, "What a marvelous Christmas present! I don't know how I can ever thank you."

He kicked the edge of the fireplace. "Thank me? You should be wishing me to perdition. I should have seen you settled back in England myself, but it was easier to assume you were more comfortable with your parents. And then I should have looked into the matter sooner rather than suspect you of any hugger-mugger."

"But you couldn't have known. And I think you are taking on too much responsibility. I should have asked to see Tony's papers."

Leland was about to explain that looking after those dependent on him *was* his responsibility as duke, when the butler cleared his throat in the doorway. "Your Grace?"

"Yes, Milsom, what is it?"

"I thought Your Grace might be wondering about the slight disturbance. The fire is out now." He bowed and backed out of the room.

Leland resumed his pacing. "So what about the reverend? What shall you do?"

"I shall cast up my accounts if you don't stop moving to and fro," she said in exasperation, rubbing her temples.

Leland smiled. "See the power of money? A bit of a windfall and no more meek little sparrow. The humble widow is already giving orders to dukes. Not that you were ever quite humble," he amended, taking a seat across from her. "But seriously, you don't have to stay in your father's house any longer."

Graceanne pondered her choices. "My suddenly taking a cottage in the village would be degrading to my mother. And it would leave her and my sister no better off. They'd still be at Papa's mercy."

"You could move in here," he suggested. "The boys being my heirs, no one would think anything of it."

No one would think anything good of it, he should have said. Graceanne could just hear the gossip now. "I think not." Rather than discussing his reputation, she said, "It wouldn't be healthy for the boys to live so far above our station. Think of the comedown when you marry and have heirs of your own, as I am sure you'll eventually do."

"What, do you think I'll toss Tony's family out into the snow?"

"Of course not, Your Grace." But his wife might.

"I thought you had agreed to stop 'Your Gracing' me, Graceanne. Please, Leland is adequate. *Cousin* if you insist on the formality."

She did. "Cousin. Besides, I am not sure Ware Hold can survive the twins."

He laughed. "You're right. It's withstood siege for only two or three hundred years. Well, if you won't move into the castle, perhaps you'd consider Ware House in London?"

"With Lady Eudora? No thank you! I think that would merely be substituting one form of tyranny for another. Maybe I should move away altogether, be truly independent for the first time in my life. Bath, perhaps, or Brighton, where the boys can play on the beach in the summer."

Leland got up and walked toward the desk, where a decanter and glasses stood. "Madeira, Cousin?"

"No, thank you, my father thinks imbibing is—why, yes, Cousin, I do believe I would enjoy a sip of sherry."

While Leland poured, he spoke. "I shouldn't like you to move where I cannot see the boys."

Leland really meant he'd miss seeing the sprouts grow up, miss the riding lessons he was already planning and the hunting, fishing, and swimming expeditions his own father never took him on. Grace thought his words must imply a threat. His Grace was being agreeable now, but cousin or not, he was still the imperious duke. And he held the power and the pursestrings. She mustn't forget that for a moment. "I suppose I'd hate to move where I knew no one."

Out of relief that she wasn't emigrating to Canada or something impossible, he handed her a glass and said, "Well, you know me. My offer of a cottage in the woods still stands, or a little house in Kensington . . ."

She did know him. And she must never, ever forget that he was a rake of the first water. She slammed the wineglass down on a table beside her, hard enough to rattle the collection of ivory figurines there. A drop of wine sloshed out onto the carved cherrywood. Graceanne hurriedly used her handkerchief, the duke's actually, from when she was weeping, to dab at the spill. "That is not, and never will be, an option, Your Grace."

"Back to 'Your Grace' again, eh? I suppose I owe you another apology, ma'am. Just as you cannot help mopping at spills, I cannot help flirting with a pretty girl." Which wasn't true at all, Leland admitted to himself. There was something about this woman ... "At any rate, you won't want to decide anything till after Christmas, when I'll have a chance to visit the bank. Do you want all the bills and such sent to me to handle?"

Graceanne was taking deep breaths to try to regain her composure. Then she decided to take a sip of wine instead. The tingle on her tongue worked better. "I am not a nodcock, Cousin, who has never seen an account book. I am sure I can manage my own finances."

"It's not the way things are usually done, a woman in charge." With misgiving he eyed the fragile wineglass, the delicate ivories, and the spark in her blue eyes. "But I suppose we can try that arrangement for now. I'll make provision for the funds to be at your sole disposal at the first of every month, with no one else to have access without my approval. That should put a crimp on the reverend's sticky fingers."

Graceanne nodded her satisfaction. "Then on the first of January I shall be free to make my own decisions for once. A new life for the new year." She savored the freedom, and the wine. One of the unfamiliar experiences gave her the courage to ask, "Do you think ... that is, I hate to bother you. It's vulgar to speak of money and such, but might I have an advance or whatever?"

"What, outrunning the bailiff already?" he teased. "And here you just assured me you could manage to live within your means." But he stood up and went to the desk, where he opened a drawer and then a cash box. "How much blunt do you need, my dear?"

Her cheeks were warm; that must be the wine, not the familiarity. "Oh, just enough for Christmas. I'd like to send something to Tony's batman in Dorset. He was injured trying to save poor Tony, only to lose him to a fever, and he returned on the ship with us, seeing to our comfort the whole way."

"Confound it, I should have seen to him." He added a few more bills to the pile in his hand.

"And I'd like to buy some gifts, even if there's not much time to shop. Do you think there will be sleds for the boys here in Warefield? Cook says it will snow for Christmas, and they could have so much fun. And a new set of dishes for Mother, a dress length or two for Prudence. Velvet, I think. A new uniform for Meg. No, a new uniform and another nursery maid!"

Leland kept adding to the stack, smiling. She hadn't mentioned anything for herself, so he did. "And a new bonnet, I hope, for me and the boys."

"A bonnet? Whatever could you and the children want with a bonnet?"

"So we don't have to look at that monstrosity you've been wearing. Save it for the snowman we'll build if Cook is right. And get yourself some prettier gowns, too. Tony wouldn't like you looking the dowd."

She looked down. "No, he wouldn't. Perhaps one or two if I find the time to sew."

He laughed. "And you said you were a downy one. You don't need time, sweetheart, you have money! The village seamstress will stay up Christmas Eve to see you outfitted properly, for enough of the ready."

"A new gown for Christmas would be lovely, even if it must be black."

"Make that two or three. I'd like you to be here with me and Aunt Eudora on Boxing Day to help give out the gifts, so Willy can meet the tenants. My relatives should certainly be dressed as well as the farmers." He shrugged and emptied the rest of the cash box into a leather purse which he handed to her. "My Christmas present." Before Graceanne could argue about the money coming from her account, he asked, "But what about your father? Should I speak to him?"

Graceanne clutched the purse and raised her chin. "No. If I am to stand on my own, I shall do it. And I intend to ask him for the return of the money he spent."

"*Brava!* Stand firm, my Grace. Kick him where it hurts most"—she inhaled sharply—"in his pocketbook. Ah, and here are the boys, just in time."

Milsom carried the exhausted twins, one under each arm.

"Did you have a good time, darlings? Thank Cousin Leland for the visit."

One look at his butler's face and the duke said, "I think we should thank Mr. Milsom, too." And double his Christmas gift.

The boys made their proper bows and thank-yous, then: "I peed in a water closet, Mama! You pull a chain and the water goes whoosh and ends up where the moat used to be."

Graceanne clapped her hand over Leslie's mouth. She didn't get to Willy in time.

"And I peed behind some bushes."

Trying not to laugh, Leland asked, "What, did you go outside, then?"

Milsom stared over their heads. "I believe that was the conservatory, Your Grace. The orange trees."

Chapter Eight

"*G*od gave Adam sovereignty over all the creatures of the earth," Reverend Beckwith preached. "Including Eve. It isn't right for a woman to have that kind of authority."

Unfortunately for Graceanne, she was the sole recipient of this day's sermon. She'd come back from Ware Hold and handed the twins over to Meg for a nap—they did not resist, for once—then confronted her father in his study.

"I have spoken to His Grace, Papa," she began to say.

"And I suppose he filled your head with all manner of nonsense."

"If you call a handsome competence nonsense, yes." Then she went on to explain that while Reverend Beckwith might have used the money for reasons he deemed worthy, Tony would not have agreed. She did not agree, and the Duke of Ware did not agree. It was only the invocation of Leland's name, and his threats to hold the vicar to account, that had Beckwith cease his diatribe about preserving the past, the revered texts. "I doubt the sacred writings would crumble to dust without my children's patrimony. Some other cork-brained collector would be happy to keep them for posterity's sake. I am not."

The vicar grumbled, "And I suppose you'd rather let

Ware gamble the whole thing away, or spend it on his ladybirds."

"I'm not saying the duke is a saint, but I cannot imagine him misusing the funds left in his trust. Nor could he possibly need more wealth. Besides, he truly wants what's best for the boys. He likes them."

Beckwith snorted, ruffling the hairs in his nose. "Hah! You always were as green as a goose. It's called petting the calf, you moonling. So you'll move in with him and he'll have his heirs, his fortune, and a ready-made mistress. Well, don't come crawling to me when my lord rakehell gets tired of you and those hell-born babes, missy."

Graceanne tried to keep her tongue in check. This is your father, she kept repeating to herself. Aloud she said, "It's not like that at all. I am not going to move into Ware House."

"What, he didn't offer you carte blanche? It must be because he doesn't want the brats underfoot."

If Beckwith weren't so busy caressing the pages of his latest, and most likely last, acquisition, he'd have seen his daughter's flaming cheeks. "He did—that is, he likes the children. He did invite us to live at the castle, but I know how small minds work." She ought to, from living at the vicarage. "So I refused his offer. I thought I might stay on here for a while, for Mother's sake." When she saw how his eyes lit up, she added, "I'll pay my fair share of expenses, but no more. And I'll go over the household accounts with you so we are both satisfied."

The vicar was thinking of how he could put some of that corrupt, worldly money to holy use. "And the bills will go to Ware's man of business?"

"No, His Grace agreed that I can be trusted to look after my sons' welfare. I shall see every bill that comes across this desk, and I shall pay only those I authorize."

That's when the good vicar began quoting Genesis.

"Furthermore," he added in a burst of last-ditch effort, "God made woman's brain smaller. He wouldn't have done that if He'd wanted them to understand finances."

Graceanne knew better than to argue Scriptures. "That's absurd. Mother handled the account books for years."

"And squandered half our income on the poor," Beckwith griped, but still making his point. "And look what happened because she overtaxed her mind. Now she's in a wheeled chair most of the time."

"Papa, she's in a wheeled chair all winter because this house is too cold for her arthritis. You won't permit enough fires to be burned to keep the place warm. That's going to change, too."

"Now, wait a minute, girl. You can fritter away your inheritance on furbelows and folderols for those limbs of Satan, but no woman is going to dictate how I spend my money."

"I wouldn't think of it, Papa, my brain is too small. When I put such bills in your pile, I'll just consider that you're repaying what you borrowed from Tony's estate."

Prudence was not happy with Graceanne's new circumstances either at first. "It's just not fair! You got to marry a handsome soldier and go to a foreign country and be a duke's relation and now this! You always get everything! Why, Papa won't even let me go to Squire Maxton's Christmas ball! And Liam asked me for the first dance!"

"Liam Hallorahan had no business asking you anything, when he knows Papa does not approve. And you'll have plenty of chances to find a handsome beau next year, when you are eighteen. I'll make sure of that."

Prudence began to see the advantages of having an older sister with deep pockets, especially when she accompanied Graceanne on her first-ever shopping spree. Of course Pru pouted and stamped her foot when Graceanne insisted an orange silk gown was too old for her, but she allowed as how the peach sarcenet was as pretty as anything Lucy had, after Graceanne threw in a Kashmir shawl, new slippers, and a painted fan. Honestly, Graceanne thought, dealing with the twins' tantrums was easier. They were less costly to bribe back to smiles, too.

70

Other than that temporary setback, the shopping trip was a great success. Henry Moon and his son were willing to make the sleds. They couldn't be varnished in time for Christmas, but they'd be sturdy enough, the blacksmith promised, even for her little demons, ah, darlings.

Mr. Anstruther at the local emporium had toys for the twins and trinkets Prudence couldn't live without, although she'd managed to for seventeen years. He didn't have any "quality" dishes, however. There was no need, he explained, since Ware got its china ordered special from London or direct from the manufacturers, and even Squire's wife went to town once a year for her fancy household furnishings. No one else thereabouts had any call for porcelain dishes. Mrs. Anstruther, however, did uncover some color plates of china patterns they could order up Birmingham way. She'd send a boy straight off if Mrs. Warrington was certain that's what she wanted, expensive plates that wouldn't last a day with those hellions—no, honeys—in the house. They'd be there by Christmas morning if it didn't snow.

Graceanne next visited some of the less fortunate of her father's parishioners and hired the women to finish her mittens and scarves, and their husbands and sons to whittle tops and wooden animals for all the Sunday-school children.

The milliner's was the last stop. Prudence snatched up a chip straw bonnet with jonquil ribbons, just the thing for her new gown. Graceanne knew she'd get no peace unless that, too, joined the pile of parcels filling the pony cart. Pru was a selfish, spoiled chit, but she was Graceanne's sister. And really, she deserved some joyful spots in her life, too. Graceanne was happy being able to provide them. She was even happier finding a black satin bonnet with lavender lining and ribbon rosettes that was far and away the prettiest hat she had owned since her wedding. No matter that it was black, it would match her new lace-trimmed black gown of finest merino and the velvet one with satin ribbons. Her cheeks seemed rosier next to it, her blue eyes brighter. Or perhaps that came from thinking if His Grace would like it.

Foolish beyond permission, she told herself. She had no business thinking such things, not with her husband dead less than six months. And certainly not about a confirmed rake like Ware. He was far beyond her touch, Graceanne reminded herself, and further, beyond her experience. Whatever else, she must not let the recent amity between them blind her to his autocratic nature. Just as she'd considered a velvet toque, then chose the black satin, His Grace could change his mind about Willy. The same way she decided what she wanted, then purchased it, Ware could have anything he wanted, including her son. The power that came from funds in hand was new to Graceanne, a blessing; she must never forget that Ware considered such power his birthright. Still, it did feel good to look presentable. And maybe next month she'd buy the toque.

The last days before Christmas were too few by half, with all the new things Graceanne wanted to do: shopping, fittings, hiring extra staff for the vicarage, and some new furnishings, too, so the place would look respectable if not festive. Her father grumbled, but he did find the funds for his share someplace, likely the same place he kept deference to his noble patron.

Ware did ride over the next day on a huge roan stallion, and he did give each of the boys a turn up in front of him while Graceanne stood wringing her hands in front of the door of the vicarage. The children were ecstatic, of course, and begged, "Faster, Collie, faster." Any faster and Graceanne would have palpitations. Ware's grin was as wide as the boys'.

He was still grinning later, after a session with the vicar in Beckwith's study. Graceanne couldn't hear what was being said, not over Willy and Les's whoops as they rode the broomstick ponies Ware had brought, but her dealings with the vicar were easier after that. Not more pleasant, just easier.

Another lightening of Graceanne's burdens came when Prudence surprisingly offered to take over choir practice. Since this was the first and only unselfish act Graceanne could recall her sister performing, she distrusted it immediately. Liam Hallorahan's fine tenor voice just might have something to do with Pru's commitment to the choir, Graceanne suspected. His handsome looks and green-eyed admiration for the chit might have even more to do with it.

With no Catholic church in miles, Liam had taken to attending Warefield's chapel. "For certain and it's the same God, no matter the name on the door," Liam declared, and "B'gorra, aren't we all God's children anyway?" Not even Vicar Beckwith could bar the church to someone who wanted to worship, especially when he attended in company with the second most influential family in the neighborhood. Squire Maxton was a reliable parish donor, his wife one of the leading do-gooders for the community. Unfortunately, Mrs. Maxton loved music. Her warbly soprano insisted the choir needed Hallorahan.

What the choir didn't need was Pru making eyes at the good-looking young Irishman behind the vicar's back, but that's what it got every Sunday until Graceanne took over as director and insisted on a little more decorum. She supposed she ought to be keeping an eye on her hoydenish sister now, to save her from heartbreak later, but Liam would be leaving in a month or so anyway. Pru would get over her infatuation soon enough. Besides, Liam and Pru weren't her problem just then; replacing the old but newly shredded wallpaper in the hall was, where the broomstick ponies had lunged out of control.

"Not a shilling of mine will go to that, daughter!"

"If the paper weren't so old and shabby, it wouldn't have ripped."

"If those urchins had an ounce of discipline, it wouldn't

73

have ripped. Why, I've a mind to use those broomsticks where they'll do the most good."

So Graceanne bundled the twins into the pony cart and went about her errands. Despite all of her new tasks, she couldn't let the usual parish duties fall behind. The sick still needed visiting, for instance. It was amazing what an improvement a visit by Graceanne and her boys made. Why, May Turner got right out of her bed and shooed them out the door.

"I'm feeling so much better, Mrs. Warrington, after these few minutes, I think I'll go visit my brother. I'll have to hurry now, looks like it's coming on to snow." ·

Little Letty Brown with her broken leg took one look at the twins and started hopping around the room, gathering her toys. "There, I told you she'd be walking soon," Graceanne told Mrs. Brown.

And the baker's wife, who was almost near to term, was so encouraged by seeing two such happy, healthy, energetic little boys, she decided to stop fretting and go help her man downstairs immediately. "And you know how important it is to humor women who are breeding, I'm sure. Otherwise they might have twi—twitches."

Only Old Man Hatchett seemed to have a relapse. "Oh, no," he called through the closed door. "Don't come in, ma'am. I'm suddenly feeling that poorly, I'm afeared it might be something contagious. I'd never forgive myself an' your precious bairns come down sick."

Somehow her duty calls always seemed shorter when she took the boys along. Graceanne's other visits to the village, without the twins, seemed to take longer than ever these busy days. Everyone wanted to stop her and congratulate her on the good news they'd heard as soon as the vicarage placed its first robust order for groceries.

There wasn't a man, woman, or child in Warefield who wasn't happy for that nice Mrs. Warrington. No one deserved it more, losing her husband so young and having to live with that nip-farthing Beckwith. Troubles seemed to come in pairs for the sweet young thing. Now maybe she'd be able to hire a proper nanny for those terrors, or send them off to school. Or the navy.

If the villagers wanted to take time to rejoice with Graceanne over her good fortune, callers at the vicarage wanted to know its precise amount. The squire's wife came for tea as soon as she heard they'd hired a decent cook. Her questions bordered on the discourteous, but she had a nephew bordering on River Tick. In an attempt to deflect the inquisition, Graceanne had the inspired notion of having the twins down to take tea with the adults. No, Mrs. Maxton wasn't ready to share Leslie's macaroon or Willy's watercress sandwich, without the watercress, naturally. And no, she didn't think she'd invite that nephew down for Christmas after all.

Graceanne was irritated at all the time the entertaining took, especially when the ladies insisted a good coze was impossible with little ears present. Her mother, though, was delighted with the influx of new company, especially since Mrs. Beckwith didn't have to be so ashamed of her parlor. For her mother's sake, Graceanne poured out the tea and passed the plates, and smiled at the nosy old biddies when she would rather have been wrapping gifts or finishing the pageant costumes or any of the thousand other things on her list.

Graceanne was so busy, she didn't miss His Grace's presence for the two days he was gone to visit friends in Oxford. The duke had stopped to see if Graceanne had any commissions for him before he left, but she didn't, not with the sleds and the dishes already ordered. She wished him Godspeed and watched him drive off in his elegant curricle, caped greatcoat over his wide shoulders. Then she went back to consulting with the sexton over decorations for the church.

No, she didn't even notice the duke's absence, except when the vicar forbade her to put the evergreen garlands in his church, and made sure their cost was added to her side of the ledger. And she didn't wish Ware would come back soon, except for the children's incessant questions: "When is Collie coming home?" and "Do you think he'll bring us something?"

No, she didn't miss him at all.

Chapter Nine

*C*hristmas came, as it usually did, whether anyone was ready for it or not. Had there been more time, in fact, Graceanne would have found more to do. Now that it was the afternoon of Christmas Eve, all she had to accomplish was a dress rehearsal of the Nativity play in the empty church, minor repairs on the twins' costumes, and a nap. The boys couldn't be expected to stay up later than their usual bedtime without a longer than usual nap; nor could they be expected to understand that concept, especially as agitated as they were. Leland's return hadn't done much to dim their excitement, not when he mentioned a surprise or two for good little boys—tomorrow.

Every other minute a dark head would pop up from the pillows to ask if it was tomorrow yet.

Finally Graceanne took them down to her own room, where the three of them could share her bed. She cuddled their little bodies next to her, pulled a quilt over them all, and started to tell stories and sing carols.

When she awoke, Willy smelled of her rosewater and Les was wearing her new slippers on his hands. They must have slept some, for her slippers didn't smell of rosewater yet and the rest of the room was more or less intact. At least Graceanne was refreshed. And at least it was now time to get the boys bathed and dressed, with Meg's help.

Then it was Graceanne's turn, with no help. She tried to ask Prudence which gown she should wear that night, which to save for Christmas Day, the velvet or the merino. Pru was too busy complaining that Mary had to wear a shawl on her head, and how was she supposed to go out caroling with the choir later if she looked like a scarecrow?

Graceanne chose the velvet, with its satin ribbons. She put on the pearls Tony had given her in honor of the twins' birth and went down to supper, to her father's lecture about the pitfalls of vanity, avarice, and trying to catch Lord Ware's eye. Prudence came in for her share of strictures on modesty and filial obedience. Even Mrs. Beckwith was censured for getting above herself, entertaining gentry, and serving three courses at supper. Of course, Graceanne noted, her father didn't turn down any of the new cook's offerings. They all said, "Yes, Papa," and "No, Mr. Beckwith," and went on eating the best food to grace this table in anyone's memory. The silence was broken only when Beckwith remembered another fault, another sin.

Graceanne couldn't help contrasting this meal, with its varied selections, to the plain fare at the nursery dinner, where the children laughed and sang and chattered about everything. Perhaps she should take her meals there from now on, she considered. What were a few spills or stains?

Then it was time to put on their warmest cloaks and walk across the path to the church. Even Mrs. Beckwith was going, all wrapped up and leaning on the arm of the new maid. Sick or well, servant or master, young or old, everyone in the little village of Warefield would be attending church that night. The twins skipped ahead of Meg, darting off into the darkness, then giggling at the nursemaid's frantic calls. Graceanne didn't want to call them to heel yet; better they expend those high spirits outside the church doors.

The party from the manse separated once they were inside the stone church, where the sexton already had the candles lighted, reflected in the stained glass windows. The vicar took up his robe and stood by the pulpit, meditating. Mrs. Beckwith settled onto the bench reserved for the minister's family, along the wall nearest the lectern, while the servants filed into back pews. Prudence took her seat in the small choir section behind the vicar, where the chairs had been pushed to one side to leave room for a few bales of hay, a makeshift manger, and a ladder draped in dark fabric.

Graceanne and the boys stayed in the tiny vestry, gathering the other Sunday-school students who were to be actors for this night. While the congregation assembled in the church, she adjusted headpieces and located props and soothed anxious nerves. Just before her father started the service, she handed out the children's Christmas gifts, their mittens, little tops, and clothespin dolls, to keep them quiet. One of the mothers was to stay with the cast while Graceanne joined the choir for the first hymn.

From where she was sitting she could look past her father's rigid back to her mother's uncertain smile. Graceanne nodded in reassurance. Past them, nearly every row of the small church was filled, both sides of the aisle, with some parishioners standing by the door in the rear. That was more to make an easy exit when the vicar got going, she knew, than from lack of seats. The unfortunates in the first few rows had no such option, sitting almost immediately under the vicar's watchful eye. They couldn't even choose to sit farther back in the darker recesses, where one might have a catnap during Beckwith's orations, since these parishioners had their names on the pews, like Squire's family. Graceanne saw that Lucy Maxton had brought her betrothed along, but she couldn't see what had Prudence in such a swivet about him. The young man had no chin. And Mrs. Maxton must have purposely forgotten to air her furs until that afternoon again, for she was swathed in beady-eyed boas, and Squire was already sneezing and wiping his eyes. Graceanne knew from her childhood that the wheezing was bound to get worse halfway through the vicar's sermon. She used to make mental wagers over which would give out sooner, her father's voice or Squire's patience.

The very first row, of course, was reserved for the Warringtons. If His Grace got up and walked out, it wouldn't be his mortal soul in danger but the vicar's job, so for tonight, at least, they were assured a shorter than usual harangue. Thank goodness, she thought, for the children's sakes. And then she thought, Goodness, didn't His Grace look fine tonight!

He wore cream-colored pantaloons and a brown velvet coat that almost matched the color of his hair. His shirtpoints weren't as high as Lucy's intended's, nor his gleaming neckcloth so intricate, but Leland was the one who seemed better dressed and more confident in his attire. Besides, he had a strong, firm chin, with just the hint of indentation. He was definitely a man to the fiancé's youth.

As much as Graceanne had been studying His Grace during the invocations, he had been watching her watching him, and now he smiled. Mortified, Graceanne quickly lowered her eyes to the prayer book in her lap. But she knew it by heart, and soon enough her mind started to wander again, right in his direction. It must be the diamond in his neckcloth that drew her eye, or the heavy gold ring on his finger that flashed when he turned the pages, or the tiny sprig of holly in his buttonhole. Or the light in his eye when he caught her staring again. This time he winked.

Graceanne forced her concentration back to the matter at hand. This was church, and Christmas! She had no business staring at one of the worshippers, no matter how attractive. Besides, it was time for the next hymn.

At least the choir was paying attention, Pru's and Liam's voices melding gracefully around the others'. So they had practiced, contrary to her fears. The only jarring notes to the ancient hymn came from the congregation: Mrs. Maxton's warbly soprano and Ware's aunt Eudora's off-key squawk trying to drown her out. Graceanne looked up—she just couldn't help herself—to see that Ware was mouthing the words, with no sound coming out that she could hear.

Tony had been tone deaf; most likely the duke was, too. Somehow that made Graceanne feel better, that he wasn't entirely perfect. She also felt better when she noticed the black armband he wore in respect for his cousin. Good, she thought. If he respected Tony's memory, he would respect Tony's widow. There would be no more of his shockingly indecent proposals.

Papa had begun his sermon while Graceanne daydreamed of what being such a man's mistress could mean.

"I see faces I haven't seen in this church since last Easter. What, does God celebrate only holidays? I hear voices I know have taken the Lord's name in vain. Are you not ashamed now to sing His praises? I know there are those of you who have lusted and coveted and lied and cheated. Repent of your sins, I say, lest you burn in the hellfires of eternity."

A less self-righteous man might have figured out by then why he saw some of his parishioners so infrequently. Not Papa. But how could even Papa be talking of sin on this of all days, when he was supposed to rejoice with his flock in the birth of hope? Then again, she'd been thinking of sin, so she was just as guilty. Squire started coughing again.

"I know there are those among you"—the vicar's eyes were fixed on the first pew, and Graceanne didn't think he meant Aunt Eudora—"who have gambled and fornicated. On Sundays!"

Squire harrumphed, and Pru giggled from beside Graceanne. Gracious, whatever the duke said to Papa that day in the study must have been dire indeed, to call down such retribution. His Grace was looking thunderclouds back.

"And I know there are those among you who would profane the sanctity of Christ's birth with merrymaking and overindulgence, with pagan rituals and self-serving avarice."

Now a great deal of the congregation began squirming. Maybe they'd been sitting too long; maybe they'd been thinking of the lamb's wool back home, the goose dinners, and the presents.

Just when the vicar was winding himself up for the grand finale of calling damnation down on all their heads if they didn't repent, a small voice from the back of the church called out: "Mama, is it time to go home yet? We're going to miss Christmas!"

Graceanne mightn't know which child it was wandering down the center aisle, but she definitely knew whose child. With her face as red as the new mittens her son wore, Graceanne watched Meg dive for the child and miss. Two footmen in the duke's livery managed to corner the boy between them and lead him back to the vestry while the rest of the parishioners laughed.

So furious he could hardly speak, the vicar pounded on the lectern, but it was too late. No one was listening, no one was going to take him seriously when his own family didn't. Glaring at his elder daughter, he signaled for the final hymn.

With the closing refrains, the choir began to walk down the aisle toward the back of the church, and the sexton dimmed some of the candles, enough that the congregation could pretend not to see the frantic scurrying as the chairs were moved back and the hay bales were moved forward.

Then Squire's youngest son took his place at the lectern and began to read: "And it came to pass . . ."

When he reached the lines where the shepherds were out minding their sheep, the blacksmith's boy, with white robes and crook, herded his small flock down the center aisle. The matching lambs, woolly headpieces, red mittens, and all, gamboled in front of him making sure their furry tails wagged.

"And, lo! A star arose."

From the top of the shrouded ladder a silver star appeared. One of the lambs breathed "Ooh!" but the shepherd managed to get in his lines about being amazed.

"And an angel spoke to them."

The Anstruther girl was atop the ladder now, her brother

holding on to her ankles. One wing was lower than the other and her halo kept falling into her eyes, but she told the shepherd to follow the star, so Toby Moon did, herding his little lambs around the perimeter of the church and back to the vestry. One lamb baaed the whole way, one woofed.

Then it was Mary and Joseph's turn. Pru's pillow stuffing was realistic, and she drooped convincingly over Joseph's arm as they wearily limped toward the altar, where the Anstruther boy came out from behind the ladder to point toward the hay bales. There was no room at the inn. But there was a cow. Timmy and George Bindle could still be heard arguing over who should be the front end, forgetting to moo. Annie Carruthers was the horse. Her father's prize Percheron had a shorter tail now. There were two feathered creatures who alternately quacked and honked, and one pig in a dyed-pink pillowslip who was so embarrassed, he refused to oink.

Mary was masterful, though, kicking the pillows aside and retrieving the blanket-wrapped "infant" from behind the bales of hay while all eyes were on the animals and their antics. As she placed the baby in the rough manger, the star rose again and the angel's sweet young voice rose in a song of joyful adoration. Mary gazed adoringly—at the redheaded Irish Joseph, who still had his arm around her. They sang a duet of rejoicing.

The shepherd and his lambs followed the star again, then the three kings, bearing gifts and retrieving fallen crowns, wandered toward the altar and made their speeches. By this time one of the lambs remembered the spinning top in his pocket, and the other remembered he hadn't relieved himself after dinner. As the rest of the choir filed back in for a reprise of the angel's hallelujah, this time carrying lighted candles, Graceanne grabbed Willy and his top. Then she looked around helplessly, wondering what to do with him while she took Leslie outside. She couldn't hand him to her father, that was for sure, unless she wanted poor Willy served up as mutton, and Meg was all the way in the rear of the church.

"Rejoice, rejoice, a King is born," sang the choir, the kings, the congregants.

"Mama, I've got to—"

The duke stood and took Willy from her, and sat back down with the child in his lap as casually as if he'd taken a pinch of snuff, one-handed. He winked again as she fled outside with her other son through the nearby side door.

Graceanne reentered the church just in time for the closing benediction. The duke must have been watching for her, since he nodded and patted the empty space next to him. Lady Eudora was still cackling on his other side. Gathering up the remains of the duke's quizzing glass first, Graceanne put Leslie down in that spot next to Ware and started to move farther into the pew. The duke merely lifted Les onto his other knee and gave her an innocent smile. The vicar cleared his throat. Graceanne sat.

For the very first time, Tony's widow and sons took their places in the Warrington pew with the duke's family while her father blessed them all. Not a one of them believed he meant it.

Chapter Ten

"*S*orry I cannot shake your hand, Vicar," Leland said as he left the church, "but as you can see, my arms are full." He could have handed one of the sleeping boys back to their mother, but Graceanne was busy gathering hats, mufflers, and sheepskin costumes. She was also accepting laughing congratulations from all the villagers on the success of her pageant.

"Never seen it done better," beamed Mr. Anstruther, his own arms around an angel and an innkeeper.

Everyone was smiling, wishing each other the joys of the season, patting backs, sharing hugs, shaking hands. The vicar's "Rejoice in the Lord" struck a somber note, but only until his flock reached the outside and Squire's wife started "God Rest Ye Merry, Gentlemen," and everyone joined in on their way to the carriages or as they began the walk toward the village in the silent, starry night.

Aunt Eudora was already in the duke's crested carriage, rapping her cane impatiently on the floor. She had even less Christmas cheer than the vicar, Leland thought, looking around for Graceanne.

She hurried to his side. "Goodness, I didn't mean to leave you there like that. Here, give me the boys so you can see Lady Eudora home before she catches a chill."

"That woman is so cold-hearted, she could give an iceberg lessons," he joked, handing over one of the twins. "Aunt Eudora will find the flask I left in the coach soon enough, then she'll be content for a minute while I help you home. The boys are too much for you to carry together. You take Willy and I'll follow you to the vicarage."

"This is Leslie," she said with a smile at his muttered frustration. "It takes time. Thank you, and for your help during the service. The boys can be a trifle, ah, rambunctious at times."

"Just a trifle?" he teased. "But they were the highlight of the pageant. Why, they even stole the show from that precious angel on her ladder. You did a superb job of directing, Mrs. Warrington."

Graceanne opened the vicarage's side door and proceeded down the hall. She tiptoed past her father's study, where light shone under the closed door. Beckwith must have already retreated there to pray over the wickedness of mankind, and the servants would be celebrating with their own families or in the kitchen. "Gammon," Graceanne whispered. "Drury Lane has nothing to fear. Did you see the three kings almost come to blows at the end? And Prudence's shocking display—why, I thought Papa would suffer a brain storm right there."

If he hadn't before, he would now, seeing Pru and Liam alone in the vicarage parlor, where the carolers would assemble later. The way they jumped apart didn't look like choir practice to Leland.

Graceanne pursed her lips. "Prudence, I think you should go help Cook fix the hot cider. The others will be here soon, and you'll want to serve them and be on your way. Liam, perhaps you could start checking for the lanterns. They might be in the barn."

And they might be right in the front hall closet, where Graceanne had made sure days before that they'd be handy for those going wassailing.

"Masterful, my dear," Leland congratulated her, after

Prudence stomped off and Liam nervously bowed and hurried in the opposite direction. "But surely your mother . . ."

"Would have found her bed by now. Her delicate nerves, you know."

He knew that Graceanne had too much in her dish if the Beckwiths expected her to play duenna for that harum-scarum miss. He frowned as he followed her up the narrow stairs, and up again to the children's rooms under the eaves. His brows lowered even more when he saw the humble accommodations.

"Oh, I haven't finished decorating," she hurried to explain, misunderstanding his scowls. "I wanted to leave something for a surprise in the morning. I'll work on it later. This should be a Christmas they'll remember forever."

It would be if he had anything to say about it.

She led him through the nursery room and into the boys' tiny bedchamber. "Watch your head," she cautioned too late, for he was already rubbing it.

Tarnation, the newest tweenie at Ware Hold had better quarters. "Lud, you'd better stop feeding them."

Graceanne didn't even smile at that. She'd been worried herself that the boys would bash their skulls on the low eaves. Even when—and if—her father deemed them civilized enough to take up residence on the family floor below, there was hardly enough room. Perhaps when Prudence married. She had put Leslie down on the bed and was reaching to take Willy from the duke.

He, meanwhile, was looking around for another bed. "Is there another room, then?"

"What, for two tiny children? This isn't the castle, Your Grace." She didn't mean to be so belligerent, she was just embarrassed for the conditions. "Most of your own tenants make do with less."

"But these are not tenant children, these are my cousins." He held up a hand when he saw how she started to get that pinched look, then he patted Willy's back and put him on the bed next to Leslie. "No, I don't mean to pull caps with you on such a night. Even I would find that sacrilegious, brangling over babies on the night of the Christ child's birth. But pulling caps reminds me that I haven't had a chance to compliment you on your new bonnet. It's lovely, Cousin."

"Thank you, Your—Cousin." Graceanne busied herself with unbuttoning Leslie's shoes so he couldn't see her blush. Leaning over the bed, she told him, "Even if there were another room, they'd never sleep apart. As infants they were fretful without each other's company in the same cradle. Later, when they were ready for cots instead of their crib, I had two made. Every night I'd put them each to sleep in his own little bed. Every morning I'd find them tangled together in one bed or the other. Now I just give them a wider mattress." She looked up quickly. "I do expect them to outgrow it, like other children stop sucking their thumbs or carrying favorite blankets around."

"Hopefully that will happen before they go to university." He bent over the bed, too, working on the other twin's boots, and his hand brushed her arm.

Even through the layer of fabric she felt uncomfortable with his touch. The tiny room, the sleeping children, the feeling of being a family—but they were not a family, and she must not forget. "I can do that, Cousin. Thank you."

"Surely you have help?"

"What, to undress two little boys? It's only dukes who forget how to put on their own clothes! Remember, your aunt is waiting in the cold carriage."

"She'll keep. She's eager to get home only to the hand of piquet I promised her, to give her poor abigail an evening off. Aunt Eudora is likely in the coach now, marking a new deck."

"She cheats?"

"That's why she's always so desperate to get up a game. None of her cronies will play with her anymore." He removed Willy's shoe and stocking and stared at the little foot he held. "It's so small."

His very reluctance to leave bothered Graceanne. She wanted him to like the boys. Why shouldn't he? Everyone else did, except Papa, but she didn't want him to like them too much. She wasn't jealous, she told herself, that the boys already adored their cousin Collie. This was different. This was fear of a man who was used to getting what he wanted. She quickly tossed a blanket over both children and made sure Willy's foot was tucked out of sight. "They'll do better like this until I see you out. And I can warm their night-shirts by the fire downstairs while I make sure the carolers get off on their way." She stepped back toward the door so he would have to follow. "Don't worry, they won't wake up."

Leland stood up, and bumped his head. "Blast! Pardon." He stared at her as he rubbed at the same sore spot. He'd been just as aware as Graceanne of their proximity, the intimacy of the setting. He could still smell her rose perfume. (Or was that Willy? By Jupiter, the lads needed a man's influence!) And he was just as conscious of that accidental touch. Except, of course, that it wasn't accidental at all. The nearness of that midnight velvet had proven irresistible. Frowning at his own lack of scruples, he asked, "You still don't trust me, do you?"

"I . . ." She couldn't lie. He must have known the answer anyway. "No."

Guiltily, he told her, "You shouldn't."

He meant she shouldn't trust him not to try his damnedest to seduce her. She thought he meant she shouldn't trust him not to kidnap her children. She almost pushed him out the door.

"But I'll try to restrain myself, I promise."

He'd try to restrain himself from stealing her babies? What kind of promise was that? Graceanne vowed to return to her cheese-paring ways, saving every shilling—wasn't she her father's daughter?—in case she had to flee.

. The duke laughed now. "Don't look so horrified. I am still a gentleman. I'd never do anything without your permission. Like asking for a good-night kiss."

Now she was truly appalled, and he laughed the harder. "The boys, I meant."

He leaned over and kissed each boy's cheek, without waiting for her permission, Graceanne noted. So much for that vow. Still, she was a little relieved. Enough that she didn't smile too brightly when Leland stood up—and gave his head another resounding thump on the pitched ceiling.

She had to stop being such a clinging mother, Graceanne told herself after she had the boys in their warm nightshirts and tucked under the covers again. They were safe, they'd have a happy Christmas, Leland would be a conscientious guardian to their inheritance. So why couldn't she leave them and go about her other chores? Instead, she wanted to hug them and squeeze them until they were almost part of her again.

They were growing too fast. Graceanne remembered when the boys were infants sharing one cradle in her bedroom, in their tiny suite. Tony would carry the cradle into the parlor when he came on his rare visits. They'd laugh about keeping their privacy, but she'd always move the cradle back as soon as he left. Now she was worried her sons would get too big to stand in this little room without bumping their heads!

Giving herself a shake, Graceanne went to fetch the rest of the ornaments to be hung. That garland of evergreens Papa wouldn't permit in his church went in the nursery room, but the foil stars, red bows, and paper icicles got hung on strings from the curtain rod to the doorframe, so Willy and Les would spot them as soon as they awoke. Too bad she couldn't see their faces then, but she'd be there when they found the sleds and other toys in her bedroom later. That would have to be enough.

Even after the last bow was hung, Graceanne lingered in the room. She pushed aside a hanging star and opened the curtains enough to look out. She could just see the candles and lanterns of the carolers making their rounds through the village, although she couldn't hear the songs. Humming one of her favorites, she stood and watched the lights bob through the night. They reminded her of the native celebrations in Spain, when the people of that poor, war-ravaged country all gathered with candles and prayers and songs of joy to celebrate *Feliz Navidad*, Merry Christmas. They filed through the streets and hillsides in a seemingly endless line of smiling faces. They were dirty, tattered, sometimes hungry, but they had their faith and each other, their candles in the dark.

And she was alone.

No, she would not get melancholy about Tony, not on this night. She hadn't seen him for months before he'd been killed, so it wasn't as if she had any fresh memories of him. She hardly remembered more about him than his smile and his good-byes, anyway. Instead, thinking about Spain reminded her of the trinkets he'd brought her whenever he made one of his infrequent and short visits. Combs, fans, lace mantillas—they were all packed in boxes in the attic because Papa took one look at them and declared them heathen trumpery, frivolous to boot.

Graceanne picked up a candle and hurried across the hall to the attics. A moment's search found her trunks, and the box with the mementos of Tony's careless affection. Yes, there was a black veil she could be wearing, and the combs weren't trumpery at all, but exquisite works of art. She'd wear a pair for Christmas, another present from her husband, along with her gowns and bonnet and the new independence his money gave her. "Thank you, Tony," she whispered. "Especially for our sons."

Under the laces, as she remembered, was a little hand-carved Nativity. Tony had given it to her last Christmas, sheepishly, because he'd forgotten to buy her a real gift and that was all he could find at the last minute. It would be perfect for the boys' mantel, especially since they couldn't reach it. Let them remember their father, too, despite the new affection for their cousin Leland.

Thinking of the duke made her look out the little window on this side of the parsonage, where she could see Ware Hold guarding its hillside. All those lighted windows for

Leland and his aunt. She wondered if he ever got lonely in that enormous pile, if he ever missed his deceased wives.

Graceanne had seen his first duchess once, when she was still in the schoolroom. She wasn't introduced, of course, but then, almost no one was. The duchess kept to herself and her houseguests. Ware's second wife was too sickly to get out, Graceanne remembered hearing. The second duchess had her own chaplain attend her at the castle, so she never attended church in the village. But did she love her husband? Or was theirs an arranged marriage, a convenient economic merger? More important, did he love her? Graceanne guessed not, if he could treat other women so casually, like commodities.

No, she didn't trust him a bit.

She went back to the boys' room and arranged the Nativity set over the fireplace just as the sexton rang the bells for midnight, Christmas midnight. Peace on Earth, goodwill to all men. Well, she'd try.

Parting the curtains again, Graceanne looked for the carolers' lights. They'd be returning soon to deliver the poor box donations, and she had to be on hand to serve the hot cider that was all the vicar would permit. She made sure there would be coffee and tea, too, for those who had tasted enough wassail on their waits. Just as she was about to close the drapes, a snowflake drifted past, then another. Her boys would have snow for their new sleds after all. Thank you, Lord. Happy birthday.

Finally she pushed aside stars and bows and icicles to kiss her sons good night. And bumped her head when she stood up.

His Grace was also listening to the midnight church bells, watching the first snowflakes, and thinking of Tony Warrington's twins.

After the carolers left, young Prudence hanging on her Irishman's arm, and castaway, too, if he didn't miss his guess, Milsom had brought up a new bowl of wassail. Then the servants gathered in the Great Hall for the lighting of the Yule log. At the first tolling of the bells, His Grace had lit the enormous ash log in one of the huge fireplaces, using a bit of last year's wood. He hadn't the slightest idea if it was last year's wood or yesterday's, actually. Hell, he'd been at some dull house party or other last year, and the year before that, but Milsom would have carried on. He always did.

The butler had handed over the burning ash splinter, then toasted the House of Ware when the new fire caught. The servants lifted their glasses of wassail and said, "Here, here." If the log burned till Twelfth Night, tradition went, Ware's house would prosper.

How the bloody hell could it prosper if the butler had to light the fire and the servants make the toasts? There was supposed to be family and friends assembled, not paid retainers and one crotchety old cardsharp who needed two footmen to hold her up after an evening at the punch bowl. And he, Leland Warrington, the Duke of Ware, was supposed to pass that burning ember to his son, blast it! Damn his past wives!

Chapter Eleven

The stars, the sleds, the storybooks—nothing compared to the snow! In all of her thinking what fun the children could have with their new sleds, Graceanne had forgotten that the boys had never seen snow. There was nothing to do but to push the presents to the side, bundle the twins in their warmest clothes, and let them loose outside.

Oh, the wonder of it! Oh, the wetness of it! Thank goodness for the new mittens and caps and mufflers, for Les and Willy needed three sets of dry clothing, once before breakfast, once after, then again before church. Graceanne didn't mind, hearing their laughter.

They danced in the snow, rolled in it, tasted it, tossed it. Heaven and the stained glass windows be praised, the boys were too young for hard and heavy snowballs, but they did manage a lopsided snowman with Graceanne to lift the head on. She did not dress the snowman in her old black hat, as Cousin Leland had suggested, not when every Christmas-morning worshipper could look out the church windows and recognize it. And not when she needed it for mornings like this, rather than ruin her new satin bonnet with such child's play. Instead, she fashioned a merry wreath of holly and ivy for a crown, and cut up some of the foil stars for eyes and a nose. With a big red bow around his neck, the snowman looked as happy as she felt, even in her old black gown.

Breakfast in the nursery was a hurried affair because she'd promised to teach the boys how to make snow angels as soon as they were fed and dry again, and because their noisy excitement couldn't be restrained in the still-sleeping house.

Outside again, Graceanne found there was no way she could explain the concept without lying down in the snow, waving her arms and legs up and down, then hopping up to show the boys the impression in the snow. *Now* the old black bonnet was ready for the dust bin. Willy and Les filled the parsonage yard with angels, then swore they weren't too wet or tired to try their new sleds.

The hill behind the church wasn't much of an incline, at least so Graceanne thought before she helped drag those sleds up it a hundred times, or so it felt. Leslie screamed the first time he went down, and every time after that. Willy just grinned. She finally convinced them they'd wear the sleds out if they didn't stop soon. Besides, there were gifts for the rest of the family. Didn't they want to see?

The Beckwiths were still at the breakfast table—Papa had thought a longer than usual grace was called for that morning—when Graceanne in her new black merino and the boys in their new nankeen suits entered the dining room.

"What's this, daughter? You know I don't permit those—"

"It's Christmas, Grandpa! Look what we helped wrap!"

Willy handed the vicar a wad of tissue paper that Graceanne had to peel apart, the vicar refusing to touch it, to reveal a new pipe. Leslie held out a piece of paper, a ribbon, and a warm muffler.

"Very nice, very nice, I am sure, but you know I don't approve of—"

"Here, Aunt Pru, all these boxes are yours. Mama didn't let us help wrap."

"Mama, how come Aunt Pru got more presents than Grandpa? Wasn't he as good this year?"

"Hush, darlings, let your aunt open her gifts."

Prudence dutifully pretended to be surprised by each new delight she uncovered, the peach sarcenet, the hat and gloves and fan, just as if she hadn't whined and wheedled over every item. She permitted each boy to kiss her cheek, then wiped it.

When it was Mrs. Beckwith's turn, Graceanne left the room.

"It was too heavy, Grandma," Willy explained.

"And too fra-fra—Mama said don't touch."

"That's 'fragile,' darling," Graceanne said, wheeling in the tea cart. Both shelves of the cart were filled with the new dishes—cups, saucers, bowls, serving platters, teapot—all in a dainty pattern of violets and vines.

Mrs. Beckwith held up one teacup to see the light shine through the delicate porcelain, and started weeping.

Willy frowned at his mother. "I told you plates weren't a happy present." But Leslie put his arms around his grandmother, who clutched the teacup to her breast, and said, "Don't cry, Grandma, you can play with our toys."

The boys were so good—and so tired from their morning in the snow—that Graceanne felt comfortable leaving them beside her mother in the family pew during the church service. She was so happy today, in fact, that she didn't even resent that no one in her family had thought to buy the boys any gifts. That her father should have done so was out of the question, and her mother hardly left the house, but Pru? That she might have spent a ha'penny of her pin money on her own nephews never occurred to her. Graceanne shrugged and joined the choir behind the pulpit, determined that nothing was going to spoil the rest of this perfect day.

The joyous uplifting of voices in song that she expected was not quite so joyous, not nearly perfect. There were some stuffed noses and scratchy throats among those who had spent the chilly night out caroling, and there were some bleary eyes and unsteady hands among them, too. One seat was empty altogether. When a particularly sour note sounded next to her, Graceanne shuddered and turned to her sister. Yes, Pru was definitely off key today, and off her looks, too. In fact, Graceanne noted, the chit had a decided greenish cast to her complexion. The one piece of dry toast on her plate at breakfast must not have meant Pru was waiting for the noonday feast after all.

Good, Graceanne thought, and not just because Pru hadn't bought the children Christmas presents or complimented her on her new gown and hairstyle. Maybe Prudence would learn from experience if her head ached enough, Graceanne thought, for surely neither Papa's sternness nor Mama's vagueness were teaching the girl moderation.

When Graceanne turned back to check on the twins, her mother was sitting alone on the bench. Before she could panic overmuch, Graceanne saw the boys ensconced on the seats next to Leland, in the Warrington pew. Lady Eudora was asleep, snoring slightly, and the duke was his usual handsome, elegantly attired self, smiling at her when he noticed her attention. He, at least, seemed to admire her new look.

She'd gathered her hair into its usual bun that morning, but then raised the knot of hair higher on the top of her head, held with two tortoiseshell combs. Then she'd draped the black lace mantilla over the whole. It wasn't quite a match for the lace on her soft woolen gown, of course, but with Tony's pearls, she felt quite the thing. Leland's warm regard seemed to agree with her assessment. It brought a flush to her cheeks, too.

The boys were playing with the duke's quizzing glass, a different one from last night's, necessarily so. Gracious, he must have a drawerful of the things, that he let three-year-olds play with them. After he collected all the pieces, he offered the boys peppermint balls from a little sack in his pocket. He must have come prepared, Graceanne thought, unless the highest peers in the realm usually carried sweets with them to church. She doubted it, and felt warmer toward Ware because of that, warmer than she wanted herself to feel.

After the service, Graceanne had to endure the comments of all her longtime neighbors about how nice it was of His Grace to take such an interest in the boys. She smiled and nodded, yes, it was. And she was looking a real treat, too, Squire remarked in his tally-ho voice. "One thing doesn't have aught to do with t'other, does it, missy?" he asked with a wink and a grin before his wife pinched him and dragged him to their carriage.

Of course the duke was next to greet her. Where else would he be when she was wishing the ground to open up, but right there to see her embarrassment? His hazel eyes were twinkling, but Leland merely bowed over Graceanne's hand and asked if he might call after taking his aunt home, for he had a few trinkets for the boys he'd like to deliver.

"For the boys? You didn't need to buy gifts for them. I told you I was going to. All that money you gave me . . ."

"I didn't have to. I wanted to. Isn't that the spirit of Christmas?"

The spirit of Christmas was hopping up and down and running to the window every other minute to watch for their beloved Collie's arrival.

"But it is snowing again, darlings. His horses might have trouble getting through the drifts." Two identical lower lips started to tremble. "But I'm sure he'll try. Come, let's look at the new picture book until he gets here. If he doesn't come, we'll go play in the snow again." Where His Grace and his curricle had better be, ditched, for disappointing little children on Christmas Day.

But no, they soon heard carriage wheels crunching in the snow. The boys scampered down the stairs, which they were never supposed to do, squealing, which they were certainly not permitted to do in this part of the house. They were trying to open the door—another taboo or Graceanne would never know where they were—but luckily they were still too short to reach the latch.

Graceanne shooed them aside, straightened her skirts, and said, "Now, remember to bow, and do not ask if he brought you anything." Then she opened the door.

His Grace was framed in the doorway, his curls all wind-blown and the shoulders of his greatcoat powdered with snow. He was wearing a grin as wide as the one she'd put on the snowman, and his booted foot was raised to kick at the door for entry, since his arms were heaped with mounds of packages.

"A few trinkets for the boys, you said. Why, you look like Father Christmas himself!"

"They are not all for the children," the duke told her as she led him into the parlor. Where else was she to entertain a visiting nobleman? Upstairs in the nursery again? Her family prepared to depart when Leland added, "I was having such a fine time shopping that I bought gifts for everyone."

Prudence, who had been drooping over a fashion magazine, perked up like a half-dead seedling that's just been watered. She wasn't getting to attend the party at Squire's tonight, despite having a new gown, but Lucy Maxton never got a gift from a real live duke. Pru hurried to help relieve Ware of the gifts, so he could shrug out of his greatcoat.

Of course it was left to Graceanne to take the damp coat to hang in the hallway and go to the kitchen to order tea. When he raised an eyebrow as if to ask why she was still acting the menial, Graceanne laughed and said, "It's the maid's day off. Oh, how I have wanted to say that like some grande dame come down in the world. But it truly is the new maid's holiday, and I really don't mind, if you'll promise not to let the children act like pigs at the trough of your gifts while I am gone."

It was Pru, however, who was in a snit when Graceanne returned. The duke had let the brats each open a present, sets of wooden jackstraws, but he made the rest of them wait for Graceanne's return. "What took so long, Gracie? You should not keep Cousin Leland waiting."

"Cousin Leland? His Grace is no cousin of yours, Pru."

"He is too, by marriage."

Graceanne looked toward her mother to remonstrate with Prudence over her coming ways, but Mrs. Beckwith was anxiously trying to explain jackstraws to Willy, and why it wasn't a good idea to stick them in his ear. Leslie was playing with his set on the floor between the duke's legs while Leland conversed with the vicar. Leslie's chubby little fingers wouldn't manage that game for a few years, but he seemed to be having no trouble whatsoever shoving the narrow pieces down His Grace's high-top boots.

"Leslie, Wellesley, come get our present for Cousin Leland. No, Your Grace, do not—"

There was a crunch, a snap, a "Blister it! What the deuce?" and another crackle.

"—stand up. Yes, well, I apologize for taking so long, but we seemed to have misplaced the gift the boys and I made for you."

The package the boys proudly handed to him seemed to have been misplaced in the dustbin. There were crumbs and smears and a few rips in the paper. "You shouldn't have," he said, and sincerely meant it.

"Open it, Collie, open it!"

So the duke stepped back, gingerly, and sat down again. He untied the string. Actually, he had to cut the knots with his pocketknife, which he hastily tucked back in an inside pocket. The paper fell off by itself to reveal a dirty sheepskin square protecting—what?

"It's a pen wipe, Collie! We made it out of the lamb hats from the pageant. See, we colored it here, and Mama showed us how to put your initials here. See?"

"I see it's the finest pen wipe I have ever owned," the duke nobly swore while Prudence snickered and the vicar snorted, "At least I got a pipe."

Leslie was looking uncertainly from one adult to the other. Willy was frowning.

"But I do not smoke," the duke whispered to the boys, "so this is a much better present."

Then he started handing out gifts, with only an occasional cracking sound as he moved around the room. To the vicar he gave a leatherbound volume, *A Dissertation on the Proof of the Existence of Angels,* by a well-known Oxford don. "I visited my old religion professor and had him sign it for you. It's not ancient, but it might be a worthy addition to your collection."

"You mean you know Robert Jordan? I believe him to be one of the foremost theologians of our day. Why, he—"

The reverend would have gone on, but Ware had turned to Mrs. Beckwith with a soft, flat bundle. Inside was a tablecloth runner and napkins, the finest damask embroidered with clusters of violets. "However did you manage that?" Graceanne asked when her mother seemed struck speechless.

He grinned. "I cheated and bribed Anstruther to lend me the illustration of the dishes you ordered. While I was in Oxford I had a clerk at one of the linen-drapers search out anything that matched."

"All that trouble," Mrs. Beckwith cried. She was weeping again, and one of the boys, dashed if Leland knew which, told him not to worry. "Grandma didn't like her dishes either."

"Lud, I never thought of that. I can exchange them—" So he had to be reassured that Mrs. Beckwith adored her new dishes, and her new linen.

The duke next handed Graceanne a small box that looked ominously like jewelry. "I cannot accept . . . that is, it wouldn't be proper for me to . . ." What she meant was that she'd die of mortification if Leland handed her the diamond bracelet or whatever expensive frippery gentlemen gave their mistresses.

"Nothing improper at all, Cousin. Open it."

He was right, there was nothing to take exception about in a plain gold locket, except that it was empty. "I meant it for locks of the twins' hair," he explained. Of course there was nothing to do then but for Graceanne to find her embroidery scissors and cut a curl from each boy. Prudence gnashed her teeth. The children were showing more forbearance.

Pru's gift, when Ware finally got around to her, was too big for a jewelry box. She wasn't quite successful in hiding her disappointment, no matter how inappropriate such a present might have been. Graceanne was relieved when the chit managed to show proper enthusiasm for the charming ceramic dresser mirror with its painted figures on the back, though she wished her sister could have refrained from throwing her arms around the duke in appreciation. He stepped back hastily enough, she noted, saying something about a pretty bauble for a pretty reflection, calculated to feed the young girl's vanity. Which was just what Prudence didn't need, Graceanne thought.

"Mama says pretty is as pretty does. What does that mean, Collie?"

"Uh, it means it's time to open another of your presents, bantling. Here, these two, I think. They are to share." One was a small tin trumpet, the other a little drum.

Prudence left off admiring her blond ringlets in the mirror to groan, but a frosty glare from Graceanne kept her in her seat. The next package contained a pair of child-sized wooden swords.

"So you can play at pirates and soldiers, all kinds of games, even St. George and the dragon."

Graceanne half expected him to produce the dragon next, but it was Mrs. Beckwith who groaned this time, thinking of the vases they could knock over, the furniture those swords could gouge. "I think I'll just take my lovely gift to the dining room before the table gets set."

Prudence and the vicar both offered to wheel her, but Pru won, so Beckwith decided he could get a bit of reading in before luncheon.

"Will you join us, Your Grace?" Mrs. Beckwith asked from the doorway. For once she was not at all embarrassed to make the invitation, not with a fine goose cooking,

Graceanne's minced meat pies heating up, and her new china. Why, her table would be fine enough for the Prince Regent himself.

"I am sorry," the duke said, "but I am expected home for nuncheon with my aunt. Another time, perhaps. But I would like to invite you all for tea this afternoon. The kitchens have been busy, although there are just two of us. And the castle is looking quite festive."

The vicar declined at the word *festive*. He intended to spend the afternoon of this holy day in church, praying. Mrs. Beckwith, torn between the pleading look on Prudence's face and the disapproval on her husband's, was decided by Willy's "Us, too, Collie?"

And Ware's "Of course you, too, halfling."

"I think I've had too much excitement for one day, Your Grace, but thank you. Yes, Prudence, you may go without me, if Graceanne accepts."

The boys were tugging on her skirts and Pru was looking like she'd cosh her with the mirror if Graceanne said no. Outmaneuvered again, if her plan was to avoid the licentious lord, she nodded. Pru made her best curtsy and sighed, "Until later, Cousin Leland." Good, he'd be busy fending off her little sister.

When all the Beckwiths were gone, Ware let the boys loose on the rest of the packages. Under the maelstrom of wrappings and ribbons, Graceanne saw puzzles and picture books and tin soldiers, but also some vastly inappropriate gifts, like cricket bats and dart sets.

After everything was unwrapped and the children were playing with the boxes, Leland asked, "Will you excuse me? I have to—"

"It's out back," Leslie told him.

"Empty my shoe."

He must have been like a child in the toy shop, Graceanne reflected while Leland was gone, buying everything that appealed to him, without regard for age or ability. Cricket bats and swords and darts, my goodness. He might as well hand the boys a cannon and be done with it. And

103

that drum and trumpet were enough to give a mother a headache just looking at them.

Leland came back with yet another gift, another horror for Graceanne. This one wiggled and barked, and had a red bow around its neck. "Oh, dear, Papa will never let them keep a dog."

Leland was on the floor with the children and the pup. "Then the little fellow can stay at the castle, and the boys can come visit."

"You tell them that," she answered with a touch of bitterness. The twins were delirious. A dog of their own was even better than snow. And it wasn't just any dog, Ware declared, it was a real, honest-to-goodness, purebred collie. So the twins instantly and simultaneously named the dog Duke, since their own duke was Collie.

"Makes sense to me," Leland agreed. "Duke it is."

Graceanne felt she was drowning. "But are you sure it's a boy?"

"Yes, Mama. See, here's his—"

"I think Duke needs to go outside. Run get your coats and mittens." Graceanne started to gather some of the toys, the catastrophes waiting to happen. Then she turned to the duke, still sitting on the floor with the puppy, looking up at her like a naughty boy. "I can't help but see a pattern here, Your Grace." She held up the dart set and waved it at him. "This is the stuff of a parent's nightmare. Cricket bats for three-year-olds? And a dog? Come, you had to have known better."

He just grinned, the same grin Willy and Les wore when they escaped Meg and picked Mrs. Beckwith's last flowers, "For you, Mama."

"I didn't think you'd find me out so soon." Leland stood and looked down at her, seeming not at all like a little boy anymore. She took one step backward and would have toppled over the toy drum if he hadn't put his arms out to steady her. Leland removed his hands from her shoulder, but not instantly. He gave her one more smile, then bent to pick up the drum.

"I bought everything the vicar would hate the most, the noisiest, most destructive toys I could find." He grinned again. "That way, he'll throw you out and you'll have no choice but to move to the castle."

Chapter Twelve

*D*angerous. · The man was positively dangerous. And endearing, which of course made him more dangerous. He returned after luncheon to fetch them in a sleigh, for the twins' sake, he said, but his own face was glowing with excitement. Graceanne couldn't have thought of a better treat for a snowy Christmas afternoon. Prudence could. Her hair would be mussed, her complexion wind-damaged. She went anyway, rather than sit home bored when all her friends were getting ready for the party at Squire's. Besides, none of the other local belles had been invited to her cousin the duke's, so she went, but not graciously.

The twins, on the other hand, were in alt, even though Duke got left behind in the barn "to keep Posy company." It was a big sled, with two large, shaggy farm horses to pull it and bells ringing everywhere. They tried to keep their wet boots from Prudence's skirts, they really did.

Not even Prudence could keep to her crotchets when she entered Ware Hold's Great Hall. Graceanne and the boys had already seen the immense room decorated, of course, but not like this.

"I wanted it to be a surprise," said Leland, standing proudly to one side, right where the liveried footmen would have been if they both hadn't succumbed to the grippe right about the time they heard who was coming to tea. Leland's surprise was a magnificent fir tree, eighteen feet high at least, decked top to bottom with glowing candles in holders. When his guests had looked their wide-eyed fill, Prudence even clapping her hands, he explained, "It's a Christmas tree. Actually it's a German tradition, called a *tannenbaum*. Princess Caroline had one, and the idea took hold in London. I found them so charming, I wanted one for the castle."

Pru giggled then. "Papa would have conniptions! Not just heathen, but Hanoverian to boot. Why, I thought he'd go off in a swoon when you mentioned Father Christmas this morning."

Graceanne smiled, too. "That's a lovely tradition and this one is . . . is wondrous! It's magnificent, Cousin Leland, but are you sure it's safe?" She kept a steely grip on each boy's wrist.

"Of course it is. Milsom here wouldn't let anything untoward happen to his castle. Look over in the corner, where there are buckets of water. And a footman is on duty whenever the candles are lit, although dashed if I know where he's gone. Milsom will see someone in his place, I'm sure."

"Stop being such a spoilsport, Gracie."

The duke laughed and swung one of the boys up in his arms. "Willy?"

"No, silly, I'm Leslie!"

He shrugged and turned to the boys' mother. "Yes, Grace, don't be a marplot. It's Christmas, time for magic, not worrying! But come, Aunt Eudora is waiting in the Adams parlor, with the wassail bowl."

"Oh, good," chirruped Prudence, not soothing Graceanne's nerves a whit.

The Adams parlor was to the rear of the castle, in the modern wing. It wasn't quite as large as the Great Hall, just large enough to fit the entire congregation of the Warefield church. Instead, it held one old lady and another Christmas tree. This one was only ten or twelve feet high, and it was decorated with red bows instead of candles.

"See, nothing to worry about."

Nothing except the Axminster carpet, the Queen Anne chairs, the Chippendale tables, the Dutch Masters paintings, and the old lady.

"Don't expect me to play nursemaid while you get up a flirtation with some mealy-mouthed vicar's daughter, nevvy."

Thinking she was the object of the supposed flirtation, and delighted that it be so, Pru replied for the duke: "Oh, I'm not at all mealy-mouthed, Lady Eudora. And you don't have to worry about the children. Gracie hardly trusts me to watch them, so she wouldn't let an old tartar—that is, she wouldn't expect anyone else to baby-sit the brats."

Graceanne didn't know where to look, except at Leland, who was covering his laughter with a cough. Lady Eudora banged her cane on the floor a few times, then declared, "At least this one's got some spirit. Do you play, girl?"

"Play? The pianoforte? Only indifferently, my lady. Gracie usually plays while I sing." She fluttered her eyelashes in the duke's direction. "I've been told I have a pretty voice." She'd been told she sang like an angel and looked divine by the candlelight atop an instrument. "Would you like me to perform?"

"Faugh," Aunt Eudora answered. "Every prunes-and-prisms chit in London trills her notes and thumps away at the pianoforte. I meant do you play cards?"

Pru's face fell. She'd really wanted to impress the duke.

"Our father would not permit gaming," Graceanne reminded the old lady, who started to hobble away in disgust, back to the wassail bowl.

"But I've always wanted to learn!" Pru almost shouted, lest Ware think her some country gapeseed, which she was, of course.

Eudora turned around. "That's more like it. You'll do, gel. What did you say your name was?" And she started to lead Prudence away, toward a card table set up at the opposite end of the room.

Pru looked back helplessly. "But I thought His Grace ..."

"M'nevvy's feeling patriarchal. It's enough to make a person bilious. Come. And bring two cups of that lamb's wool."

"Not for money, Aunt Eudora," Leland called after them as Graceanne murmured, "Oh, dear, and you said she cheated."

"What, are you afraid I'll be having your sister raiding the poor box like that skinflint father of yours?" Lady Eudora turned back to Prudence. "Don't worry, gel, I'll lay out your stake. Pennies only, makes the game more interesting, don't you know."

"And I can keep whatever I win?"

"Oh, dear," Graceanne said again, louder.

Leland chuckled and took her arm. "I think Miss Prudence can handle herself." He led her toward an inlaid table where the wassail bowl sat. The boys had already found the tray of sugarplums next to it. Graceanne had no way of knowing how many the platter used to contain, but she suspected the Ware staff would not send up a half-empty plate. Well, it was Christmas.

"A toast," Leland was saying, holding out a cup of the warmed brew. When she took it he poured another and raised his. "To Christmas. To good cheer and goodwill."

"To peace," Graceanne added, taking a cautious sip. It was delicious, this mixture of ale and spices. She sipped again. The duke, meanwhile, was offering a taste to each of the boys from his own cup. "I don't think they should—"

"A tiny bit won't hurt, just to toast the holiday. Besides, they need to experience more of the world, more than they ever will in the vicarage."

Oh, well, she thought, it was Christmas.

Leland was leading the boys across the room toward the decorated tree. "Do you know, I think Father Christmas made a mistake this year."

"Grandpa says there's no such thing, Collie."

"Ah, then perhaps that's why he got confused. You see,

Father Christmas cannot deliver presents where no one believes in him, that's the rule. So he had to leave some gifts here instead of at the vicarage."

"Do you believe in Father Christmas, Collie?"

"Well, I'd like to," Leland said, rummaging under the low branches to the rear of the tree. "But I particularly wished for a pair of matched grays for my new phaeton, and look what he delivered instead." He pulled out from underneath the tree two identical wooden rocking horses, with real manes and tails, leather harness, and glass eyes. The boys jumped aboard and neighed and whoaed and rocked until Graceanne nervously started chewing on her lip.

"That is a most wonderful surprise, Cousin. But are you quite sure . . . ?"

"That they can't pull my phaeton? Definitely." He brushed pine needles off his shoulder, then led her to a nearby sofa, where she could watch the boys' antics. "Come, you must learn to relax more. They'll be fine, I promise. You cannot keep them wrapped in cotton wool, you know, and expect them to grow up to be decent men."

Graceanne hadn't been thinking of the twins so much as the carpet.

"I couldn't bring the rocking horses with me in the curricle this morning, of course, so I'll have someone haul them over to the vicarage in a wagon as soon as the weather clears. My man will make sure they get up to the nursery, out of the vicar's way."

Good, then she'd only have to worry about them wearing holes in the wood flooring and falling through into Papa's bedroom. She had another sip of the wassail. Leland was right, there was no use worrying today. She stared over at him as he watched Willy dismount and ask Les if he wanted to ride the other horse awhile. The fond affection she saw in the duke's smile made her say, "You'd make a wonderful father."

He sat up straighter and, she swore, puffed his chest out.

She might have complimented his prowess with the ribbons or at culping wafers. "I would, wouldn't I?"

"Well, yes, if you ever managed to tell your children apart."

"Unfair, Gracie, you've had three years to work with your peapod brood! Furthermore, I have the perfect solution right here." He took a small box out of his pocket and called the boys to him when they seemed to be tiring of the wooden horses. "Here, my lads, is one last present on this most special of days."

Les climbed into his lap and Willy leaned against his leg for a closer look. "That's girl stuff, Collie," he said when the box was open.

"Not at all. See, I have a ring on, and a stickpin. I thought of getting you signet rings, but your fingers are growing too fast, so I settled on these. Look, these are your initials, *L* for Leslie, *W* for Willy. They are stickpins for your neckcloths, just like mine."

"Silly, we don't wear neckcloths. We're just boys!"

"Yes, but you have lapels on your coats, and collars on your shirts. Boutonnieres are au courant."

"What's a 'boot on ears'?"

"What's 'awker aunt'?"

"It means all the fashionable gentlemen are wearing pins in their buttonholes."

"Especially those who don't know their name," their mother teased with a giggle. "Perhaps you'll even start a new fashion for gentlemen who tend to get castaway, little pins with their addresses engraved on them, so the Watch can send them home in a hackney." She giggled again.

The duke eyed her narrowly, then moved the wassail cup away from her reach. "Enough of that, my girl, or you'll be the one needing help finding your way home. Here, Les, Willy, not only will you be all the crack, but no one can mix you up again."

"But we don't get mixed."

"And Mama doesn't get mixed."

"But poor, old, silly Cousin Leland does, so won't you

help him out?" At their nods, he took the *W* and reached for the boy on his lap. Graceanne coughed delicately. He switched to the boy by his leg. When he had both pins affixed on their collars, Leland sat back with a satisfied smile. "There. Now, why don't you go ride the horses a few more minutes before Milsom comes to get you for tea?"

"They really should have a nap," Graceanne worried.

"On Christmas? Gammon, they can sleep the rest of the year."

While the grown-ups were debating, the level of Graceanne's wassail cup was descending. By the time Milsom arrived, both boys were sound asleep under the Christmas tree. Ware sent him off to fetch tea for the adults, except Aunt Eudora, who was also sleeping, her head on the card table. Pru wandered around admiring the furnishings and the decorations, then joined Graceanne and the duke when two footmen and the butler brought in the tea things.

As soon as everything was laid out to Milsom's satisfaction, he snapped his fingers to the footmen and nodded at the sleeping children. Small boys sprawled on His Grace's carpet did not fit Milsom's dignity. The twins were removed from the parlor like so many dirty dishes.

After an elegant tea, the three adults moved to the pianoforte in the corner, the finest instrument Graceanne had ever played. Prudence had recovered from the morning's indisposition and sang beautifully, directing her voice and soulful gaze at the duke. Graceanne joined in for some of the old carols and Ware hummed along. He truly had abominable pitch, but, begging their pardons, enjoyed himself nevertheless. Then Pru sang some Gaelic carols by herself. Graceanne didn't want to know where or how she learned them, not today.

They stopped singing when the boys ran into the room, energies back to full gallop. Milsom bowed.

Leland told Graceanne, "See, no loud noises, no alarums."

"I do see. Thank you, Mr. Milsom."

Milsom bowed. "My pleasure, madam. And the steward says the door to the wine cellar can be repaired tomorrow, Your Grace."

His precious wine cellar? With the bottles laid down in his father's time?

Her babies put to sleep in the damp, dark caverns beneath this place?

Prudence was tired of being ignored. "Do you know, Cousin Leland, you've done such a lovely job of decorating for the holidays, I don't understand how you forgot the mistletoe." Milsom sniffed and bowed himself out as Pru struck a pose next to the fireplace. "I helped Lucy Maxton make the kissing bough for the manor, and I think it's quite one of the nicest Christmas traditions, don't you?"

"Oh, quite!" He gathered up both boys, one under each arm, and carried them toward Prudence, who was, of course, standing under a beribboned bunch of the berries. "Les, Willy, here's a lesson a gentleman should learn early in life: Snatch kisses whenever you can!" And he held them up to kiss the cheek Prudence begrudgingly presented. He lightly bussed her forehead, almost as an afterthought, before bending down to the twins' level. "Now, why don't you try getting your mother over here, Willy, ah, Leslie?" He looked in vain for an initial. "The deuce! Did you lose the pins already?"

"We put them on the horsies, Collie."

"So they don't get mixed in the wagon!"

He sighed. "Bright lads. Now, why don't you be even more clever and drag your mother under the mistletoe?"

They giggled, Prudence bristled, and Graceanne said, "Come, boys, it's time we went home."

Then the butler was at the door, handing out the wraps. "Blast, Milsom, this is not the time to be so dashed efficient!"

"Yes, Your Grace. Your mittens, Master Wellesley."

Leland waited, but no one corrected the butler. "Lucky guess. Fifty-fifty odds, anyway." Milsom sniffed.

Graceanne almost purred with pleasure on the sleigh ride home. "I think this was the nicest Christmas I've ever known, surely the best the boys have had. The pageant, their first snow, Christmas trees and sleigh rides, rocking horses and a puppy."

"And a pen wipe."

She laughed. "It's the stuff dreams are made of, a memory they'll cherish all their lives. I know I will. Thank you for making it so very magical."

Her warm regard almost made up for that missed kiss under the mistletoe, Leland told himself. Almost. That and how she'd said this was her favorite Christmas, not one from her childhood, not one with Tony. It had been one of his finest Christmases, too. His youth wasn't spent in a strict religious household like hers, but his parents were cool and distant, his tutors and servants merely polite. He never remembered such joy as a child, and never the pleasure of creating such happiness for others. Recently there'd been only stuffy house parties, inane flirtations, the repetitive rounds of London celebrations.

But today, with his family near him, or the closest he had to one, his house brimming with children's laughter, yes, today was magical. Almost enough to make him wish that—no, it could never be. For now he'd be content with a nearly perfect day. After all, only one boy puked on the ride home. On Prudence.

Chapter Thirteen

The glow of Christmas continued. On Boxing Day, when all the tenants and servitors came to toast their lord's health and receive his blessing, and his largess, in return, Leland wanted his cousins at Ware. It was important for the boys to meet those dependent on the Warringtons, the duke felt. Graceanne felt this was foolish, when the boys weren't remotely likely to inherit, but, as the duke pointed out, this was part of their heritage, too, prospective noblemen or not. Every man from titled gentleman to yeoman farmer should know the source of his income, respect it, and care for it. That's what this day was about.

Respecting the source of *her* income, Graceanne accepted, although she was nervous about the reception she was likely to get from the duke's tenants—and their wives. So she dressed with extra care and took her place near the duke and his aunt in the Great Hall, shivering despite the warmth from the two huge fireplaces. Milsom handed her a glass of sherry.

Once the visits began, she realized she had nothing to fear. She'd known most of these people all her life. They weren't suddenly going to think ill of her for appearing at the duke's side; most thought it about time she and the boys took their rightful place. She didn't receive one slighting remark from the women, not one suggestive leer from the men, except from His Grace, after he'd raised his glass one time too many. After the tenth or twelfth farmer's toast, Graceanne and Milsom made sure Leland's cup was filled with the children's punch, not the potent lamb's wool.

The boys had a wonderful time, helping hand out presents, playing in the snow with the tenant children, being introduced and admired by everyone. The old-timers told Graceanne the twins were the spitting image of His Grace as a lad, and a rare hellion he was, too. They told Ware that it was good to see children in the old fortress, good to see a new generation of Warringtons running up and down the ancient halls. Continuance, that's what one old gaffer called it, so they toasted continuance, and Ware was well satisfied. The water closet wasn't working properly and Willy's ball was missing, he'd have the devil's own headache on the morrow, but his line had continuance. And the physician reported that Aunt Eudora would make a full recovery.

The week after Boxing Day, Leland called at the vicarage often, going sledding with the twins once before the snow melted, making sure the rocking horses were delivered, consulting about Duke the dog's training. He brought a collar and leash his stableman had crafted, fruit from Ware's succession houses, a box of toys from his own nursery days. When Graceanne protested that he should save such treasures for his own son, he replied that since that son was not even a twinkle in anyone's eye, the twins may as well enjoy the stuff rather than let it molder in an empty nursery. Besides, she could send the box back when he got around to having a son; Willy and Les would have long outgrown such childish pursuits as tin soldiers. Judging from how His Grace spent hours on the floor with the twins configuring miniature battles, Graceanne doubted a boy ever outgrew the pastime.

He was everything thoughtful, and she was careful not to be alone with him.

She refused the invitation for another party at Squire's

house on New Year's Eve because of her mourning period, and couldn't help feeling that Leland decided to visit friends in Oxford for the holiday on that count. Prudence reported he'd already accepted, then canceled, throwing Mrs. Maxton into a swivet. Pru was in the sulks again because she wasn't to go either, the vicar's excuse being that she was still too young, her mother was too weak to chaperon her, and there might be bad influences among the unknown guests. Pru hardly came out of her room the entire week, claiming an indisposition, which was almost as much a relief to Graceanne as Leland's departure. Pru's petulance was aggravating; Leland's kindness and consideration were all too tempting. Speak of bad influences!

Graceanne always hated New Year's Eve. She disliked that false, spirits-generated joy of noisy fetes at the embassy in Portugal, and she used to dread the prayerful, contemplative New Year's Eves the vicar celebrated. She'd always felt stranded in the parsonage with nothing but her life speeding by, reminding her of what she was missing. New Year's Eve made her feel alone. This year was looking rosier. She no longer had to worry about her sons' futures; now she could dream for them, with hope.

Les could be a soldier like his father. The cavalry, of course. He'd be brave and dashing, ready for anything. She'd start praying now for an end to war. And Willy might take up the law. He had more patience than Les for books and quiet pursuits. The clergy likely wasn't an option: This household was enough to make anyone a nonbeliever. Perhaps both boys would go into trade, sail off to new lands to find fortunes. No, she couldn't bear that. Leland would say she was tying her apron strings too tightly, but she was having enough problems facing pony lessons in the spring; she couldn't contemplate her sons' leaving. That was the problem with New Year's Eve, and being alone.

Then it was Twelfth Night, when three castaway kings from the village made the rounds, handing pennies to the children. And the decorations had to come down lest they bring bad luck in addition to the vicar's wrath. So Christmas was over, the magic and the melancholy.

The duke was leaving. Of course. He had his glittering London life to lead, parties, not piquet with his aunt. He had the theater, not the blacksmith, the butcher, and the innkeeper's brother done up as Wise Men. Lobster patties instead of flavored snow; high-bred horses instead of highly polished ones; bucks and bloods and blades for friends, not babies. And ladies of his own class.

Graceanne told herself it was good that he was leaving. The boys were getting too used to him and his extravagant lifestyle. He spoiled them. With their own competence they could enjoy a comfortable life, but they were not nabobs' children. And it was better he left now, before they were too dependent on him.

Graceanne knew she was in as much danger of relying too heavily on Leland for companionship, for intelligent conversation, and shared joy in the children. She had an allowance. For the first time in her life she could be independent, make choices about her life and her sons' lives—after he left. It was too easy to let him decide the boys were old enough for ponies, not old enough for a tutor, that skating was too dangerous, but rolling down hills *sans* sleds wasn't. Those should have been her choices, but he'd smiled and teased and made her loosen the leading strings.

She would miss him, too much already. She feared that the longer he stayed, the more she'd miss him when he left. And he would leave. 'Twas better he went now, before he took part of her heart with him.

"What, the widow sent you haring back to London in the dead of winter with a flea in your ear about claiming one of her children? Told you it was a bacon-brained idea."

"No, Crow, you told me it was an excellent idea, that she'd be more than happy to part with one of the nuisances." The two men were in White's, which was less than a quarter filled. Crosby Fanshaw was in his peacock plumage, Leland was in much more somber garb. His mood matched. She hadn't quite sent him off with a flea in his ear, not at all. It was more like a tickle, a tingle, a whispered siren's call. He'd had to leave Warwick if he was to stay a gentleman. But he wasn't happy about it.

Fanshaw polished his quizzing glass. "Well, can't figure women at the best of times. There was m'sister, trying to foist her brats off on the mater constantly. So I suggested she send the worst of 'em, the middle boy, off to join the navy. Midshipman, don't you know. They take 'em small. Make a man out of the little savage. Caught the brat using my four best neckcloths to tie his sister to a chair. He said they were playing Joan of Arc. My four best, I say! Anyway, m'sister starts shrieking, babies start wailing, m'brother reads me a lecture about family feeling, and I start packing." He shrugged his padded shoulders. "Bachelor quarters is better'n that, even if town is thin of company. Tailors ain't so busy, besides." He raised a glass. "Glad to see you back, though."

The duke stared into his glass of cognac, swirling the amber liquid around. Ware House wasn't exactly bachelor quarters, but it was certainly quiet and empty and dreary after the Hold. No decorations, no neighbors calling, no children's laughter, no—

No, it was just after-holiday megrims, he told himself, that had him blue-deviled. He'd get over it as soon as he found a new diversion.

"So what was she like, Tony's widow? A drab? A dasher?" Crosby wanted to know.

Leland studied his drink some more. "No, not a drab, once she had some decent clothes. Not a stunner, either, that was the sister. A regular Diamond, that one."

Crow perked up. "Ah-ha, a bit of dalliance there?"

"What, my wards' aunt? Besides, the chit is seventeen, a mere babe."

"You're the one who said it was experience that counted, not years."

"Yes, but this one is a gorgeous bit of fluff and knows

it all too well. That's about all she knows. Graceanne, ah, Mrs. Warrington, has it all over her for intelligence."

"So the widow wasn't an antidote after all?" Crosby refused to believe his friend had spent nearly a month in the countryside without getting up a flirtation with some fancy piece or other.

Leland smiled, but at his memories, not at his friend. When he saw Graceanne Christmas morning, with that veil over her blond hair, singing in the choir, then on Boxing Day, when she held the children to wave to the departing tenants, he'd thought her more beautiful than any Madonna ever painted. Even sledding, her hair coming undone, her nose red, and her cheeks rosy, she'd been so enchanting that he would have tumbled her right there in the snow if it weren't for the children, and a still-healthy respect for her self-defense methods. No London Incomparable had that vibrancy, the brilliant warmth he saw in Grace that made her so very exquisite. Despite their beauty, the town belles were as sterile as a framed portrait in comparison.

"No, Mrs. Warrington was not an antidote," he finally answered. "Very attractive woman, actually. You said yourself Tony had good taste. The usual nice blond hair, pretty blue eyes." Like summer sunshine was nice, like azure tropical seas were pretty.

Crow nodded, careful not to disturb his neckcloth. "New arrangement, don't you know. Devised it m'self. Call it the Fanshaw Fall."

Leland studied the intricate arrangement, happy enough to change the subject. Two or three pieces of linen had to be used to give that thickness, that height, that stranglehold. "Looks deuced uncomfortable to me. You'd do better to name it the Crow Killer."

"Your taste in women was always better than your taste in clothes," the baronet retorted, not a bit concerned over his friend's less than enthusiastic response to his sartorial ingenuity. He was also not a bit deterred from pursuing details of Ware's latest *affaire*. "So the pretty widow was warm and willing, eh?"

Now Leland laughed, but without a great deal of humor. "Not at all. She is a vicar's daughter to the core. You know, good works, good thoughts. I do believe she is that rarest of *aves*, an honest woman."

"Good grief, that's the worst kind." Crow shuddered delicately. "Good thing you fled, old man, you might have found yourself leg-shackled."

"Don't be absurd. You should see the family she comes from. The father's a moralizing old jackstraw who'd rob his parishioners blind if he thought I'd let him get away with it. The mother's a cripple, in spirit more than body, I think. And that sister is bound to land them all in the scandal broth. I don't know what Tony was thinking of, to ally himself with such a sorry bunch. At least the children turned out all right."

"So your heir passed muster, did he?"

"My heir is the best—no, one of the two best children there could be. You should just see them, so bright and sweet and trusting. Learning their letters already, they are."

Crow wrinkled his nose. "Now you're sounding like m'sister-in-law cooing over her latest rug rat. At any rate, you've got your heir and can stop worrying about sticking your spoon in the wall and the Crown getting all of Ware."

The duke's fingers drummed on the table next to him. "But I don't have the rearing of him—them—dash it. She'll spoil them, smother them. That vicar will try to bleed the spirit out of them. I can take a hand if things get bad enough, but they aren't mine. I have to step back and let Graceanne do her job." As much as it rankled him, she was the boys' mother. "And your mention of sticking my spoon in the wall reminds me I have a job I'd like to ask of you."

"Not a very useful sort of chap, you know, but anything I can do."

"I'd like you to stand guardian to my wards if anything should happen to me."

"Me? Children?" The quizzing glass dropped to the end of its ribbon. "Haven't you been listening, Lee? I'll send 'em off to the navy! How old are the brats, anyway? They must be old enough for school!"

"They're practically babies, you clunch, and I'm not asking you to be nursemaid. Graceanne is a good mother, just a trifle overprotective. But if something happens to me, Willy will be rich beyond Vicar Beckwith's wildest expectations. You'd have to protect the boys and their mother from him."

"Unless she's remarried by then."

Graceanne remarried? Leland hadn't thought of that at all. And he didn't like the notion above half. What, some other man raising Ware's heirs, most likely living in Ware Hold, holding his widow? No, Tony's widow, confound it! "Damn and blast! She cannot remarry!"

"Can't stop her, in the blood it is. Widows remarry. Especially ones with looks and full purses, which she already has. You cock your toes up, some lucky chap gets himself a real plum, calling a duke his son." .

"Deuce take it, there'd be fortune-hunters and basket-scramblers sniffing 'round her skirts before I was in the ground."

Crow nodded. "If not sooner, on expectations."

The two friends were silent for a moment, contemplating. At last Leland pounded the leather armrest of his chair. "Blister it, none of that would happen if I had a wife and babes of my own!"

Crow shook his head sadly. "And here I thought seeing the infants would cure you of that rumgumption. Looks like the opposite. Lady Sefton's holding a rout next month. May as well start looking there."

He may as well. He couldn't worry about some other man raising Tony's children, and he couldn't live the rest of his own life in Graceanne's pocket, either. Besides, now that he was in London he had other interests to take care of, not just heirs and the Hold. There were other investments, other properties that needed tending. There were definitely more willing women.

* * *

Before Lady Sefton held her rout, and the newest crop of debutantes made their curtsies, Leland received a note from the Foreign Office. There was some trouble with the Prussian allies—power, money, the usual things—that called for his skills at diplomacy and his sober head at the stalled peace talks in Vienna. No Duke of Ware had ever refused the Crown. He'd have to go.

Before he left, Leland wrote to Graceanne in Warwick, assuring her that her finances were secure, as they'd discussed. His man of business, Eric Olmstead, would keep an eye on her accounts, and Milsom, who was now at Ware House, Grosvenor Square, London, could always get a message to him through the Foreign Office in case of emergency.

A ha'penny's worth of good that was going to do her, Graceanne thought as she read his letter. By the time Ware got any of her correspondence, Pru·would be long gone.

Chapter Fourteen

$\mathcal{D}$ays were easier than nights. Dreary January gave way to a brighter February, and Graceanne settled into her new, more comfortable life. Even the vicar reluctantly agreed their situation was improved. There were enough candles for him to read as late as he wanted, enough food that his stomach didn't rumble embarrassingly during his sermons, and enough servants and nurserymaids that his pesky grandsons were not underfoot as much. Through his new correspondence with Professor Jordan, he was able to purchase some modern, modest texts, but still worthy additions to his collection.

Mrs. Beckwith recovered some of her health and some of her animation under the new regimen. She even began to make social calls now that she was not ashamed to reciprocate, and parish visits, since bringing bread to the needy did not mean taking it off her own table. Graceanne or one of the servants—they now had a cook, a man-of-all-work, and three girls who came from the village every day to clean and serve and help Meg in the nursery—would drive her in the pony cart.

At first Prudence was also reaping the benefits of Graceanne's windfall. Not that she ever did much, but even fewer chores fell on Pru's shoulders now. Therefore she could spend most of her days with her bosom bow, Lucy, at the manor, to everyone's relief, from Graceanne to the children to the servants, who were all targets of Pru's derisive and demanding nature. Prudence was helping Lucy plan her trousseau, she claimed, and Graceanne hoped it was so, and not helping Liam Hallorahan supervise Squire's new racing stable. Pru was filling out under the new cook's plain but decent cooking, growing more womanly by the day, and Graceanne worried the young Irishman might find her sister even more appealing.

Somehow Graceanne's days were as full as ever, even if she didn't have to do all the baking and shopping and parish work. She still taught Sunday school and still helped her father make clean copies of his sermons, mostly to keep the peace with him. She still saw to the running of the household to conserve her mother's strength, and she still kept the household accounts. In addition she spent hours over her own bank statements, making budgets, figuring interest, trying to plan for emergencies so she would not have to call on the duke. That extra money each month meant her security, so she stayed careful with her pence and pounds and did not turn into a spendthrift overnight.

Whatever excess of time Graceanne might have found was devoted to the boys. She took them on long tromps on nice days, to exercise the dog and the children. The sheepdog seemed to know his job by instinct, having adopted the twins as his own small flock. Duke always kept Willy and Les in sight, and tried his best to keep them together and out of danger. Unfortunately, he perceived the sexton as a sheep-stealer and the village dogs as wolves, but Graceanne was working on that. She was also working on teaching the boys their letters and numbers, after swearing to Leland that they were too young for formal schooling. The only fault he'd be able to find with their education was the lack of schoolbooks: Indoors they read from picture books, outdoors from tombstones in the church graveyard next door.

Her days were busy, but Graceanne no longer fell exhausted into her bed right after dinner. Now she had time to sit with her reading, mending, or letters, and think of all the time she had yet to fill. Endless hours, countless nights.

Then Liam Hallorahan came to ask Vicar Beckwith for Prudence's hand.

The vicar said no, to no one's surprise, not even Liam's, Graceanne suspected. She was only surprised Mr. Hallorahan managed to leave with all his skin.

After that there wasn't a restful night's sleep to be had, what with Prudence alternating between shrieking and sobbing and slamming doors. The first night the twins woke up crying; the second night Mr. Beckwith moved a cot into the church; the third night a trembling Mrs. Beckwith pleaded with Graceanne to talk to her sister.

"You're what?" Graceanne sank down on the one chair in Pru's room. Prudence was stretched out on the mattress, a blanket over her head. Maybe she heard wrong. "You're not really . . . ?"

The blanket nodded, yes.

"Dear Lord, how did that happen? No, I know how it happens. That wicked Irishman had his way with you, didn't he? Why, that dastard should be shot. If I were a man, I'd call him out, I would."

There was a mumble from under the bedcovers.

"What do you mean, it wasn't his fault? There was somebody else, too?"

Now Prudence sat up, indignation writ on her tear-puffed face. "Of course not, you gudgeon. I meant it wasn't Liam's fault. It wasn't even his idea. I thought Papa would let us marry if I wasn't a . . . you know."

"But now you're breeding!"

"Well, I didn't *know* that would happen, did I? No one told me!"

No one thought she needed to know. Graceanne wanted to tear someone's hair out—her own or Pru's, she couldn't decide. "You should have found out, for heaven's sake! And you should have known better in the first place. What were you thinking?" she wailed, well aware the nodcocks hadn't been thinking at all.

"I was thinking that I had to get out of here, that's what. That if I stayed another year I'd grow old and ugly without ever going to parties and having fun. That I'd never meet any young men and I'd be on the shelf and living with my parents forever. Or end up marrying a farmer and having his grubby brats."

"Now you'll have Liam's grubby—er, children." Graceanne couldn't quite see how a horse breeder was much above a wheat-and-barley farmer or a hog grower, but she didn't have a chance to clarify that.

"Well, I never wanted a baby. I just wanted to go places. Liam goes to Tattersall's twice a year to the auctions. That's in London, you know. And he goes to horse fairs all the time. He said I could go along."

Graceanne doubted any of those venues were proper places for a lady, and certainly not one with an infant. "When is the baby due?"

Pru rolled over, tired of the conversation. "Oh, I don't know."

"What do you mean, you don't know? Haven't you been counting? Pru, you have to know, to make plans!"

"Stop shouting at me! Everyone's always shouting at me! And I made my plans: I am going to marry Liam and get out of here. I didn't want any baby, I told you. And no one ever told me I had to count. What, did you think Mama was going to tell me about breeding?"

No, Graceanne couldn't picture their anxious mother explaining the marriage bed to her seventeen-year-old daughter. Mrs. Beckwith never told Graceanne a thing, not even on her wedding day. Tony only laughed and said he'd show her.

"I thought I could get rid of it somehow if I didn't want it."

Some of the army wives had hinted about such things, but Graceanne certainly didn't know of any.

"But Liam said that would be a sin."

And laying with an innocent girl wasn't? No matter, what was done was done, and if it couldn't be undone, or redone differently, had to be fixed. "Papa said no?"

"He said he'd see me burn in Hell before he let me wed a Papist. I think they are one and the same to him. And no one else will marry us, since I am underage."

"But did he know about the baby? Surely that must make a difference, even to Papa."

"Liam was supposed to tell him when he asked permission for us to marry." She sat up in the bed. "*You* can go talk to him, Gracie. He listens to you."

If the Almighty himself was whispering in Beckwith's ear, the vicar wouldn't have listened. No daughter of his was going to marry out of the only true church, and that was that.

"But what do you expect Prudençe to do, Papa? This isn't just a flirtation she'll grow out of if you forbid her to see the young man. This is a baby!"

The vicar slammed shut the Bible he'd been studying as though he could slam shut this conversation. "Then she can have it at the workhouse for all I care. Or let her go live in sin with her stableboy. She has already sinned, what difference can it make to her immortal soul?"

"But what about the child, Papa? Will you permit your own grandchild to be branded a bastard? Its life would be ruined forever, through no fault of the baby's."

"That is no grandchild of mine. Prudence is no longer my daughter." He opened the Bible again, to the front, and pointed to the family listings. *Prudence Lynne Beckwith* was drawn through with a heavy black line. Several. If Graceanne hadn't known the name, she couldn't have made it out.

She shook her head. "You foolish old man. Did you think crossing her out of the family Bible was going to make the problem go away? Your daughter, your daughter Prudence, sir, is upstairs in her bedroom here, growing bigger with child even as you contemplate her life in the hereafter. What are you going to do about that, sir?"

"I'm going to write next Sunday's sermon, girl, that's what. About serpents' tongues and disrespectful children and silver-tongued devils. You think something should be done about your sister's condition, you do it. Get that . . . that Jezebel out of my house. You're the one with the money and the influential friends, so go make your wicked arrangements. I blame you for the whole evil mess anyway." He opened the Bible and began to read, his lips moving.

Graceanne wasn't being shut out. "I? I am to blame, Papa? How can you say such a thing? I never encouraged her to meet with Liam, I never left them alone. I think she's been planning this since before I came home from the Peninsula."

Without looking up, without hearing her logic, the vicar growled: "Yes, you. You challenged my authority, you and your twice-damned duke. You're the one who put ideas in her head, ideas above her station, made her want what she couldn't have."

"That's unfair, Papa. Just seeing what Lucy Maxton had was enough to make Pru jealous when she had so little. Why, if you'd just let her laugh and dance like the other girls, she may have paid more attention to your lectures. You lavished everything on your precious books." She waved her arms toward the glass-fronted cases. "And ignored the needs of your own family. You didn't even give her your affection, Papa, how could you expect her not to look elsewhere?"

"Bah. To an Irishman? He cannot even vote."

"Neither can women, but what's that to the point?"

"The point is you encouraged her to think she could make decisions for herself, contrary to mine, counter to the natural order of things. Now she has to pay the price. Or you do, since you think money is more important than religion. Get out of my sight, girl, you are keeping me from God's work."

* * *

If there was one thing Graceanne was sure of, it was that not even God could want Pru's baby to be born out of wedlock. Mary and Joseph were married, weren't they? If He wasn't going to take care of the situation, and the vicar wasn't going to take care of the situation, Graceanne was damned well going to have to take matters into her own two hands.

Thinking this was very much a case of slamming the barn door after the cow ran out, Graceanne went to see Liam Hallorahan at Squire's. She didn't stop at the manor or pay her respects to Mrs. Maxton; she didn't stop to think what gossip would arise. She just drove Posy around back to the new paddocks and stable complex. She pulled up alongside the cleared racing oval and handed Posy's reins to one of the grooms who was standing around watching the training runs. Liam's red hair stood out in the knot of men observing at the rails, and Graceanne marched purposely toward him, giving Squire a brief nod.

"A moment of your time, Mr. Hallorahan?"

"Sure and I wouldn't deny a pretty lady, ma'am. Excuse me, Squire. Carry on, lads."

Graceanne was fractionally aware, in one tiny corner of her mind, that Squire's mouth was hanging open and some of the stablehands were sniggling and elbowing each other. "Choir business," she firmly declared. In a way it was, although Liam and Pru had been making a lot more than music.

With her arm resting lightly on his, Liam drew her away from the others. When they were in full sight, but out of hearing, he grabbed her hand and asked, "Pru? She's all right, Mrs. Warrington? Nothing's wrong?"

The desperation in his voice reassured Graceanne. The handsome Irishman hadn't just been leading her sister down the primrose path; he seemed to care. She bit back her first answer, that no, Prudence was not all right, she was *enceinte*. He already knew that. "Yes, she is fine," she said instead. "Or as fine as can be expected while expecting. I, ah, came to ask your intentions." Good grief, Graceanne thought, that sounded like a cheap melodrama. Her lines should have been declaimed by a maiden's father or brother or someone who at least stood higher than the villain's shoulder. Not that Liam Hallorahan was a true villain. He didn't even look the part. He was tall and broad, but his sun-weathered face had laugh wrinkles and freckles, and he was running hard, callused hands through his hair in a distracted manner.

"I'm sorry," she began again. "I know you asked my father in an honorable fashion for permission to marry Prudence. I meant, how shall you accomplish that, in light of his refusal?"

"And how soon, you'll be after wanting to know, I'm sure. B'gad, and it's all I've been worriting over meself."

Graceanne noted that his brogue returned under duress. She patted his arm the way she would have comforted one of the twins, except Liam had muscles of iron under his corduroy jacket. She nodded. "And I came to offer my help. I have some money put by, if you need it to purchase a special license. I don't know how expensive they are, do you?"

Liam smiled at her, showing dimples—he really was a most attractive man, not that hard muscles and dimples were any excuse for Pru's fall from grace—and gently touched her cheek. " 'Tis a fine lady you are indeed, Mrs. Warrington, but things are nary so simple. Aye, a special license would do the trick, but archbishops don't hand dispensations to poor Irish Catholics. Your highborn English lords could get a license to marry their stepsisters, likely, given enow money and influence. I misdoubt they'd let me in the door unless I had that pot o' gold I've been seeking me whole life."

Graceanne suspected he might be right and cursed the duke again for being out of the country. "Then it will have to be Gretna Green."

"Aye, they're no so fussy over the Scottish border. But that spaleen vicar—pardon, your da—said he'd have me ar-

131

rested for kidnapping should I take Miss Prudence away. I'd pay the old blighter no never mind, but happens there's another problem. I've promised Squire here I'd take three of his best mares back to Ireland and me father's stud this month to be bred. He's already made all the arrangements and bookings. And me da needs the income."

"And Ireland is in the opposite direction from Scotland," she finished for him.

He nodded. "And there's some't else. I never thought to take a man's daughter without his blessing. That's laying bad cess on a marriage. I'm thinking we'd better go to Ireland with the horses and get me own da's blessing."

How nice, Graceanne thought, then the three mares and Pru could all be breeding at the same time.

Chapter Fifteen

*G*raceanne made all the arrangements.

First she had to meet with Liam again, since Prudence wouldn't come out of her room. He didn't come to choir practice or church, not with the vicar around, so she met him outside the lending library in the village and set tongues to wagging again. That was as good a camouflage as any, Graceanne thought, for keeping Prudence's secret.

Liam was so relieved to have any kind of solution offered to him and was so appreciative of her help that he kissed her hand. Then he kissed both her cheeks.

"Mr. Hallorahan!" she exclaimed, blushing furiously under the Misses Macgruders' gasped shock.

" 'Tis a brother's affection I'm showing, lass," he whispered in her ear, "merely a brother's." But he was flashing those dimples. The town was getting a diversionary smoke screen indeed, and Prudence was getting more than she deserved.

But not in Pru's estimation. "But I always wanted a pretty wedding like yours. And if I can't tell Lucy, what good is it? Some skimble-skamble wedding over the anvil is not at all what I had in mind, Gracie. Besides, by the time I get to Gretna Green, I'll be so fat even their filthy blacksmiths will laugh."

As patiently as she explained to the children that while birds could fly, little boys must not jump off the barn roof, she told Pru there was no choice. Somewhat less patiently did she listen to her sister's new complaints.

"I don't see why I cannot just drive off with Liam when he takes the mares next week. At least that would be romantic."

"What, and advertise your disgrace in front of the whole village? Perhaps I should have the Sunday-school children strew orange blossoms in your path."

Pru screwed her face into a pout. "It's not as if we aren't going to be married as soon as we find someone who'll do the thing. Besides, I don't care if I never see this place again. Good riddance, I say. So why should I care what these cabbageheads think, anyway?"

"So Mama can hold her head up in Warefield, that's why." And so the Duke of Ware doesn't learn that his wards' aunt is no better than she ought to be, Graceanne hoped, but she didn't say to Pru. She just plotted her intrigues a little deeper.

She made sure that they both went to bid Liam a polite farewell at Squire's, and she made sure Pru went to church—with her cloak kept on against both the chill and prying eyes. Let everyone see the chit wasn't grieving; let no one see she was swelling like a dead cow on a hot day. Then Graceanne drove Prudence to visit Lucy briefly, to announce her carefully rehearsed good fortune: a friend of Gracie's, another army officer's widow, was going traveling, possibly to Austria for the peace talks, and she wanted a companion. What luck!

One week after Liam left, Graceanne drove Pru out of town in a hired carriage to meet her friend in Worcester, she told Mr. Blanchard at the local hostelry as he helped load all the bags and boxes. Pru had insisted that it would look odd if she didn't have new, fashionable clothes for her journeying. Her old clothes didn't fit, anyway. Graceanne's purse did.

Liam was supposed to be waiting in Worcester, resting

the mares. The hired driver and post boy mustn't know this, of course, so Graceanne dismissed them to return to Warefield without her, saying she was going to visit with her friend a day or two before returning home. Graceanne and Pru took a room at a respectable inn, at Graceanne's expense, to await the friend's arrival. Pru wanted only to see the shops; Graceanne wanted only to see her gone before someone recognized them.

Liam finally appeared, with a cumbersome traveling coach he'd managed to hire. It wasn't as fancy as the one Graceanne had chosen for the ride, nor as well sprung. According to Pru, it was also odorous, drafty, and the squabs were bound to hurt her back. Furthermore, Liam was going to drive it himself to save expenses and to keep an eye on the mares tied behind.

"We're going to take forever just getting to Cardigan, I know it. And I'll have no one to talk to the whole time, Gracie."

"Of course you will. You can ride outside with Liam."

"What, in the cold and the wind? Besides, you were the one who worried what people would think."

"Yes, but they are now supposed to think that you are already man and wife, so there is nothing odd in your traveling together."

"But I don't have a ring," Pru slyly noted. "Innkeepers' wives are sure to notice such things."

So they had to go buy her a ring, at Graceanne's expense. Liam needed his money for their traveling costs.

Pru was still not resigned to that old coach. "I don't understand why you can't accompany me, Gracie, at least till the Welsh border."

"This is my first night ever away from the boys, Pru, and I am as anxious as a broody hen. I couldn't bear to be away a moment longer than I have to."

"For pity's sake, Gracie, the brats don't need you. You left four nursemaids to watch them."

Graceanne smiled. "Wait until you are a mother, Pru, then tell me how you feel about leaving your baby behind."

"I won't feel like that, I know. If you think I am dragging a puling brat around with me when we go to London, you are even more harebrained than I thought." She tugged her new fur-lined mantle closer about her. "Truly, Gracie, the slow pace is sure to make me queasy with nothing to do and no one to talk to. Couldn't you at least hire me a maid?"

"You can sleep or read those books you insisted I purchase for you or start sewing baby clothes. You've never had a maid a day in your life, Prudence Beckwith, and you're not going to start now on my sons' income. If I thought my budget could spare it, I'd hire a girl for myself so I don't have to spend tonight alone at an inn. At least you'll have Liam."

"Smelling of horses," Pru muttered angrily, but she gave up and got into the coach without so much as thanking Graceanne for her efforts. It was Liam who hugged Graceanne good-bye and swore to take care of her precious sister. Graceanne walked back to the inn, shaking her head. That poor man.

Despite her widow's blacks, the veil, and air of distraction, Graceanne still got looks from the men in the taproom that left her uncomfortably wishing she had a maid after all. She ordered her meals brought up to her room and resigned herself to staying there until the next morning.

There was no noise. That's what she noticed first. No listening for cries or calls of "Mama," no smashes, crashes, or thuds. There might be a murmur from the common room, an occasional clink barely heard through the walls and doors, but no one was going to come looking for her. How was she expected to rest?

Graceanne decided to spend her solitary evening writing to Ware in case someone informed him of her doings. She supposed the steward at Ware Hold was in contact with his man of business in London, and she suspected that all of her bank transactions were reported back to His Grace as a matter of course. He'd wonder about her withdrawing all of her reserve and most of her March allowance. She'd left herself just enough for household expenses, unless she put some of Prudence's dressmakers' bills off till next month. Graceanne took the pins out of her hair and shook it loose, feeling some relief from the headache she was developing at thoughts of her budget. And here she'd felt rich for all of a month.

She wrote to Ware that there had been some unforeseen expenses in the family, nothing he should worry about. The boys were fine, learning their alphabets. They already knew *L* and *W*, and recognized *R*, *I*, and *P*. She wished him well and closed with another reassurance that she was not living above her means.

The next morning she rode home on a carter's wagon to save the cost of hiring a carriage. She was half frozen, but there were her twins shouting a welcome, the dog barking, and only one of the nursemaids crying. She was home.

The innkeeper at the Crown and Feather where Grace-anne stayed got busy the next morning. Three carriages of sporting gentlemen pulled up, demanding accommodations for the mill to be held the next day outside of town. So he didn't put the widow's letter in the post that day. He put it in his pocket instead, where it stayed until his breeches were due to be cleaned. Which was after enough ale had been spilled on them that the local sot could get castaway on the fumes as mine host walked past. That's when Graceanne's letter got mailed.

The note went from Worcester to Ware's London house, where his secretary debated about the fate of such a scruffy letter. Should he consign it to the dustbin? Open it? Forward it, since the handwriting, as far as he could make out on the blurred address, was feminine? His Grace had no business dealings in Worcester, to his secretary's knowledge. For three days the letter sat on the man's desk with dubious charitable requests and questionable investment offerings. Then arrived a letter from His Grace's aunt, some correspondence from a university professor, and a ballot for a policy vote from one of the duke's clubs. The secretary gathered these and the waif from Worcester into a pouch to be sent to the Foreign Office for delivery via diplomatic couriers and embassy mailbags.

All in all, it was mid-April when Leland received Grace-anne's note. By then he'd already had a message from his man of business that Mrs. Warrington had gone through her entire account for January, February, and March. He'd written back to increase the funds. She wasn't a henwit who would turn into a wastrel in two months. And he could afford the additional expense. Why, he'd won and lost more than her monthly income on one roll of the dice the previous night. He'd bought his current mistress, a highborn lady of the Austrian court, a diamond bracelet whose price would have fed and clothed the twins for a year. What he was spending on bribes to collect and dispense political information—his government's request, his pocketbook—didn't bear thinking about. And he was hating every minute of the whole thing.

The talks were going nowhere but from bedroom to ballroom. Any important decisions would be made quietly, privately, away from this circus. Vienna was London times two, wealthier and wickeder. In a word, decadent.

In the back of Leland's mind was the niggling worry that his life, this glittering world of power and money, was nothing but dross. And soon enough he'd have to select a wife from the haut monde, to perpetuate the race of hollow, empty people like himself.

He could have his pick of any of the women attending the Congress, but none appealed to him except for an evening or two of pleasure. He wanted an English wife, not one of the exotic foreign beauties who were weaned on intrigue. He didn't want anyone else's English wife, either, although bored British brides were waiting outside his apartments every night. There were more than a few beautiful widows on the prowl for a proposal or a protector. When Leland asked about their children, the Diamonds laughed and waved manicured fingers. Nannies, tutors, schools—la, who cared? A handful of debutantes fished the matrimonial waters of the peace talks. Sharks they were, smelling out titles and fortunes like blood on the water. The Duke of Ware was no one's supper.

Jupiter, he was getting too old for this life! Moreover, it was getting on toward spring, and he'd promised Willy and Les ponies and riding lessons. Let the diplomatic society swap lies with every handshake or kiss, Leland vowed to keep his word to two little boys. You couldn't trust a groom to do the thing properly, he was convinced, forgetting that it was John Groom who'd set him on his first pony and dusted off his breeches till he got the hang of the thing. No, servants didn't care enough. Then again, should he find one pony, because it would be easier to watch one child at a time, or two ponies so they could all ride together? He wondered if Graceanne rode. And did the ponies have to match?

The hell with the peace talks. With rumors of Napoleon's return flying around, any decisions would be moot anyway. Let the puffguts waste their efforts on these endless debates. They could dashed well do it without the Duke of Ware. Leland was determined to get home before someone else, some sap-skulled suitor of Tony's widow, made cow-handed riders out of the boys.

There were obligations, however, that not even the Duke of Ware could shunt aside, not without creating an international incident. While his departure was delayed, Leland notified his secretary, his steward, and his man of affairs to open his houses, send his yacht, and watch the horse sales for a pair of well-trained, even-tempered ponies.

He also wrote to tell Graceanne that he was coming home, that he was keeping his promise about the ponies. His letter was carried that same day to the British embassy, taken by special courier to London, and hand-delivered to the parsonage in Warefield. Where the vicar tore it up. Leland was too late; Graceanne was already gone.

Not quite by chance Graceanne picked up the post in the village one day. She'd been eagerly awaiting some word from her sister, word that her father would have read or ripped up, she knew, no matter who was the addressee.

Pru's letter did not relieve her trepidations. Prudence hated the trip. The carriage made her as ill as she knew it would, and the packet sail was positively hellish. She might never recover. Liam was hateful. He cared more for his precious horses than for her, which was no wonder, she was so ugly and bloated. And they hadn't found anyone to marry them, so they were staying at his father's horse farm, which was dirty and isolated. Liam was going to London on horse business, the letter went on, lines crossed and recrossed, and refused to take her. He lied to her about getting married, about his family's prosperity, and about the fun they'd have. Now he was leaving her alone with people who barely spoke English.

Prudence begged Graceanne to come rescue her. Or to send money so she could hire a maid. There went most of April's money.

Chapter Sixteen

Liam arrived almost in time with the May deposit. He was at his wit's end and had left his business at Tattersall's to come beg Graceanne for help. Pru was sickly. She wouldn't eat or leave her bed.

"And she says she hates the wee bairn."

"Never!" Graceanne couldn't begin to imagine such a thing. She remembered how she felt carrying the twins—a beached whale being the closest picture called to mind—but still exhilarated, gloriously enraptured of the new life she bore.

"Aye, she hates the babe," Liam repeated. "And Old Mara the midwife is that worried, she is." Liam shook his head, the red of his hair catching gold sparks from the sunshine. They were sitting outside the schoolhouse, in full view of the whole village. It wasn't Graceanne's choice, but there was no alternative.

There were other problems, too, Liam went on. No one would marry them. The Anglican curate wouldn't perform the ceremony because Prudence was underage; the Catholic priest asked Pru to adopt their ways and swear the babe would be raised a Catholic. She refused. Graceanne could hear the bitterness in Liam's voice when he told her this last; he'd been willing to renounce *his* church. They could have held an old Irish hand-fast ceremony, but Pru declared it wouldn't be recognized in England, and worse, Liam's father was saying that if they weren't married in a Catholic church, they weren't married in the eyes of God. So Prudence was a soiled dove in their town. None of the women but Old Mara called, not even to offer sorely needed advice. And Pru and Gilly Hallorahan, Liam's father, were constantly at daggers drawn.

"So you can see I have nary a choice but to leave me wee dearie there. She's too poorly to travel, and I made better time, just me and the horses I brought to auction, sleeping out in barns and such." He rubbed at a stain on his leather breeches. "I had to come away now, b'gosh. We need the money the sale will bring, and to keep abuilding on the reputation of the Hallorahan stud, don't you see."

Graceanne saw that they'd all be better off if the Hallorahans had stuck to breeding horses. She also saw that she had no choice but to give Liam what money she could, along with the address of His Grace's man of business in London, Mr. Olmstead. "He'll know how to go about getting a special license so an English priest will marry you. I'll write out a blank bank draft and request him to release whatever funds are necessary, as an advance on my income. We'll worry about making that child your lawful issue first, then worry about the eyes of God and your father later."

Liam stared at his work-roughened hands. "I don't know if Pru will wed with me anymore."

"That is *not* an option, either. The child's life shall not be ruined because Pru is in one of her takings, not if I have anything to say about it."

As she'd known all along, Graceanne was also out of options. She had no choice but to go to her sister, bringing aid, comfort, what assistance she could—and see the ninnyhammer married.

The vicar was no help, not that Graceanne had expected anything else. "If you leave my house," he fumed, "you leave forever. Don't come back. Both my daughters are as good as dead to me."

Graceanne turned to her mother, who was weeping into the handkerchief she clutched in trembling hands. "Mama," she said, "we are your daughters, too." Graceanne knew how she'd feel if anyone tried to keep her from her sons. "Mama?" Mrs. Beckwith cried harder. Graceanne went to start the packing.

Burning Beckwith bridges was one thing, defying the duke was another. He didn't want her to remove the twins from his domain. He'd be displeased if she took the boys away where he couldn't see them, he'd said.

Then he shouldn't have gone off to Austria having a high old time, Graceanne said to herself, tossing undergarments into a trunk. How much was he seeing Willy and Les from there? She read the London papers when they came her way, and couldn't help hearing as the residents of Warefield village kept track of "their" duke. She even knew the name of his Austrian mistress. A princess, no less. Graceanne wished her well. Just let the woman keep Ware happy and busy, she prayed, and out of the country.

She didn't think the duke would withhold her monthly funds on principle, not after he was reported to have bought the princess a bracelet worth a hundred widows' mites. And she refused to entertain the belief that the Duke of Ware, no matter how angry or imperious, would let his wards go hungry out of pique that his every want and wish wasn't being catered to. He was authoritative, not cruel.

There was no question of leaving the boys behind, of course. If the duke were home, with the estimable Mr. Milsom and that army of servants, an entire nursery wing, and extensive grounds, she might have considered parting with her cherubs for the duration. It was a measure of her confidence in His Grace's affection for the boys that she'd even entertain the notion of leaving the darlings behind. That and the dread of spending days or possibly weeks in a closed coach with her precious angels. Even a mother's love has its limits.

She and Liam hired the most comfortable carriage in Warefield, the most reliable driver, a footman who had young brothers of his own. Unfortunately the nursemaid Meg refused to leave the young man with whom she was keeping company; Susan was needed at home; Bertha was subject to travel sickness; and June was petrified of crossing the sea. In other words, they'd all rather go to Hell in a handcart than to Ireland in a rolling insane ward.

If no maid would travel with them, the dog would not be left behind. The moment Duke saw one box of the boys' clothing being packed, he was never out of sight. Besides, the vicar would have the collie tossed out on his silky ear the second Graceanne's carriage turned the corner. Then, too, Duke was the only loyal baby-sitter she had.

When they were ready, Graceanne withdrew the rest of her account and wrote to the bank to forward her next deposits to the address Liam gave her, care of his father in Wicklow, Ireland.

They set out, then separated. Having seen Graceanne's party safely on the road, Liam was to ride as fast as possible to London to transact his own business. Then he had to see Mr. Olmstead, deliver Graceanne's letter for His Grace that explained her actions, get the special license, and meet her at the ferry dock in Cardigan Bay.

Graceanne packed puzzles and books and baskets of toys. That took care of the first morning.

The rest of the journey could not be described in polite conversation. Graceanne hoped the children liked Ireland: She'd set up housekeeping there for the next ten years rather than face another such expedition.

Once the carriage was unloaded, the driver and groom treated themselves to a two-day drunken celebration—after they'd put half a county between them and the Warrington ménage. Now it was just a matter of waiting at the inn Liam had recommended.

The rooms were clean, the food was adequate, and the staff there was friendly. Graceanne was learning to trust the boys with strangers more. She had no choice if she was to have a second to herself. Thank goodness for Duke, who always went along.

Days went by with no sign of Liam. No messenger, no mail. Graceanne was alone with two small boys, running through her money, with the staff at the inn growing less friendly by the hour. What could have happened to Liam? An accident, Graceanne supposed, but he would have sent word. Unless he was dead. No, a strong, healthy young man like Liam wouldn't just cock up his toes like that. The alternative was almost worse, that he'd taken her cash, her blank check, and the letter releasing her funds—and left for parts unknown.

Could she really be abandoned, stranded in Wales, where the people spoke an incomprehensible dialect? It certainly looked that way. *Now* Graceanne had a choice. She could take the boys home—not to the vicarage, for she had no home there—but home to England, to London. She could throw herself on the mercy of the duke's Mr. Olmstead, who would make some provision for her and the boys, she was sure, until Ware could be contacted and advised of her idiocy. Or she could continue without Liam across the channel to Ireland, where her next allotment of funds should be waiting, to save her sister from Mr. Gilly Hallorahan, who sounded as rigidly moralistic as their own father.

Ireland was closer.

"She did what?" The rafters of Ware House, Grosvenor Square, fairly shook with the roar of shattered illusions. Leland could hardly believe that Graceanne Warrington, that most virtuous of all widows, that female of hitherto Madonna-like purity, had run off with an Irish groom. Hell and damnation, she'd turned down his own amorous overtures! Such was the message from Ware Hold's steward, however, and here was her bank withdrawal of every last groat, confound it!

He could not even hare off to Warwick, not without duly presenting himself at Whitehall for interminable conferences about the course of the peace negotiations and rumors of the Corsican's return. By George, what was one more opinion about the future of European politics compared to the fate of two little boys? Ware's celebrated skills at diplomacy were sadly challenged over the next sennight, before he could order out his curricle and tear off to his country-seat.

What he found there challenged his composure even more. The steward swore he'd seen Mrs. Warrington and Liam Hallorahan together, cozylike, outside the schoolhouse.

His housekeeper, when called forth by Milsom, who had as usual accompanied his master into the country, reported that she'd seen the two of them kissing and hugging on the main street, bold as brass.

No, it was the younger sister, Prudence Beckwith, who was keeping company with Squire's Irish horseman, Leland swore.

The housekeeper swore right back that the whole village knew Miss Prudence had gone traveling with a wealthy lady companion well over a month earlier. She bought pretty new frocks right in Warefield, too. Word had it she was headed to Vienna and all the fancy parties. She'd be a great success, would Miss Prudence.

If Prudence was in Vienna, Leland thought, he was a monkey's uncle. The chit would have been hanging on his coattails from the minute her feet hit the ground. That or she'd be the latest comet of the demimonde.

Milsom was sniffing his disapproval of His Grace's gossiping with the servants, so Leland took himself off to Squire's. Hallorahan had left, all right, Maxton confirmed, and he was sorry to see the lad go. "Dab hand with the horses, don't you know." Of course, Squire was also glad his Lucy was promised to a respectable young gent, else he would have had to send the boy packing ages before. "Dab hand with the ladies, too, don't you know. Why, the pretty little sister leaves town, doesn't the chap take up with the widow. Not that Gracie's not a beauty in her way, but it's Pru who's the real dazzler."

The man's eyesight and intellect were so deficient,

Leland decided, his comments could be dismissed. Not so Vicar Beckwith's.

"I neither know nor care," the man snarled when pressed for the whereabouts of Prudence and Graceanne. "Fancy clothes, fancy men, fancy ideas in their heads. All of my teachings gone for naught, and their mother here weeping herself into an early grave while the household is going to rack and ruin. No, I do not want to speak of those wanton jades. I have no more daughters."

Leland slapped his riding crop against his booted leg. "And your grandsons?"

"Hah! Taking those fiends from Hell with her and the Irishman was the only decent thing the strumpet did. I have no more grandsons."

"Then perhaps you'll have no more position as vicar here, if you cannot show more generosity of spirit and for-giveness. I thought that was what you were supposed to preach, Beckwith, not vituperation and scandal-mongering."

The duke took himself back to Ware Hold, ordered his bags packed and his curricle brought around. He set out on the main road, but turned back toward the castle after a quarter of a mile or so, at the first intersection. Returned to the Hold's drive, he threw the reins to his tiger, stomped up the steps, and pounded on the door.

"Milsom!" he shouted when a surprised footman opened the heavy portals. "Where the devil is my yacht anchored anyway?"

Chapter Seventeen

At least there were ponies.

Hallorahan's stud farm was a green gem where Thoroughbred mares and their foals pranced between neat fence lines on a sunlit hillside. It was everything Liam had boasted about.

The Hallorahans' house was everything Pru had complained about. It was dark and dirty and hadn't seen a woman's touch since Liam's mother's death, eight years before. Unfortunately, it hadn't seen Liam since he set out for London, either.

His father, Gilly, was more concerned with the missing money from the Tattersall's sale than with his missing son. His quarterly rent to Lord Asquith was nearly due, and that English dastard would use any excuse to seize the farm now that he saw how successful Gilly and Liam had made it.

Besides, as he made plain when he grudgingly carted in Graceanne's boxes and trunks, the last thing he needed was to be saddled with another useless, hoity-toity English female. And this one had brats to be fed.

"Ye let 'em go next or nigh me horses, the plaguey little vermin, an' I'll feed 'em to the wolves. Didn't know Ireland had wolves yet, did ye? Aye, great hairy droolly beasties what chew on English bairns for breakfast. For dessert they nibble on fluffy dogs."

The boys ran shrieking behind Graceanne's skirts, dragging Duke with them. Welcome to Ireland, Mrs. Warrington.

Liam's father might have been labeled an old curmudgeon had he been old. Gilly couldn't be more than forty-five, and in fine condition from working with the horses. Graceanne saw a lot of Liam in the older man's face, but with more weathered lines, fewer smiles.

"Can you cook, girl? T'other one's about as useful as tits on a bull."

On the plus side, a check had arrived from Mr. Olmstead with a generous increase in her June allowance, to offset the costs of travel. Part of the boys' education, the man's note said, since travel was known to be a learning experience. Graceanne was certainly finding it so.

With the money she was able to soothe Gilly and, more important, hire a maid and a housekeeper so she could see less of housework and more of Prudence, who was indeed doing poorly. Pru's already low spirits were not raised by Liam's desertion, either.

"It's because I'm ugly," Pru cried, and she was. One look at her sister and Graceanne knew something was wrong. A further outlay of money brought a real doctor, who was no more encouraging than Old Mara. He had serious doubts of a happy outcome, he confided to Graceanne, or of Pru carrying the babe to term. Old Mara's herbs being as good a prescription as any he knew, his only suggestion was to keep Pru quiet and off her feet.

Gilly snorted when Graceanne told him. "An' ye needed to spend yer blunt to hear that? This female ain't done nary a lick o' work since she got here. Won't be no hardship keepin' 'er at rest."

Graceanne and the new maid helped Pru wash her hair, then they braided the long blond curls and got her into an attractive gown whose fullness concealed some of Pru's ungainliness. Pru felt so much better that she permitted them to help her to a sofa in the parlor, which had been tidied and brightened with new curtains and pillows. She even smiled and coquetted with Lord Asquith when he came to see if Liam was back with the money. The English landlord would be put off only a bit longer; he wanted this all settled so he could summer in Scotland for the hunting and fishing. Meanwhile, he didn't mind the flattering attention of a little English strumpet.

Gilly spat tobacco juice out the window when Asquith left. "Too bad ye're breedin'. Looks like his highness'd take t'rent money out in trade."

Pru glowered at the crudity and began to cry. Scowling at both of them, Graceanne had to help her sister back to bed, then go stop her sons from practicing spitting out the window.

At least there were ponies for the boys, and lots of children for them to play with, red-haired, freckled children who rode bareback on sturdy little cobs, and stablehands galore standing around to watch out for them. For every maid missing in the house, there were two brawny lads to muck out the stalls. No wonder there was not enough money to pay the landlord. By dint of careful reasoning, then shouting, which he seemed to respect more, Graceanne made Gilly aware of his extravagant overhead.

"I never did have a head for figures," Gilly admitted, " 'cept th' female one, a' course." Graceanne accepted the first, ignored the second, and started helping with the book-keeping in exchange for Gilly teaching the boys to ride properly, so they'd be safe. Duke stayed with them, thank goodness, for Graceanne was afraid to leave her sister for long. Prudence grew restless and weepy if left to her own devices, remembering every tale of death in childbirth she'd ever heard.

"That's nonsense, Pru," Graceanne tried to reassure the younger girl. "If I had no trouble giving birth to twins, you should do fine with just one baby. And whatever pain I had was worth it, to have my precious boys."

Prudence moaned and cried some more.

Willy and Les, meanwhile, were growing tanned and strong, like farm children frolicking in the hayloft. Graceanne hardly saw them except for meals and bedtime and an hour or two in the morning, when she herded them and whatever other children were around into the parlor for lessons. She was not going to give Lord Ware the opportunity to accuse her of neglecting their education, in addition to whatever other grievances he held against her. She thought he'd be pleased to see the children so much less dependent on their mother, learning a rough-and-tumble, boyish life of horses and dogs, fishing and swimming. She hated it and missed her babies.

They did have a bedroom where she could stand up, she reminded herself, looking for silver linings. They'd never bump their heads on this roof no matter how fast they were growing. Of course, it was thatched, and she could hear mice scurrying in it sometimes, but she wouldn't think about that, nor the bruised elbows, the scratches from berry picking, the wet, ruined clothes. The boys seemed happy.

Not so Prudence. As the weather grew warmer, she grew more uncomfortable and more demanding. With no word of Liam, she became angrier: at him, at his father, at the baby she carried. And her anger seemed to sap what little strength she had.

Then Tattersall's sent a bank draft to Gilly. They'd held a successful auction, the note said, but no one had come to collect the earnings, minus the fee, of course. Graceanne insisted that Mr. Hallorahan use some of the money left after paying Lord Asquith to hire a Bow Street runner to find Liam. Liam wouldn't run off without that money even if, as Gilly claimed, he had gotten cold feet about marrying Pru.

"B'gad and that horse money would have bought a lot o' warm socks," Gilly allowed, relieved now that his stud farm was safe for another quarter.

Graceanne wrote to Mr. Olmstead in London as soon as Gilly agreed to send the funds. She promised to add to the price if necessary from her next month's income if that would help. The boys could go barefoot all summer; Prudence's baby wasn't going to wait that long before needing a father.

Having ascertained that his yacht was in Portsmouth having its sails refitted, His Grace took himself off to London to wait, with Milsom's blessing. The butler chose to stay on in Warwick for the nonce, overseeing the spring-cleaning and underseeing His Grace's foul temper.

Leland decided that he'd meet the yacht in Bristol in a few weeks rather than face countless nights at indifferent inns, and endure the hired horses and wretched roads of a drive. Going by sea would get him to Ireland soon enough. Well, not soon enough, since he was already too late, but in plenty of time to fetch the boys back before they were ruined entirely. He thought the novelty of a boat ride might console Willy and Les at the separation from their mother if Graceanne decided to stay with her lover, damn her doxy's heart.

A visit from Olmstead revealed that the Irishman had called on Ware's own solicitor some time ago, bringing Graceanne's request that her money be sent to Hallorahan's place in Ireland and asking about a special license. That confirmed the rumors, and changed matters. If Graceanne married the man, could Leland really call her an unfit mother and take the boys away? Blast it, an Irish horse trainer raising his heirs! He went to Gentleman Jackson's parlor to polish his boxing science. Every sparring partner seemed to have red hair; the only thing that saved them from having their freckled heads knocked off was the fact that Hallorahan hadn't come back to get the license. The only reason Leland didn't set off for Ireland on horseback that same day was a raging storm that was reported to have washed away whole roads.

The same storm kept his yacht in Portsmouth an additional sennight. So Ware was still in London when Graceanne's latest letter to Olmstead arrived after a long, weather-related delay. This time she wanted to hire a Bow Street runner to find the Irishman. The bastard had shabbed off on her? After sending her to Ireland? Ware didn't bother going back to Gentleman Jackson's. He went straight to Manton's shooting gallery.

A report came directly from Bow Street. Mr. Liam Hallorahan was easy to trace, having last been seen leaving Tattersall's on his way to his hotel. He wasn't staying in one of the better lodgings, naturally, but had taken a room in a respectable inn which was, unfortunately, in a less than respectable neighborhood. Said neighborhood was visited that very evening, it happened, by a press gang for His Majesty's Navy. Liam Hallorahan, the report concluded, was now en route to the Americas, protecting His Majesty's foreign interests.

Prudence went into labor the day after the letter came, at least a month earlier than anyone predicted. It was an easy birthing by most standards, if you discounted the mother's screams. To Prudence it was the most painful, disgusting event in her entire life, and she wanted only to have it over and done. She refused to look at the child.

Old Mara whispered at Graceanne not to insist, for the babe hadn't a chance of surviving. Why break the poor lassie's heart by showing her that pitiful scrap? Mara had to blow into its mouth just to make the infant let out a thin, feeble wail. It was as if all of Prudence's screams had used up the baby's voice, too.

The child was bluish and tiny, as scrawny as a baby bird. Graceanne had never seen so small an infant, and she marveled as she wrapped her new niece in the softest blankets, holding her to keep her warm, comforting the tiny body so she wouldn't use up her tenuous hold on life in crying.

"It's a beautiful, perfect little girl, Pru," Graceanne lied. Or perhaps she meant it, her heart having gone out to the fragile infant the moment she took her from Old Mara, and love being notoriously blind. "What shall you name her?"

Prudence turned her face to the wall.

"Best to hurry, missus, an' have in Father to get her

blessed," Old Mara warned. "Th' wee bairn's too frail to make it through till morning, I reck."

"Not the Catholic priest, Gracie," Pru insisted, but Old Mara took another look at that tiny pinched face and said she didn't think there'd be time to fetch in the Anglican minister. Then Gilly swore he'd have only the Catholic priest in his house, and Prudence started screaming again.

How could they be arguing over which church should baptize the baby? Graceanne wondered. Didn't any of them care that the infant might—no, most likely would—die? Was she the only one to sorrow for this pitiful little rag fighting so hard for every breath?

"Gilly, fetch your Father Padraic, he's closest. If God wants another angel, He won't care who sends her. Pru, stop that carrying on, you'll only weaken yourself further. Tell me what you want to call the baby."

"I told you, I don't want the thing! I was going to send it to the orphanage anyway. Let them name it, if it lives long enough."

"Prudence! You cannot mean such a thing." Even for Prudence, that was a shockingly heartless thought. "You're just overwrought from the birthing. You couldn't give away your own flesh and blood!"

"No? Watch me, Gracie. Father Padraic runs the orphanage. He'll take the brat if it's still alive."

Tears running down her face, whether for her new niece in her arms or for her sister, Graceanne swore, "I'll never let you."

"Fine, then you keep it. You name it. The brat is yours if it lives. Have someone get you legal papers if you want, Gracie, and hurry, for as soon as I can get out of this bed, I'm leaving here—without a sickly little Irish bastard."

The priest came, and Graceanne tried again to make Prudence give her child a name.

"I won't! Just give it something pretty, something silly, not like Prudence or Grace."

Father Padraic was waiting, the baby trembling in his arms.

"Antonia," Graceanne choked out, giving this infant the name she had selected for Tony's daughter. "Antonia Faith."

"Antonia Faith Warrington," Pru called.

Graceanne gulped and nodded. She'd do it. She had to. Prudence wasn't going to change her selfish mind, and Graceanne wasn't nodcock enough to believe she would. Even if Pru did have a change of heart—or any kind of heart—and decided to keep the babe, where could they go, how could they live? No, Antonia would be better with an aunt who already loved her. And no one, well, almost no one, knew when Tony had died. She'd claim little Nina as her own, his posthumous child, so there'd be no scandal. Pru could have her own life back to make of it what she could, and Graceanne would have the girl child she always wanted. If she could keep her alive.

Chapter Eighteen

*W*et nurses didn't come cheap, not even in Ireland, where children died at an appalling rate. Father Padraic found Shanna McBride for Graceanne in the workhouse, where the poor girl would never be able to work off her debts. Tossed out on the street from her indentured position in an alehouse when she was found to be breeding, Shanna had begged and wandered homeless until her time. Her impoverished family couldn't take her back; they'd had to put her into bond-servitude in the first place just to feed the younger children. So Graceanne paid off the indentures, then the poorhouse costs, and what the parish had outlaid to bury Shanna's stillborn infant. Feeling dirty, like she'd just purchased a slave, Graceanne watched the magistrate filling out forms making Shanna her property. But Antonia had to be fed.

Pru almost laughed when Graceanne suggested she try nursing the infant. "What, and never get my figure back?"

Graceanne laid out more money for a solicitor to draw up papers, making everything legal. Prudence gladly signed, although she kept swearing there was no need; she was never going to try to reclaim such a sorry specimen. Why Graceanne wanted to go to all the fuss and bother was beyond her anyway, for the child couldn't live out the first fever or influenza.

Gilly also had to sign. He was all too happy to put his signature on the papers if it meant he'd never have to pay out good blunt to support the pawky bastard. "Never sure it were me boy's in t'first place," he muttered with a sour look at Prudence, who was smiling at the middle-aged solicitor. Pru slammed a book down on top of Gilly's favorite clay pipe. The noise woke the infant, who set off a feeble wail.

"Hush, *cara mia,* hush, *niña.*" Graceanne cuddled the infant, rocking her back to sleep while she scowled at the others.

Antonia was now Graceanne's, hers and Tony's. She'd simply move the date of his death forward a month or two, if anyone asked, and wear her blacks a month or so longer. She was sick of them, but there was no money for a whole new wardrobe anyway. Antonia would need dresses and sweaters and caps and more blankets to keep her warm, even in the Irish summer.

And Antonia, little Nina, was another day old. She was not thriving, hardly suckling according to Shanna, but alive. If a heart could be kept beating on strength of will and prayer, Nina had Graceanne's. And Willy and Les's, who thought she was the best thing they'd ever seen, uglier even than the pink baby mice that fell through the roof last week. And a sister might be nice, they allowed, for when they played knights and dragons. Duke never liked being the captive maiden waiting to be saved. He never wanted to wear a hat.

Every day the baby gained a bit. Her breathing was still ragged, her lips were still blue, and she was taking so little nourishment, Shanna was afraid her milk would dry. Then they'd just have to get a goat, Graceanne declared, not giving up. She held the baby as if her body warmth would keep her with them. She talked to Nina constantly, promising a world of wonders, pretty gowns she was even now embroidering, doting brothers, dolls.

If the baby was slow to gain, Pru was quick to lose. She dropped the extra pounds as fast as she could, almost overnight, and with them the drained, pulled look. She started eating decent meals, taking walks in the fresh air, and sleeping as much as she thought she needed, which was, of course, twice as much as Gilly thought any female needed.

One day Pru begged a wagon ride to the little village to buy a new hat, which she charged to Graceanne without a by-your-leave when Lord Asquith told her the bonnet was a perfect companion to her beauty. Graceanne was too busy with the fussing baby to argue, and too relieved to have Pru out of the house and out of Gilly's way. For the most part, Prudence spent her time reworking her gowns, taking them in, adding new trimmings. Not even she dared to ask Graceanne for money to hire a seamstress.

Lord Asquith took to calling, and Graceanne was happy enough when Prudence acted as hostess in her stead, pouring the tea, making conversation about people she never met. Graceanne had enough to do between the boys' lessons, the new baby, the household, and trying to keep some peace between Gilly and Pru.

One month after Nina's birth, the baby was almost as big as a normal newborn and almost healthy in color and breathing. Graceanne was almost ready to stop worrying that every time Nina went to sleep she might not awaken. And Prudence was almost ready to leave.

"Lord Asquith is going to Scotland for the rest of the summer," Prudence announced one day. "He's asked me to accompany him."

"To accompany him? That's an odd synonym for marry, Pru."

The younger girl brushed her sister's qualms aside. "Perhaps he'll come around by the time we get to Scotland." She didn't seem concerned. "He owns property in Jamaica, too, and says he'll take me in the fall."

"Oh, Pru, that's not the way it should be. It's wrong!"

"What's right, then? For me to go back to the vicarage and sing in the choir? Even if Papa would let me, that's not what I want, that's not what I've ever wanted. Besides, Gracie, not even you with your rosy outlook can have forgotten that I am already ruined. I can't make my reputation any worse. Instead of putting on sackcloth and ashes, I may as well wear silk."

After Prudence left, Graceanne had a lot to think about, although not much spare time to do it in. What about her own life? And the boys' and Nina's? It was time she thought of their futures, too. The twins were content enough, but they were nearly savages except for their two-hour lessons. How could they learn to be proper English gentlemen fit for polite drawing rooms if they were running wild in the hills? If, Heaven forbid, Willy got to be duke, he'd need to know more than how to tickle fish out of streams. And Nina would always be a by-blow of Liam Hallorahan and an English doxy around here, no matter what name she bore. The country people had long memories, besides every superstition and prejudice Graceanne could name.

No, they shouldn't stay there. Gilly wasn't even family. And he was beginning to look at her in a way she did not like.

Things came to a head one day when she was sitting in the sun next to the kitchen garden behind the house. She was watching the twins gather peas, Nina on a blanket next to her.

Gilly stepped out of the kitchen door, pipe in hand, and sat next to her on the ground, too close for comfort. She pretended to fuss with Nina's blanket, as an excuse to put more inches between them.

"Ye know, ye could do worse'n settle here," Gilly started to say. "Ye seem to fit in the way of life hereabout. None o' them prettified ways about ye." He nodded. "That's good."

Well, it wasn't much of a compliment, but Graceanne bowed her head and murmured a thank-you.

"No telling if Liam'll ever get back, I be thinking," he went on. "An' I need brawny sons to help run th' place.

Your two ain't fallen off th' roof recently, nor tried to burn th' barn down but that onct."

"It was an accident! And they're just babies, not the stablehands you keep trying to make them into."

"They'll grow" was all Gilly said. "An' I'm not too old to have more sons meself. A man needs a woman. Been a long time without." He let the implication drift off, that while she was there, he couldn't entertain another.

"Does this mean that you are asking me to . . . marry you?"

"Aye, ye're a bonny enough lass, for an Englishwoman. Good mother, hard worker . . ."

Graceanne said she needed time to think about it.

Gilly did offer security, and he was decent enough in his way. She'd seen him in his cups only twice, once when the letter came saying Liam was impressed, and the other time when Pru had given birth to the only grandchild he was liable to have, and that one a sickly female. Gilly already treated the boys with casual affection and her with a modicum of respect. She supposed Willy and Les could learn the ways of a gentleman when they went off to school. And she could convince Gilly to install a real roof as a wedding present.

But was a real roof over her head enough? Here was another man who wanted her sons and her warm woman's body. Gilly was more honorable than the duke, but the whole came down to the same: Graceanne was a commodity, not a person wanted for her own self, not a woman to be cherished. She couldn't do it. And if she was going to reject Gilly's offer, she definitely couldn't stay.

She couldn't face the return trip on her own either, not with the addition of a fragile infant, a young wet nurse, and an uncertain welcome in England. She almost wished the duke were back in London. He'd know what was best to do. Surely he had a small bit of property where she and her family could settle for a new start. Somewhere he wouldn't visit too often, with his too-tempting importunities. No, Graceanne told herself, she did not need any more complications, only an escort. She recalled how Tony's batman Rawley had seen her and the boys home from Portugal, taking care of their every need despite his injury. She'd had one letter from him after Christmas, thanking her for the gift. And no, he hadn't found work by then except helping out in his brother-in-law's apothecary. There wasn't much call for a one-armed veteran, he'd written.

Graceanne sat down and wrote to Rawley that very day. A one-armed veteran was precisely what she needed as pathfinder, protector, and provider of a male influence for the twins. Tony's cousin Ware was being generous, she wrote, so she could hire Rawley's services as equerry if he was still free. She enclosed a check for his expenses and asked him to hurry, since she found herself in a rather uncomfortable position in Ireland. She didn't mention the new baby; Pru's lapse was better explained in person.

Graceanne didn't get her knight in sergeant's uniform quickly enough. She got an escort fit for a princess instead, and she only wished the princess had managed to keep him.

His Grace finally got under way. Dead calms turned into thunderstorms which turned into gales. This was a bone-headed notion in the first place, taking the yacht to Ireland. What if the twins got seasick? What if they fell overboard? Grace would never forgive him. Besides, he could have been there ages ago if he'd driven. What if she needed help, with Liam taken up by the press gang? All in all, Lord Ware had too much time on his hands and too many worries on his mind. If not for the handsome wages he paid, the duke's crew would have jumped ship the third day out. By the time the Emerald Isle hove into view, they were considering tossing him off the side of the yacht, the salaries bedamned.

Totally unaware that his foul temper had nearly caused a mutiny, Leland hailed the first fisherman he saw on the docks at Wicklow Head and asked for directions to Hallorahan's stud farm. Then he asked again at the livery stable, where he hired the likeliest-looking beast. And again from a shepherd at an unmarked crossroads. The deuce take it if he could understand a word these people spoke. So what the hell was Graceanne doing here, especially if Liam wasn't?

He got his answer soon enough, when Graceanne, looking more beautiful than he remembered despite the blacks she still wore, with a warm sun-glow to her skin and paler golden highlights to her hair, introduced him to Gilly Hallorahan. Liam's father refused to leave her side, even when Leland suggested they had private matters to discuss.

"Reckon ye do, but not in my house. High-nosed English toffs ben't in such high odor, Duke."

So that was the way of it. She'd left with the son, then took up with the older man—not too old; Leland noted the strong forearms and well-muscled thighs—when Liam involuntarily deserted her. Leland sat stiffly, his face a rigid mask of controlled fury.

At first Graceanne was delighted to see Ware, even allowing herself a moment to believe he cared enough about her to come fetch her home. Not with that aristocratic disapproval writ on his stony countenance, he didn't. She quickly realized he wanted the boys, that was all. Chiding herself for being a peagoose, she called them in and took up her sewing.

Watching Leland with the twins was like watching an iceberg melt. They threw themselves at him in an ecstasy of welcomes, raining hugs and wet kisses and shouts about their ponies and their friends and the mice in the roof all at once, while Duke pranced in circles, adding to the noise with excited barks. The twins wanted to show Collie their swimming pool and the foals and the barn cat's kittens and the new baby and their ponies.

"Whoa, bantlings," he told them, tossing one after the other up in the air and pretending to stagger when he caught them, so big had they grown. "Let me talk to your mother, then you can show me all your marvels."

When Willy and Les rushed out to tell the stablehands

that their cousin Collie, who was really a duke, was really here, Leland straightened his clothes. He brushed a smudge of dirt off his fawn breeches. "The boys look well, sturdy and solid. They've lost some of the baby roundness, and their voices have deepened. They speak much better, too, even if they still both talk at the same time." And he still couldn't tell one from the other. "And Duke has turned into a handsome animal."

Graceanne was wishing they hadn't stormed in like unmannerly urchins, dressed like ragamuffins and climbing all over the immaculate nobleman. Even Duke had forgotten his training. "They're still young," she said by way of an excuse—for the boys, not the dog. "Only four."

"Are they?" They'd been three at Christmas. Leland felt a pang for the changes he'd missed seeing, the birthday he hadn't acknowledged with gifts, the blasted ponies some jumped-up horse-coper was providing! He addressed the older man, still hovering behind Graceanne: "I heard about your son's impressment. I'm sorry."

Gilly barely nodded, so Leland turned back to Tony's widow. "As soon as I heard, I started arrangements to have him brought home."

"How generous of you. Isn't that kind, Gilly?" Gilly grunted.

Ware said, "Yes, well, I'm sure you'll be glad to see him."

Graceanne wasn't sure at all, not if she had to explain about Pru traipsing off with Liam's landlord, and not if Liam was going to cause trouble about the baby.

She must have murmured something suitable, for the duke went on. "Of course, it may take some time. Meanwhile"—he cleared his throat; confound it, there was no polite way of putting this—"I'd like to take the boys back to England on my yacht. And you, too, naturally, if you wish to come. I, ah, believe the twins belong in their own country."

Graceanne studied the tiny cap she was embroidering. "Yes, I have been thinking it was time we returned home."

"Here now," Gilly put in, "I thought ye've been thinking on my offer." He turned to Ware, fists clenched at his sides. "An' an honorable offer it do be, too, Duke. Ye've got yer yacht an' yer mansions an' yer piles of blunt, but I've got a wedding ring to put on her finger. Can ye match that, Duke?"

Something inside Leland turned to ash. It was true, then. Grace and this rough countryman had an understanding. And with the boys so obviously flourishing, Leland knew he couldn't take them away from her.

Graceanne died a little in the awkward silence after Gilly's question. Then, "Don't be a fool, Gilly," she said. "His Grace is only showing proper concern for his wards' welfare. He has always been a most excellent guardian."

Gilly spat out the window. Graceanne suddenly wondered what he did in the winter, with the windows shut. With any luck, she wouldn't be here to find out. Setting aside the sewing she was too nervous to stitch properly, she asked Gilly to check on the boys while she and His Grace continued their conversation.

"I cannot return to my parents' home, Your Grace."

"Leland. And I should hope not. There are a few extra rooms at Ware Hold," he teased, inordinately relieved that she was considering coming away with him. "Just a few. And Ware House in London is almost as empty. On the boat ride home we can discuss where you'd like to live."

"I have other reservations, Your—cousin." He gestured for her to continue, schooling himself not to grin, not to show he was willing to agree to almost anything. "At first you wished to have only Willy, your heir, come to you. I need to know that you'd not favor him over Les."

"Confound it, Grace, that was before I met either boy. You must know I'd not love one more than the other, or make them compete with each other for my regard."

"And you'll not establish Willy as your heir, confer titles and such on him, while you are still in your prime? I'd not have him disappointed later."

He nodded, liking that she thought him still young. Compared to Liam's father, Gilly, he was practically a lad. "I shan't dub him viscount until I'm at least fifty, and without male issue. Will that do?"

Graceanne thought the duke would be virile well into his seventies, but she didn't say so. She was thinking how best to put her most pressing concern. He was so good with the boys and would be such a loving father. She had no real cause to distrust him, yet his world did not accept children like Nina. The members of the *ton* kept their dirty linen hidden in the deepest closets. Hers was going aboard that yacht, first class, or none of them were going. "So you'll care for all my children, be a fair and even-handed guardian?"

"I said so, didn't I?"

"I would have your handshake, Leland. It's that important to me."

This was not time to quibble about a man's word, not when he was so close to filling that gaping hole in his life. Leland stood and took her hand in his. "I solemnly swear to love both your children the same, with no favoritism."

"*All* my children," she corrected him.

He shrugged. "All."

Chapter Nineteen

The duke returned to his yacht. He wouldn't have accepted Gilly's hospitality, nor was it offered. Furthermore, he had to alert the crew and rearrange the bunks in the cabins, since Graceanne insisted the children needed their nursemaid Shanna. Leland couldn't but think the Irish girl would be miserable away from home and family, but the chit convinced him she'd never leave Mrs. Grace, not after all she'd done for her. So be it. Shanna could sleep with the boys, leaving the widow's wide bed half empty. And his own the same, of course, if by any stroke of Gallic magic she preferred to sleep there.

He did not see much of Graceanne the next day, since she was busy with the packing, so he went with the boys on their farewell rounds of stalls and paddocks. He wondered if Graceanne knew that their favorite activity at the horse farm was watching the stallion perform. They were too excited at the prospect of a boat ride to worry about the horses left behind, especially when the duke described the ponies he had waiting for them at Ware.

Leland hired a wagon to transport the trunks, bags, and boxes to the dock, and a carriage for Graceanne, the nursemaid, and the boys. Willy and Les wanted to ride on the wagon with the dog, though, so he tossed them up, with firm instructions to stay seated and hold on tightly over bumps, while the widow and the maid settled themselves in the coach.

As he walked back to the carriage, Leland heard an odd sound. He looked under the wheel to see if a spring was damaged. No, it wasn't that kind of noise. His brows lowered, the duke pulled open the carriage door, then shut it quickly, backing out. The nursemaid was holding an infant to her breast.

Graceanne opened the door again and stepped down, but she stayed close to the carriage. "I should have told you."

"You should have told me?" he thundered. "You bloody well should have mentioned that you were bringing an unwed girl and her baby aboard my boat! And why the devil would you hire a—"

Before he could go any further with that thought, Graceanne quietly said, "It's not Shanna's baby."

If it wasn't the nursemaid's baby . . . dear God, he thought, a baby. He staggered back from the carriage.

Graceanne reached in and lifted out a small blanket-wrapped bundle. She cuddled it, gazing down in such tenderness, his heart gave a lurch. My God, a baby.

Still staring at the infant, she told him, "I should have told you, but I was afraid you wouldn't want to travel with an infant. She won't be any problem, I swear."

Leland wasn't listening. He was calculating. The bundle was so tiny, what was nine months back from yesterday? He couldn't think. Could she have been breeding over Christmas? He recalled the velvet gown she wore, oh, so well, but it was cut in the latest style, with the waistline under the bosom. But Tony'd already been dead for months by then. Too many months.

"By all that's holy, woman, how could you?" His well-bred, aristocratic indifference gave way to abject anguish.

Graceanne didn't notice. What, did he think she should have tossed Pru's baby in the dust heap? "How could I not?" She looked up and read disgust on his handsome face. She held the baby closer to her breast. "She's mine, so speak now if you will not acknowledge her. But I swear to you, the boys and I will go elsewhere if you cannot accept Nina."

Still reeling, he automatically said, "I could force you, or take the twins. The laws . . ."

"But you said you would not. I hold you to your word. Nina is part of our family."

"Nina?" It was the gasp of a dying man.

"Antonia Faith. Little girl, *niña*. Nina."

"You named the bas—er, baby—after Tony? Tarnation, woman, does your boldness know no bounds? The gall, the absolute nerve!"

Her shoulders went back. "Tony would understand. He had a generous heart." Not like some others she could mention but didn't.

A generous heart, Tony Warrington? Ware was positive his hotheaded cousin would kill her, Liam, Gilly, and every horse on the farm. Leland wanted to himself. It was all he could do not to strangle the jade.

"And you hope to pass the child off as Tony's?"

"No one has to know the exact date of his death. It's not as if he died in a specific battle or anything. And the timing is not that many months far from possible. Nina deserves that, Your Grace. She fought so hard."

"What, is she sickly besides?"

"She's just delicate." Graceanne uncovered the infant's head and held her out toward him to see. "She won't be any problem."

All he saw was a pinkish red tinge to the downy hair on the infant's head. Like Liam's. Or Gilly's. That was problem enough. He turned away. "And you don't feed her yourself?" He jerked his head toward the carriage and the waiting maid. No, she wouldn't let a nursing babe interfere with her finding a new protector.

"Of course not. How could I? Why, you think . . ."

She was too late. Leland had already climbed aboard the wagon with the boys and given the driver the office to start.

Graceanne carried the baby back into the carriage, and

168

the groom raised the steps. They were off. Graceanne sank back on the cushions, shaking. He thought that little of her? She knew he'd never seen her as a lady of his own class, but to think she'd fallen so low? And he'd never even asked, he just assumed she was Nina's true mother from the beginning, she realized now. Well, let him, then, she thought, her chin coming up despite the tears that threatened. Let him think the worst since he was determined to anyway. Graceanne Beckwith Warrington, vicar's daughter and soldier's widow, was not about to go begging his priggish lordship's pardon.

Perhaps traveling by sea was not such a good idea. If the crew was ready to keelhaul their captain before, now they were ready to abandon ship altogether. The twins were just a bit hard to keep out of trouble among the ropes and sails and masts, hammocks, longboats, and oilskins. Leland didn't dare take his eyes off them for a moment, lest one or the other decide to go swimming or fishing or repeating the sailors' expletives when they found the boys underfoot.

The nursemaid was no assistance. When she wasn't feeding the infant, she was cowering in her bunk, leaving Graceanne to deal with the baby instead of the boys. The superstitious chit heard one of the sailors say that now he understood why it was such bad luck having women on board, and she was positive they were going to sink. And the dog was even less of a help. Duke never found his sea legs and was sick as a pup—all over the *Silver Lady's* teak decks. Furthermore, the dog could not be trained to use a chamber pot or the buckets provided for such a purpose, so yet another section of teak decking had to be designated as the dog's necessary. The twins, on the other hand, delighted in aiming their spigots between the railings, especially when they sailed close to shore or another vessel.

The sleeping arrangements were also less than satisfactory. Mrs. Warrington insisted on having the baby in with her, since Shanna was a heavy sleeper and might not hear her cries. After the first night Leland didn't believe a deaf man could sleep through the infant's bawling. He didn't, nor any of the crew. And she was so small! With Shanna awakened to tend to that scourge, the twins could not be left alone in case one woke up and wandered to the deck. So the widow shared her lovely bed with a mewling infant, and the Duke of Ware in the captain's luxurious quarters was lumped in bed with two little boys who wriggled all night. The wet nurse, the blasted wet nurse, was the only one to have a cabin to herself.

The other thing Leland was finding awkward about shipboard travel was how hard it was to avoid his passenger. If they'd gone by carriage, he could have ridden alongside, or taken up the ribbons. Even a good-sized yacht like the *Silver Lady* did not offer a great deal of privacy. But the duke did his best, since seeing her—especially seeing her with that infant in her arms—made his stomach turn, and he was never seasick. Luckily she didn't like taking the infant on deck because of the wind and the sun, so Graceanne stayed mostly in the elegantly appointed stateroom. Leland stayed mostly outside on the deck.

There was one blessing to the boat trip: On the first day out Les fell and cut his chin on a cleat. Now Leland could tell his wards apart.

Graceanne was enjoying herself enormously. The duke was keeping such careful eye on the boys that she did not have to worry about their safety, and he was keeping so consistently out of her company that she could rejoice. He was uncomfortable in her presence? Good. The less she saw of that blackguard the better.

And for once she didn't have to see to the cooking or cleaning. The cook almost had a seizure when Graceanne stepped into the cramped little galley and offered to help. There was a steward whose sole job was to attend the needs of the passengers, and a cabin boy for everything else. Best of all, Nina was getting stronger. Even her complaints were growing louder than whimpers. Never had an infant's crying sounded so sweet. Graceanne was content to hold her and sing to her and plan their future. She wasn't quite sure where they'd live, Graceanne crooned to the infant, but she promised they'd live happily ever after, just like in fairy tales.

"Life is not make-believe, madam, and you do the child a disservice by teaching her otherwise." Leland took off his oilskin coat and sat as far as possible from Graceanne and the baby in the stateroom. The twins were in his cabin napping at last—he'd insist they have an afternoon rest until they were fourteen at least—with the cabin boy guarding the door. With a summer rain squall raging on deck, Ware had no place else to go. "Perhaps we should now discuss where you and the children will live."

"Yes, you said we could decide it aboard the yacht. The boys have been asking."

He got up and began pacing. "There is nothing to discuss. We go to London." At first, on his outward journey, Ware had pictured an idyllic family summer in Warwick, with picnics and simple country pleasures. Then, he'd planned, they'd all go to town for the fall Little Season. The twins would have nannies and tutors, and Grace would have a new wardrobe. Once she was out of mourning, he'd see she was eased into the life of the beau monde. Then, if she could find her place in his world . . .

Leland had never let his planning go beyond convincing himself that Tony's widow deserved pretty gowns and parties.

But now? Summer was nearly over and the villagers in Warefield would never accept soiled goods. And there was no telling whom she'd run off with next. In London he could keep a closer watch on the widow, and since she was keeping up this perverse pretense of mourning, he wouldn't have to introduce her to the *ton*, which could be even more morally narrow-minded.

"I prefer the country, Your Grace. It will be healthier for Nina."

"Why? You said she wasn't sickly."

"She's better, merely delicate."

Something in her voice made Leland pause in his pacing and take his first good look at the infant. "Gads, if that's delicate, I'd hate to see what you call ailing." The child had a pinched look to her face and a bluish cast to her complexion. She trembled and jerked her hands around spasmodically. "By Jupiter, we should have gone by carriage."

"No, I think that would have been worse, with the dust and the drafts and the jouncing around. The yacht is better appointed than many an inn we'd have to patronize."

He nodded and resumed his pacing. "Ware House in London is even more comfortable. It will be easier to put it about that the child is Tony's post-obit."

Graceanne insisted. "The children and I will be happier in the country."

"But I have business I need to attend to in London and duties at the Foreign Office, so that is where we are going." He pounded on the chart table for emphasis, sending maps rolling in every direction.

"I know what it is," Graceanne accused him. "You are making the trip longer, hoping Nina dies before you have to acknowledge her!"

"My God, woman, what you must think of me!"

"No worse than you think of me, I'm sure," she shouted back.

"I never wished a child dead! How dare you accuse me of such a thing!"

"Then why won't you ever look at her?"

"I just did! And if I hadn't already decided to go to London, I'd change my mind. There are better physicians there."

"Nina doesn't need a physician; she just needs time and love. You never even bothered to look at her before. How can you know what she needs?" Now Graceanne was up and pacing to calm the baby's fretfulness at the angry voices.

"That's because all I ever saw was her red hair."

"My mother had red hair. Everyone in Warefield will remember that."

"I still have business in London."

"Gammon, I can just imagine your business. What is it this time, an Oriental empress? Let us go on without you. If not to Warefield, then some other quiet place. You cannot want a houseful of children interfering with your 'business' in the city."

"No!" he shouted, setting the infant to wailing again. "My wards stay with me."

"Then, here," she yelled, thrusting the red-faced bundle into his unsuspecting arms and heading for the door, "here's your latest ward. Get used to her."

Sergeant Rawley arrived in Wicklow, Ireland, a few weeks later. What he heard about Mrs. Warrington sent him riding neck-or-nothing back to England without a day of rest. According to Hallorahan, that "generous" duke had come claiming the major's widow, along with a baby Rawley knew nothing about, except that it sure as hell couldn't be the major's. Major Warrington hadn't been next or nigh his sweet young wife for over six months before taking that fever what killed him. Hadn't Rawley been a-nagging at him the whole time to go visit the missus? That little darling wasn't increasing then, and she sure as bedamned didn't get in an interesting condition on the way home from Portugal. It sounded to Rawley like his lady needed more than an escort.

He'd taken the King's shilling and given his arm; even without Mrs. Warrington's blunt, he'd give that duke what-for.

Chapter Twenty

$\mathcal{E}$ven the longest journey comes to an end except, perhaps, the journey to self-awareness. By the time they reached London, Lord Ware had devised a story to tell Aunt Eudora, and thus all of town. Milsom would see it reached the servants' grapevine, and hence to Warefield.

Despondent after Christmas, so Leland related, Mrs. Warrington fell into a decline because Tony would never see his new child. Her megrims were worsened by the offer to go traveling from a fellow officer's widow, an offer she had to refuse because of her condition, but which she was happy to have her sister accept in her stead. Prudence's departure made life at the vicarage more dreary, with more chores and less time to spend with her sons or resting for the baby's sake. With Ware's active encouragement from abroad, therefore, and his man of business's contrivance from London, Mrs. Warrington was sent to Ware's old retired nanny for her confinement. Liam Hallorahan was good enough to escort her on his way home; the duke left the peace negotiations to bring his cousins back with him.

"Humph!" Aunt Eudora snorted. "If you weren't a duke, my friends would laugh in my face."

"But I am a duke, Aunt, so they shall smile and nod politely and congratulate you on your new grandniece, as long as you accept Antonia as your kin."

"I don't doubt she's my kin, boy, it's which side of the blanket she was born on that has me flummoxed."

"What, you think the infant is mine?"

"I ain't blind, boy. I saw how you panted after the widow last Christmas." She pounded her cane on the floor for emphasis. "And you better not be acting like a stag in rut unless you want everyone else to think so, too."

Having carefully inspected the new arrival, Milsom drew his own conclusions, which he was certainly too well trained to discuss with his employer, or anyone else for that matter. "Very good, Your Grace," he said after being spoon-fed a bowl of hogwash if ever he saw one. "Major Warrington would be proud of his wife and new daughter."

Leland swallowed his own retort and dismissed the butler to spread the word.

Ware's friend Crow Fanshaw needed a bit more convincing. He'd stopped by when he heard Leland was back in town, and the duke was forced to introduce him to Graceanne. Ware knew he couldn't keep her hidden away like the family skeleton, not if he wanted the *ton* to accept his story, but did she have to tote that blasted infant around with her like an extra shawl? Having the boys down to tea was one thing; let Crow see that not all children were barbarians, like his sister's tribe. It was bad enough that Les—or Will—asked his Tulip friend how Crow turned his head without poking out an eye on the high shirt collars he wore, but did Grace have to show off the half-pint Hallorahan?

Crow was polishing his quizzing glass later at White's when the inevitable came. "I say, Tony's boys couldn't be more alike if you held a mirror to 'em. Of course, the younger one—Leslie, was it?—is going to be the better dresser. You can tell."

"You can tell which is Leslie?" Now that Les's chin was healed, Leland hadn't a clue which twin was which. He was ashamed to admit it to a man-milliner like Crow, however. "That is, you can tell which has better taste?"

"Of course. And deuce take it if they aren't little Tony Warringtons come to life. Ah, can't say the same for the infant."

There, the question everyone was going to be asking, but not out loud. There was only one answer: "Mrs. Warrington's mother was a redhead."

Crow nodded and replaced his glass in its special pocket. "That explains it, then. Lovely female, Tony's widow. Too bad she's still in mourning."

Too bad he couldn't plant his best friend a facer, but Leland sipped his wine and smiled his agreement.

"She didn't seem too in alt about being in London. Not like m'sister, anyway, who can't wait to leave the country no matter if she has to drag the brats along with her. I mean, even if Mrs. Tony can't do the fall Season because she's in mourning, there are still the shops."

There had been words spoken over Graceanne's refusal to have the duke pay her modistes' bills. Ware was not willing to trust her with more than pin money, so she still wore her country-made gowns. Not that he'd wash the family linen for Crow's ears. "Mrs. Warrington is used to a quieter life, and you must have seen she is a devoted mother."

Crow didn't know if it was devotion or being dicked in the nob, letting those rug rats climb all over her. He did know that he'd not be taking tea again at Ware House anytime soon.

Leland was going on: "She's concerned about the children here in London. I found an excellent tutor, a university student on convalescent leave, but that's only an hour or two a day, the boys are so young." And the tutor so weak. "But we cannot seem to find a suitable nanny, so Graceanne has the full burden of their care most times, in addition to the infant."

Actually they'd found three suitable nannies on three successive days. None of them lasted through the night.

The employment agency was referring Milsom to their competitors down the block.

Crow was shaking his head knowledgeably. "Finding a decent nanny is the devil of a job." He spoke from his sister's experience. "You want one that'll keep the brats out of your hair, without worrying if she's got them chained in irons. M'sister finally found one who actually seems to like the little beasts, and they like her back. At least they pay attention to her. First time I ever saw them not trying to murder each other. Nanny Sprockett's almost got them civilized, by George."

So by ten o'clock the next morning, Milsom had bribed Nanny Sprockett to Ware House. In two days she had the boys eating out of her hand—sugarplums and ginger nuts—and the fussy baby eating some kind of pap to make her grow. She even convinced the Irish wet nurse to stop putting milk out for the little people—and every stray cat in the neighborhood. Then she threatened to slap Aunt Eudora's hand if she dealt from the bottom again.

Graceanne was pleased with the new nanny, except that suddenly she had too much time on her hands. She had no chores and no one on whom to pay calls. She had no money to visit the shops unless she was willing to have all her purchases, from toys to tooth powder, from bonnets to bonbons, credited to the duke's account. She wasn't.

She was amazed how the lack of funds made her feel so defenseless, especially since she hadn't had money in her own hands for all that long. For those years before, she'd never realized the helplessness of her position. Now she did. She didn't feel quite like a servant, since she had nothing to do in the vast, well-run mansion, but more like a poor relation. It didn't help when Mr. Milsom deferred to her in household matters he could have handled in his sleep, after she asked to be of assistance.

No, she had to have this situation out with Ware. Graceanne's pride wouldn't let her tell him the truth about Nina; neither would it let her be a nonentity the rest of her life. Ware was used to giving orders and expecting them to be obeyed, but Graceanne's days of "Yes, Papa" and "No, Papa" were over.

"Your Grace, a moment of your time?" She had to disturb him in his library, a room she'd never entered lest she meet him there. He'd been avoiding her assiduously, so this was her only opportunity. Bearding the lion in his den seemed to fit her mood.

Leland gestured her to the seat facing his desk. She was not going to start this conversation being dwarfed by the wide leather chair or being intimidated by the expanse of polished wood between them. "I prefer to stand," she said, "but you may sit, of course."

He could do no such thing, of course. He did lean his tall frame against the desk, though, managing to look relaxed and confident, blast him.

"About my bills," she began.

Leland held up his hand. "All of your expenses are being paid, Mrs. Warrington. No reasonable requests will be denied, I promise you. Every shopkeeper in town knows the address, so you merely have to place your order and give your direction." He crossed his arms across his chest, satisfied.

Graceanne wasn't, and was determined to make him understand. "But I don't have any accounting, whether I am overspending my allowance or not. And I have to ask Mr. Milsom every time I need to tip a footman or a delivery boy. I don't even have pin money to put in the poor box at church without asking Mr. Olmstead. It is degrading."

"So is having to chase you to Ireland."

Graceanne blushed, but managed to say, "I never asked you to come after me."

"And I never asked you to account for every pound and shilling."

"Your generosity is not in question, Your Grace. It's a matter of trust that you won't grant me the wherewithal to take a hackney across town, much less across the continent. And I am not permitted to hire my own servants."

"I thought you liked Nanny Sprockett."

"I did *not* like the dresser you hired for me."

Leland shuffled some papers on his desk. "I admit the first choice was not felicitous." He hadn't stolen that one from Crow's sister, but from his sister-in-law, who was always turned out in the height of fashion. "How was I supposed to know she did not like children?"

"And the second one? She took one look at my wardrobe and announced she wouldn't be seen dead in my castoffs."

He tried to hide a smile. "I daresay she was dressed better than you."

"Immeasurably, I'm sure. Now that Nanny Sprockett is here, I might take the time to do some shopping, if you will show me an accounting of my bills, but that's not the point. The point is, I do not need you or one of your hand-picked watchdogs overseeing my every move. I never had a dresser before in my life, and I do not require one now."

"Oh, you know the right shops to patronize, do you? Fair prices so no one overcharges you? Unsavory neighborhoods to avoid?"

Graceanne had to admit that she didn't.

"Furthermore," he went on, on the attack, "a lady is never, I repeat, never, seen abroad without escort in London."

"Are you implying that I am not a lady?" It was a good thing she wasn't sitting at the desk; the letter opener was a safe distance away.

"I am implying that without a maid in attendance, you are subject to worse insults than that."

"They couldn't be any worse than the way your aunt looks at me." Or the way he did, like she'd crawled out from under a rock. With Nina in tow.

"You are not that naive, Grace. There are a great many indignities you'd find more offensive than Aunt Eudora's disapproval. If it's any consolation, she is more incensed with me than with you." He tidied another pile of documents. "She, ah, believes me to be the infant's father."

"You?" And she laughed, which was possibly the worst insult to Ware's pride of all.

"Is that all?" he asked, taking up his pen to signal the end of the conversation. "See Mr. Olmstead about an accounting and an allowance if that's what you wish, but for your personal needs only. The boys' expenses are part of my household. And hire your own abigail, if you want to be bothered with references and such. Hire any blasted servants you want, as long as you don't go out of this house without one of them. And," he added without looking up from his papers, "as long as you aren't using them and my blunt to shab off again. Believe me, the consequences of another runaway liaison will be far worse than having to suffer Aunt Eudora's lectures."

Graceanne wasn't sure, but she thought she'd just won the battle yet lost the war. He was never going to trust her, and she was never going to be more than a prisoner in his house; a prisoner whose every want and need was met, who was treated with distant courtesy, but a captive all the same.

As for the duke, he was grimly satisfied that he'd made his points: His wards' mother was going to behave with propriety, and he wasn't financing another tryst. "Good day, Mrs. Warrington."

The words still left a bitter taste in his mouth when he returned with the boys after their riding lesson at an indoor rink. Lesson, hell, Hallorahan had made the twins into regular Lilliputian centaurs, although the Warrington blood had to get some credit. He had only to stand back and watch, and make sure they didn't attempt any jumps higher than their ponies could take. They'd be ready for Hyde Park any day now—any day he wouldn't be embarrassed to be seen bear-leading his little cubs. He was already a laughingstock at White's, having been caught teaching them to roll hoops in Grosvenor Square. Then there was all the time he devoted to their riding and taking them places. Boys new to London had to go to Astley's and the menagerie at the Tower and Gunter's for ices, didn't they? He couldn't very well entrust them to that weak-kneed tutor, no matter how his friends chuckled behind his back. Besides, the twins were better company than those rashers of wind at the Parliamentary sessions he was missing these days. His business ventures were also suffering, and his social life, too.

He couldn't seem to enjoy himself at the rounds of routs and ridottos now that summer was over and the *ton* was coming back to town. He'd think of Graceanne sitting in the house every evening with her endless sewing, or being fleeced by Aunt Eudora at cards, and the champagne would seem flat, the conversations insipid. More often than not, he just spent the nights at his clubs. Drat the woman, she was cutting up his peace more every day!

Then Sergeant Rawley got to town. The first jarvey he asked directed him right to Ware House. The door was opened by the starchiest butler Rawley'd ever seen. Why, if the fellow hadn't been wearing an old-fashioned wig, Rawley'd think he was the duke himself. The chap took his blessed time fetching Mrs. Warrington, too.

Graceanne came flying down the stairs, baby and all, shouting his name when she got the message. She pushed the infant into Milsom's arms, then threw herself at Rawley's massive chest, weeping her happiness into his shirtfront.

Leland stepped out of his library to see what the commotion was in the hall, and did not like what he saw at all, Graceanne in the embrace of a large, rough-looking individual.

Rawley didn't like what he saw any better. Crying, was she? So was the infant. And that toff in the niffy-naffy pantaloons was looking as jealous as a ram with one ewe. So Rawley planted him a flush one, right-handed.

Now Ware didn't have to worry about any bitter taste in his mouth or any champagne going flat. He wasn't going to be able to eat anything for a week. And he wasn't going to have to fret over spending so much time with the twins, either, for Graceanne hired the man while His Grace was unconscious, to be the boys' mentor and her personal servant.

She also explained to Rawley about the baby and her sis-

181

ter, and how the duke didn't trust her. Rawley wished he'd hit the makebait harder.

So Graceanne had a loyal friend, and Ware had a malevolent giant on his payroll, one who was idolized by the duke's own wards. Resting in bed with an ice pack on his jaw, Leland decided he really had to do something about finding himself a life. A wife, he meant, a wife.

Chapter Twenty-one

They said Miss Eleanor Ridgemont had three offers her first season, two her second. This was her third, however, and if she didn't settle soon, the gossip went, she'd be on the shelf, Diamond of the first water or not. They said she was holding out for a better offer, a higher title, a heavier purse . . . or true love. They shook their heads.

The reigning Toast was certainly exquisite, tall and stately, raven-haired and alabaster-skinned. She was the daughter of an earl, an heiress in her own right, a talented watercolorist, and a graceful dancer. In other words, she'd make the Duke of Ware a perfect duchess. She'd not find a higher title, since Prinny preferred older women, and few unwed gentlemen in town had deeper pockets. As for true love . . . Leland shook his head. If she was that much of a peagoose, he didn't want to marry her anyway.

As September gave way to the opening of Almack's, the galas at the theater, and the endless private balls of the fall Season, His Grace had given serious consideration to finding himself a wife.

Between Rawley, Nanny, and Grace, he hardly got to spend time with the twins. He got reports from their tutor, of course, and brief onslaughts of boyish enthusiasm when the twins were between jaunts with their uncle Rawley, or when the sergeant was temporarily out of the gruesome war stories on which Willy and Les seemed to thrive. And Leland did make a practice of visiting the nursery after the children's supper when his schedule permitted, after Rawley was gone for the day and before Graceanne came to read stories and tuck them in. Nanny Sprockett smiled over her knitting as the boys related the tricks Uncle Rawley was helping them teach the ponies, and the steam engine Uncle Rawley had taken them to see, the battles he reenacted for them with the tin soldiers. Leland wasn't smiling. He may be spending more time with the twins than the average father of the haut monde, but by no stretch of the imagination could he convince himself he was actually raising them.

Not that he was complaining about their upbringing, and not that his complaining would do much good, after he'd promised Grace she could hire her own servants. It was natural Tony's children should be army mad, especially with a bigger-than-life warrior in their midst. After all, Leland couldn't expect them to be interested in land management or the workings of Parliament, things his own sons would need to know. When he had sons of his own.

The widow was finding her feet, too. She'd hired a middle-aged abigail, unexceptional according to Milsom, and was dressing more like a comfortably circumstanced officer's relict and less like a ragpicker, although still in those infernal, hypocritical blacks. She was going about with Aunt Eudora to afternoon teas, musicales, and the like, nothing out of keeping with her mourning period, but she was getting to meet society's old tabbies. She was passing their inspection, too, Aunt Eudora reported, except for a few raised eyebrows when the infant was brought forth at Ware House at-home days.

She was back to doing charitable work, he heard from Olmstead. Milsom and Nanny Sprockett had dissuaded her from volunteering at the foundling home, where she was too liable to bring infectious diseases back to the children. So Grace and Rawley and her abigail visited a veterans' hospital mornings when the boys were at their lessons. She wrote letters for the men or read to them, while her abigail did their mending and Rawley gleaned more barbaric tales to fill the twins' heads with gore. "An estimable female," Mr. Olmstead declared, which was high praise indeed from that noted misogynist.

So it was Leland who found himself at loose ends in his own venue. The parties were stale, his friends' conversations flat, the wagers and dares puerile, and the current crop of birds of paradise held all the appeal of plucked chickens. Every time he thought of taking one of the actresses or opera dancers back to her rooms, he saw Graceanne's lovely, sad face. She might have a child out of wedlock, that look seemed to say, but she was still a vicar's daughter. The rumors and gossip of his every move still shocked her, confound the woman.

Then, too, he heard some of the whispers. Not to his face, of course, but when his back was turned at a race meet or in a theater box. It seemed Aunt Eudora wasn't the only one to suppose a reputed rakehell like Ware was dallying with his cousin's pretty widow. See how he doted on those twins? There was even a bet on the books at White's that a certain duke would be pushing a perambulator in the park next. When hell froze over!

He kept even more distance between himself, the widow, and the infant, to dilute the scandal broth. He did it for her sake, Leland convinced himself, and his wards', so they wouldn't grow up having to defend their mother's honor. That was another reason for him to marry, if he needed another one: to end the rumor-mongering about Mrs. Warrington.

So he watched and he listened. He spent all of October propping up columns at debutante balls, playing whist for chicken stakes at Almack's, meanwhile scrutinizing the current harvest of Quality daughters. Miss Eleanor Ridgemont was definitely the cream of that crop.

Leland wasn't about to rush his fences, however, not after the disasters of his first two marriages. He wanted to know Miss Ridgemont's attitude toward child-rearing, child-bearing, and country living. Even Willy could have told him what a clunch he was being. Miss Ridgemont felt just as she ought, which was however the rich, handsome Duke of Ware wanted her to feel. Until she snabbled him, at least.

In an effort to get to know the black-haired beauty better, Ware invited her for a drive in the park. In order to get the duke to come up to scratch, Miss Ridgemont was dressed in her most becoming day gown, which was too thin for a brisk afternoon in an open carriage even if it was only early November, too narrow in the skirt to allow her a graceful ascent and descent, and too low cut to permit Ware's eyes to wander toward any other female.

Ware was indeed absorbed between watching his mettlesome cattle and watching her chest take on a bluish tinge. He did manage to spot two small figures in the distance, though.

"My wards," he told her, happy that she'd get to meet them so soon. The boys were on their ponies, with Rawley right behind them on a huge rawboned gray, the dog trailing behind. Leland turned his pair in their direction.

"Oh, but we mustn't leave the carriageway," Miss Ridgemont protested. "My reputation, you know." She batted her long black eyelashes, all but daring him to sweep her behind a bush and steal a kiss.

Instead, he told her not to worry, his tiger was up behind them for propriety. He did notice that at least the chit didn't seem averse to lovemaking. A cold wife would not suit his purposes at all. A shawl, he was pleased to note, would fix Miss Ridgemont's temporary discomfort. He offered the carriage blanket in the meantime. Eleanor gritted her teeth and declined.

When the boys saw him, they waved and shouted for Cousin Leland to come watch them put their ponies through their paces. How could he refuse? He pulled up next to the sergeant, and his tiger jumped down to go to the horses' heads.

"Will you get down, Miss Ridgemont?" the duke offered, climbing out of the curricle before she could protest.

Eleanor hadn't come to the park to be ogled by a hulking manservant and a grinning tiger. She'd accepted Ware's invitation so everyone could see she was fair on her way to making the match of the Season. "It really is quite chilly, Your Grace. I don't know what I was thinking when I chose this gown." She tugged the neckline a smidgen higher.

So he shrugged off his greatcoat and tossed it over her shoulders. Then the duke left her alone in the carriage to go watch some children ride in circles. Worse, she wasn't alone for long when the dog decided to join her, to make friends. The coziest Eleanor Ridgemont ever got with an animal was when she wore furs. She screamed, which caused one of the ponies to miss its footing. Luckily no harm befell Les, though Leland was there in a flash, ready to catch him. Rawley had more confidence in his lads, so when he came to order the dog out of the curricle, he just frowned in disgust at the bit of fluff His Grace was driving about.

The children had to go, Eleanor decided. This fascination Ware had with the infantry was unbecoming. In truth, identical twins might make charming pageboys, quite the amusing novelty, but as the duke's wards? She'd have them sent away to school before they could spell Jack Rabbit. As for the servant, it was the outside of enough for Miss Ridgemont to be scowled at by a great lunk of a lackey—and a repulsive cripple to boot. She'd get rid of him quickly enough, as soon as Ware returned to the curricle and took up the ribbons, in fact.

First she had to suffer an introduction to the brats. Ware led them over on their ponies. "Miss Ridgemont, may I present my wards. This is Wellesley, and the other handsome chap is Leslie."

She nodded her head fractionally, but the children nearly fell off their ponies, laughing. Ware looked confused; there was Willy up on his Patches, Les on his Peaches. Anyone could tell the ponies apart.

"A good rider has to sit more'n one horse," Rawley explained with a sly grin at Ware's discomfiture in front of his ladybird, "so I switch 'em off, Your Grace. Do you mean you couldn't tell?"

"Insolent bastard," Ware muttered as he gave his tiger the nod to release the horses.

That was just the opening Eleanor needed. "Precisely, Your Grace. That man insulted me with an insolent look."

Leland rubbed his oft-aching jaw. "Be happy a look was all he gave you."

"And he should have kept better care of that vicious dog."

"Duke? There's never been a sweeter-natured dog, unless you threaten the children. It was my fault for not warning you. I beg your pardon, my dear, that you were frightened."

Only partially mollified by his handsome apology, Eleanor persisted: "But the man has one hand!"

"Yes, otherwise he'd still be with the army, so I suppose we are lucky. He was the boys' father's batman, you see." He rubbed his jaw again. "Almost fanatical in his devotion, actually."

Eleanor was nothing if not determined. "But he obviously cannot manage two active children with that . . . that hook."

"Oh, he threatens to disembowel them with it if they misbehave. Works every time."

Now Miss Ridgemont's alabaster skin took on a greenish cast instead of blue. Leland wondered if she was sensitive or merely squeamish. He couldn't help but compare her attitude to Graceanne's, who spent her free time visiting wounded and maimed soldiers.

He didn't want a Lady Bountiful, Leland told himself, he wanted a duchess, an aristocrat. Miss Ridgemont was definitely that.

* * *

So His Grace was courting Eleanor the Iceberg, was he? If that was the type of woman Ware was going to install as his wife, Graceanne wanted to be elsewhere. She refused to contemplate why the thought of his bringing home a wife, any wife, gave her the dismals. But *this* prospective duchess was known to be particular in the extreme. And Graceanne had another bone to pick with the nodcock who put on his own blinders.

Once more she knocked on his library's door. This time she carried ammunition. Nina.

"Your Grace, you have not fulfilled our agreement."

Eyeing the bundle in her arms with misgivings, Leland put down his newspaper. "What agreement was that, Mrs. Warrington?"

"You swore to treat all my children equally."

He frowned. A lesser person would have fled. "A cheap trick, ma'am. A vow gained by dishonorable means is worthless."

"And is it worthless to Antonia to know some love and affection when she sees her brothers receiving it? Is she supposed to grow up thinking she is inferior because you are too enamored of your own deluded sense of honor to accept her as a person in her own right? I do not wish her to grow up in a cold, unloving household."

"What are you suggesting?"

"That you let us, the boys and Nina and myself, find a cottage in the country somewhere on our own, where you won't have to be reminded of us and our supposed sins."

"No!" he shouted. That was all.

That was it? No explanation? He was even more pig-headed than Graceanne thought. "May I remind you that your actions—or nonactions—toward Nina are branding this innocent child precisely what we have been at pains to avoid. The servants are talking that you don't treat her as a beloved cousin. Soon the *ton* will be spreading their gossip. Then what?"

Blast it, she was right, Leland acknowledged. "If I let

you run off to the country, the rumors will have you exiled from polite company. So what am I supposed to do?"

"You could try being the doting guardian to Nina that you are to the boys. Here."

What he knew was coming came: an armful, nay, a handful, of wriggling infant. Confound the woman.

"It's been months since you've so much as held her." Graceanne folded back a corner of the blanket so he could see the child better. "See how far she's come?"

Reluctantly he looked down, straight into blue eyes the color of tropical seas, Graceanne's blue eyes. And a smile. Wet and gummy, but a smile for all that. Lud, he must have traded his soul to win a smile like that, for he had no will of his own. "Do you think she'll be happier in the country, then?"

"I think the air is cleaner and the food is fresher. And I'd like to show her to my mother."

Who had red hair once, Leland reminded himself. By George, the infant—no, he had to start calling her by name, Nina—was going to be a beauty. She was still tiny, but now she was rounded, with dimples. She even had dimples on those tiny hands reaching out to grab his neckcloth and put it in her mouth. He'd be fighting off her suitors with an ax. No, pistols. One in each hand. Just let some bounder try to get near her. Of course.

Of course, she still wasn't the sturdiest-looking thing he'd ever seen. Maybe the London fog was affecting her lungs.

"Actually," he said, "I have been thinking about a house party at Warefield over the holidays." He'd been thinking for about twenty seconds.

Chapter Twenty-two

*A*ctually, a house party was not such a bad idea. Leland could invite Miss Ridgemont and see how she got on with the children, the countryside, and him. In the city there were too many social boundaries to keep them from getting to know each other well enough for such an important decision. One dance an evening—two would have shown too much particularity—did not reveal their compatibility, or lack thereof. At Ware Hold they could easily find themselves apart from others to carry on real conversations instead of the polite chitchat. And the mistletoe was a perfect excuse to find if they'd be compatible otherwise. Begetting his sons was his duty; he didn't intend it to be a chore. If all the dibs were in tune, then a New Year's announcement of the engagement would be in order.

He could not invite solely Miss Ridgemont and her companion, of course. That would be tantamount to a declaration he wasn't prepared to make without further deliberation. He needed some other young, marriageable females to throw dust in the eyes of the rumor-mongers, and so as not to raise false hopes. Then he'd need young, marriageable gentlemen to keep the chits happy and occupied so he could pursue Miss Ridgemont. Unattached females always came with mothers, fathers, chaperones, and maids. Then there were the valets and grooms and drivers from their carriages. Suddenly his little house party was taking on the proportions of a Carlton House fete. Milsom could handle it, of course, but was it fair to Graceanne to pitchfork her into a *ton*ish celebration when she was looking forward to a quiet country Christmas like last year's?

He consulted his friend Crow.

"Don't see why you think you have to make excuses for the widow," the baronet told him over dinner at White's. "I've seen her doing the rounds with your aunt. Good-looking female, pleasant manners. Even m'sister-in-law says so, and you know how starchy she is."

"Still, it's such a different way of life."

"From a vicarage perhaps, but didn't you say Wellington was your heir's godfather? If Mrs. Warrington was on such terms with Old Hokey, she can't be that much of a turnip."

"Tony did install her at the embassy," Leland reflected.

"There. Give over and tell me how goes the courtship of the ravishing Miss Ridgemont."

The duke was still pondering a flock of harpies alighting at Ware, getting their talons into Graceanne's history, shredding her reputation and her composure. "I don't know, she comes from a different world."

"Miss Ridgemont? Born and bred right here in London, old chap. Father was an earl, don't you know. Silver spoons and all that tripe, same as you."

"No, Mrs. Warrington." Ware had barely touched the roast capon in chestnut sauce.

"Seems to me if a pleasant female like the widow can't fit into your world, maybe it's your world at fault." Crow took a mouthful of escalloped veal while the duke digested that bit of wisdom. "Besides, you've got the widow on your mind more than's healthy if you're pursuing another female altogether, especially the elusive Eleanor. Why don't you marry Mrs. Warrington and be done with it if all you want out of the match is sons? Lud knows she's fertile enough."

Ware couldn't tell Crow that was part of the problem:

He'd never know if he was the father of his sons or not. No, he had to get over this fixation with Tony's wayward widow. Miss Ridgemont was the best alternative. "But you don't think a house party is a bad idea? You'll come? Or are you promised to your family?"

"Not in good odor with m'sister these days, don't you know, not after telling you about that nanny. Uh, you wouldn't have your eye on my valet, would you?"

Ware surveyed his friend through his own quizzing glass, the hair *à la* Brutus, the neckcloth *à la* Polyphemus. "Devil a bit, my friend, devil a bit. Your man is safe from my evil designs. So you'll come help entertain the debs and do the pretty with their mamas?"

"I wouldn't miss this chance to watch you make a cake of yourself for the world. Not every day a fellow gets to see his best friend stick his own neck into parson's noose, don't you know."

Aunt Eudora wouldn't travel with the twins. The boys wouldn't leave their ponies behind. Shanna wouldn't travel on the thirteenth of the month, Graceanne didn't want to be traveling toward her father's vicarage on a Sunday. The baby and Nanny had to be kept warm; Milsom's imported delicacies had to be kept cool. And the duke didn't want to have to rely on Warefield or even Oxford to do his Christmas shopping. This year he was getting to buy dolls and wanted to make sure he had the best selection. While he was at the toy shop, of course, there were a few other incidentals he thought might suit the boys and Nina. No matter the company, he vowed, the children were to have a fine Christmas, better than last year, even if it had to be a private celebration upstairs in the nursery.

The Three Kings might have managed a smaller caravan. And made better time.

And that fire at the last inn had nothing whatsoever to do with the duke's explaining to the twins the advantages of the modern sulfur matches over an old-fashioned flint box.

Graceanne did make His Grace promise there would be no candlelit Christmas trees in the nursery.

By the time they reached Warefield, unpacked, and·got everyone settled, there was no time to decorate the castle before the company was due to appear. Milsom came to Graceanne for advice, to her gratification, and she suggested that they leave the gathering of greenery to the young guests when they got there. Otherwise, she feared, they'd find Warefield dreadfully thin of entertainment. Before the Londoners' arrival, though, Graceanne had to call at the vicarage.

"There will be no scandal, Papa, unless you make one. Ware has been more than understanding," she lied, "and you can do no less. After all, Nina is your granddaughter."

Mrs. Beckwith was already christening the infant with her tears.

"If you don't accept Nina into the family and get over this foolishness of saying I am no longer your daughter, then I cannot come to church or bring the boys. Ware will hire a chaplain of his own, I'm sure, rather than see his wards snubbed. How will you explain that to your parishioners when they are looking forward to glimpsing the London nobs? Or to the bishop? Come, Papa, it's Christmas."

Beckwith hemmed and hawed a bit, then allowed as how he'd not turn a Christian away from his church doors. "But I won't have any of that wicked pageantry folderol like last year. You see where that led."

"Oh, but little Antonia will make a perfect baby Jesus," Mrs. Beckwith cooed.

"And the boys will be so disappointed if they can't be the cow. His Grace did mention he'd purchase new pews for the church, since he was inviting so many guests to see his wards perform."

So Graceanne had the pageant to organize, too. Luckily her angel, shepherd, and three Wise Men were still available, the costumes preserved. The Bindle brothers happily agreed to take over the sheep roles instead of the cow.

Mary and Joseph were harder to find. Heaven alone knew where last year's players were.

Graceanne enlisted Shanna for Mary. If they could have a red-haired, Irish Joseph one year, they could have a red-haired, Irish Mary this one. Surprisingly, Rawley volunteered to play Mary's husband, giving rise to much speculation upstairs and down. At least he'd keep the barnyard animals under control while Shanna managed the baby. Satisfied, Graceanne was ready to greet the duke's guests. She even put on one of her new gowns, having decided to use Christmas as an excuse to come out of mourning, finally.

She donned colors—mostly darker ones rather than pastels—for the children's sake, she told herself, not to impress anyone or to feel more on a par with the London guests. The boys never noticed and Nina cried until she recognized her mother under the curled hair and russet velvet. Leland noticed and heartily approved, if his smile was any judge. Then he remembered himself and put on his forbidding ducal disapproval, but she'd seen the light in his eyes, and that was enough. She was finding it hard to hate him when he was so kind to the boys and now Nina; she hoped he was finding it as hard to hate her.

The first guests to arrive were Sir Crosby Fanshaw, escorting Miss Eleanor Ridgemont and her companion. Graceanne had been up in the nursery trying to calm some of the twins' Christmas fever by reading from a storybook, when they heard the carriage approach. She left them with the book to make her way down the staircase to the Great Hall, where Leland and his aunt waited. She wasn't putting herself forward; the duke had requested her presence to show they were all one family. Furthermore, she'd been helping Milsom and the housekeeper assign bedchambers, almost as if she were the hostess here.

Wraps were taken, hands were kissed, introductions were made. In fact, Miss Pettibone, the companion, was the only person not at least casually acquainted. Graceanne had met both Miss Ridgemont and Sir Crosby over various teas.

Poor Miss Pettibone blushed and tried to hide behind one of the suits of armor when she was made the center of attention. She alone was relieved when a noise from the upper story made everyone crane their necks up the stairs.

"My God, no," prayed Graceanne.

"Heaven help us!" swore Ware.

"Disgraceful!" thumped Aunt Eudora.

"By George, look at them go!" enthused Crow.

"I'm going to faint," threatened Miss Ridgemont, but she didn't.

Miss Pettibone did, without saying a word, but taking the armored knight with her in a horrendous clatter.

Milsom was quiet, too, merely positioning himself at the bottom of the stairs and indicating to a footman to follow suit. Milsom plucked one small body out of the air as Willy soared off the waxed banister. The footman was not so deft with Leslie, who flew into the midst of the openmouthed company. Rather, he flew over Miss Pettibone's supine body and landed, splat, against Miss Ridgemont's chest.

The lady went down, shrieking.

Graceanne pulled Les off the hysterical woman and half hugged him, half shook him. "If you ever, *ever* do such a thing again, I'll—" She started to cry.

Leland had the other twin by the back of his collar, dangling. "Do you see what you've done to your mother? How you've upset everyone? I've a good mind to—"

Miss Ridgemont shrieked the louder for being ignored, and swatted away the hand Crow offered to assist her to her feet. She preferred the marble squares, it seemed, for she drummed her feet on them.

"Heaven help us," repeated Ware.

"Throw a bucket of water on her. It works on squalling cats," offered Aunt Eudora.

"I think Miss Pettibone needs smelling salts," said Graceanne from that lady's side, behind the fallen knight.

"M'sister uses burnt feathers," offered Crow, staring at Miss Ridgemont through his looking glass.

Milsom was, as ever, quietly efficient, signaling the gathered footmen to fetch wine, the housekeeper, Nanny Sprockett, and a vinaigrette. But the boys were trying to be helpful, to make amends. Willy grabbed up Miss Ridgemont's fallen shako-style bonnet with its towering plumes, and ran toward the massive fireplace to light the feathers. Les pulled the hothouse roses out of a Sèvres vase and was ready with the water, but he couldn't recall which lady Aunt Eudora said needed the bath, so he just tossed it between both of them. Which luckily put out Willy's burning hat.

Miss Pettibone was duly revived and guided to a chair by Nanny while the housekeeper made a special tisane, which was more tender attention than the companion was used to receiving. Miss Ridgemont was restored to order, more or less, with a glass of brandy provided by Milsom.

Then she demanded the children be beaten, birched, banished.

"I am dreadfully sorry, Miss Ridgemont," Graceanne began, "and the boys will certainly apologize. And they will never slide down the banister again, I swear."

"At least not until they are nine, I think." The duke appeared to ponder the matter, his eyes twinkling. "Yes, I believe I was nine before I managed a creditable dismount. Tony didn't manage it till he was nearly eleven, if I recall. Do you remember that scar on his chin?"

Eleanor was still sputtering about boiling the boys in oil, and Graceanne was threatening to give the boys' ponies away to some deserving children who didn't scare their mothers out of their wits.

"Well, my buckos." The Duke of Ware knelt down in the wet and rose-strewn hall. "Which is it to be, boiling in oil, no ponies, or your promise not to slide down the banister until you are nine years of age?"

They solemnly chose to give their word to wait five years, holding out their hands to be shaken. Then they ran like hell, lest their cousin change his mind.

The duke watched them race up the stairs, still smiling. "I think the greenery should go up tomorrow just to be on the safe side," he told Graceanne and Milsom. "You know, garlands wrapped over the posts and the railing." Then he rubbed his chin, still looking up at that shiny banister. "But that's tomorrow, Crow. What say we give it a go tonight?"

"Are you daft?" Graceanne wanted to know, but Leland was grinning at his friend. "A friendly wager?"

Crow was torn. His clothes might be. On the other hand, a gentleman never turned down a bet, and the banister did look inviting, except for the newel post at the end. "I'm willing if you are, but you're the chap so desperate for an heir."

Aunt Eudora snorted. Graceanne bit her lip and told them they were acting worse than the little boys. And Miss Ridgemont, furious she was being disregarded, that her hat was ruined and the brats weren't to be punished, stomped off to her room—right through the wet, slippery roses. This time she slid directly into the other suit of armor, which landed atop her in a most suggestive pose. Miss Pettibone fainted again.

Fanshaw put down his quizzing glass and patted his friend's shoulder. "And here you were afraid the house party might be dull."

Chapter Twenty-three

*H*ow could holding the wrong woman feel so right?

After Miss Ridgemont and her companion were carried off to their rooms by the housekeeper, the nanny, two footmen, and the butler, and after the Great Hall was mopped and restored to medieval splendor, Graceanne dissolved into tears. She just couldn't help herself.

And His Grace just couldn't help himself from gathering her into his arms to comfort her absurd blubbering about how she'd ruined his lovely house party. All she ever wanted was a little cottage somewhere for her and the children, she wept into his shirtfront while Crow studiously examined the slightly dented knights. She'd never wanted to associate with toplofty lords and lace-bedecked ladies, she cried. And look what happened when she did.

"What happened, Gracie, was two imps got up to mischief and two ladies' tender sensibilities were offended. That's all," he responded in his least toplofty voice. "They'll recover, and so will you, my girl. Now, dry your eyes lest Crow here think I give every woman of my acquaintance the vapors."

Graceanne accepted the handkerchief he held, although she had a perfectly good one in her own pocket, and made her excuses to Sir Crosby.

"The excitement, I don't doubt," he gallantly assured her. "Think nothing of it."

Graceanne left to make repairs to her appearance before any more guests arrived, and Leland took Crow off to the library for a sorely needed brandy.

Looking in her mirror upstairs, Graceanne realized she was more shaken by the duke's embrace and by his tender words than by the other events of the day. She'd felt so comfortable, so comforted in his arms—and he wasn't the least arrogant at all! She even thought he might—no, she was certain he did—like her! And oh, she was mortally afraid that she liked him back, despite his stiff-rumped pride, his autocratic intolerance, and his distrust of her.

Graceanne knew she'd have to tell him the truth about Prudence and Liam and Nina for the baby's sake, she told herself, but in all honesty she knew she'd have to tell him for her own sake. She'd have to swallow her own not inconsiderable pride, or regret for the rest of her life that she let him think the worst of her.

She'd tell him as soon as the guests left, she decided, if he hadn't already offered for Miss Ridgemont. But that was foolish. Once he offered for the lady, Graceanne's confession would be too late. She'd never know the answer to What if.... She owed it to them *both* to find out.

Leland was also shaken. Blast, once Grace was in his arms, he'd never wanted to let her go. If Crow hadn't been standing around, he'd have kissed her, stroked her, petted her, done his damnedest to get her upstairs to his room or to the bearskin rug there in the library. He hadn't cared. And it was more than lust, too. He'd seen enough women's tears in his lifetime to be inured, but Grace's nearly broke his heart. He'd have taken on the Mongolian hordes to keep her from crying anymore. Deuce take it, he must really care for the impossible chit!

How, he asked himself, how in bloody hell could he love a woman born to genteel poverty? True, she was a lady to her fingertips in most respects. But how could he love a female who turned down his carte blanche to bear an illegitimate child with a horse trainer? How could he think of making such a one his duchess? He couldn't. He wouldn't. He didn't.

He'd just have to give Miss Ridgemont more opportunities to show her better qualities.

Eleanor was at her finest that evening, sparkling like her diamonds among the other guests. She was stunning in a red satin gown, one long black curl draped over a pure white shoulder. She laughed, she flirted, she was a butterfly.

Graceanne was a moth in her quiet brown velvet and Tony's pearls. She sat with Miss Pettibone and the mamas of his other guests, Leland noticed. She was polite and friendly to the young bucks and Crow, without encouraging them to stay among the dowagers. Leland was glad she wasn't casting out lures to his friends, but why the devil did she consider herself one of the chaperones? Dash it, Graceanne couldn't be much older than Eleanor. She needed some gaiety in her life, too.

So he suggested dancing—informal, of course. Fortunately for his intentions toward Miss Ridgemont, Graceanne volunteered to play the pianoforte for them while the footmen rolled back the carpet. Unfortunately, Leland was aware of a sharp disappointment that he wouldn't get to hold the widow in his arms again.

Eleanor was a superb dancer, light and lissome. She was witty, too, chatting knowledgeably of the latest books, poems, and theater productions when the figures permitted. Yes, she'd do well as a social hostess.

She wouldn't do quite as well as a country wife, however. Before they parted for the night, Leland invited the company to go out with him the following morning to collect greens to decorate the Hold. Miss Ridgemont gaily laughed and informed them that she never left her bedchamber before noon, and certainly not to go tromping through the woods, ruining her boots and her complexion. And didn't holly have prickers, anyway?

No one missed her, least of all Ware, who with the others chased his wards and their dog from one end of the estate to the other, followed by wagons and carts to collect their armfuls of ivy and evergreen and mistletoe. Much giggling from the young ladies told him he couldn't forget the mistletoe. They marked two large firs as the Christmas trees for the estate woodsmen to chop down, and managed to locate a huge fallen log that the twins were sure would burn for the twelve days of Yuletide.

A laughing, happy, rosy-cheeked group arrived back at the castle. Graceanne's face was glowing more than anyone else's, Ware observed as she skipped along, a twin's hand in each of hers, teaching them the words to a new carol.

But Miss Ridgemont was an enchanting picture, too, posed at the Adams room window with her lap easel and her watercolors. She was attempting the delightful view of the topiary gardens, she informed them all with a self-deprecating tinkle, as a present to their host. Miss Ridgemont was truly gifted, they all agreed, even the boys who crowded in to see the painting before they went up to the nursery for luncheon.

She could do another painting tomorrow, the duke insisted. Eleanor was so talented, he was positive the next would be better. As for his gift, it was the thought that counted. He'd pay for a new gown, of course.

After lunch everyone again gathered in the Great Hall to fashion the mounds of greens into wreaths and garlands and kissing boughs. Graceanne and Milsom returned from the attics with ribbons, bells, candleholders, and glass ornaments, and the footmen brought ladders, scissors, string, and hot punch.

The boys were taking a nap, thank goodness, exhausted from the morning's exertions. So Graceanne was able to devote her energies to persuading the dowagers that their weaving and sewing skills were crucial if they hoped to have enough garlands. She also had to convince the ladies that three kissing boughs were really enough, and Crow and the other gentlemen that emptying the punch bowl really wasn't part of their job so much as getting on those ladders and hanging the festoons and mistletoe. Which, of course, necessitated that same giggling among the young ladies.

The Great Hall resounded with Christmas cheer, except for Eleanor's corner, where she sat in state directing the Duke of Ware precisely how she wanted her kissing ball hung. No, the archway was too high, the mantel too low. Miss Ridgemont's creation was a massive affair of interwoven grapevines, ribbons, apples, and candles, which she'd shamelessly coerced Miss Pettibone into making. Ware put up with her dictatorial behavior as long as he could, in compensation for her lost painting, although he was itching to join the others as they laughed and sang. He could hear Grace's pretty voice again as she led off carol after carol. Of course, he thought, she was used to directing the church choir. He wondered if she missed that.

Soon Graceanne had them all singing, even Miss Ashton-Highet's deaf grandmother. His own voice wasn't quite that bad, Leland judged. Finally he gestured to Crosby Fanshaw. "Here, old man, you'll be better able to advise Miss Ridgemont in placing her decoration. I'm afraid I don't have the exquisite taste the two of you share."

He left the two most beautifully turned-out people in the room arguing over the location of that monstrosity while he breathed a sigh of relief. He should *not* be feeling relieved to leave his prospective bride's company, he reflected.

That evening the young ladies performed in the music room, the usual set pieces of German composers to the usual polite applause. Then Miss Ridgemont took her place at the front while two footmen dragged forth the harp. Leland groaned inwardly, but devil take it if the chit couldn't play divinely. And she'd come prepared to emulate the angels, in a white satin gown with a net overskirt. What a perfect picture she made! How long she played!

His applause was entirely sincere at the completion of her piece.

Then he groaned again. Graceanne was the only female left to perform. She had a pleasant voice, he knew, and was competent at the instrument, but she couldn't have had any formal training like the others. Coming after Miss Ridgemont's superb recital, well, she'd look no account, like a poor vicar's daughter among these peers' progeny and earls' offsprings.

Graceanne seemed to know it and smiled self-consciously. "I cannot hope to emulate the superb performances we've heard tonight, but perhaps you might like to hear what our brave soldiers in the Peninsula heard at Christmastide." She picked up a Spanish *quitarra* from behind the pianoforte, tuned it, then began to sing a Spanish carol. Almost no one in the audience could understand the words, but they all heard the love and joy in the message as her voice sang with the glory of the season. Miss Pettibone wiped a tear from her eye. After another song Graceanne put the instrument down and switched to the pianoforte and "Adeste Fidelis," motioning them all to gather round and join in.

Leland swallowed the lump in his throat.

The next day he decided to give Miss Ridgemont's mothering aptitude another go. The twins could be a bit, well, boisterous, he admitted, so he went to the nursery after lunch to fetch Nina while the other young ladies went for a walk with Graceanne to the village shops. The gentlemen were content at billiards, and the older ladies were resting. Miss Ridgemont had stayed behind, claiming a headache, but actually disdaining rustic markets. She hoped to get some time alone with His Grace, besides.

He wasn't quite alone. Nanny warned that Miss Nina was teething and apt to be fretful, but he ignored the advice. "My precious *niña*'s never been anything but a perfect lady for Cousin Leland, have you, sweet pea?" He chucked the infant under the chin and she smiled and blew bubbles.

She was still smiling when he handed her back to Nanny Sprockett, but not even the most devoted of guardians could claim she smelled anything like sweet. Another of Miss Ridgemont's dresses would have to be burned. Leland's ears burned with her recriminations.

Well, they weren't her children, Ware reflected. A woman couldn't be expected to take just any infants to her bosom, could she? And a lady like Eleanor shouldn't be supposed to have the familiarity with infants Graceanne did. Lud, he hoped not. Still, he remembered the widow last year, leading all the village children through their paces at the pageant, knitting those endless mittens. And she'd held every one of his tenants' infants last year at Boxing Day, he recalled, sharing their mothers' pride. Damn and blast, he hadn't been this confused since his salad days.

One last try, that's what he'd give Miss Ridgemont. The mistletoe test, he laughed to himself. She'd grow used to children once she had her own, he was convinced, but if she cringed from his kiss the way his first wife did, or stood passively like his second, he'd rather name Willy his heir and be done with it.

He caught Eleanor under the kissing bough when no one was around the next afternoon, not a difficult feat, as Miss Ridgemont seemed to station herself there whenever he was near.

He laughed about the joys of the season as he placed a chaste kiss on her lips and then, when she did not draw back, deepened the embrace. She put her arms around his neck; he put his around her back. His lips teased and she answered with passion. She was everything he could have wanted: warm and responsive without being as bold as a lightskirt, and with a truly magnificent bosom pressed willingly against his chest.

And he felt—nothing. Nothing but her lips and her breasts. There was no stirring blood, no soaring senses, no raging need to throw her to the floor and make wild love in the daytime. He'd be hard pressed to get up the enthusiasm at candlelit night, he decided, between silken sheets on a feather mattress, after champagne and oysters. He felt nothing, nothing but the wish that she were someone else.

Chapter Twenty-four

*B*eing a gentleman had definite drawbacks. Lord Ware could not, for instance, tell Miss Ridgemont that they would not suit, not when he'd never made a formal address to her in the first place. Nor could he tell her and her giggly, gaudy friends to get the deuce out of his castle so he could enjoy the holiday season with his own family, not after inviting them to stay through the New Year.

And he certainly couldn't grab Mrs. Warrington and press heated kisses on her lips as he was aching to do with every ounce of fevered blood that pulsed through his body. But he could catch her under the mistletoe! He could steal a legitimate kiss, by Jupiter, if she stood still long enough. Between entertaining the oldest members of the party and keeping the youngest out of everyone else's way, Graceanne was busy conferring with Milsom and the housekeeper over meals, menus, and Boxing Day gifts for the tenants and the servants. She was rehearsing the pageant and making new costumes, and, yes, helping with choir practice. Leland hardly had a chance to see the elusive widow, much less entice her under the kissing bough.

He half feared that kiss, anyway. What if it branded him, seared her memory into his soul for all time? He was half afraid it was too late.

And he still had to play the host. The Duke of Ware was nothing if not a gentleman.

It was time to stir the pudding, Graceanne announced to the guests. Everyone was invited to the kitchen to make his or her Christmas wish, from the lowest potboy—in fair warning to those high-in-the-instep dowagers—to the youngest child—in fair warning to Miss Ridgemont. Eleanor went anyway rather than remain above stairs all by herself. She also wanted to keep an eye on that Mrs. Warrington; Ware was being altogether too watchful of the dowdy widow.

When they were all gathered in the kitchen—a ridiculous idea in the first place; ladies did not belong in hot, messy places—Miss Ridgemont found herself wedged between a footman and Miss Ashton-Highet's deaf grandmother, which served her notion of propriety even less well. "This is absurd," she muttered, "making wishes on a lump of potage."

The deaf ancient didn't hear her, but the twins did. They were waiting their turns with Shanna the nursemaid, and it would be hard to tell who of the three was the most excited.

"It is not!" piped up Willy.

Leslie added: "How else will Father Christmas know what to bring for Christmas?"

Eleanor was delighted to get revenge at last. "You poor, simple brats, don't you know there is no such thing as Father Christmas? I'm surprised, Mrs. Warrington, that you permit such outrageous mummery in a good Christian household."

So the boys started to cry.

"Why, next you'll teach them to believe in fairies and elves and leprechauns."

So Shanna started to cry.

"Enough!" shouted the duke in his most awesome voice. The pots and pans shook on their hooks on the walls, half the servants disappeared without making their wishes, wishing to keep their positions more than anything else. "In this house," he thundered, "pudding wishes come true. And Father Christmas is real, Miss Ridgemont, because I say he is. And finally, if the little people talk to Shanna, perhaps she is more fortunate than the rest of us."

"Well, I never—" Eleanor began.

"No, and you damned well never will!" the Duke of Ware forgot his gallantry enough to say.

So Miss Ridgemont started to cry.

The next day Miss Ridgemont received an urgent summons, which never passed through Milsom's hands, to attend a sick relative. She begged her friends to bear her company in this time of woe, which was due to last until they reached the Earl of Cranshaw's house party.

Crow brought the lady to Warwick, so he was honor bound to escort her to her destination. He stopped to have a last toast with his friend while his valet was packing, a time-consuming task. Ware was worried that he'd placed a heavy burden on Crow's padded shoulders, but the baronet reassured him that it was no such thing. "In fact, Lee, I came to ask if you'd mind me cutting you out with the lady."

"I'll hand you the saber, my best of good friends," the duke replied. "Good luck to you. But are you sure? I mean . . ."

"Oh, I know the chit's rep, how she's hanging out for title and fortune, but we're well matched. Same interests, don't you know. Everyone says we make a handsome couple. She'll run out of dukes and earls soon, and I'll be waiting."

Ware shook his friend's hand, careful not to crush the fingers between the rings Crosby wore. "Then I'll wish you luck, Crow, and my best wishes."

By the time the company had all departed, some in better cheer than others, the afternoon of Christmas Eve had arrived. Graceanne decided she had to tell Leland now about

Pru and the baby, before attending the holiest of church services with lies and distrust between them. She was well aware they'd never be social equals, but the hurtfulness had to end. And after all, Miss Ridgemont was gone; half of Graceanne's Christmas wish had already come true. She sought his direction from Milsom.

Ware was determined to get her alone at last. He asked the butler where she might be found.

Milsom *almost* said, "Waiting for you, you nodcock," but he hadn't had quite that much of the lamb's wool yet.

They met in the Adams room, and were admiring the newly installed Christmas tree and discussing how many carriages were needed to transport their diminished group to church that evening, while they each tried to get up the courage to speak.

Milsom cleared his throat from the doorway. "A military man has called, Mrs. Warrington."

"Oh, one of Tony's friends, I suppose."

"No, madam, this is a naval gentleman, a Mr. Hallorahan. Are you at home?"

Not only was she at home, she was out of the parlor and into Liam's embrace in the Great Hall in a flash. Leland stayed where he was, staring into the fire.

The deuce take it, he thought, he'd even pulled strings to get the fellow sent back. Now she'd go off with him again, and he couldn't do a blasted thing about it. Leland wouldn't stop her, not if it meant Grace's happiness. He knew that now, that he could never be happy if she wasn't.

Then he heard her ask Milsom to send someone to fetch the baby downstairs. Of course, the duke despaired, it wanted only that. How could he go on without the children? Her children. Liam's child. His life.

He didn't know whether to go offer his felicitations, forbid her to take the boys, or beg her to stay. He couldn't just do nothing, he told himself. He had to move, to try. He went toward the open door and heard the Irishman's voice.

"Aye, e'en if she'll have me own carroty thatch, she's a bonny, bonny lassie. Just like her mum, b'gor."

"Yes, and she has the sweetness Pru used to possess before our father's meanness changed her."

"Ah, but she wanted only a bit of liveliness, did Pru. She was a good girl, I know. I could make her happy enow to bring back the sweetness."

Graceanne didn't want him to get his hopes up, when he kept swearing he was going to find Pru and marry her. "I'm afraid she's dreadfully spoiled. Your father's house on the farm . . ."

"Aye, and don't I know that cottage is no place for Pru? I don't intend to go back, and so I told my da. I liked the seafaring life, I did, and did well at it, too, after I found my way about. Saved the captain's life during an engagement and got promoted right on deck. Now I mean to take my prize money and buy into a shipping firm. I can take a wife to all those places Pru wanted to see, b'gad."

"That's no life for a baby, Liam."

"No, more's the pity," he said, looking down at the infant in his arms.

Graceanne sighed. "And I don't think I could part with her now."

"And I wouldn't ask it of you. I could never offer all this"—he waved his hand around the opulent hall—"and I can see how you love the wee girl as your own. She's yours, and God bless you for taking her in. The good Lord willing, there will be bairns aplenty for Pru and me when I find her, and after she grows up some. She's just a babe herself, is my Prudence."

"You are much too good for her, Liam Hallorahan, but I wish you Godspeed, that you might find her."

"Merry Christmas to you, Mrs. Warrington, and God bless you and keep you, my darling babe. Forgive me."

Liam left without looking back, not even seeing the duke standing in the hallway.

Leland wanted to rush in and gather Graceanne into his arms, but she already had a baby in hers, getting wet from her tears. He put his arms around both of them anyway. "I

211

have been such a fool, Grace. It is I who has to beg for your forgiveness, for distrusting you even for an instant."

Graceanne smiled through her tears. "I've been stubborn and too prideful to tell you. Can you forgive me?"

Leland finally got his kiss with the infant between them. It was necessarily a chaste kind of kiss, a bit distanced and much too quick, but enough to set his heart singing. If Miss Ridgemont's fervent kiss was a pleasant jog in the park, this tender touching was winning the Breeders' Cup at Newmarket.

Graceanne handed him the baby, worrying that if her knees were weak, so might her arms be. Of course, then they still had Nina between them, stupidly. They shared one more awkward kiss, though, which started bells ringing. Actually, they were the church bells.

"Oh, dear, the pageant!" Graceanne left him with the baby and a volume of unspoken words, to rush off to make sure the boys were ready.

Leland looked down at the babe in his arms, who was staring anxiously after her disappearing mother. "Don't worry, precious," he told her, "she's coming back. And I've got you." He buried his face in Nina's soft talcum smell, making her chuckle again. "I've got all of you now."

The pageant went well. The cow mooed from both ends, but Joseph and Mary were properly reverent in their roles, and Nina in her swaddling didn't complain too much about the rough homespun next to her skin.

Afterward they went home to greet the carolers, to light the Yule log with great pomp and ceremony, Ware guiding Willy and Les's hands holding last year's burning sliver to the new log. It was amazing how much warmth the traditional fire put out when done the right way. Then they all toasted the season with wassail, even Nanny taking a sip.

Finally it was time for the boys to go to bed and for Graceanne to put out the last nursery decorations and the gifts for the twins to find in the morning. The duke had to go wrap the last of his presents and make sure those purchased in London were assembled just right under the tree in the parlor.

While he was gone, Graceanne slipped off to her own bedchamber, where she lay awake listening to the distant carolers, holding her Christmas wish to her heart. She wished by every good luck charm of Shanna's, and said a prayer or two of her own.

On the morning of Christmas Day, Graceanne brought the children down to the parlor before breakfast. She was wearing an emerald green velvet gown and the boys had matching green velvet coats and short pants. They wore brand-new caps they didn't want to take off, even to open the mounds of packages under the tree. Graceanne complained again that he was spoiling the children, but Leland was enjoying every minute of watching their delight, almost as much as he'd enjoyed shopping for the unicycles and croquet sets, the small-sized pocket watches and tiny high leather riding boots. There was even a huge wooden castle, complete with carved knights on chargers, to match Nina's new dollhouse. And there were dolls. At least six of them stood or sat around the base of the tree, from rag babies to porcelain-faced beauties to peddler dolls with trays of tiny wares.

Leland shrugged off Graceanne's "Six dolls? You bought a tiny infant six dolls? Why, some of them are bigger than she is!"

"I couldn't decide," was all he said.

"Silly, all Nina needs to make her happy is a simple teething ring." Then she called the boys to her side and whispered into their ears. "But we have a gift for you, too, don't we, my angels?"

"Another pen wipe?"

"Better." The twins giggled, then together took off their new caps. Where Leland was used to seeing the twins with brown tousled heads, the riotous curls were all trimmed off and their hair was neatly combed—with parts on different sides!

"Les on the left, Willy on the wight," they chanted merrily.

"That's the best present of all! It's one of my Christmas wishes come true! I do have to confess I cheated and made two. No, I cannot tell you what the other one is yet. I have a present for your mother first." He turned to Graceanne and took a small box out of his pocket. "I hope you'll be happy with a simple ring like your daughter."

It was no simple ring at all, not with diamonds and sapphires, to match her eyes, he said. Graceanne had a horrible moment of doubt, that the ring was too ornate to be anything honorable.

But Leland was quick to read her smile's disappearance. "No, no, the one that matches is the plain gold band, but you don't get that one until you marry me, dear heart. Will you, and make my other Christmas wish come true? Do say yes, darling, for I don't think I can live without you, I love you so much."

"Me or my children, Your Grace?" she had to know.

"All of you, each of you, but none more than you, my Grace."

"Then yes, Leland, for I love you just as much, and now my wish can come true, too."

"And ours!" chorused Willy and Les, jumping up and down.

No such thing as Father Christmas? Don't dare tell the Duke of Ware, or his duchess.

Merry Christmas!

Christmas Wishes

Chapter One

$\mathcal{J}$uneclaire wished she did not have to spend another Christmas at Stanton Hall. "You would have liked the way Christmas used to be," she told her companion, Pansy. Pansy just grunted and continued her investigation of all the parcels being wrapped and put into baskets for the servants' and tenants' Boxing Day gifts. Bright ribbons, shiny paper, and mounds of presents and treats were spread on two tables and the floor of the rear pantry Miss Juneclaire Beaumont was using to assemble Lady Stanton's largess. Lady Stanton was being very generous this year. She had directed her niece Juneclaire to knit mittens for all the children, to hem handkerchiefs for all the footmen and grooms, and to sew rag dolls for the little girls on the estate. Juneclaire had also been sent to the nearby village of Farley's Grange to purchase new shawls for the tenants' wives and whistles and tops for the boys. All week she had been busy helping Cook bake plum cakes, decorate gingerbread men, and create marzipan angels, after tying colorful ribbons around pots of jam from the berries she had collected all summer and fall. She also made sachets of the lavender she had drying in the stillroom and poured out rose water into little bottles for the maidservants. The orchards provided shiny apples, and Uncle Avery Stanton provided shiny coins. Oh yes, and Aunt Marta Stanton provided a new Bible for each of the servants, whether they could read or not. Last year the gift was a hymnal, the year before a book of sermons. Aunt Marta was very consistent in her Christian charity.

Lady Stanton was so consistent, in fact, that her own niece would receive one of the Bibles and a shiny coin as her Christmas gift and naught else.

It wasn't that she minded being treated worse than the servants, Juneclaire reflected, pausing to share one of the crisp apples with Pansy. Nor did she mind all the work, though that was considerable at this time of year, with helping the maids air the unused rooms for holiday guests and directing the footmen in hanging the greenery after Juneclaire fashioned it into wreaths and garlands. No, she was used to being useful. What she could not and would not get inured to was being used, to being considered a serf with no salary or self-respect. Juneclaire acknowledged that she was a poor relation and that she owed Lord and Lady Stanton her gratitude for the very roof over her head. How could she not accept the fact, when Aunt Marta reminded her daily?

"Still," she told Pansy, pushing a soft brown curl back under her mobcap, "they could have been kinder." Pansy was too busy redistributing a pile of apricot tarts to notice Juneclaire wipe a suddenly damp brown eye with her sleeve. "Here," Juneclaire said, looking over her shoulder, "you'd better not let Aunt Marta see you nibbling on those or we'll be in the briers for sure." She tied a bow on a pair of warm knitted socks and sniffed. "She could at least have let us stir the Christmas pudding and make a wish with everyone else."

Lady Stanton did not believe in such nonsense.

2

She thought such superstitions were heathenish and not at all suitable for a Stanton of Stanton Hall or one of their household. She could not stop the kitchen staff, naturally, not if she wanted a smooth pudding to serve her guests, but she could see that her niece was kept too busy for any pagan rituals. If it were up to Lady Stanton, Christmas would be spent on one's knees, in church. There would be none of this mad jollity, this extravagance of entertaining and gifting. Aunt Marta was religious, proper, strict—and cheap. She wouldn't even distribute Boxing Day gifts if it were not for Lord Stanton and the fact that to discontinue the tradition would disgruntle the dependents and, worse, make her look paltry in the neighborhood. Lady Stanton was very careful of her standing among the local gentry, especially since her own roots did not bear close scrutiny, with their ties to Trade. She had worked hard to earn that "Lady" before her name and intended to enjoy its rewards. If being accepted as the first family in the vicinity meant showing off her generosity once a year, Juneclaire could handle the details. If it meant giving hearth space to her misbegotten waif of a niece, Juneclaire could at least be put to work and molded to Lady Stanton's measure.

Juneclaire kept wrapping bundles, trying to make a happy Christmas for those less fortunate than she was. At least she tried to convince herself that the servants were less fortunate, even though they got an actual wage and could move to another position; the tenants were less well established than Juneclaire, although they worked to better their own lives and had families who cared about them.

"Things were not always this way," she informed her companion. Aunt Marta would have been horrified to see Juneclaire's hands go still while she recalled earlier Christmases, when Maman lifted her up to stir the pudding and make her wish. Papa used to smile at the English ways and tousle her curls. He always knew her wish anyway, and he would laugh. His *petite fleur* only wanted a puppy or a kitten or a pony. Juneclaire received gloves and combs and books and dolls and sweets and, at last, a pony, despite a lack of funds.

Then she and Maman returned to England without Papa, without her pony, to this cold and damp Stanton Hall with its disapproving ancestors frowning down on her from their portraits on the wall. That year she wished that the horrors in Papa's homeland would be over soon and he would send for them. Maman gave her a locket to wear, with a tiny painting of her and Papa in it. Juneclaire touched it now, under her worn brown wool gown.

The next Christmas, when they knew Papa was not coming for them, Juneclaire wished Maman would be stronger in her loss, but she was not, and then Juneclaire was nine years old and alone. For the next ten years she tried not to wish for what could never be.

Juneclaire tried to be grateful for the grudging charity, truly she did, winning the respect of the servants, at least, with her quiet acceptance of her lot. They considered Juneclaire a true lady, sweet and caring, not like some they could mention, with jumped-up airs. Of course, Juneclaire's being a lady set her apart. The staff could take pity on the orphaned chit, and they could be kind to her when Lady Stanton was not looking, but they could not be her friends, not if they wanted to keep their positions. Aunt Marta did not condone familiarity between the classes. For the same reason she did not permit her niece to play with the village children. Juneclaire wasn't good enough to merit a governess or new frocks or a maid to wait on her, but she was too genteel for the locals: her mother was a Stanton. So Juneclaire had no friends.

She did have her cousins, however, if two loud, unruly imps of Satan could be consolation to a gentle female. She was as relieved as everyone else on the estate except Lady Stanton when Rupert and Newton finally went away to school. In earlier days they had made her life an endless hell of creepy things in her bed, slimy things in her slippers, crawly things in her porridge. She was the unwilling plunder when they played pirate, the dragon's victim when they played at knights. They tied her up, locked her in closets, terrorized her in dark attics. And if *her* hair got mussed, *her* pinafore got soiled, she got a lecture from Aunt Marta and no supper. Dearest Rupert, Juneclaire's age, and baby Newton, a year younger, were just high-spirited, according to their fond mother. The Root and the Newt, as their not-so-fond and often-hungry cousin termed them, had no redeeming virtues whatsoever, except that she could listen in on their lessons and ride their ponies when the boys outgrew them.

If Christmas seasons were never joyous for Juneclaire at Stanton Hall, now they were less so when the boys came home for holiday with the only knowledge her scapegrace relatives seemed to have absorbed at Harrow: carnal knowledge.

At age eighteen, Newt was a thin, spotty-faced budding tulip, with yellow pantaloons, high shirt collars, and roving hands. Nineteen-year-old Root was short and stocky, with sausage fingers and damp lips with which Juneclaire was growing altogether too familiar. She'd taken to avoiding dark corridors and to carrying a darning needle slipped through her lace collar as a weapon. Even if Juneclaire were willing—and hell would freeze over first—she thought she'd be without more than her supper if Aunt Marta caught her in one of her darlings' embraces. Root and Newt were so stupid, though, they thought she was just playing hard to get, as they nursed their various pinpricks.

Aunt Marta would not have anything as indecorous as a kissing bough in her house, of course, but the brats had discovered a patch of mistletoe and took great joy in bedeviling Juneclaire in public places, where she could not retaliate. Unaware of her own prettiness, Juneclaire could not understand why they did not share their ardor with a willing housemaid, the way Uncle Avery did. She did not think she could mention this to the randy rattlepates, however, nor could she complain to her aunt, who would only find Juneclaire at fault for her wanton looks. No matter how hard Juneclaire stared at her mirror, she could find nothing siren-like about brown hair, brown eyes, and thick brown eyebrows. Her mouth seemed too full and her nose too short, especially in comparison with her beautiful mother's miniature. And Juneclaire knew for a fact there could be nothing seductive about the shapeless, drab gowns she wore at Aunt Marta's insistence. They were so high-necked and loose-fitting that Root was eighteen before he even discovered she had a bosom. Unfortunately, octopus-armed Newt was not as mutton-headed.

Juneclaire could have gone to Uncle Avery with her problems, she supposed, but he would likely have patted her head and handed her a shilling, the way he used to when he found her in tears. Now she stood taller than the short, portly frame Root had inherited, and she had a fair stock of shillings. She also felt too sorry for her uncle to bring him more difficulties. The poor man hated what he called mingle-mangles, which meant he avoided his lady and her sons every chance he got, contenting himself with his pigs and sheep and cows—and housemaids. To say he was henpecked was a vast understatement. If he were a slice of bread, there'd be no place to spread jam. So Juneclaire made sure her door was locked at night and wished every year would be her last Christmas at Stanton Hall. This year just might be the one.

"What, are you still at this foolish task, you lazy girl? You should have been finished hours ago. I need you to make out the place cards for tomorrow's dinner, Claire." Aunt Marta could not bring herself to give Juneclaire her proper name, considering it too foreign, too affected for one in her niece's position. Lady Stanton unwrapped an apricot tart and held it up to her sharp nose before biting into it. She poked her bony fingers into the various boxes and trays. Lady Stanton had as much meat on her bones as she had human kindness in her heart. "I am placing you between Captain Fancroft and Squire Holmes. You may ask the captain about the war, but remember that no gentleman expects or wishes a lady to be knowledgeable. Whatever you say, do not disagree with him. Squire Holmes is interested in his children and the hunt. You shall *not* express your queer notions of sympathy for the fox. Do you understand, miss?"

"Yes, Aunt Marta. No, I shan't, Aunt Marta," Juneclaire replied from long practice.

"And see that you don't take off your gloves. No need for anyone to see your hands ain't as smooth as a lady's."

"But I am a lady, Aunt."

"Hoity-toity, miss. You'll stop putting on airs, too, if you hope to snabble an eligible *parti*."

Juneclaire rather thought she did, even if she wouldn't have used those terms. This year she was being permitted to join Aunt Marta's annual Christmas Eve gathering, in hopes that she would attract some gentleman's eye. There was to be no

7

London Season for Juneclaire, not even a come-out ball in her honor, for Aunt Marta was too nipfarthing and too ashamed of this product of a runaway match between Miss Clara Stanton and her dancing master. Even if Jules Beaumont had been son to a *duc*, he was the third son of an early victim of the Terror, the family wealth confiscated by the upstarts. Juneclaire saw nothing to be embarrassed over in her heritage, even if her parents did not marry until reaching France, and in a Catholic church at that.

Now she raised her chin and said, "I do not think my birth will count against me with a true gentleman, not if he cares for me."

"Poppycock, just see that you don't give them a disgust of you. Holmes needs a mother for his brats, and Fancroft wants an heir while he can still sire one."

"But . . . but aren't there to be any younger men at the party?"

"Not for you there won't be. What did you think, some storybook hero was going to fall in love with your doe eyes? Young men don't offer marriage to dowerless chits with tainted names. They offer *carte blanche*." Aunt Marta checked the hems of the handkerchiefs.

Ah, well, perhaps the captain would be knowledgeable on closer acquaintance, or the squire kindly. She wouldn't mind children, not if it meant a house of her own, away from Stanton Hall, if the gentleman Aunt Marta picked out was nice. She made the mistake of asking.

"Nice? What has that to do with it? You'll take the first one that offers for you or you can go to the poorhouse, for all I care. It's time and enough someone else paid your bills and bought your clothes."

Juneclaire knew the threat of the poorhouse was only that. Aunt Marta would never let the neighborhood see her treat a blood relation in so miserly a fashion, nor would her aunt part with an unpaid servant so easily. No, Fancroft and Holmes must be warm enough in the pocket to offer Lady Stanton handsome settlements for her niece's hand, which meant Juneclaire dared not refuse. And what choice did she have, after all, but to marry a man of her aunt's selection? She never met any strangers, sequestered away at the Hall and traveling no farther than Farley's Grange, and she was ill-equipped for anything but marriage. She was not well-enough educated to go for a governess, she was too shy to go on the stage, and she did not sew quickly enough to be a seamstress. Mostly, she did not have enough patience to continue on as her aunt's lackey.

With the optimism that came with youth and the season of surprises, Miss Beaumont hoped for better than an aging roué or a beleaguered widower. If only Juneclaire could have made her pudding wish, she would have asked for a handsome cavalier, no matter what Aunt Marta said.

At least she had her pretty new gown. White velvet it was, with a high waist and low neck and tiny puff sleeves. Aunt Marta meant her to look like a debutante of the ton: respectable, virginal, à la mode. If all went well, she could be married in the same dress, avoiding additional expense. Juneclaire had spent some of her precious shillings for green ribbon to trim the gown and had woven a crown of holly for her hair. She thought she would do very well, with her mother's pearls and the Norwich silk shawl she knew Uncle Avery meant to give her. Perhaps there would be a young beau who did not need to marry for money or consequence. Aunt Marta didn't know everything, Juneclaire thought with a smile. She didn't know about Uncle Avery's housemaids.

Lady Stanton was checking the names on the

filled baskets, peevishly hurrying Juneclaire along toward her next chore. She removed the bottle of rose water from the package marked Lily; Juneclaire's smile faded. Then Aunt Marta caught sight of Pansy.

"What is that . . . that *creature* doing here?" she shouted, her thin frame going rigid in anger. "I told you yesterday Cook was looking for her in the kitchens! I abhor these unseemly friendships you insist on striking up, Claire, and I won't have it. What if Squire Holmes found out? Captain Fancroft would be revolted, I am sure. I won't have your disobedience, do you hear me?"

Juneclaire was sure the whole kitchen staff heard her, and she blushed with embarrassment. Pansy ran to hide behind Juneclaire as Aunt Marta slammed the door behind her. Lady Stanton stomped off, insisting for the rest of the household who might have missed her earlier screaming that she hadn't raised up a penniless orphan out of the goodness of her heart just to be made a laughingstock, and where was that bobbing-block of a husband of hers when she needed him to do something about his niece and her willful ways.

"Don't worry, Pansy," Juneclaire whispered, leaving the boxes and baskets, leaving the pantry, but not leaving Pansy in the kitchen.

Now, Juneclaire might have been willing to sacrifice her hopes and dreams on Aunt Marta's altar of greed and meanness, for she was a dutiful girl. She might have put on the prettiest gown she'd ever owned and put herself on display for her aunt's guests, hoping to impress them with Lady Stanton's beneficence. She was even ready to try to charm some overweight old seaman into a declaration to please her aunt. But not Pansy. She would not let Aunt Marta sacrifice Pansy just to puff off her own consequence, just because Pansy was little and lame.

Well, wishing hadn't brought Maman or Papa back, and it would not bring her any handsome and wealthy knight riding to her rescue. Wishing was certainly not going to save Pansy. That Juneclaire had to do herself. So she did. She gathered her few belongings, including the velvet gown and her heaviest cloak, a gray wool that used to be her aunt's. The rabbit lining looked more like rat fur after all these years, but she would need the warmth if she and Pansy were to reach London, where Mrs. Simms, the old housekeeper, resided. Juneclaire hastily estimated that by nightfall she could reach the market village of Strasmere, where not many people would recognize her, especially with the hood of her cloak up. Tomorrow she could find a farmer going to Bramley, the nearest posting stop, and then in a day she would be in London. She counted out her hoard of shillings and nodded. They ought to be enough. Juneclaire wrapped half of them and her mother's pearls in a stocking, which she tucked inside the loose bodice of her gown. The rest she placed in her reticule, along with Mrs. Simms's last letter. She wrapped a white muffler around her neck, knotted off an unfinished pair of mittens, and put them on, not caring that one was shorter than the other. Then she went to the kitchens, where she filled every nook of her carpetbag and every pocket of her cloak with bread and cheese and apples and sliced meats. "For the poorhouse," she told the gaping scullery maid. "Do they have a better Christmas, too."

Juneclaire left Stanton Hall without looking back. She did not leave a farewell note. She did not leave her aunt's Christmas dinner.

Unfortunately, Juneclaire's almost instant planning did not take into account Pansy's lameness.

The poor dear couldn't walk far or fast. Miss Beaumont had also not considered that many others would be on the road for the holidays and that there would, indeed, be no rooms at the inn at Strasmere, or the next down the road, or the next. Sheltered as she was, Juneclaire never would have guessed that most innkeepers and their wives would not accept a single woman, traveling without servants, on foot, and in dubious company.

"I run a respectable establishment, I do," she heard over and over. "I'm not having the likes of such a one at *my* inn, I'm not."

Juneclaire raised her determined chin and lowered her thick eyebrows. She was not going back to Stanton Hall, not even if she had to sleep under hedgerows. She would get to London, even if she had to walk the whole way, carrying Pansy.

Chapter Two

$\mathcal{L}$ord Merritt Jordan, the Earl of St. Cloud, wished he did not have to spend Christmas at home. He flicked the whip over the leader's left ear as the curricle straightened after a turn that sent the outer wheels two feet in the air. His groom, Foley, took the liberty of long years in service, and a short glimpse of eternity, to speak up. As soon as his insides righted themselves, Foley shouted from his perch behind the driver's seat that he'd rather eat his mincemeat pie than be one. "An' the way you been cursin' about havin' to be somewheres you don't want, I can't figure why you're drivin' like the Devil hisself is behind us, my lord, and catchin' up fast."

St. Cloud frowned, not at the familiarity but at the truth. Damn and blast, he was in no hurry to get to the Priory in Berkshire. He obligingly slowed the pace a fraction. "Now the Devil won't have to run so hard." Why should he, when hell was waiting up ahead?

Foley shook his grizzled head but relaxed a little. Now they were traveling at death-defying speed, not necessarily death-wishing, and there was no one he'd trust with the ribbons more than his master. If Lord St. Cloud didn't have the lightest hands with the reins, aye, and the surest eye toward horseflesh, besides the truest aim with a pistol, the neatest right in the ring and the sharpest skill with the pasteboards of any gentleman in St. James's Street, Foley would eat his hat. If it hadn't blown off a mile outside London. Blister it, if Lord St. Cloud didn't have his black moods like now, he'd well nigh be the best employer in London Town. He was fair and generous, not toplofty, and he didn't truck with women.

Foley had no fondness for the female species; they only distracted a man from the important business in life, like war and wagering. What with their weeping and clinging and flirting and spending every groat of a chap's income, they were more trouble than they were worth, by half. It was a good thing, in Foley's opinion, that Lord St. Cloud was not in the petticoat line. Not that the silly geese wouldn't be littering my lord's doorstep if he smiled on them. With his wealth and title, the debutantes would be pawing each other aside to catch his attention. With his wealth and finely muscled frame the demireps would be clawing one another's eyes out. And with his dark, brooding looks and well-chiseled features, green eyes and cleft chin, every other female from sixteen to sixty would be gnawing on him like a bone, with or without his incredible wealth. If he smiled at them.

Luckily for Foley's misogynistic peace of mind, Lord St. Cloud seldom smiled at anyone, and at women least of all. The groom spit over the downwind side of the careening carriage. Give him his horses anytime. Many years ago, when Foley was a jockey, a waitress at the Green Knight had run off with a linen draper's assistant; the shop boy's hands were clean, she said, and he didn't smell of the stable. That's why Foley frowned if a pretty gal looked his way. Foley never understood about his master's dour expression and dark humors.

"I don't see what's got you in such a takin'," he muttered now, hanging on for dear life as the earl dropped his hands for the grays to pass a mail coach. "After all, it's Christmas and you're goin' home."

Foley couldn't see St. Cloud's sneer from his position at the earl's back, even if the groom's eyes weren't shut as they missed the coach by inches. Home, hah! Merritt Jordan had felt more at home on the French prison ship. At least there he'd had friends among the other captives. He'd only had to worry about disease, vermin, and hunger—not his relatives. Spending any holiday at St. Cloud Priory at Ayn-Jerome outside Thackford, much less Christmas and his birthday, was more like doing penance for being born.

They would all be there, all the vultures. His mother would see to that, filling the moldering old pile with relations, guests, and hangers-on, just so she did not have to face him alone. And they'd all want something of him, as always: money, favors, compliance with *their* standards for *his* behavior. Cousin Niles would have his usual sheaf of tailors' bills and gambling debts to be paid, and Cousin Elsbeth would still be whining for a London Season. Lord Harmon Wilmott, their father and St. Cloud's uncle, would shake his jowls and issue another lecture on St. Cloud's duties and responsibilities. St. Cloud was the last of the Jordan line, Uncle Harmon would intone; he owed his ancestors a continuance. Mother's brother undoubtedly meant that the earl should marry Elsbeth, saving Lord Harmon the expense and aggravation and keeping the wealth in the family, the Wilmott family, that was.

St. Cloud clenched his fists, and the horses took exception. When he had them back under his perfect control and Foley had quit muttering, he returned to his musings of what lay ahead. Grandmother, blind as a bat for the last five years, would be nagging at him that she wanted to see her great-grandchildren, and soon. And every female in the county who could scrape up an acquaintance would be calling, with hopes of becoming the next Countess St. Cloud, by come-hither hook or by compromising-situation crook. He dare not walk in his own shrubbery without an escort or sit at ease in his own library unless the door was locked. Hell and damnation, he thought, not for the first time. The Priory already had enough Lady St. Clouds, and those two did not even speak to each other, not without his grandmother, the dowager, shouting, or Lady Fanny, his mother and current countess until he married, weeping.

The closer his carriage got to the Priory, the more St. Cloud understood how a winded deer felt surrounded by wolves. But he was not defenseless, he reminded himself. He was no longer a child who had to abide by adult rules. He was a grown man, twenty-nine years of age, and Uncle Harmon was no longer his trustee or warder. St. Cloud had made that plain four years ago, the day he came into his majority, after waiting a young lifetime of oppression.

Merritt Jordan had, like most of his class, been raised by wet nurses, nannies, and nursemaids. He seldom saw his parents, his mother being too high-strung for the duties of motherhood and his father not being interested. Then came his father's "accident," as they called it, and subsequent death two years later, when St. Cloud was seven years old. Lady Fanny's nerves deteriorated to such an extent that she could not bear to have her son near her. He was too noisy, too active. He might break something.

Her father took over the management of the estate since there were no male Jordan relatives. Lord Wilmott and Grandmother had such rows about raising the new tenth earl that Lady Fanny took to her bed for a year. Lord Wilmott moved his own family from Motthaven next door into the Priory, and the elder Lady St. Cloud moved to the dower house. Uncle Harmon took over the guardianship when he ascended to his father's baronetcy and later brought his own motherless children to reside under the Jordan banner—and checkbook.

Niles and later Elsbeth could run wild over the estate; St. Cloud had to be groomed for his future dignities. Niles could go off to school at thirteen; St. Cloud at the same age was too delicate to jeopardize among the other sons of the upper ten thousand. Of course his life was precious to the Wilmotts. Without St. Cloud they would have to live on their own neglected property, within their own modest means, for the earldom reverted back to the Crown.

On the one hand, he was wrapped in cotton wool, given the fattest, most placid ponies to ride, kept away from guns and swords, swaddled like an infant prone to croup. On the other hand, he was force-fed a rigorous education by one sanctimonious, sadistic tutor after another. The last was a young curate, Mr. Forbush, who licked his lips when he birched the young earl at every excuse. Lady Fanny cried and did nothing. She was as in awe of her overbearing brother as she had been of her dictatorial father and her grim husband. Uncle Harmon saw nothing wrong with beating the impertinence out of a young boy who questioned his trustee's cutting in the home woods, raising the tenants' rents, or selling off the Thoroughbred stud farm. He approved of Mr. Forbush to such an extent that when St. Cloud finally went to university, Uncle Harmon kept the curate on as the family's spiritual adviser. The hypocrite rained hellfire and brimstone down on the household every Sunday in the old Priory's chapel of St. Jerome of the Clouds. Lady Fanny was confirmed in her belief that she would burn in purgatory, and Uncle Harmon was convinced his self-righteous sacrifices on his nephew's behalf would be rewarded in the afterlife.

The earl enjoyed the partial freedom of university life. He excelled at his studies, but he also found outlets for the years of anger and neglect in athletic pursuits, honing his whip-tight muscles and deadly skills. None of the other lads was foolish enough to think St. Cloud was merely competing for fun. Fun did not seem to exist in the young peer's vocabulary.

St. Cloud's dream, when he came down from university, was to join the army like his deceased uncle George Jordan, whose name was never mentioned. The dowager ranted, Lady Fanny wept, Mr. Forbush prayed. And Uncle Harmon refused. Merritt Jordan was still the last St. Cloud. No Corsican upstart was going to capsize Wilmott's gravy boat.

Defeated, St. Cloud threw himself into Town life like a sailor on shore after months at sea. He followed his frivolous cousin Niles into gaming dens and bawdy houses. He surpassed him in reckless wagers and hey-go-mad stunts. He ran up debts and ran with lightskirts. He skirted the law with innumerable duels and became known as Satan St. Cloud, a deadly rakehell who took his pleasures seriously. Except that he found no pleasure in such an existence, beyond aggravating Uncle Harmon.

On his twenty-fifth birthday, St. Cloud waited until Mr. Forbush had given his Christmas sermon, not about the Holy Child and Peace on Earth, but about the sins of the fathers, blasphemy, adultery, murder. Forbush stared at St. Cloud and licked his lips.

One step outside the chapel doors the curate found himself in an iron-hard grip, being dragged to the gatehouse, where the Earl of St. Cloud celebrated Christmas his own way, beating a man of the cloth to within an inch of his life, then tossing him over the gate like a sack of refuse.

St. Cloud strode back to the house and his astounded relatives with a look on his face that could have been a grimace on anyone else's. London bucks would have recognized it as the St. Cloud smile and fled. The earl notified Uncle Harmon that his services were no longer required; a bailiff had been hired. With a green-eyed look that could stop molten lava in its course, St. Cloud informed him and Niles that the London solicitors were already advised to direct Wilmott bills to Motthaven, not the Priory. He told his mother that if she did not put off her blacks and cease the weeping after nearly twenty years, she could very well go live with Lady St. Cloud in the dower house.

Having turned the Priory nicely on its ear, the earl returned to London to purchase his own commission. Prinny himself refused the request, unless and until St. Cloud had assured the succession. He almost went to marry the first Covent Garden doxie he could find, out of spite, but not even Satan St. Cloud could go through with such an affront to his ancestors. Besides, in the nine months it would take to beget a son, Bonny could be defeated. Or the child might be a girl.

Instead the earl took the offered position of liaison between the War Office and the quartermaster general. The Regent asked him to accept, to see why the troops were not properly outfitted, why ammunition did not reach Wellesley's men in time. A request from the Regent was as good as a command, so St. Cloud became a paper merchant, by damn! He saw enough graft and corruption to disgust even a politician and ended by using some of his own blunt to expedite orders. Three months later he convinced his superior that the only way to see where deliveries were running afoul was in person—St. Cloud's person.

With every intention of joining up with some regiment or other in Spain, St. Cloud boarded a convoy ship for the Peninsula. The ship was attacked and sunk. The earl was wounded and captured and imprisoned on a French barque, without ever touching Spanish soil. Whitehall was not best pleased to have to trade four French officers of high rank for his release, and St. Cloud was furious that part of his parole—negotiated by Uncle Harmon, indubitably—was his word as a gentleman not to take up arms against his captors again.

No longer in good odor at the War Office, St. Cloud took his seat in the Lords and did what he could there for the war effort, for the returning veterans. Fusty political pettifoggery satisfied him as little as bumbling bureaucracy, so he resumed his Town life, but with some new moderation. Merritt Jordan had nothing left to prove and only himself to aggravate with outrageous behavior, like now, when the headache he had from too much drink and too little sleep was pounding in his temples with each beat of the horses' hooves. He should have known better than to start the journey so late. Hell, he thought, neatly turning the grays into the courtyard of the Rose and the Crown with inches to spare between them and an overladen departing carriage, he should have made some excuse to avoid the Priory altogether. He usually did.

While the grays were being changed for his lordship's own matched chestnuts, sent ahead three days ago, St. Cloud was ushered into the inn's best private parlor, also reserved. Over a steaming mug of the landlord's renowned spiced punch, St. Cloud mused that no matter how much he struggled, some bonds never came undone. When Uncle Harmon tried to inflict his opinions on his nephew, St. Cloud could stare him into silence, without even hinting at irregularities in the trust's bookkeeping. St. Cloud could control the wilder excesses of his basket-scrambling cousin Niles with pocketbook governance, and he could challenge any man whose loose tongue overcame his instincts for self-preservation enough to probe the St. Cloud family history. But he could not deal with his womenfolk at all.

He could not frown them into submission, for Grandmother was blind and Mother always had her eyes covered with a damp cloth or a lace-edged handkerchief, albeit not a black-bordered one any longer. He could not affect their behavior through the purse strings either, since both widows' jointures were generous, and he could certainly not still their querulous demands with threats of physical violence. All he could do was stay away.

For two groats he'd have spent the holidays in London, where his latest mistress would have found some way of enlivening his birthday. Instead he was on the road to Berkshire to face the ghosts of his past, literally.

Tapping in the wainscoting, wailing through the chimneys, disappearing foodstuffs—the Priory ghosts were walking the halls. Murdered monks, squirrels in the secret passages, or bats in Lady Fanny's belfry, his mother's letters had gone from her usual vaporish complaints to hysterical gibberish about divine retribution. And company coming.

St. Cloud tossed back another cup of punch and called Foley out of the taproom. At least he did not have to travel in state, cooped in a stuffy coach for

21

endless hours. His bags and valet had gone on ahead yesterday, so he could have the pleasure of tooling the curricle and his priceless cattle through the cold, barren, winter-wrapped countryside. The dreary scenery matched his mood, and Foley knew better than to complain about the speed again, until the chestnuts showed off their high spirits by nearly wrapping the curricle around a signpost.

"I thought you meant the beasts to make it through the next stages an' on to the Priory without a change," Foley shouted over the wind. "They'll be blown way 'fore that, at this rate."

"I think the horses have more heart than you do, old man," St. Cloud replied. "They'll do. I intend to slow down before long to give them a rest anyway, but you want to get to a warm bed tonight, don't you?"

"Aye, and I'm thinkin' there'll be some eggnog and spice cake waiting. So I'd as lief get there in one piece, if it's all the same to you, my lord."

Eggnog and spice cake and Christmas carolers. Marriageable women, skittish women, swooning women. Ghosts and ghouls and noises in the night. "Bloody hell."

The expletive may have been for Foley's impudence, or it may have been for St. Cloud's black thoughts, or perhaps for the tree fallen across the roadway. Foley did not know. He got down to assess the situation as soon as the chestnuts came to a halt, and St. Cloud reached into his greatcoat pocket. Too late. Two men rode out of the screening bushes, and one of them already held his pistol on the defenseless groom.

"Stand and deliver."

Chapter Three

"*B*loody hell."

"Nothing to get riled over, Yer Highness," the man with the gun called out from Foley's side. He was big and broad and had a scarf pulled up over his mouth and a slouch hat pulled down low over his eyes. "Just raise yer hands up slow, like, and everything will be aces."

The other highwayman had dismounted and was holding the chestnuts' bridles. He was also bundled past recognition, but he was smaller, slighter, and as nervous as the horses he was trying to calm. He did not have a weapon in sight, so St. Cloud weighed the odds.

"None of that, Yer Highness," the first man said, catching the earl's tentative movement. He used the butt end of his pistol on Foley's head, then turned the barrel on St. Cloud.

The other robber jumped. "What'd you go and do that for, Charlie? You never said nothing about—"

"Shut your mouth, boy. Do you want to make him an introduction? Can't you see the toff is a real out-and-outer? He was going to go for the gun sooner or later, and much help you'd 'a' been. I couldn't keep both of 'em covered, now, could I?"

"But you shouldn't've hit him so hard. What if he's dead?"

"If he is dead, Charlie," the earl said in a voice that was like cold steel, "your life is not worth a ha'penny."

"Fine words for a gent what's got his arms up in the air," Charlie blustered, but he dismounted and nudged Foley with his toe until the little man groaned. "There, now can we finish this argle-bargle and get to business? You toss the pistol out first, real slow so I don't get twitch-fingered. And remember, I ain't tenderhearted like my green friend here."

St. Cloud's wallet was next, then his gold fob, quizzing glass, silver flask, and emerald stickpin.

"And the ring, too, Yer Highness," Charlie said, searching Foley's pockets for the groom's purse but never taking his eyes, or the gun, off the earl.

"It's a signet ring with my family crest on it. No fence would give a brass farthing for the thing, for they could never resell it; if you're ever found with it, it's your death warrant for sure."

"Let it be, Charlie," the youngster begged. "We have enough."

"Chicken gizzard," Charlie grumbled, leading his horse closer to the curricle to pick up the booty from where St. Cloud had thrown it to the ground. A quick shake of the earl's leather purse had him agreeing and getting back on his horse. "Reckon it's a good day's work, and it is the season for givin', ain't it? Stand back, boy."

The youth let go of the horses, but before St. Cloud could lower his hands and find the ribbons, Charlie fired his pistol right over the chestnuts' backs. "Merry Christmas, Yer Highness," he shouted after the rocketing curricle.

* * *

The thieves were long gone by the time St. Cloud could catch up the reins and slow the frenzied animals, then turn them back to find Foley. The groom was limping toward him along the verge, holding a none-too-clean kerchief to a gash on the side of his head. St. Cloud jumped down and hurried to him, leaving the chestnuts standing with their heads lowered. There was no fear of their spooking anymore this day.

"How bad does it hurt, Foley?" he asked, pulling off his own neck cloth to make a bandage. "Can you hold on to the next inn or should I come back for you with a wagon?"

"Don't fatch so, m'lord, I'll do. 'Tain't my head what's botherin' me as much as my pride anyways. The chestnuts could've been hurt in that panic run. And you, too," he added as an afterthought, seeing the twitch in the earl's lips. "To think I was taken in by that old trick like a regular Johnny Raw, why, I'm slumguzzled for sure."

St. Cloud helped the older man back up to the curricle, wishing he had his flask, at least. "Whatever that is, don't blame yourself. I shouldn't have been wool-gathering either, but who would have thought there'd be bridle culls on this side road in Berkshire?"

"Amateurs, they was, you could tell."

"Yes, I was able to convince them to leave my ring, when any flat knows the thing can be melted down for the gold."

The groom spit through his teeth in disgust. "An' only one gun between them."

"It was enough," the earl answered, trying to keep the chestnuts to the least bumpy portion of the road. "And now they have mine." He was trying to recall how soon they could expect to come upon the next inn. He'd lost track of their position in the headlong rush and in truth hadn't been paying proper attention before then. There had to be something closer ahead than the Rose and the Crown was behind, even a hedge tavern. He didn't like Foley's color.

The groom was barely conscious when St. Cloud turned into the yard of a place whose weathered signboard proclaimed it the Fighting Cock. Dilapidated, in need of paint, and with one sullen stable hand to come to their assistance, this inn was a far cry from the Rose and the Crown. There was a vast difference in their style of arrival, too. Now the horses were lathered and plodding, the curricle was scraped and spattered, the earl was disheveled, and his groom was bloody and sagging on the seat. And there was no pocketful of coins to grease the wheels of hospitality.

Their reception was commensurate with their appearance. The earl had to rub down the horses himself while waiting for the doctor. He had to leave his signet ring as pledge for the surgeon's bill and the laudanum he prescribed as well as for Foley's bed and baiting the horses. The innkeeper offered to throw in some stew as part of the bargain, but St. Cloud was too furious to eat. There were no horses to be hired, not on tick, and no room for the earl, not on Christmas Eve.

"You can't mean to set out so late," Foley complained from his rude palette behind the kitchen stairs. "And without me." He tried to sit up.

The earl pushed him back down. "Stubble it, you old hen. I'm not your only chick. There are a few hours of daylight left, and we're not that far from St. Cloud. Anyway, it looks to be a clear night ahead. I'll send a carriage back for you at first light."

"But the chestnuts, m'lord, they're tired."

"They've had their rest, and I'll travel slowly. Besides, I wouldn't leave my cattle in this cesspit."

Foley grinned as the laudanum pushed his eyes closed. "Aye, but you'd leave me."

St. Cloud tucked the thin blanket around his man. "No choice," he told him. "Lady St. Cloud is frantic enough as is. If my bags arrive and I don't appear as promised, she'll send out the militia. Blast all females and families."

"And footpads and fools."

"And clutch-fisted innkeepers."

St. Cloud was still furious an hour later. Two hours later, when he got down again to lighten the load as the chestnuts strained up yet another hill, he was furious, footsore, and hungry.

Some other traveler must have had trouble with the incline, he observed, spotting a small pile of books by the side of the road. The books were neatly stacked on a rock, off the damp ground and in full view, as though waiting to be picked up. St. Cloud did not think they were left for anyone in particular, for night was coming on, this country byway was practically deserted, and the books were neither wrapped nor tied. No, the chap must simply have grown weary of carrying the heavy volumes. The earl picked them up, thinking that if he came upon his fellow traveler, he could offer a ride and restore his belongings.

Oddly enough, the books were all religious in nature. Who would bother to carry a hymnal, a Bible, and a book of sermons, only to discard them on Christmas Eve? A heretic making a quiet statement? A distraught mourner abandoning his faith? With nothing better to occupy his mind but his own sour thoughts as he paced beside the horses, St. Cloud idly thumbed through the pages. More curious yet, the Bible was written in French, with no inscriptions or dedications. What, then? A spy shedding excess baggage as he fled the authorities?

27

No, a fugitive would have hidden his trail, not left the evidence for the next passerby to find. Furthermore, the French pedestrian could not be a spy; St. Cloud had had his fill of adventure for the day.

The earl chided himself for his flights of fancy, using some poor émigré bastard to take his mind off his own empty pockets and empty stomach.

That poor émigré bastard had food. Midway up the next hill St. Cloud discovered an earthenware jug on an upturned log, with crumbs beneath it that the forest creatures hadn't discovered yet. "Damn," he cursed. The jug was empty, naturally. All that was left was a whiff of cider, just enough to make St. Cloud's mouth water. He stowed the jug under the floorboard, next to the books.

So the Frenchman was too poor for wine, and he was not far ahead. He could read, bilingually, and he was countryman enough not to leave an empty bottle where it could injure a horse and rider. St. Cloud hoped to catch up with him soon and hoped the fellow had something more to eat, to trade for a ride.

The earl stayed afoot, looking for signs of his would-be companion. If he had been mounted or traveling faster, he would have missed the next bundle, a paper-wrapped parcel carefully placed in the crook of a tree.

The earl looked around then, feeling foolish. He shrugged his broad shoulders and untied the string holding the soft package closed. Then he felt even more foolish for the previous observations he'd considered astute. Either the Frenchman was going to have a cold and lonely holiday after abandoning his *chère amie*'s Christmas gift, or the Frenchman was a female. She would come just about to his chin, St. Cloud estimated, shaking out the white velvet, with a delicately rounded figure indeed, he knowledgeably extrapolated. The gown was not up to London standards, though an obviously expensive piece of goods, in good taste and the latest fashion.

Not even St. Cloud's fertile imagination could figure a scenario for a young woman—the gown was white, after all—strewing her possessions about the countryside on Christmas Eve. If this was some local ritual, it was a dashed dangerous one, with shadows lengthening and highwaymen on the prowl.

He rewrapped the parcel and took it to the curricle, where the chestnuts were cropping grass. This time he climbed up and set the pair to a faster pace. The sooner he had some answers, the better—for his own peace of mind and for the woman's sake.

Nothing prepared him for the answers he found around the next bend. Hell, the answers only led to more questions.

The woman trudging ahead was covered head to toe in a gray hooded cape. She carried a tapestry carpetbag over one elbow and an infant slung over her shoulder! What in the world would a mother and child be doing out alone miles from nowhere?

Then she turned to face the approaching carriage as he pulled rein alongside of her, and all rational thought fled from his mind. She was exquisite, with a soft, gentle look to her. Thick eyebrows were furrowed to mix a touch of uncertainty with innocence in her big brown eyes. The babe's head was covered by a blue blanket, reminding him of nothing so much as a Raphael masterpiece. He expected a donkey to trot out of the bushes at any moment to complete the tableau.

Instead the woman noticed her dress parcel on the seat beside him and smiled. "Oh, you found my gown. I was hoping someone would, who could use it." She was well spoken and her voice was low, with no French accent or country inflection.

"Had you tired of it, then, ma'am?" He lifted the books from beneath his feet. "Or these?"

She smiled again, a quicksilver thing, like sun peeking from behind clouds. "You must know it was no such thing, sir. I simply had not realized when I set out how few wagons I would meet along the road, nor how heavy Pansy would seem after a few miles."

"You have been out on the road by yourself for more than a few miles? I would say that is remarkably poor planning indeed," he said in an angry tone. "Almost criminally cork-brained, in fact, considering, ah, Pansy."

Juneclaire took a step back, wondering at this stranger's hostility and wondering what else he thought she could have done about Pansy. As her heavy brows lowered in displeasure, she informed him, "We are not so far from Bramley now, sir, so I shall be on my way."

Bramley was at least two hours away, by carriage, and in the opposite direction from the Priory. St. Cloud cursed under his breath at the idiocy of what he saw before him and at what he was about to do. There was no decision, really. Not even the most stone-hearted care-for-naught could leave a fragile, gently bred mother and her baby on the road alone, afoot, in the dark, on Christmas Eve. Not if he was any kind of gentleman. "I am headed to Bramley myself, ma'am. May I offer you a ride?"

Juneclaire had been hoping for that very thing, but now she was hesitant. The man's accents were those of a gentleman, but he was scowling and speaking as if he thought she enjoyed her difficult situation. Did he think she would have left herself open to insult from every passing sheepherder on a whim? She was not reassured by his travel-stained appearance either. His greatcoat was caked with dust, and his cravat was missing altogether. The carriage was none too neat, and the horses were spent. A gentleman down on his luck, Juneclaire decided, no one she should know. Which was too bad, she regretted, since the dark-haired stranger might be very attractive if only he would smile. She bobbed a shallow curtsy with Pansy still in her arms and said, "Thank you for your kind offer, but it would not be proper for me to accept."

"Not proper? How can you consider propriety at this late date? And even if you were some innocent miss who had to protect her good name at all costs, how could you put such thoughts ahead of her welfare?" He nodded toward the blanketed bundle in her arms.

Now that was unjust! Juneclaire turned her back on him and set off down the road.

St. Cloud cursed the caper-witted female, then drove the chestnuts up to her. He started to get down, but he saw the woman shrink back and glance furtively to either side, as if seeking a way to run. He sat down, hard, his green eyes narrowed. "You're afraid of me," he stated matter-of-factly.

Juneclaire bit her lip. "You are angry."

"I am always angry, ma'am. Now I am enraged. I have been set on and robbed, my groom injured. I have been treated worse than a horse trader at a miserable inn, and my feet hurt. I am tired and hungry and dirty. Soon I will be cold. If that's not enough to try the patience of a saint, which I am not, I come upon a woman in circumstances no female should be forced to endure. *That* makes me furious."

"You are mad for my sake?" Juneclaire asked quietly, disbelievingly. No one had ever taken her part in anything before.

"I have been trained since birth to recognize damsels in distress, ma'am. The books never tell you they are so reluctant to be rescued, nor that

31

they might be more afraid of the knight errant than the dragon. Truly, I only wish to spare you the dangers and discomforts of the road."

He was not looking nearly so fierce, Juneclaire thought, and the holdup could account for his bedraggled appearance. She realized that although his voice bespoke education and refinement, he could still be a plausible villain, but the very idea of highwaymen in the vicinity sent a shiver down her spine.

He saw her tremble and held out his hand. "Come, ma'am. At the rate you were going you would have no possessions whatsoever by the time you reached Bramley. And I don't eat babies, I promise."

She looked down at Pansy and smiled, then took a step closer to the carriage. She had the feeling that her stern-faced savior would not take no for an answer anyway.

"There, why don't you hand the baby up first."

She flashed him a quick grin that was more naughty schoolgirl than dignified matron and lifted Pansy to his waiting arms. The earl had a hard time tearing his eyes off the enchanting sight of her dimples and transferring his gaze to the unfamiliar burden.

"I've never held a—"

Christmas pig.

Chapter Four

St. Cloud threw his head back and laughed. Then he looked at Pansy on the seat beside him, a bristly black-and-white Berkshire pig with stand-up ears, little pink eyes, and a pink snout wriggling up at him. He recalled his promise not to eat her and laughed till tears ran down his eyes.

Juneclaire clambered up and took Pansy in her lap, laughing, too. She was right—he was attractive when he smiled. Actually, he was the most stunningly good-looking man she had ever seen, but since she hardly saw any men except for the farm workers, the vicar, and her uncle, she thought her judgment was suspect. The smile took years off his age and made his green eyes sparkle. He no longer wore that hooded, forbidding scowl, and Juneclaire settled back on her seat, contentment easing her tired muscles.

St. Cloud patted Pansy on the head before giving the horses the office to start. "Thank you for the joke. That was the most fun I've had in years."

"You should laugh more," Juneclaire said, then followed the startling familiarity with an explanation of sorts. "She really is a fine pig, you know, and a very good friend. I've had her ever since Ophelia stepped on her by mistake."

"Ophelia?" His lip quirked. "Never tell me that's the sow? Then the boar must be Hamlet?"

"Of course. It wasn't fair that Pansy should be the runt and lamed, too, so McCade—he's Uncle Avery's head pig man—gave her to me to feed and raise."

"She seems, ah, well behaved, for a pig."

"Oh, she is. And smart and clean, too. I bathe her in buttermilk to keep her hair soft, and then she licks it up for a snack."

"How efficient," he teased, knowing full well what was coming next, with a tenderhearted girl and a tender-meated piglet.

"Yes, well, you can see then how I could not hand Pansy over to the butcher just so Aunt Marta could impress her fine London guests. She wanted a boar's head, the way she thinks things used to be done, but McCade wouldn't part with Hamlet, of course."

"Of course," he solemnly agreed, his eyes on the road so she could not tell if he was bamming her again.

"Then Aunt Marta settled on a suckling pig, with an apple in its mouth, but there were no new litters. It isn't Pansy's fault she's so small, but Aunt wouldn't listen. All she cares about is putting on a show for the toplofty London titles visiting in the neighborhood, without spending a fortune. The peers only come for the party anyway. Those snobs will never accept her in the highest circles no matter what she does, in spite of Uncle Avery's title. Aunt Marta's father was in Trade," she confided.

St. Cloud was suddenly sobered, the habitual frown again marring his fine features. His passenger wasn't a mother, a matron, or a married lady. She wasn't a seamstress or a serving girl. By the Devil's drawers, she was a cursed highborn virgin, a runaway, and a pig thief! Oh Lord, what had he got himself into now? Perhaps if he knew the family, he could just sneak her back with no one the wiser.

"I'm sure your family must be worried about you, Miss . . . ?"

She must have read his intent, for she sat up straighter. "No, they are not. They never did before. And it's Juneclaire. One word."

"Very well, Miss Oneword, I am Merritt Jordan, at your service." He was not about to put notions in her head by mentioning his title. He couldn't bear to see that typical calculating gleam come over her guileless brown eyes. Besides, she seemed to have a low-enough opinion of the shallow Quality already. Heaven knew what she would think of Satan St. Cloud. For some reason her thoughts mattered.

Juneclaire was studying him, fitting his name to the strong planes of his face, the cleft in his chin. "I suppose your friends call you Merry?" she asked doubtfully.

Friends, relatives, acquaintances, everyone called him St. Cloud and had since he was seven. "Only my uncle George used to call me by a pet name. 'Merry Easter, Merry,' he used to say. 'Merry Christmas, Merry.' That's my birthday," he told her, not examining how easily he revealed personal details to this chance-met waif. He doubted if anyone outside his immediate family knew his birthday or cared. And he never mentioned George to anyone, ever.

"How wonderful for you! I suppose Christmas is your favorite day of the year, then."

"Hardly. That's the day Uncle George died."

"Oh, I'm sorry. I didn't know." Juneclaire was upset, thinking sorrow turned his lips down.

"Of course not, how could you? And no, the rest of my doting family does not call me anything half-charming," he went on. He heard the bitterness in his own voice and saw regret in her serious little face. Dash it, the chit felt sorry for him!

The earl quickly turned back to the horses to hide his scowl, but Juneclaire huddled deeper in her cloak, squeezing Pansy to her so hard the piglet squealed in protest. She did not understand this man at all, and his uncertain temper unnerved her.

"I told you I don't bite," he said gruffly, then added, "I would be honored if you called me Merry, if you like. If your chaperon"—a nod toward Pansy—"permits this breach of etiquette. I think the circumstances are such that formal rules need not apply." There, she was smiling again. St. Cloud released the breath he didn't know he'd been holding.

"Thank you. My family calls me Claire, or Clarry. I hate both of those," she confided in return.

"Then I shall never use either," he vowed, again enraged at the way the girl's family seemed to hold this rare treasure in so little esteem, so careless of her feelings and well-being. If she was his . . . sister, he'd be out scouring the countryside. For sure he would have found her before some stranger with who-knew-what on his mind could offer a ride. Or worse. The earl masked his outrage at her poor treatment as best he could, with so little practice at hiding his ill humor. He'd quickly realized his little innocent could be startled by the slightest hint of anger, like some wary forest creature. He made a conscious effort to ease the set muscles of his face into an unfamiliar smile. "I shall call you Junco, then, for a gray-and-white snow bird in the Colonies." He reached over to touch the gray cloak and the white muffler she had wound around her neck. His gloved hand briefly grazed her cheek. "It's not quite the *rara avis* I think you are, but a brave and cheery little fellow. Do you mind?"

Juneclaire shook her head. Then, to hide the color

she knew was rushing to her face at his words, at his touch, she bent to the carpetbag at her feet. "Would you like something to eat, Merry? I have some bread and cheese and—"

"I thought you'd never ask!"

Later, after a silence broken only by the steady beat of the horses' hooves and Pansy's vocal table manners, the now content earl asked, "You do have friends waiting for you in Bramley, don't you?"

He had a hard time holding on to his temper and his new resolve not to look like thunderclouds when she gaily answered, "Why, no, I am just going to meet the coach to London there. I was hoping to make the afternoon mail, but now I shall have to wait for tomorrow morning."

St. Cloud ground his teeth in an effort not to curse. "Tomorrow is Christmas; no coaches will run."

"Oh, dear, I hadn't thought of that."

"I warrant there are a lot of things you hadn't thought of, miss. Do you have enough brass for a respectable hotel? For sure I cannot help you there. The thieves barely left me the lint in my pockets."

Juneclaire suddenly found a need to inspect behind Pansy's ears. The piglet complained loudly, which hid Juneclaire's whispered "No."

"Did you say no? You ran away without enough blunt to hire a carriage or put up at an inn? Of all the cork-brained, mutton-headed ideas, why, I—"

Juneclaire was pressed against the railing at the edge of her seat. St. Cloud took a deep breath and unclenched his jaw. "Forgive me, Junco. I am just concerned for you."

Concerned? He looked ready to strangle her! "The money doesn't matter. I do have enough for my London coach fare and a night on the road, Mr. Jordan, and perhaps an inn in Bramley, although not the finest. But the inns are all filled with holiday travelers, and they don't seem to want unescorted females at any price. Or pigs."

There went St. Cloud's plan to drop her off with some respectable party in Bramley and proceed on his way before anybody recognized him. "Just what had you intended to do, then, if I might ask?"

She didn't like the sarcasm and raised her straight little nose in the air like a duchess. "I intend to sleep under a hedgerow as I did last night, for your information. It's not what I would like, but don't worry, Pansy and I shall manage."

Don't worry? Tell the Thames to stop flowing! Didn't the chit know what kind of villains roamed the roads? Thieves, beggars, gypsies—if she was lucky. Didn't she understand that she was ruined anyway? One night away from home was enough to shred her reputation. One hour in his company had the same effect, and that's how well she managed.

He could make up some Banbury tale about being brother and sister and pray no one recognized him, the chestnuts, or the crest on the side of his curricle. That close to St. Cloud? Hell, he may as well pray the pretty bird-wit turned into a bird in fact and flew off. And her damned pig with her. St. Cloud could hire her a coach and four and send her on her way, except that the banks would be closed, and tomorrow, too! What a coil. For twopence he would take her home, beat some sense into her relations, and be back on his way before midnight. He would, if the chestnuts weren't spent and she did not look so appealing, with her brown curls tumbling around her hood and a crumb on her chin.

"How old are you anyway, little one?" He wondered if he could throw her back, like a too-small fish.

"Not so little. I am nineteen, old enough to be out on my own."

"So ancient." She looked younger, he thought, with that untouched look. She did not have the brittle smile or the coy simper of a London belle years younger. "If you are such a mature age, how is it that you are still unwed? Are the men around here blind?"

"I do not go out in Society, so I do not know many men. But thank you for the compliment, if such it was."

Gads, she couldn't even flirt, and she was going to make it to London? "It was, Junco. But are you in mourning that you had no come-out?" he persisted.

Juneclaire picked at the unfinished hem of her mitten. She'd have the thing unraveled if he did not stop asking his probing questions, but she felt she owed him her answers, for his caring. "My parents died many years ago. Aunt is . . . embarrassed. They ran away, you see, and their marriage was irregular by her standards. But I am not quite on the shelf. Aunt Marta is looking for a husband for me, among the widowers and older bachelors."

No, he would not take her back, even if he knew her direction. He noticed that she was careful not to mention an address or a family name. At least the peagoose had some sense. St. Cloud wondered if she would trust him enough to hand over her coach fare so he could hire job horses and drive her to London himself. It meant a long, uncomfortable night, but he'd had worse and she would be safe, he thought. "Who is it you go to visit in London, Junco? You and Pansy?"

"Mrs. Simms, our old housekeeper. I thought she might find me a position in the mansion where she is employed."

Juneclaire had to grab Pansy to keep the pig

from falling off the seat, so the curricle stopped suddenly, and she was sure the words coming from Mr. Jordan's lips were not meant for a lady's ears. She knew he would have that ugly look on his face, but by now she was confident enough that he was not going to turn violent on her. He simply had a volatile temper, no patience, and a colorful vocabulary. Juneclaire had nearly reached the end of her tether, too, however. "I know my plan is caper-witted," she shouted back at him. "But I have no-where else to go. And not just for Pansy's sake. I'd rather go into service—be a scullery maid or such—than be married off willy-nilly to some overweight sea captain or a snuff-drenched squire whose only conversation is about what animal he killed last. I have no choice! I am not a man, who can join the army or take religious orders or read the law. No one will even teach me a trade! All I have is Pansy. What am I supposed to do?"

Two days on the road had taken their toll on Miss Beaumont's courage. A short tirade against this scowling stranger was the best she could manage before tears started to well in her eyes. Silently St. Cloud handed her a fine lawn handkerchief and then clucked the horses into motion.

That tore it, he conceded. There was no choice but to take the chit to St. Cloud Priory, but heaven knew the little pigeon deserved better than the flock of vultures there. He'd get fresh horses at Bramley one way or another and then turn around. The earl did not know how Miss Juneclaire Oneword was going to accept his high-handed decision. Not well, he guessed from her last burst of indignation. He'd face that hurdle once they reached Bramley.

As a matter of fact, where the hell was Bramley? They had turned off the Thackford road miles back at a cross sign and should have reached the town, he thought, although he did not know the way so well from this direction. "Ah, Junco, is this the road to Bramley?"

"How should I know?" she snuffled into his handkerchief. "I've never been here before."

Chapter Five

They were lost. Juneclaire was glad she could not see her companion's face in the gathering darkness. He was on foot, leading the horses up an uneven dirt track they were hoping led to a farmhouse. So many muffled imprecations came back to her through the cold night, Juneclaire began to wonder if Mr. Jordan had ever been a sailor. He certainly was not a countryman, stubbing his toe on every stone.

"Oh, look," she called out to distract him, "the evening star. Let's make a wish."

"Ouch! Bloody bastard bedrock." She'd distracted him too much. "I wish you to Jericho, Miss Juneclaire—ooph."

The one word he uttered was not even in her mental dictionary, thank goodness. With her breath making clouds in front of her face, Juneclaire stated, "Then I shall have to wish for you. I shall wish for your heart's desire."

"Right now my heart's desire is a hot tub and a warm brandy. If you can produce those, Junco, I shall believe in leprechauns, genies, and brown-eyed goddesses. Otherwise, wishes are for schoolgirls."

She made her wish anyway, not for his bodily

comforts but for his troubled soul. The man might be an aristocrat, but he was not happy. Juneclaire had finally taken a better look at the cut of his coat and the quality of his horses, after she got over being terrorized at his arrogant ill humor. She refused to be embarrassed by her earlier remarks about the nobility, not if he was unabashed at his profanity. He *was* toplofty, refusing to let her go on alone, looking down his distinguished nose at her plans. He was obviously not used to being disagreed with, she thought with chagrin, recalling the row that had ensued when he tried to blame her for getting them lost, as if she should have known to bring a map with her when she left home. He had not demurred when she called him "my lord" either.

No matter, Lord Merritt might have everything in the world he wanted—not at this moment, of course—with no need to make wishes, but Juneclaire thought otherwise. She thought he was so cynical, he'd lost the capacity to believe in miracles. Perhaps he had been disappointed too many times. Juneclaire mightn't have a home or a loving family, a fortune or a settled future, but she still looked for magic. So she made her wish for his inner contentment.

Ice-cold well water for washing and tepid lemonade for drinking were not what Lord Merritt requested, his lowered brows reminded Juneclaire, but she smiled complacently. He was much happier now that they had found this old barn. He even whistled while rubbing down the horses. There were no lights at the farmhouse, but the barn was half filled with workhorses. St. Cloud thought the family must be off visiting for the holiday. He put his chestnuts in a loose box near the end of the row and swept out two other stalls with no signs of recent occupation. There was fresh hay for the horses, straw for their own beds, and a lantern by which to eat the rest of her hoarded food. Pansy was having a wonderful time, rooting around in the corncrib, and Juneclaire was pleased.

"Why are you wearing that Mona Lisa smile, Junco? We are miles from nowhere, with an irate farmer liable to burst in on us at any minute, and our next meal has just eaten more than her fair share of this one."

Juneclaire wasn't worried, since he was scratching behind the little pig's ears while he spoke. "This is a great improvement over sleeping under a bush," she told him, then lowered her eyes. "And I feel safer with you here."

He snorted, or Pansy did. "I daresay I am more protection than the porker, but not much. Some hero I have been. In one day I have gotten myself robbed and lost. I have no money, no pistol, no map, and I am eating your food."

"And you shouted at me."

"That, too. You should be demanding my head on a platter instead of feeding my pride. Any proper hero would have found you a proper bed."

Juneclaire settled into the straw and began to take her hair down. "But you found me just what I wanted. I have always dreamed of staying up all night in a barn on Christmas Eve to see if the animals really do speak at midnight, as the old tales say."

"Do you believe they will?"

She did not notice the way his eyes watched her, green glitters in the lantern's light. "Goodness," she said after removing the mouthful of hairpins to her pocket, "I have no idea and won't until I see for myself. Aunt Marta would never let me, of course. She was petrified that I might find myself

44

alone with the grooms and stableboys. Aunt Marta is a terrible snob, you see."

"I daresay she would be relieved that you are alone with a wellborn rake," he noted dryly.

Juneclaire paused in her efforts to brush her hair out of the thick braids that had been wound into a bun at her neck. "Are you really a rake?"

St. Cloud leaned back in the straw, a reed in his mouth. He watched the way the lantern cast golden highlights through her soft brown hair, way past her shoulders, covering her . . . cloak. He sat up. "I suppose I was, once. Now? Maybe it depends on one's definition. Are you afraid for your virtue?"

She looked like a startled fawn, those brown eyes wide open, thick brows arched high. The thought had never occurred to her. "Should I be?"

The earl had given over thinking of Juneclaire as Madonna-like hours ago. Now he was rearranging his impression of this hobbledehoy waif. The translucent beauty and the purity were still there, but Miss Juneclaire was no child. She was a damned desirable woman. He could think of few things he'd rather do than run his hands through those silky masses or feel her soft lips smile with pleasure under his kisses or—

"No," he answered curtly, getting up to snuff out the lantern. "I don't seduce innocents."

"Oh." Juneclaire could not keep the wistfulness out of her voice. She'd never even met a rake before and was hardly likely to again. She sighed and thought she heard a chuckle from his makeshift bed in the neighboring stall. She must be wrong. Her stone-faced savior was not much given to light humor. "Merry?"

"Yes?"

"Don't you find me attractive?"

That was a definite chuckle, followed by his own sigh. "Very, minx, but I find I am still somewhat

45

of a gentleman. You are under my care, and that means you are safe, even from me. Especially from me. So stop fishing for compliments and go to sleep, Junco. It's been a long day and you must be tired. I am."

He rolled over in the straw. Juneclaire pulled Pansy closer for warmth but did not shut her eyes. She could see starlight through the chinks in the barn's roof. Every now and again one of the horses would stamp its foot.

"Merry?"

He turned around again, bumping his elbow on the wooden partition. "Blast. Woman, do not try my patience."

"But, Merry, I do not wish to sleep. Then I will never know about the animals. Won't you talk to me a bit so I stay awake?"

He grumbled, but she could tell he sat up. "What do you wish to talk about?"

"I don't know. . . . What do you do all day? Usually, I mean, when you are not traveling about the countryside saving silly girls?"

So he told her about his clubs and his wagers, Gentleman Jackson's and Manton's, the House and the War Office, agricultural lectures and investment counselors. He told her about the opera and the theater and balls, thinking that's what a rural young miss might care about. None of it whatsoever seemed interesting to him: neither the telling nor the living. Juneclaire, however, seemed to be swallowing his tales as eagerly as Pansy relished the windfall apples stored in another unused stall.

Juneclaire was thinking that she was right: he was indeed a man of means. His lordship's life was full and glamorous, dedicated to his own pleasure. He was as far above her as the stars overhead. She never felt her lowly status so much as when he asked what she did all day and she had to tell him about going to church and visiting the sick, helping Cook and directing the housemaids, mending and polishing and tending the flower gardens.

St. Cloud thought again of seeing her relations drawn and quartered for turning their own flesh and blood into a drudge. They hadn't managed to ruin her spirit, though, for he could detect the pleasure she derived from her roses and her sugarplums, the pride she took in seeing her aunt's house run well. Juneclaire was a real lady, and a rakehell such as he was not fit to touch her hem.

That did not keep the earl from moving his pile of straw to her side of the partition, though, so they could talk more easily. Juneclaire scrunched over to give him more room. St. Cloud did not want to talk about tomorrow, when he would have to force unpleasant decisions on her, and Juneclaire did not want to discuss the future, when this enchanted interlude would be only a memory to savor. So they talked about the past, the happier times before his father was injured and her father was killed, before his mother turned him over to tutors and hers slipped away. They talked of Christmases past.

"When we were in France, the whole family gathered in the kitchen to stir the Christmas pudding. Did yours?" she wanted to know.

"The children, sometimes. I doubt my mother even knows the way to the kitchen. What about you? Aunt Marta doesn't sound like one to take her turn after the potboy."

"She thinks it's all pagan superstition," she said regretfully, then added, "but I used to sneak down and have my turn anyway. Cook would call for me last, just before it was done."

"And would she put in the ring and the key and the penny? I cannot remember the other charms that were supposed to bring luck or wealth or whatever."

"No, Cook never dared to put the lucky pieces in the pudding she made for the family. I think she made another just for the staff."

"It was rigged in my household anyway. Aunt Florrie always got the little silver horse. She would cry otherwise. Aunt Florrie is not quite right," he explained, wondering if he should also mention his hysterical mother, wayward cousin, devious uncle, blind grandmother. No, he decided. Why chance giving the chit nightmares? And that was without reference to the ghost. He pictured Juneclaire crying out in the night, her hair tumbled over her shoulders, throwing herself into his arms in the straw. He shook his head. Unworthy, St. Cloud. "Oh yes, and once she was permitted at the table, Cousin Elsbeth always managed to receive the piece of pudding with the ring in it. It never helped, for she is twenty and still unwed."

"Then she must not have wished hard enough."

"I suspect it has more to do with her ambitious expectations and her shrewish nature. But I am certain you must have made a wish, fairy child that you are. What did you wish for?" He thought she'd confess to seeking a visit to London, fancy clothes and balls, like Elsbeth.

Suddenly shy, Juneclaire answered, "Just the usual schoolgirl fancies, I suppose." She was not about to tell him that her wish was going to be for a handsome cavalier to rescue her from the corpulent captain or the smelly squire. That had already come true, without her even making the wish! "I know," she declared, changing the subject, "let's make our Christmas wishes anyway. No, not for a hot meal or anything silly like that, but something special, something important. It's supposed to come true by Twelfth Night if you are deserving, so your wish must be for something worth being good."

"Do you mean only the righteous can have their

wishes answered? I thought those were prayers," he teased.

Juneclaire considered. "Being good never hurts."

Oh, doesn't it? he wondered, pondering the ache in his loins to think of the dark-haired beauty not two feet away from him and two lifetimes apart. "You go first."

"I suppose I should wish for an end to the war and peace for everyone."

"No, no. That's being too good. Take it as a given and wish for something personal. After all, it's your one and only Christmas wish, practically in a manger. It's bound to come true, little bird." He reached over and found her hand.

"Do you know what I wish, then? I wish for a place of my very own, where I am wanted and welcome and no one can send me away or make me ashamed to be there."

He squeezed her hand, there in the dark. "I think . . . Yes, I think I wish for fewer people dependent on me, fewer responsibilities, and not having to listen to them tell me what's right for me. Then I mightn't feel so inclined to do the opposite."

They were quiet for a moment, lost in their own thoughts. Then Juneclaire started to hum a Christmas carol, and Merry joined in. They went through all the old songs they knew, English and French. His fine baritone held the tune better than her uncertain soprano, but she knew more of the words. They might have done better the other way around, but the horses and the pig did not complain.

Despite Juneclaire's determination to stay awake, her eyelids were too heavy to hold open when they ran out of songs. She had put in two long, hard days, even for a country girl used to physical exertion and fresh air. They drifted into sleep nestled in the straw, their hands entwined, the pig between them.

49

Chapter Six

*V*oices! It was true! Animals really could—A hand was clapped over Juneclaire's mouth before she could sit up and exclaim over the wonder of it all. The lantern was lighted, so she could see Merry's face inches from her own, scowling at her. He shook his head no. She nodded and he took his hand away but stayed so close, Juneclaire could feel his breath on her cheek. There were miracles and then there were—

"I tell you, Charlie, old man Blaine will have our hides for using his horses."

"Shut up, boy. Who's to tell him? He'll come back tomorrow an' be none the wiser if you bed 'em down proper. Left you in charge, didn't he? 'Sides, it wouldn't do to take my own cob out, now would it? I swan, you got less brains'n a duck, Ned Corbett. Riddles is back in the livery over to Bramley for all the world and his brother to see. For aught anyone knows I'm tucked up tight, and you been here watching the Blaine place all day and night just like you ought to be."

"That last carriage was too close to here, Charlie. Magistrate'll be here in the morning asking questions."

"Not on Christmas Day, he won't. Lord Cantwell

likes his stuffed goose too well. And if he does, you didn't hear nothing anyway. 'Sides, that last coach was a bonus, you might say, for a good day's work. Who'd expect some widder lady to wear all her diamonds to midnight service? Finish up with them horses, boy. I want to divide up the take and be gone."

"I still don't like it. I wish you hadn't gone and hit that groom this morning. He dies and we could hang, Charlie."

"Stop worritin' at it, Ned. We could already hang for highway robbery, boy. What do you think, they hang you twice?"

"And you never said nothing about pulling a gun on no swell."

"What did you expect, boy? His nibs was going to hand over the blunt if we asked him pretty please? You're acting like a bloody schoolmarm."

"I never wanted to go anyways, Charlie. My ma finds out, she'll die."

"You're forgetting why you agreed to help me in the first place. You needed money for medicine, 'member, else she'll die. Sounds like she's going to cock up her toes anyway, may as well go in style."

"You leave my ma out of this, you makebate! She always said you'd end on the gallows, and she was right."

Juneclaire could hear the sound of a scuffle. She moved to poke her head over the wood to see, but St. Cloud quickly held her down with his body across her chest. All she could hear was heavy breathing. No, that was hers.

"Let that be a lesson, boy. No one messes with Charlie Parrett. You just cost yourself an extra yellow boy I was going to throw in for your ma. You'll think twice about giving me lip next time."

"There ain't going to be no next time, Charlie. I ain't going out with you again."

There came the sound of a heavy slap. "You ain't with me, boy, then you're against me. I'd never know when you'd give my name over to Cantwell for the reward money. O' course, the second they take me up, I'll shout your name so loud, your ma will hear even in heaven."

"I wouldn't cry rope on you, Charlie. I just don't want to do it again."

"You already been on the high toby, Ned, so there's no backing down. You don't come with me, I'll have to leave town and this easy-picking territory. Afore I go, naturally, I'd be sure to send a message to Cantwell, asking him where you got the ready for your ma's doctorin'. Now stop your sniveling and take your money, you poor, tender little dewdrop. Why, you're nothing but a whining pansy."

So Pansy went out to investigate. She slipped past St. Cloud while he was still lying across Juneclaire. Juneclaire held him and her breath.

"What's that?"

"What do you think it is, you looby, the lord-high sheriff hisself come to arrest you? It's a bloody pig."

"Farmer Blaine doesn't keep pigs."

The next sound Juneclaire heard was the cocking of a pistol.

After that, a blur. St. Cloud hurtled out of the stall with a shout, and Charlie swung the pistol around. The earl was on the bigger man before the thief could take aim. Ned jumped up, but Juneclaire hit him on the back of the neck with a bucket. The two older men fought for possession of the weapon, one hand each on the gun, St. Cloud's other hand going for Charlie's throat, Charlie's trying to gouge at St. Cloud's eyes. Juneclaire was ready to brain Charlie Parrett with her bucket when she had a clear shot. Ned started for the pitchfork near the door but tripped over Pansy and went down. June-claire hit him over the head again. When she looked up, his lordship and Parrett were rolling on the ground, the pistol between them.

They rolled into the upright where the lantern hung, sending the light flying. Now they struggled in the dark, with harsh panting noises and grunts the only sounds, till Juneclaire heard the crinkly rustle of loose straw catching on fire. Then Ned was rushing by her, stamping at the burgeoning flames. The horses started to kick at the walls of their stalls, and Pansy was squealing. Juneclaire found the other bucket, the one she'd washed with, and tossed the water on the fire. Then she took her cloak off and threw it over the sparks and started stomping up and down on it while Ned scraped the unlit straw away with his hands, leaving just bare dirt that could not burn. Then the pistol went off.

Juneclaire froze in place. Not Merry, she prayed, not even thinking of her own devilish situation if the enigmatic gentleman was hurt. There came the scrape of flint and a tiny glow. Whatever was keeping her knees locked upright, whether bravery, fear, or stupidity, gave out when she saw who lit another lantern. She sank to the ground on top of her wet, charred cloak and hugged Pansy so hard, the pig squealed loudly enough to wake the dead, but not Charlie Parrett.

Ned dashed for the door, to be stopped by an iron-hard clasp on his wrist. The boy made retching sounds, and St. Cloud shoved him toward one of the buckets.

"I guess I should have let him go," he said in disgust, watching Juneclaire hand the boy a hand-kerchief—St. Cloud's own. "Are you all right, Junco?"

"Yes, I think so. The fire is out. And you, my lord?"

"All in one piece, at least." He gingerly explored a bruise on his chin, which, from its feel, would add a less-than-festive touch to his appearance by the morning. Juneclaire thought he looked more human with his hair all mussed and his face dirty. He certainly was more endearing, though she could not go toward him to wipe away the smudges or push the dark curls back off his forehead. Not with Charlie at his feet.

"Is he . . . ?"

"Quite. We've saved the county the price of a trial." St. Cloud dragged the limp figure into one of the empty stalls, out of sight. He came back to poke through the pile of loot. His silver flask went into his greatcoat pocket, along with his fob, gold quizzing glass, and stickpin. He kept his pistol in easy reach and his eye on Ned while he counted out coins and bills. "Of course, this leaves us with a tad of a predicament, my dear, especially since I am sure you wish to be involved with investigations and your name to be brought out at inquests as little as I do. It could be much simpler, really. You know, a falling-out among thieves . . ."

"Merry, you wouldn't, just to save yourself some trouble!"

"Please, my lord, my ma—"

St. Cloud gave the youngster a look that sent Ned back to the bucket. "We heard all about your mother, sirrah. How proud she'd be to see her baby now," St. Cloud said with a sneer. "How much her health would improve to see you hang."

"But, Merry, he's just a boy!" Juneclaire pleaded.

"Just a boy who terrorizes the countryside, robbing and injuring innocent travelers. What about justice, Juneclaire?"

"But it was Charlie who hit your groom. And Ned said he wasn't going to do it again, and he did help put out the fire. And we can give the money back now. What's the justice in hanging a boy who looks after his mother the best way he can? Someone should have been helping them before, the parish or landlord. Then this wouldn't have happened."

St. Cloud had a dark inkling who was the title holder for these miles around St. Cloud Priory, in the vicinity of Bramley. It was only an inkling, mind, so he thought he'd keep it to himself while Miss Juneclaire waxed eloquent. Ned must have appreciated her defensive oratory as well, for he looked up and said, "Thank you, ma'am. It's Miss Beaumont, from Stanton Hall, ain't it? My aunt keeps house for the vicar at Strasmere, and we visited once before Ma took sick. She mentioned a Miss Juneclaire Beaumont, who decorated the church and taught Sunday school to the children."

So much for squeaking though this coil without trumpeting their identities to the countryside, the earl thought, angrily stuffing what he determined his share of the thieves' haul into his wallet. He checked to make sure his pistol was loaded.

"No!" Juneclaire screeched, rushing to put her hand on his sleeve, having correctly interpreted the earl's aggravation if not his intent. "He won't tell anyone I was here, will you, Ned?"

"No, ma'am. Never. I'll do anything you say, my lord."

St. Cloud patted her hand, taking a moment to think. "Very well, Junco, you've won your case. Ned, you'll take Farmer Blaine's horses out again, with a lantern and your friend Charlie. You'll ride to Lord Cantwell's house to head him off from coming here. Tell him you were asleep . . . where? The loft over the cow barn? Fine. You heard a shot, went to investigate, and found this suspicious character dead in the stable, the horses in a lather, a sack of jewels and gold next to him. You don't know anything else, did not see anyone run off, but suspect

55

it was as we mentioned, an argument over the split. The other chap must have shabbed off when the shot woke the house. You had no pistol, so you couldn't give chase.

"That should keep Cantwell happy, with the money returned." The earl fixed Ned with a penetrating stare. "And be assured, bantling, I know exactly how much is left in that sack to be returned to the victims."

"You don't have to worry, my lord, I wouldn't touch a groat. Not now."

"Very well, I believe you. How long should that take?"

"No time at all. Bramley's right over the next rise, around the bend."

St. Cloud called curses down on the vagaries of fate while he searched in his pockets for a pad and pencil. "When you are finished with the magistrate, you will have to ride back to the Fighting Cock. I am sure you can get there and back before morning riding cross-country, even in the dark."

Ned nodded, while St. Cloud tore a page from his book. "The note is for my groom. You needn't see him, just give it to the innkeeper and redeem my signet with the purse I will give you. If you are back here with my ring, say, an hour past dawn, we can forget the whole bumblebroth. If not, young Ned, I will go straight to Lord Cantwell. And you can bet your bootstraps that Uncle Hebert will take my word over yours."

Ned was nodding, swearing on his mother's head that he'd do everything his lordship ordered, as fast as the horses could fly. He'd try to hold back dawn for an hour, too, if his lordship wanted.

"But what *about* his mother?" Juneclaire wanted to know. "They'll be in the same mess."

"I'll see that the mother is taken care of," St. Cloud promised, "if I see the son in the morning."

Juneclaire was satisfied. Her knight's armor wasn't tarnished.

"Oh, by the by, Ned, there is no need to mention me or the lady in any context whatsoever. If, however, someone is looking for her by name, you may inform him or her that Miss Beaumont's fiancé was escorting her to his family home for the holidays when there was a carriage accident."

Juneclaire's contentment shattered into rubble. Her knight's armor must have been made of cheesecloth instead of chain mail, that he received such a grievous blow to the head to addle his wits.

Ned knew there had been no female in the curricle that morning, but he also knew he was lucky to get out of the barn with his skin on. This devil could best Charlie, who was bigger and a dirtier fighter, and he had a look that could freeze a fellow's blood right in his veins. If the swell wanted him to swear, Ned would say his lordship was marrying the pig!

The earl helped the boy take the body out and tie it to one of the horses. Juneclaire tried not to look. She draped her cloak across one of the partitions in hopes it would be dry by morning. Then she started shivering.

When St. Cloud came back, Juneclaire found it the most natural thing in the world that he should hold his arms open and she should walk into them. He wrapped his greatcoat around her, rubbed her back, and feathered kisses on the top of her head until the trembling stopped.

"I'll never be a disbeliever again, Junco," he murmured into her hair, sending shivers through her again, but not from the cold this time. "And you must have been very, very good to compensate for my wickedness, to get our wishes answered so quickly."

"I don't understand." She didn't understand any of the feelings she was feeling either.

"Your wish, Miss Beaumont, for a place of your own. It's cold and dreary, but I'm sure you can change that in jig time with one of your smiles. They work for me, you know."

Juneclaire looked up at him in such muddled confusion, he had to kiss the tip of her nose, which was cold, so he held her closer still. "My house, goose. Your house when we marry."

She pulled back as far as his arms would let her, perhaps a quarter of an inch. "Oh, pooh, you don't have to marry me. I know you were being honorable and all that for Ned's benefit, but he'll never talk. You put the fear of God into him."

"God would be more forgiving if he doesn't get back. And I was not being honorable just for Ned. I am a gentleman, as I keep reminding you. The boy won't talk soon, but someone might see us in the morning, and sooner or later he'd mention your name. You have to be a respectable married lady by then."

"But you cannot want to marry me."

"To be honest, I haven't wanted to marry anyone, but why not you? You are kind and brave and loyal, and handy with a bucket. You're beautiful and you make me smile. What more could I ask? You'll be getting the worst of the bargain, but I need you to make my wish come true."

"All those responsibilities and people dragging at you?"

"Exactly. One of my responsibilities is to produce an heir, and now you'll keep me safe from all the matchmaking mamas and predatory females."

"Silly."

No one had ever called the Earl of St. Cloud silly before. No female had ever fit so perfectly next to his heart before. No matter what he told Juneclaire, he'd known their fates were sealed from the moment she stepped into his carriage and proved to be a lady. The matrimonial noose had been tightening around his neck with every mile until he could barely draw in his last gasps of freedom. Now the idea did not seem so bad, as he whispered reassurances in her ear until she fell asleep in his arms, his greatcoat spread over both of them. The pig whiffled in the corncrib.

Chapter Seven

$\mathscr{T}$he earl awoke to the sound of church bells. The sun was well up, but St. Cloud did not want to disturb Juneclaire by searching out his fob watch. She still slept next to him under the greatcoat, not even the top of her head showing. St. Cloud shut his eyes again to savor the feeling. He almost never woke with a woman in his arms, never caring to stay the night with any of his paramours. Now he thought he might enjoy starting the days this way. Not with unfulfilled desires, naturally, but a special license would take care of that problem. He expected the other, the feeling of comfort and joy, just like the old carol they sang last night, to last for the next fifty or sixty years. God rest ye merry gentlemen.

Time didn't matter anyway. St. Cloud was already long overdue at the Priory, and Juneclaire had no coach to catch in Bramley, even if they were running. And the boy had returned. He could hear Ned whistling about his tasks and jingling harness. Tactful lad.

St. Cloud wondered what Juneclaire would be like in the mornings. Some women, he knew, were querulous if roused early. Not even the earl dared approach the dowager Lady St. Cloud until Grandmother had her fortifying chocolate. Others, like his cousin Elsbeth, were vain of their looks until safely in their dressers' hands, and his mother had to lie abed all afternoon if forced to bestir herself before noon. Junco was not temperamental, conceited, or missish. St. Cloud could not wait to find her reaction to being kissed awake like Sleeping Beauty. He himself woke up amorous.

He raised the coat to stroke her smooth cheek—and his hands touched hair more bristly than his own side-whiskers. His eyes jerked open to stare into little red-rimmed beady ones, with absurdly long white eyelashes.

St. Cloud jumped up. Pansy jumped up. St. Cloud shouted: "What the hell!" And the pig raced off with a piercing whee that sounded like the gates of hell swinging shut.

"Stop that, you confounded animal," the earl ordered. "You weren't hurt, so quit overplaying your part, you ham. Your mistress must be out talking with Ned, so you're wasting your time trying to get sympathy." St. Cloud felt he was the one who deserved pitying, denied the pleasure of waking his bride-to-be. On his way out of the barn he tossed Pansy an apple saved from Juneclaire's hoard the night before. "There, and don't tell anyone I tried to kiss a pig good morning!"

Juneclaire wasn't polishing tack with Ned. She must be using the convenience, or be out by the pump, washing. This would be the last time in her life she'd use icy water or sleep on the ground, St. Cloud vowed.

Ned jumped off the upturned barrel and touched his cap. Then he fumbled in his pocket and withdrew St. Cloud's ring. "Here, my lord. I was back by first light, I swear, but you didn't say nothing 'bout waking you up."

The earl could see that the curricle was clean and

shining in the wintry sun. The boy must have been back for hours, working outside in the cold. "Thank you," he acknowledged, nodding toward the equipage, and Ned blushed with pride. He was no more than twelve or thirteen, St. Cloud saw now by light of day, though tall for his age. He shouldn't have been out riding the roads all night, damn it, but he shouldn't have been mixed up with highwaymen either.

"Did you have any trouble?" the earl asked.

"Nary a bit. That widder lady went back toward Bramley, and the innkeeper sent her to Lord Cantwell at High Oaks to report the robbery. She was still kicking up a dust over to the manor. Magistrate was having to give her hospitality for the night, it seems, 'cause she was too afrighted to go back on the roads and had no money for the inn. He was right pleased to see me with the widder's purse and sparklers, I can tell you that."

"And what did he say about Charlie?"

"He said good riddance to bad rubbish, is what. Charlie'd been poaching up at High Oaks for as long as I can remember, only Cantwell's man could never catch him. His lordship being magistrate and all, he had to have proof. Charlie Parrett was too smart for that."

"If he was so smart, he should have stuck to poaching instead of going on the high toby."

Ned scuffed his worn boots in the dirt. "I reckon. Anyways, Charlie was right about his lordship and his Christmas dinner. Magistrate said he'd come out tomorrow to look over the place. No hurry today, with Charlie dead and the killer long gone, he said. And the widder had her money back, so he could stop her caterwauling and send her on her way before she curdled the cream for his pudding. Takes his supper serious, Lord Cantwell does."

"Very well, and if you just volunteer as little information as possible when he does arrive, the whole thing should blow over shortly. You can play dumb, can't you?"

The boy grinned at him. "Seems I've had a heap of practice, my lord."

"Quite. And did you do as well at the Fighting Cock?" He hadn't put his ring on yet, just turned it in his hand. "Did that innkeeper give you any trouble?"

"Nary a bit, once he saw the brass. And I saw your groom, too." Ned looked away. "I wanted to make sure he was, you know, not mangled or nothing. He was sitting in the taproom, happy as a grig, Wilton's daughters making a fuss over him on account of the bandage on his head. Said he slept the day through, then woke up for supper right as rain. He was glad to get your letter, I could tell, and wanted particular to know the horses was safe."

"Trust Foley to care more for the chestnuts than for me."

"Prime 'uns they are for true. I brushed them down quietlike this morning while you were sleeping. But he asked about you, too. Said he didn't recognize me a bit, so I was thinking I was home free, till he wanted to know why I wasn't wearing livery, and if I wasn't from the Priory, where'd I meet up with you and where'd you get the blunt to pay his shot and hire him a carriage. I didn't know what you wanted me to say, him being your man and all, so I did what you said just now and played dumb. He thinks I'm stupider'n a rock," Ned complained, "what doesn't even know its way home." He paused to look up at the man who towered over him. "Is it true you're St. Cloud? The earl hisself, who owns half the county?"

St. Cloud cursed. He wished Foley's head had

been hit just a mite harder. "I am the earl, yes, but nowhere near as wealthy as all that."

The boy whistled through his teeth. "St. Cloud hisself," he marveled. "And I brushed your horses. Wait till I tell Ma."

"You'll tell her nothing of the sort," the earl ordered, but knew the boy would burst if he didn't tell his mother, so tacked on, "until I am long gone. You'll have to figure a way to tell her without mentioning the robbery. A carriage accident, I think, and you helped. That way you can explain about the money for her doctor." He flipped the boy two gold coins. "But don't mention the lady with me."

Ned looked confused. "The lady?"

"Excellent, boy. You'll have that rock perfect yet. Now tell me, did you send Miss Beaumont to the farmhouse to freshen up? We should be on the road soon, lest Cantwell decide to do his civic duty between meals after all."

Ned was shaking his head no, and St. Cloud suddenly felt an emptiness in the pit of his stomach that had nothing to do with hunger. "She's not at the house?" He raced around the barn to the well, Ned and Pansy on his heels. St. Cloud spun back and grabbed the boy's thin shoulders. "Tell me you gave her directions to a stream or something where she's gone."

White-faced, Ned shook his head again. "She . . . she wasn't here when I came back, sir. I thought you knew."

The earl ran back to the barn to search the stalls in case she woke up and realized the impropriety of sleeping next to him. Maybe he snored. Maybe . . .

Her things were gone, except for Pansy and the blue blanket. And a page from his notepad, stuck on a nail in the stall where they'd slept. St. Cloud sank down on a bale of hay while he read.

Dear Merry, Happy birthday and Merry Christmas. You are an honorable man, and under other circumstances I would be proud and happy to be your wife. Circumstances were such that I feel I can call you Merry, instead of Lord Jordan or whatever your title, but I cannot marry you. I cannot take advantage of your nobility and generosity and am therefore leaving. I have nothing to leave you for a Christmas gift or to thank you for your kindness, except that I might help grant your Christmas wish after all. Now you shall have one less responsibility, one fewer persons hanging on your sleeve.

For your birthday I am giving you Pansy. I cannot travel well with her, and she would not be happy in London, but that is not why I am leaving her with you. She is a very smart pig, and I know you will care for her, but mostly she will make you smile. I defy any man to be a sobersides with a pig as a companion. She likes sticky buns and having her ears scratched, but I expect you already know those things.

I have borrowed five shillings, so you do not need to worry about my reaching London. I shall return them to you in care of the postmaster at Bramley as soon as I am able. I regret taking them without your permission, but you would have argued about my decision to leave, and I could not bear to see you angry again. I shall remember you sleeping instead. Thank you for your kindness and best wishes to you. Sincerely, Juneclaire Beaumont.

St. Cloud cursed and threw his ring across the barn, the ring he was going to give her as proof that *her* Christmas wish was coming true. Pansy chased it, chuffing at the new game, nosing in the straw until she found it.

"Botheration," he raged. "The blasted animal will likely eat the damn thing and choke. Then Junco will have my head for sure." As he traded the last apple for his ring, St. Cloud realized he was thinking of Miss Beaumont in the future, not the past. Never the past, gone and forgotten. He was going after her.

He wiped his slimy, gritty ring on his sleeve—the once elegant greatcoat was ready for the dustbin after these two days anyway—then put it on his own finger, until he found Juneclaire and could place it on hers. After he strangled the chit.

"Fiend seize it, she must have been gone for hours! She could be halfway to London by now if Bramley is as close as you said." The boy nodded from the doorway, miserably aware that he should have awakened the gentleman ages ago. He wiped his nose on his shirtsleeve, to his lordship's further disgust. The earl stomped back to the stall where his pistol and his flask lay.

"After all my efforts to keep her out of this scandalbroth," he growled, "she has to go make mice feet of her reputation. The Devil only knows what she'll say about Charlie Parrett or you."

Ned was inching along the railing in the barn, not sure whether to flee his lordship's wrath or stay to take the pig home after the furious gent butchered it. Ma'd be right pleased to have fresh ham for Christmas dinner and bacon for Easter. Mention of Charlie Parrett stopped him in his tracks. "Me? You think she'll go to the magistrate and turn me in?" His voice was so high, it cracked. "But she didn't want to last night."

"No, brat, she won't peach on you on purpose. She's got bottom. But if she comes from this way, the good citizens in Bramley are bound to ask if she saw anything. And how is she going to explain being on her own? And if I go after her, there are certain to be more questions."

"Naw, no one'd dare quiz a fine swell like you." Ned didn't mention that most of the villagers would run inside and slam their doors rather than ask such a fierce-looking, arrogant nobleman what he was doing in their midst.

St. Cloud was pacing the length of the barn, the piglet trundling after. He was talking more to himself than to Ned, who was filling buckets for the horses. "But if they don't talk to me, I'll never find out where she went. And if I don't give some answers, they'll make them up. I know village life; it's the same as London gossip. No, I'll have to hope no one recognizes me."

"What about your uncle Hebert, the magistrate? He has to know you."

"Prosy old puff-guts always hated me, too. He's not even a real relation, just by marriage, his sister to my uncle. The dastard's bound to ask a lot of questions."

"Like what happened to your face."

"I haven't even seen how bad it looks." The boy's grimace told him. "A carriage accident."

"And where did you sleep?"

"Under a hedge."

"And what were you doing Bramley way, when everyone knows the Priory is clear west and north?"

St. Cloud started leading out the chestnuts, and Ned ran to help. "I was meeting Miss Beaumont to escort her to my home. And if anyone asks where is my groom or her maid and how did I mislay a female in my care, I'll tell them it's none of their deuced business. Especially not Hebert Cantwell's."

Ned whistled, impressed in spite of himself. "Guess it's no wonder they call you Satan St. Cloud, telling all those bouncers, and on the Lord's birthday, too! But they're going to wonder all the same, a top-of-the-trees gentleman like yourself all mussed up and Charlie Parrett laid out dead. What'll you say if anyone asks if you killed him?"

"The truth, brat, that he was such a bungler, he shot himself with his own pistol."

Chapter Eight

*J*uneclaire was on her way out of Bramley before St. Cloud was aware she was gone.

How silly he was, she had thought on the short walk toward the village earlier that morning, as soon as the cock crowed in predawn light. How silly and how sweet, to think about saving her from gossip. But ruination was only for ladies of the ton, not poor females. Indigent misses could not afford to worry overmuch about their good names, not when they had to consider their next meal. As for Juneclaire, she had no name to speak of, so how could she lose it? Her aunt already considered her no better than she should be because of her parents' marriage. She made it plain no respectable man would have Juneclaire to wive without good reason.

Merry, Lord Jordan, though, with all his talk of heirs and London, was Quality. He was of the ton, and he respected Juneclaire enough to offer marriage when he need not at all. He thought she was good enough to bear his own name, bear his children. No one else's opinion mattered.

He said she was beautiful and brave. The thought kept her warm on the way to Bramley. She was not feeling very courageous, once wagons and carriages started passing her, local people on their way to church dressed in all their finery, staring at the outsider. She was truly alone now, without even Pansy to talk to, to watch out for. Her own solitary state seemed much magnified without the little animal, now that she was coming among strangers. Merry would look after Pansy, she assured herself, before she fell into a fit of the dismals with missing her companion. The pig, not the man, she tried to convince herself. He was a real gentleman—the man, not the pig—so Pansy would be safe. Juneclaire did not think he'd bring that formidable temper of his to bear versus an innocent creature. Not that his ill humors were a sham, she admitted, but they seemed more an ingrained habit than from genuine meanness. He was kind. He had been mostly gentle with her and more than fair with Ned. He was concerned about his groom and worried that his people were fretting at his late arrival. He was a good man. He wasn't appreciated by his relatives either, which was just about the only thing he and Juneclaire had in common, besides a night in the barn. Her mind had come full circle. That was enough to dream about, not enough to marry on.

"Do you need a lift into town, miss? Bells are starting to toll." An old couple in an antique tilbury had pulled up alongside her while she was wool-gathering. "I be Sam Grey," the man said, "and this be my Alice."

Alice took in the odd condition of Juneclaire's cloak, as well as the quality of its cut and fabric. Juneclaire felt those old eyes missed nothing, not her tapestry bag, the muddied half boots, or the mismatched mittens. Juneclaire bobbed a curtsy, lest these good people think her manners as ramshackle as her appearance, and smiled. "A happy day to you, sir, ma'am. I am Juneclaire Beaumont, and I would be delighted to accept your kind offer."

Alice smiled back at Juneclaire's pretty behavior and moved over on the seat. Her black dress crinkled as she moved, so starched it was. She had a new green bow on her black ruched bonnet, and Sam wore a sprig of holly in his lapel. "Can't think what folks is about," he groused now, clucking the equally ancient horse into motion, such as it was, "passing a little gel like you up on the way to church, and this being a holy day and all."

"You know what it is, Sam, what with highway robberies and shootings, folks think they can't trust anyone. Little Bramley has never seen the like. Our Johnny brought the news this morning, Miss Beaumont. Such goings-on."

Juneclaire only had to nod and exclaim "How terrible" a few times while Sam and Alice speculated on the unmourned demise of Charlie Parrett. Sam spit over the side of the carriage. "Should end any of this bobbery about a gang of footpads in the neighborhood. Charlie Parrett was ringleader, mark me, and you'll see no more lawbreaking roundabouts, and a sight more rabbits and grouse on Lord Cantwell's estate, to boot." He laughed and coughed and spit again.

Alice patted his hand, then turned to Juneclaire. "A nice young lady like yourself hadn't ought to be alone on the roads during such uncertain times."

There was no censure in Alice's remark, just a great deal of curiosity. Juneclaire knew her face would turn red if she tried to lie to this shrewd little woman, and her tongue would twist itself in knots. It always did, so she told the truth. "I have no choice, for I had to help a friend in need, and my own situation was intolerable, so I am going to London to seek a position. I have coach fare and a bit extra."

Sam spit again but Alice tsked. She didn't know about any friend, but she could imagine what kind

71

of trouble bedeviled such a pretty gal. "Well, you won't find the men are any different in London, Miss Beaumont. I can tell you, for Sam and I were in service at one of the great houses for years, we were, till the master pensioned us off and we came here. I suppose you have references and appointments and friends to stay with till you are settled?"

Juneclaire stared at her mittens, wishing the right one could grow an inch up the cuff. "No, ma'am, just the address of our old housekeeper. I was hoping she might—"

"Without references? You must have come down with the last rain, Miss Beaumont. And if Bramley sounds bad, with talk of highwaymen and poachers and murderers, you should see London. There's cutpurses on every corner, and that's not the worst of it. Why, a pretty girl like you would get swallowed up the second your foot touched pavement. There are folks there who meet the coaches looking for just such ones as yourself. They offer the little country girls jobs and rooms and rides—and do you know where the girls end up?"

Juneclaire didn't, but she could guess. Aunt Marta had preached about the fleshpots of the city often enough. Feeling slightly ill, Juneclaire thanked Mrs. Grey for her warning. "Now I shall know better how to go on."

"You've never been in service, have you, dearie?" Alice guessed, shaking her head.

"Not that I ever got paid for, no. But I cannot go back. Pansy—"

While Juneclaire was realizing that she no longer had to worry about Pansy's future, Mrs. Grey was bemoaning a world where gently bred females—and she did not hesitate to declare Miss Beaumont a lady—had to leave home and hearth to see their virtue intact. Alice didn't doubt this Pansy had been seduced and abandoned by some rakish lordling or other, and Miss Beaumont was next.

"Don't fret, missy, I'll talk to Mrs. Vicar Broome right after service. She knows everything that's going on in the parish, so she'll find you a ride toward Springdale. That's the next closer coaching stop to London, and folks in Bramley have lots of relatives there. Someone's bound to be going off for Christmas dinner. And we'll fix you up with some kind of letter of introduction. I still have lots of friends in London, though I wish there was another way."

During Reverend Broome's reading of the Nativity, Juneclaire thought about another way. Would she rather be a servant in someone else's household or a drudge in her aunt's? Servants got paid pittances, barely enough to repay Merry's loan, and that was assuming she found a position at all. Back with the Stantons, though, she did have a room of her own, the use of Uncle's library, all the food she wanted to eat—and no strangers whispering about her in church.

She knew she was an object of speculation, but she would have been horrified to hear her tale so embroidered. By the time Mrs. Broome had pressed a hot roll and a shilling into her hand, Juneclaire was escaping a ravening monster and ravishment. Pity the man who pursued Miss Beaumont to the hitherto peaceful little village.

Juneclaire was bustled toward Mr. Josiah Coglin, who was waiting with his wife and daughters for their coach to be brought round from the inn. The owner of the mercantile and his family were bound for Springdale, where Mr. Coglin's brother ran a similar enterprise. Mr. Coglin was all sympathy to Juneclaire's plight, quickly whispered into his ear by the efficient Mrs. Broome. Of course, the vicar's wife would never be indelicately explicit, but Mr. Coglin got the idea. So did Mrs. Mavis Coglin, who thought the drab little chit with heavy eyebrows must have invited any insults, since her looks had nothing to recommend her. Mrs. Coglin saw no reason to chance such a questionable miss with her own blond-haired, blue-eyed angels, or her husband. Miss Beaumont could ride on the seat with the driver and footman, she declared, lest the ladies' skirts get crushed. Further, if the chit wished to go into service, she'd better learn her place.

Juneclaire clutched her carpetbag in one hand—no one offered to take it for her—and waved goodbye to the Greys and Mrs. Broome with the other. Once the Coglin ladies were settled inside, the grinning footman took his seat, nearer to Juneclaire than she could like. She was already pressed against the coachman on her other side, and that man's watery eyes were more on her than the horses.

Could Stanton Hall be worse than this?

They stopped at an inn about an hour later when the younger Miss Coglin complained of queasiness. The footman, whose name Juneclaire had learned was Scully, hopped down smartly to lower the steps. All the while he was handing out the ladies and Mr. Coglin, he kept his leer on Juneclaire, hoping to catch a glimpse of ankle when she clambered down from the box without assistance. Mrs. Coglin turned her back on Juneclaire with a flick of her ermine tippet and demanded a private parlor, instantly. Mr. Josiah Coglin looked back at Juneclaire with a shrug of regret, either for his wife's manners or for missing a pretty sight.

Juneclaire brought her satchel, thinking she might take the opportunity to freshen up, but the innkeeper's harried wife was quick to direct her toward the kitchens, where the help ate.

"I am not a servant," Juneclaire stated. "Not yet,

74

at any rate." And she vowed never to accept employment with such jumped-up mushrooms. She took a seat at a window table in the common room so she could see when the carriage was ready to leave. Mrs. Coglin might just forget her guest the same way she forgot to invite her to share the early nuncheon her strident voice was demanding.

When Juneclaire managed to get the attention of the serving girl, she asked for tea and a quick snack. The maid, who looked none too clean and none too happy to be waiting on a solitary female who looked as if she hadn't a feather to fly with, took her not-so-sweet time before plunking down a tepid pot of tea, a watery egg, dry toast, and a rasher of bacon. Bacon! To keep the tears from her eyes, Juneclaire looked about the room at the other travelers. To her right was a large, noisy family whose children never stayed in their seats long enough to count. One small girl toddled over to Juneclaire, so she gave her the bacon, receiving back a runny-nosed, gummy grin. To her left snored two sheepherders, judging from their smell, with their heads on the table. Across the way was a party of loud young men still on the go from last night's wassail or this morning's ale.

One of the men was looking at her the same way Scully had looked at her, and she felt dirty again. She left a coin on the table and went to find a place to wash.

The innkeeper's wife met her in the hall and thrust a tray into her hands. "Here, you may as well be useful. Bring this in to your mistress." She jerked her head toward an oak-paneled door and bustled back toward the kitchen before Juneclaire could repeat, "But I am not a servant."

The tray had a steaming pot of tea, lovely biscuits, and golden currant buns. Juneclaire sighed.

She tapped lightly on the door, balancing the heavy tray in one unaccustomed hand, and went in.

"Put it there," Mrs. Coglin directed, again not offering to share the room or the food with Miss Beaumont. She didn't say "Thank you" either. Even Aunt Marta, the worst snob Juneclaire had ever known prior to this, always said "Thank you." She might pay her staff nipfarthing wages and treat them as interchangeable mannequins, but she always said "Please" and "Thank you."

Juneclaire demonstrated her own manners and breeding in inquiring as to the health of the younger Miss Coglin. That beribboned miss did not answer, too busy cramming biscuits into her rosebud mouth as fast as her dimpled fingers could snatch them away from her sister. Juneclaire turned to go, declining to curtsy.

"You can take this with you," Mrs. Coglin instructed, indicating yet another tray. This one held a single glass and a bottle of some reddish restorative cordial. Juneclaire thought of refusing, of giving her oft-repeated line like a bad drama, but then she thought of the miles to Springdale. She took up the tray.

Scully was coming out of the kitchens, wiping his mouth, when he spotted Juneclaire in the dark hallway with her hands full. Before she could begin to guess his intent, he grabbed hold of her and was slobbering damp kisses on her neck and cheek as she struggled to avoid his mouth on hers.

"Come on, pet, it's Christmas. Give a fellow a kiss now."

It was all of a piece that such a self-inflated shopkeeper as Mrs. Coglin would have a loose screw for a footman. Juneclaire didn't have a darning needle about her person, so she pushed at him, but he was too strong. Or the ale he'd been drinking was.

"What's the matter, lovey? Who're you saving it

for? That last gent couldn't've been any good if he sent you on the road. Scully'll show you a better time."

What Scully showed her was that he was bigger, so she'd better be quicker. Scully was Mrs. Coglin's servant; let *him* carry the blessed restorative, drip by sticky, sugary, reddish drip. Down his face, down his shirt, down his ardor.

Now she couldn't go on with the Coglins.

Juneclaire fetched her bag and left the inn just as that noisy family was departing. A gaunt woman with an infant in her arms was trying to herd her brood onto the back of an open wagon half filled with boxes and bundles and two chickens in a crate. The father chewed on the stem of his pipe and patted the workhorses hitched in front while he waited. The patient beasts' noses were pointed west, toward Strasmere, toward Stanton Hall.

"Pardon, sir, but could I ride along with you for a bit? I can pay my way, and I won't mind sitting in the back with the children."

Juneclaire was going home. Uncle Avery would never let her be thrown on the dole, and Aunt Marta would just have to take her back. It might be too optimistic to hope Lady Stanton would appreciate her niece more, now that she had a day or two of running the Hall by herself, but no matter. Juneclaire was good at it. What she wasn't good at, it seemed, was facing the world on her own. She wasn't quite that brave, no matter what Merry thought.

Despite what she saw as a grievous flaw in her character, and a disappointment to Merry if he should find out, Juneclaire was determined not to be cowed by her relations. She would *not* marry a fusty old man of her aunt's selection, not after turning down the most handsome, most intriguing rake in England. She would *not* be harassed by her cousins, not after routing Scully, and not after spending a night safe and unafraid in the arms of a true gentleman.

Juneclaire pulled the little runny-nosed moppet toward her and curled up on the hard wooden wagon bed, her satchel under her head as a pillow. She'd just rest after her adventures, and she would *not* cry.

Chapter Nine

St. Cloud thought he'd leave the pig. Then he thought of trying to convince Miss Beaumont that he was a worthy candidate for her hand without that blasted pig in his. There was no way he could look into those soulful brown eyes and tell her that he'd found Pansy a good home. Not when he was bound to recall Ned's thin frame and hungry, hopeful expression every time the boy glanced at the porker.

Then the earl had to consider that he couldn't spring the horses without seeing if pigs really could fly. Those little trotters weren't meant for clinging to a swaying bench going sixteen miles an hour, nor was St. Cloud willing to dawdle. Neither could he manage the chestnuts, fresh as they were, with one hand.

Rope, that's what he needed. Ned almost lost his front teeth, grinning at the impatient nobleman, but he did fetch a coil of hemp. St. Cloud made a harness of sorts, looping the rope under Pansy's legs, across her belly, and over her chest, around her neck, meeting in a sailor's knot on her back. The other end was snubbed to the arm rail, over Pansy's vociferous protests. The shoat was even more unhappy when, not three yards from the barn

79

door, she slid off the seat to dangle inches from the wheels, all four feet kicking in the air. The volume of noise coming from the baby swine was far out of proportion to her size and was only equalled by St. Cloud's curses.

"Is there a crate around, boy?" he demanded of Ned, who was thrilled to be enlarging his vocabulary. Ned shook his head, then learned a few more new words.

St. Cloud gave up. He unbuttoned his greatcoat and stuffed the piglet into his waistcoat. Pansy stopped complaining immediately. The earl rebuttoned all but two middle buttons of the outer garment so Pansy could stick her snout out and breathe. No one in London would believe this.

No one in Bramley would either.

It had surely been an eventful Christmas morn in the little village: that widow screeching about highwaymen, then Charlie Parrett riding in facedown, and a slip of a thing running off to London to save herself from a fate worse than death, now this bedlamite. The fellows brimming with Christmas cheer in the inn's taproom couldn't decide if the raggedy chap with the thunderous look was Charlie's killer and confederate, a rapist, or just a raving maniac. Then the hostler who led the horses away reported a well-known crest on the curricle. Worse yet, he was Satan St. Cloud.

Now, coincidences were one thing, but not one of the men gathered at the bar doubted for an instant that all the day's unlikely events circled around this nasty-looking nobleman like steel bits near a magnet. From his reputation and the ugly bruise on his face, they assumed he'd helped Charlie Parrett to the big poaching preserve in purgatory. From his reputation and his query about a missing young lady, they knew he was bent on having his way with the chit. Not in Bramley, he wouldn't, not when jobs were scarce and prices were high, with him closing down the old quarry and shutting down the wood mill, and half the farmers paying him rent without ever getting to speak their piece about repairs or crops. They dealt with his uncle or his agents, and that wasn't half-right. St. Cloud sure wasn't going to be helped in his hellraking, not when many of the local families sent their girls to the Priory to be maids and such. Not even rounds for the bar loosened tongues.

They drank his ale and watched out of the corners of their eyes when he poured his mug into a saucer and fed it to the pig. His reputation or not, none of them could figure out about the pig. None of the locals had any truck with the gentry anyway; queerer than Dick's hatband, all of 'em.

St. Cloud ordered breakfast for two and carried his mug and the pig's dish over to a table to wait, to think about his next move. On the way, he saw himself in the cracked mirror over the bar—and shuddered. Black hair sticking at all angles, purple bruises on his cheek and chin, no cravat whatsoever, and two days' growth of dark beard—it was no wonder the sots at the bar wouldn't give him the time of day. They most likely thought he'd steal it from them! In London the earl shaved morning and evening, bathed at least as often if he was riding or boxing or fencing, and changed his clothes from buckskins to pantaloons to formal knee breeches without a second thought. His valet, Todd, was liable to go off in an apoplexy if he saw the earl in such a state. Then he'd quit.

The citizens of Bramley might be more forthcoming if he didn't look like Dick Turpin, and he'd feel better, too, the earl decided after a satisfying breakfast of beefsteak and kidney pie, potatoes, hot muffins, and coffee. Pansy did not care for the cof-

fee, so he drank hers also. Then he addressed the
landlord about a room to wash and shave in. Money
still opened some doors, he was relieved to note,
although he was forced to rent the room for a day
and night, payment in advance. No amount of
money was going to see Pansy up the innkeeper's
stairs, so St. Cloud tied her to his chair and tossed
a coin to the barkeep to keep her ale flowing.

There wasn't much he could do about the bruise.
Todd would have some concoction to cover it up, but
he was at the Priory, likely steaming imaginary
wrinkles out of St. Cloud's evening attire. And
there was no hope for the caped greatcoat. It would
have to be burned. St. Cloud could wash, at least,
and didn't cut himself too badly with the borrowed
razor. The serving wench who brought the hot water managed to find a cravat somewhere, likely
some other guest's room, he didn't doubt from the
way she quickly tucked his coin down her bodice.
There, now he felt presentable again.

The maid must have thought so, too, for she
stayed to admire the earl's broad shoulders and cleft
chin.

"I don't suppose you know anything about a
young woman wearing a gray cloak, do you?" he
asked her, thinking she might be interested in talking.

That's not what Betty was interested in at all.
She shook her head. Foolish chit, refusing the likes
of this top drawer. So what if he looked like storm
clouds, he was generous, wasn't he? A girl could do
worse. "Why don't you stay the night and I'll ask
around? Maybe I'll find something out, or maybe
you'll forget about looking. The room's paid for
anyways."

The earl smiled at her, if you could call a cold
half sneer by that name, and walked by her without commenting. Something in his bleak look made

82

Betty call after him, "I heard she came through town early, but she never came by the inn that I saw. You might try the church."

St. Cloud didn't know if the suggestion was for the sake of his immortal soul, his manhood, or his quest for Juneclaire, but he had nowhere else to try.

He gathered up a sleeping pig, a sack of potato peelings and yesterday's muffins, and proceeded to the church.

The second Christmas service was in progress; maybe Juneclaire was inside praying. He eagerly stepped over the threshold, then halted. Not even the Earl of St. Cloud would bring a pig to church. Pansy barely roused when he tied her to the hitching rail outside, between a dappled mare drowsing over a feed bag and a fat, shaggy pony harnessed to a cart decorated with greenery and red ribbons. St. Cloud scattered a few muffins near the piglet just in case she woke up hungry—she always woke up hungry; in case she woke up, period—and fed one to the pony. Then he went into the little church and took a seat near the rear.

Now Merritt Jordan was not one for practicing religion on a regular basis, but never since his school days had he sat on bare wooden pews with the reprobates and recalcitrants avoiding the preacher's eye. He scowled, and his neighbors on the bench scooted over. That was one benefit of two days in the same clothes, he told himself, and sharing them half that time with a pig. Now he was free to stare at the backs of the worshipers ahead of him, those too well bred to turn around to look at the latecomer.

There was Cantwell in the first pew, the one with the carved aisle piece. St. Cloud wagered old Hebert's fat behind wasn't on any hard bench. He'd have soft cushions for himself and his family while

83

the rest of the congregation, his people, wriggled and writhed in discomfort. Cantwell's wife was the broad-beamed lady beside him with the stuffed white bird mounted on her bonnet. What kind of hypocrite killed a dove for Christmas? he thought maliciously, flicking his gaze over the rest of Cantwell's party: two washed-out blond misses, a sandy-haired youth.

The earl studied each rear view in the church. There were five ladies with gray mantles, but two had gray hair, one had black, another was suckling an infant under the cloak, and the last one's head barely reached over the pew in front. Of the brunets, in case Junco had removed her cloak, only one was of the right height and slimness, with erect posture and neatly coiled braids. He stared at the woman's back, willing her to turn around. She did and gave him a wink from one of her crossed eyes.

The minister was stumbling over "the Lord coming among us this day," and the choir was singing the final hymn. St. Cloud turned his back to study the stained-glass windows as the parishioners filed out after the recessional. When the foot shuffling and whispers had passed, the earl turned and approached the doorway, where the vicar was shaking the last hands.

"A word with you, Reverend, if you don't mind? I'll only take a minute of your time."

Mr. Broome nodded, pushing the spectacles back up his nose. He led the way back down the church aisle and out a side door to a covered walk leading to the manse.

When they were seated in the vicar's office, the earl declined a politely offered sherry, knowing the reverend must be wishing him to the Devil, with his Christmas dinner growing cold.

"To be brief, sir, I was told you might have information about a young woman passing through here this morning."

Mr. Broome polished his glasses. The earl ground his teeth. When the spectacles were wiped to the gray-haired man's satisfaction, he looked up at his caller and asked, "And who might you be?"

The earl was trying his damnedest to hold his temper in check. "Merritt Jordan," he replied, thinking to keep his unsavory St. Cloud reputation as far away from Juneclaire as possible.

The vicar blinked, then blinked again. Yes, he had that look of his father and uncle before him. Broome had grown up with the Jordans. But the young earl was said to be an intelligent man, among other things. How could he suppose that a vicar who got his living from the family would not instantly recognize his patron's name? Didn't Reverend Broome pray for St. Cloud's reform and redemption every night?

"Ah, what might you want with the young lady, if I might ask?"

St. Cloud bit back a curse. He was not in the habit of explaining his actions to anyone, yet he knew he wasn't going to hear a word until he reassured the old dodderer. "Nothing havey-cavey, I swear. I intend to marry the girl."

Thank you, Lord. The vicar raised his head with a smile. "Do you, now?"

"As soon as I find her, damn it. Excuse me, vicar. You can perform the ceremony yourself to see it's all on the square, if you just tell me where Miss Beaumont is."

Positively beaming now, Mr. Broome rose and poured out a glass of the unwanted sherry. "I'll just go speak with Mrs. Broome for a moment. She's the one who saw the young lady off, you know. She wasn't happy about such a sweet young thing out on her own, going to London, so she'll be pleased

85

as punch to make your acquaintance. I'll just be a second, my lord."

He was more than a second, and his wife was not pleased to be called out of her kitchen with her hair coming undone and her cheeks flushed from the oven fires. Red-faced, the vicar returned, while angry whispers sounded in the hall.

"I'm afraid my good wife is, ah, concerned. Not that I doubt your sincerity, mind, but, ah . . ."

"Get on with it, man. I don't have a special license in my pocket to prove my intentions are honorable, blast it. Do you want me to swear on your Bible?"

"I think you have sworn enough, actually, my lord," the vicar gently reproved, making the earl feel about six years old.

He apologized, then sipped the sherry to restore his patience. "What, then?"

"It has to do with a friend of Miss Beaumont's. Pansy, I believe."

Sherry spewed down St. Cloud's new cravat. "Pansy? Your wife is worried about Pansy? Is everyone demented? Pansy is under my care, sleeping off a drunk right now."

The vicar shook his head sadly. His wife was correct, poor Pansy's ruin was complete, and his lordship showed no remorse. "I am sorry, my lord, in that case I cannot—"

"Wait, let me get her. You'll see for yourself, and Mrs. Broome, too."

Mrs. Broome was wringing her hands when the earl returned and dumped a tipsy piglet on her polished wood floors. Pansy tried to gain her feet, scrabbling against the shiny surface. Then she gave up, collapsed in a heap, and passed wind.

"Meet Pansy," St. Cloud announced. "You should have let sleeping hogs lie."

Chapter Ten

"What do you mean, I'll have no trouble recognizing the Coglins' coach because Miss Beaumont is riding on top with the driver?" No matter that he intended to take her up in his own open carriage, without footman or tiger. How dare anyone else treat Juneclaire so roughly! He jumped up and stalked to the fireplace.

"But, my lord," the vicar's wife tried to explain, fearing for her prized collection of china shepherdesses on the mantel, "Miss Beaumont had no maid or escort, and her clothes . . . Well, Mrs. Coglin did not see her for a lady."

"Anyone with two eyes in their head can see she's a lady! Hell and damnation, what kind of bobbing-block puts a female up on the box in the middle of winter?" He grabbed up a paperweight from Vicar Broome's desk.

Mrs. Broome was wringing her hands again. She didn't know whether to worry most about her bric-a-brac, the goose roasting in the kitchen, likely burning without her, or the lace curtains, which the pig was now tasting. She didn't want to offend his lordship, of course, but he was not a comfortable guest. "Mr. Coglin is the wealthiest shopkeeper in town, so his wife tends to get a bit above herself."

"Very charitably put, my love," her husband noted, his eyes twinkling. His lordship's anger warmed Reverend Broome's heart, it did, showing just the right amount of pride and protectiveness. This wasn't some hole-in-corner affair; the earl really cared for the girl. The vicar sighed when Lord St. Cloud gave his graphic opinion of coxcomb caper-merchants and their encroaching, overblown wives. Not all of his prayers for the earl's salvation had been answered, then. No matter, Mr. Broome was a patient man; he did not expect miracles.

Mrs. Broome was scarlet-faced, having snatched her beloved snow globe from the earl's hands before he could punctuate his comments about toplofty tradesmen by smashing it onto the desk. "No matter where she's riding, my lord, if you miss the coach along the road, you'll find the family at Coglin's dry-goods store in Springdale. You'll want to catch up with them before Miss Beaumont parts company with them, so perhaps you should hurry. Please?"

St. Cloud considered asking if he could leave Pansy with them for a while but reconsidered when the pig started nibbling on the carpet fringe. He did beg Mrs. Broome for a large hatbox, which she was only too happy to fetch if it would see him on his way with the blessed pig.

While he waited, the earl wrote a check against his London bank, made out to Mr. Broome. He did not fill in an amount. "Here, vicar, buy some cushions for the back pews. I promise you'll have better attendance on Sundays."

Who said prayers weren't answered?

Mavis Coglin loved to visit her sister-in-law, Joan, in Springdale. Joan and her family had rooms over the store on the main street, a cook-housekeeper, and a shabby landaulet. Mavis possessed a fine clapboard house overlooking the village green in Bramley, employed four domestics, and had a traveling carriage plus a chaise for local calls and such.

"No, Joan, dear, don't apologize," Mavis oozed. "We don't mind being cramped in this little parlor, do we, Mr. Coglin? And I am sure whatever your Mrs. Burke prepares is adequate, though how she had the time with all her other duties . . . So I had my own cook fix some of her specialities. Scully is bringing them up from the coach now. That's the traveling coach, of course. You won't mind if Scully helps serve, will you? I know your dear little girls are used to passing dishes and such, but truly, Joan, it's not quite the thing." Mavis was having a grand time, especially when someone knocked on the shop door right in the middle of dinner.

"You see, Joan, dear, how inconvenient it is to live near the store? Every Tom, Dick, and Harry is forever ringing your bell when a button falls off or a ribbon goes missing. Isn't that so, Mr. Coglin? Why don't you let Scully get the door, Joan? He'll send the inconsiderate fellow to the roundabout fast enough. So much more the thing, don't you know, than sending one of the children. I never answer the door myself, of course, except when Lady Cantwell calls. Dear Lady C. needed to confer with me about flowers for the church altar."

"Here now, mister, the shop is closed. Just because you went and spilled some wine on your neck cloth ain't no reason to ruin gentlefolk's Christmas dinner. I got splashed some myself and I'm still serving. And it ain't going to stop me from celebrating tonight neither, when the folks is home in bed."

St. Cloud wasn't listening, not to Scully anyway.

He was hearing the sounds of the family upstairs and trying to pick out Juneclaire's soft voice.

Scully put his hand on the earl's shoulder to set him on his way. "G'wan, now, pal. Come back tomorrow."

Scully's hand was removed by an iron vise around his wrist. "You forget yourself, *pal*. I am here to see Mr. Josiah Coglin, and you shall stand out of my way."

"It's worth my job, an' I let you go up," Scully whined, his fingers growing numb from the continued pressure.

"And it's worth your life if you do not." Eyes as cold as green ice bore into Scully, convincing him. He gulped and nodded. "Here," the earl ordered, thrusting a large hatbox into the footman's arms, "guard this. And if you value your neck, don't let it out."

Don't let what out? Scully sank down on the floor between the glove counter and the lace table, staring at the hatbox. He pushed the box across the aisle with his foot and rubbed his wrist. The fellow had the Devil's own strength.

Scully did not give a thought to his employers' safety upstairs, too concerned with his own skin and what was making noises in the dread box. Weren't no bonnet, that was for sure, with moans and grunts coming from it. The greasy hairs on the back of Scully's neck slowly rose, leaving a chill right down his spine. B'gad, the thing could be a goblin or some such creature from hell, ready to drink his blood if it got out. Scully had to know.

Fellow said don't let it out, not don't look. Scully edged closer on hands and knees to where he could peer in one of the holes poked through the lid. He took a deep breath and put his eye to the opening. A red-rimmed eye with no white showing looked back. Scully was out the door before his heart remembered to start beating again. He ran around the corner, jumped into the traveling carriage, and slammed the door. He wasn't going back upstairs till that warlock left and, no matter what the limb of Satan ordered, he wasn't staying downstairs with no soul-snatching hell fiend, not in a pig's eye.

"Sirs, ladies, forgive me for intruding, but could you tell me where I might find Miss Juneclaire Beaumont? You brought her here from Bramley."

Nearly all the Coglins had their mouths hanging open. Mavis closed hers with a snap and demanded that the impertinent fellow remove himself at once, before she called for her footman.

"Your man already greeted me at the door. Please, ma'am, Miss Beaumont? Then I shall be more than happy to leave you to enjoy your meal in peace."

Mavis sniffed. "I am sure I do not know what became of the baggage. She left the inn where we stopped for refreshment without so much as a by-your-leave."

"She just left? Surely you asked her where she was going, with whom?"

"I never had the chance, sirrah. The wanton went off without a word to anyone. No one saw her leave. And you can be sure I asked, for I meant to make the jade pay for my footman's new uniform, if the stains did not come out."

A muscle twitched in St. Cloud's jaw. "How did Miss Beaumont come to be responsible for your footman's uniform?"

"She threw a bottle of wine at poor Scully. Fine return for our Christian charity, I say. Now you can leave us decent people to our meal."

"A moment more, ma'am, so I understand perfectly. You let an innocent young lady set off by herself from an inn in the middle of nowhere?"

Mavis wiped her mouth delicately with her napkin. "I told you, I made inquiries. And there was no proof that she is, indeed, a lady. In fact, the innkeeper mentioned some young bucks passing through. Perhaps she took up with them."

"Ma'am," St. Cloud ground out through narrowed lips, "were you a gentleman, I would call you out. Were you a lady, I'd see every door in London closed to you. Miss Beaumont has more ladylike grace in her little finger than you possess in your whole overdressed, overweight, overreaching self."

"Josiah, throw him out," Mavis screeched, her face swollen and splotched. "Do you hear the way this ruffian is speaking to me? Do something, I say!"

Josiah Coglin figured the intruder to be five inches taller than himself, fifteen years younger, and in fitter condition by half. Jupiter, the most exercise Josiah got was carrying the cash envelope to the bank. Besides, the fellow was right. So Josiah did something; he passed around the mashed turnips. His brother snickered, and Joan hid her satisfaction in her napkin. The children still watched, wide-eyed.

Mavis saw no one was coming to her rescue and the rudesby was still glaring at her. "Pish-tosh," she blustered, "fine words coming from a fine jackanapes with rag manners and rags on his back. What do you know about gentlemen and ladies? Bounders like you come into the shop all the time, looking for a piece of gimcrack frippery to turn the girls' heads. For all we know, you're the doxie's fancy man. I know your kind."

St. Cloud's gaze could have withered the silk blossoms at Mavis Coglin's heaving breast if they were not already dead. "No, ma'am," he said on his way to the stairs, "you don't know my kind at all. Not many earls buy their own shoe buttons or silver polish."

* * *

Scully was still cowering in the coach when St. Cloud found him. The earl banged open the door and plucked the footman out like a pickle from a barrel. He held Scully by the collar, feet off the ground. "Why did Miss Beaumont throw the wine at you?" he demanded.

Scully was saying every prayer he ever heard, including the last rites. The earl shook him. "Why?"

"N-nothing, gov, I swear. She just come over violentlike."

Juneclaire, who pleaded mercy for a young robber? St. Cloud tightened his grip and shook the weasel again. "You must have done something to insult her. What?"

"A k-kiss, that's all."

That's all? St. Cloud broke the dastard's nose and darkened both his daylights, that's all. Scully was relieved the devil hadn't sent the demon in the box after him.

Damn! St. Cloud took a swallow from his flask while he tried to think through the fog of anger clouding his mind. He absently poured some of the brandy onto a roll for the pig nuzzling at his sleeve.

She could be anywhere! She could be halfway to London or asleep under a hedge. She could have taken a ride with anyone passing by that inn or been taken by the young blades for sport. Not even the brandy warmed the chill in his gut at the thought.

He needed more people to help search. He needed more money to pay them. The earl decided to drive home and organize the armies of servants at the Priory. He'd have them combing the countryside, searching every coach and cart. He'd get rid of the pig, thankfully, and saddle his stallion so he could cover more territory. He'd get to London, hire Bow Street runners, and knock on every door in London asking if a Mrs. Simms was housekeeper.

Just let her be safe until he found her.

St. Cloud stuffed the pig back in her box and whipped up the horses, wondering at his determination to locate a chit he'd only known a day or so. It wasn't just pride, he told himself, because she had refused him, and not just how he hated to be thwarted. He wanted her, but this was more than lust, more than the thrill of the chase. He had to find her to fill that empty space where his dreams had been. He had planned on showing her the Priory, her future home; he'd pictured her in the portrait gallery, the orangery, the morning room. He could practically see her there. Now he'd be looking around the corners, staring in the mirrors, waiting for her to appear like Mother's ghost. He had to find her.

But he didn't find her, not even when his curricle overtook the lumbering old wagon full of noisy children. He didn't notice the sleeping woman among the bundles and boxes and babies and crated chickens. He kept on driving.

Chapter Eleven

$\mathscr{M}$atthew Mulvilhill shoved his brother Mark into their sister Anne, who started bawling, which woke Baby Sarah, wailing in their mother's arms. Their father, John Mulvilhill, reached behind him to clout the nearest young Mulvilhill without taking his eyes off the horses. Lucas, minding his own business, was carving his name in the planked wagon with his new pocketknife. The knife slipped, ruining his perfect L, and Lucas said a word not found in the Bible. He hopped up to get out of his father's reach and tripped over little Mary, who was cuddled next to Juneclaire, who awoke to shrieks and kicks and a suspicious damp spot on her much-abused cloak.

Christmas carols held the children's attention for perhaps a mile, at the horses' phlegmatic gait. Somewhere in the middle of a wassail song Juneclaire noticed that in addition to the general bumpiness of the wagon now that they'd turned on the larger road, and the seeming inability of the children to sit in one place for the count of ten, one of the bundles was moving.

" 'Heigh-ho, nobody—' What in the world is in that sack?"

"Kittens. We're taking them to Granny's."

"In a sack?"

"Sure, you puts a rock in with 'em and they go down fast."

"A rock? You're going to drown the kittens?"

"Pa says we have too many cats; they'll eat the chickens, else."

"But . . . but it's Christmas!"

"That's why we gots to take 'em to Granny's. Our pond is froze, but she's near a good running stream. Pa says I can toss 'em in."

"No, it's my turn!"

"I can throw the farrest!"

"Pa!"

Juneclaire had no idea where she was. She was alone on a wood-bordered dirt track with no habitation in sight. She had only Mrs. Broome's roll by way of food in her satchel, two precious shillings less in her purse, and a sackful of kittens in her hands. And it was starting to snow.

She would *not* cry. The kittens would, and did, a pitiful mewing that hurried her to a log under a tree whose branches offered some protection. When she opened the sack, four pairs of bluish eyes blinked up at her. Another pair of eyes would never open again, no matter how hard she tried to blow life into the tiny mouth.

She didn't have time to cry. The other scrawny babies wouldn't eat the roll; it was too hard. They were too cold, too thin, too weak from hunger—and she couldn't just leave the dead one there for the badgers and crows. She made room in her carpet-bag and folded the sack on top of her belongings, then carefully lifted the kittens in. There were two gray-striped ones, a patchwork brindle, and an all-black kitten who tried to suck on her finger. She unwrapped her warm scarf and draped it over the top of the satchel, one corner turned back for air.

Crying was for children. Juneclaire cleared leaves away from a spot between two jutting roots of the tree. She laid the dead kitten on the ground, then covered it with the leaves, sticks, and whatever stones she could find. Then she placed her French Bible, the hymnal, and the volume of sermons on top of the makeshift grave and set out down the country lane, wiping her eyes. For the second time in two days she left her books on the side of the road; she couldn't begin to count how many new heartaches she carried with her. But those weren't tears, they were snowflakes.

If Juneclaire were alone, she would keep walking. She'd eat her solitary roll and walk until she found a likely cottage or tidy farmstead to seek directions or hire a cart ride back to Bramley. Sam and Alice Grey would put her up for the night, she thought, or Vicar and Mrs. Broome. She'd walk all through the night if she had to, if she were alone, rather than approach the derelict thatch-roof hovel and its broken-doored barn. This place seemed too poor for a horse or a scrap of food for the kittens or a warm fire. Goodness, the hut looked so poor, the people couldn't afford to give directions!

Maybe it was deserted, Juneclaire thought cheerfully as her brisk steps took her nearer. Maybe it was the haunt of one such as Charlie Parrett. Her feet dragged.

Then a dog started to bark. It was a big, mud-colored mongrel with a hairier strip down its back, charging out of the old barn.

"Good doggy," Juneclaire called. The dog came nearer, stiff-legged, snarling, sniffing the air. "Nice doggy," she said. The cur's ridge hairs were standing up, its teeth showing. Not a nice doggy at all.

The beast was barking and snarling in earnest now, darting up to snap at the air perilously close to her ankles. Juneclaire was going to throw her satchel at it, until she remembered the kittens. The kittens! She raised the bag over her head, shouting, "Go away, you miserable mutt! You're not going to eat my kittens, not on Christmas Day!"

The outcome was still pending when a sharp whistle pierced the air. The dog dropped to its belly as if poleaxed, though it still kept a yellow-eyed gaze on Juneclaire, daring her to take one more step. An old man hobbled out of the barn. Sam Grey was old; this man was old enough to be Sam's father. He was old enough to be Noah's father. He was bent, bald, and toothless, with skin like autumn leaves. But he controlled the big dog with a simple "Down, Jack. Good boy."

"Thank you," Juneclaire said. "I'll just be—"

"Don't know what's come over old Jack." He paused to think about it. "Usually it's just cats what get him so riled."

"It's my fault, then, for that's what I've got in my bag. I'd better get on my way. Good afternoon to you." She started to back away, keeping her eye on the big dog.

The old man was peering at her from under unruly white brows. His blue eyes were clear enough, though. He took a wheezing breath and said, "Hold, missy. What's a mite like you doing out here?"

With a simple hand gesture from his master, Jack was on his feet, rumbling low in his throat. Juneclaire stopped her retreat. "I . . . I was going to London to seek a position, but I decided not," she told him, thinning the story to its bare bones. She saw no reason to mention a pig, a nobleman, a highway robber, or Scully. "Only, the family that was carrying me back had all these children, and they were going to drown the little kittens. I couldn't let them, so I got off with the cats. Only, I don't quite know where I am, and the kittens need something to eat, and yours was the first place I came to."

He nodded slowly, like a rusted hinge. No words came from his sunken mouth, so Juneclaire nervously went on, "I am heading west of Strasmere, but I have friends in Bramley. I just met them today, actually, but they are nice people. They'll help me. And . . . and I can pay my way."

Still there was no response. He couldn't have frozen in that position, could he, with the dog on guard? Juneclaire imagined them all turning into snow sculptures, the whole tableau waiting for the spring thaw. "F-forgive my manners." She bobbed an awkward curtsy. "I am Miss Juneclaire Beaumont, from Stanton Hall, near Farley's Grange."

The old man bent at the waist, and Juneclaire almost rushed forward to catch him, except the dog stood between them. "I'm Little Yerby," the ancient announced once he'd straightened and paused to catch his breath. "My father was Big Yerby. He's gone, but the name stuck. Even my Aggie calls me Little." There was another halt for breathing. "She's gone off to our daughter's lying-in with the donkey, else I'd ride you to town." He scratched his bald head. "Guess you better come in, then. Coming on to snow. My old bones've been warning me for days." He turned toward the house.

"But what about Jack and the kittens?"

"Jack does what I tell him."

Juneclaire hoped so, as she followed him toward the mean cottage, only she hadn't heard him tell Jack anything.

There were two rooms inside the dwelling, both neat as a pin. Fresh rushes covered the packed-dirt floor, and calico curtains fluttered at the windows. Vegetables and herbs hung from the rafters, and a warm fire burned in the open hearth. Juneclaire observed that Little Yerby's clothes were clean and neatly mended, as he took a copper kettle off the hob. He poured some of the hot water into an earthenware pot for tea and added a little to a saucer of milk for the kittens. Juneclaire crumpled the roll into the warm mixture and put it and the kittens, on their sack, near the fireplace.

With a mug of hot tea in her hand, Juneclaire was more than content to sit and watch the kittens attack their meal. "How could anyone think of destroying such sweet and innocent babies?"

"Be worse to let them loose to starve." Little Yerby was in a cane-backed chair, warming his gnarled fingers on the mug more than drinking from it.

"But they wouldn't eat so much."

"Big family like that, they was prob'ly scraping by just to feed their own young'uns."

"But they don't take them out and drown them if there are too many!"

"World's a hard place, missy."

Juneclaire sighed. "I know."

"Next choice is worse." Little Yerby stood up in stages, then turned and gave Juneclaire a toothless grin. "Don't know what my Aggie'll say—'tain't proper with her away and all, me inviting a pretty little thing to spend the night—but there it is. You can bunk near the fire, where my girl used to sleep. There be an old quilt somewheres." He shuffled off to the bedroom and rummaged in a chest. "Here 'tis. If you'll help with the chores, I'll add some vegetables to the stew Aggie left me. Can't chew much more'n that, you know. Still, I saved some dandelion wine for Christmas supper."

He halted at the pantry. "Sorry Aggie ain't here. It's the first Christmas since we married. Sorry my girl married away, too. What was I looking for? Oh yes, the wine. Mind wanders some, you know."

Then he slapped his thigh and doubled over, laughing. "Won't they talk down to the local, Little Yerby and a rare charmer. Aggie'll be tickled pink!"

Juneclaire smiled back. "And I'd be honored to be your guest, Mr. Yerby, and help with the chores."

"Yeah, the chores, near forgot. Not as spry as I used to be. You know anything about cows?"

"No, but I know a lot about pigs." Juneclaire was transferring the kittens to a basket he held out to her so they wouldn't wander too close to the fire.

Little Yerby slapped his leg again. "You ever milked a sow? There, you go on start; I'll put up the stew."

How hard could it be? The cows were all lined up, their heads in the food troughs. A bucket and a stool stood ready by the door. Jack sniffed at her but didn't growl or anything, so Juneclaire carried the equipment to the first animal in the line. She put the stool down, then shoved the bucket under. She removed her mittens and blew on her hands, then straightened her shoulders, sat down, and reached under the—uh-oh.

"Guess old Fred is tickled pink, too." But not as pink as Juneclaire's cheeks as she cautiously backed away.

The cows were easier. Juneclaire only got half as much on her as she got in the bucket, till she got the knack of the thing. Little Yerby skimmed off a ladle of cream and stored the rest of the milk while Juneclaire rinsed the buckets at the well.

After supper Little Yerby nodded over his pipe, and Juneclaire sat on her cloak by the fire with the kittens playing in her lap, their bellies round and full. Then Jack scratched at the door.

"Oh, dear, does he usually come in at night?"

"Just for an hour or two afore he settles down with the cows. He can stay out, though. You know, Aggie always wanted a cat. Said Jack was my dog, not her'n. Cat'd keep mice out of the pantry and the root cellar, too."

"And you have the milk for it, till the kitten can hunt on its own. But what about Jack?"

He knocked the pipe into the fireplace. "Never tried an infant before."

Juneclaire gathered the kittens on their sack. "He wouldn't . . . ?"

"Jack does what I tell him," Little Yerby answered, opening the door. "Down, Jack. Stay."

The dog lay rigid, tense, and ready to spring, the hackles at his back erect, his muzzle creased to show huge white teeth. Little Yerby nodded, and Juneclaire put the kittens down, about a foot from his nose, and held her breath.

There was a puddle of saliva under Jack's mouth by the time the kittens noticed him. He didn't move, but he growled. One kit dug its sharp claws into Juneclaire's skirts and tried to climb, one disappeared into the rafters, and another found the other room and hid under the bed. The last kitten, though, one of the gray-striped ones, arched its back and hissed. Jack raised pleading eyes to Little Yerby, who shook his head no. The kitten reached out a tiny paw and batted at Jack's nose.

"Look at that," the old man said. "Just like David and Goliath."

Juneclaire was ready to snatch the idiot cat out of harm's way, but Little Yerby told her to let them be. Jack nudged the kitten's foot, toppling the wee thing, which meowed loudly. Jack opened his mouth—and licked the kitten. Juneclaire gasped. David, as the hero was instantly christened, be it he or be it she, circled around and curled up to sleep next to the big dog's chest, between Jack's feet.

Juneclaire rounded up the other kittens and soothed them in their basket, with the familiar sack. She did not want to offend the old man's hospitality but had to renew her offer: "You have been so kind, Mr. Yerby, and I was no help with the chores at all to speak of, and David won't be feeding on Mrs. Yerby's mice for a while still, so will you not accept my shilling for his feed?"

"Nay, less, you'll be needing it more. Howbeit you can do something worth more than gold, missy. I couldn't get to church today without the donkey, not on these old legs, and I never did learn me my letters." He handed her a worn book. "Would you read me the story?"

So Juneclaire sat on the stool by the fire that Christmas night while the old man leaned back in his chair, one knobby hand resting on his dog's head, the other stroking a sleeping kitten.

" 'And it came to pass in those days,' " she began, " 'that there went out a decree from Caesar Augustus, that all the world should be taxed.' "

Chapter Twelve

*H*ome for the holidays. Oh, joy.

St. Cloud meant to head directly to the stables to begin to organize the grooms' search. Instead, he saw the gardener's boy race from the gate lodge across the lawns to announce his arrival at the Priory. Oh, blast!

By the time the earl tooled his weary chestnuts through the tree-lined drive, over the bridge at the ornamental lake, past the formal gardens and the maze, a welcoming delegation was waiting in the carriage drive.

His relatives would never be so outré as to demonstrate what might be taken for affection; they'd be waiting in the gold salon having predinner sherry and dissecting his character. St. Cloud Priory kept Town hours, even though Countess Fanny hadn't been to London in years. Instead, they sent servants to wait outside in the snow. There were two grooms and Foley to help with one curricle, three footmen to carry his bags that had been delivered the day before. His valet, Todd, took one look at the earl and about-faced up the steps to order a hot bath. Talbot, the butler, remained at attention in the open doorway and a maid was there to—Hell, St. Cloud couldn't figure why a maid was there at all, shivering. He handed her the hatbox and told her to wait inside.

He waved off the footmen and let the grooms take the chestnuts, with orders to double their rations. He held Foley back. The wiry ex-jockey was pale, with a small bandage still on his head.

"Old man, am I glad to see you. How are you feeling?" the earl asked.

"Fairly, my lord, iffen I can say the same? It's a rare takin' they been in, up to the house, with me no wiser from talkin' to that boy you sent with the blunt. I was that worried about the chestnuts, I was," the older man scolded.

"They've taken no harm, I swear. Listen, Foley, I need a groom to ride to London as soon as possible, through the night if the snow doesn't get worse."

"I'll go saddle Lightning, my lord. You have a message for me to take?"

"You're not going. Find one of the other men, someone you trust."

"You mean a younger man. I'll be handin' in my livery, then."

"Don't get all prickly and puss-faced on me, old man. Not now. You've been hurt, and I need you here."

Talbot coughed from up the stairs, subtly. "Old stone britches should shut the door if he's gettin' cold," Foley pointed out, not so quietly, not so subtly.

"Ignore him. Here is the message your man is to give to my secretary at Jordan House: I want every available footman and groom out in Mayfair, going house to house, looking for a housekeeper named Mrs. Simms. Some of the knockers will be off, but they should be able to ask around for the house-keepers' names."

Foley pulled at the bandage on his head. "I

105

thought I was the one concussed. Of all the crack-brained starts—"

"Enough, Foley. I am sure there will be more than one lecture waiting for me inside, I do not require yours."

Foley knew the short limits to the earl's patience. "Yes, my lord. And when the men find this here Mrs. Simms, what are they supposed to do with her?"

"Send for me, but give Mrs. Simms ten pounds to hold on to the lady—she'll know who I mean—and keep her safe until I can get there. I also want a man at every posting house that takes coaches coming into Town from Bramley, Springdale, or anywhere closer. They are to look for a lady in a gray, rabbit-lined cloak. She has brown hair and a smile like a Madonna. The man should follow her, find out where she goes, and make bloody hell sure she gets there safe. And send for me. I'll be in London as soon as possible. Is that clear?"

"Clear as pitch. Every man jack in London is to look for a housekeeper or a pretty chit."

"Right. Now go, get someone started while there's still light."

Foley left, shaking his head and muttering. "I take my eyes off the lad for less'n a day and there's a female involved. Should've known."

"Welcome home, my lord," Talbot intoned as he bowed the earl through the door. "Merry Christmas, my lord, and may I offer you the felicitations of the day on behalf of the staff and myself. The coincidence of your natal day with the Nativity brings double cause for joy and celebration." Talbot must have been practicing since yesterday. "The family and guests are in the gold parlor. Shall I announce you?"

"Good lord, no. I'm not fit for company, much less

106

milady's dinner table. Tell them to go in without me. I'll join them later for tea." He took the hatbox from the blushing maid, who curtsied and fled down the hall. "I have a great many arrangements to make, Talbot. I am sure Todd is seeing to my bath, but could you send up some dinner on a tray? Make that a large dinner. And a basket."

"A basket, my lord?"

"Large. And a decanter of that cognac my father put down. Large, if I have to face the family later."

Before St. Cloud could cross the black-and-white tiles of the huge entry hall to reach the arched stairways, his grandmother's less-than-dulcet tones floated down the hall: "So where is the scapegrace? Been home twenty minutes by my count, two days late, and nary a word for his worried kin. If I hadn't sent my maid out, we'd be sitting here like ninnies not knowing if he was dead or alive. Why, the jackanapes could have expired on the doorstep, and without an heir, mind you."

The dowager's words were punctuated by raps of her cane and, since she couldn't see what she was thumping, muffled oaths and tumbled footstools. "Sad lack of manners you taught the boy, Fanny. No sense of responsibility either, the rakehell. I've been sitting all day in this mausoleum among confounded strangers waiting for the whopstraw to show, instead of being home in my own comfort with my own people. Deuced if I'll stay here all night waiting on his convenience. Be like waiting for your haunt to come, Fanny. I'm going home. Talbot! Munch! Get the carriage! Where's my wrap?"

Before St. Cloud could flee upstairs past Talbot's stiff-spined, measured tread, the dowager's cane rapping started down the hall, followed by the crash of china. Lady Fanny's fluttery "Mother St. Cloud, please" came after. "What about dinner? Oh, I feel ill."

"Not in front of the guests, you ninny." That from Uncle Harmon. "Who's got the vinaigrette? Where's that blasted Talbot? No, Florrie, we won't burn feathers under Fanny's nose. Give Lady Pomeroy back her headpiece, you clunch. Elsbeth, stop batting your eyelashes at the admiral. Get over here and help your aunt."

Welcome home, my lord.

St. Cloud's silent appearance in the gold salon put an end to all the commotion except the dowager's flailing cane and demands for her carriage. "I am here, Grandmother, so you can stop enacting us a Cheltenham tragedy and upsetting Lady Fanny. I simply did not wish to present myself in all my dirt."

The dowager sniffed when he kissed her powdered and rouged cheek. "I can tell why. So what fustian are you going to give us for being two days late and near missing your own birthday party?"

"Why, Grandmother, you should know me better than that; I haven't seen fit to explain my actions since my youth. Surely you don't expect a rakeshame to make excuses?"

The dowager cackled and banged her cane down on Talbot's foot. The butler did not disgrace his calling by more than a wince, St. Cloud observed, as the earl turned to kiss his mother's brow, removing a lavender-soaked handkerchief to do so. "I am sorry if I interfered in your plans, my lady. You should know better than to fret over me."

"Dear boy, how could I not? My condition . . ."

St. Cloud was already shaking hands with his cousin, ignoring the younger Wilmott's smug looks. Niles was wearing white satin knee breeches, a white satin coat, and a white waistcoat picked out with red-and-green embroidered holly. None of it paid for, most likely. St. Cloud took great care to pat Niles on the shoulder in greeting, leaving a smudge. His cousin Elsbeth presented the tips of her fingers for his salute, her nose wrinkled. "That's more than travel dust, St. Cloud."

Uncle Harmon Wilmott did not put his hand out or step closer. He nodded curtly, frowning. "I think you could show more remorse for turning the house upside down and upsetting your mother's delicate nerves."

"Do you, Uncle?" The earl spoke slowly, deliberately, watching the color rise in the baronet's pouchy face.

Lady Fanny was quick to step into the silence, although she found interchanges between her son and her brother particularly wearing. "Yes, dearest, I was quite overset to think something must have happened to you, and there was the bother of redoing the seating plan, you know. I don't see what I would have done without Harmon's support. It's been that way for years, of course, and we mustn't let Harmon think we're ungrateful, dear."

St. Cloud bowed in his uncle's direction but did not add to his mother's words. She held a gray filmy scarf to her cheek. "You really should have been here," she reproved. "Harmon had to light the Yule log in your place. You know the head of the household holds that honor."

"I am certain Uncle Harmon found no difficulty in usurping my . . . honors." He turned to greet others of the company while his mother searched for her hartshorn.

Lord, even Sydelle Pomeroy was dressed—or undressed—to the nines. Red silk with nothing under it, unless he missed his guess.

"I knew you wouldn't forsake us, my lord," she breathed, making his appearance a compliment to her undeniable beauty.

" 'Us,' my lady? How could I forsake you when I did not know you would be here?" The sultry widow had been after St. Cloud's title as long as Cousin Niles had been after her fortune. Lady Pomeroy had been Uncle Harmon's wife's godchild and milked the tenuous relationship for all the invitations she could. She and Niles made a fine pair: cold, calculating, and conceited.

Damn, he wished they were all gone! Then St. Cloud remembered Junco—he hadn't thought of her for at least five minutes—and her wishes. An evil kind of grin came over his face, lips half quirked, eyes slightly narrowed. Only Niles recognized the St. Cloud smile for what it was and left off denigrating the earl's shabby manners. St. Cloud stepped back to the hall and returned with the hatbox.

Aunt Florrie clapped her hands together. "Oh, goody! You brought us a present!"

"My gifts to you must still be with my baggage upstairs, Aunt Florrie. This was a present given to me, which I was going to take upstairs, if I had been permitted. Since you've all made me feel so welcome, I'll share it with you."

He tipped Pansy out to the floor, and the piglet headed straight for the scent of biscuits, in ladies' hands, on low tables, and under gentlemen's pumps, where crumbs were ground into the Aubusson carpet. So Juneclaire was right, St. Cloud acknowledged. Christmas wishes come true. The room was almost clear in no time, the indomitable Talbot having the presence of mind to announce dinner. Juneclaire was right about another thing: a man with a pig really did have more opportunity to smile. St. Cloud was positively beaming.

None of those remaining in the parlor seemed to share his good humor, except for Florrie, who had tied a napkin around Pansy's neck and was helping her sip from the hastily discarded sherry glasses. The dowager was shouting to know what was going on, and how could everyone have gone into dinner without her taking precedence. Niles was snickering at more evidence of his cousin's gaucherie, and Lady Fanny had collapsed back on the sofa.

"Come, Mother, they cannot start without you." The earl half lifted his mother into Niles's arms. "Uncle Harmon, I am sure I can leave you to escort Lady St. Cloud into dinner."

Lord Wilmott was seething, his jowls quivering. "How dare you, sir, shame your mother by setting an animal loose in her drawing room? How could you bring such disgrace to this house?"

St. Cloud took out his quizzing glass, blessing Charlie Parrett for treating it kindly, and surveyed the overturned furniture, the broken glassware, and, finally, the livid baronet. "Odd," he drawled. "I thought this was my house." He bowed. "My ladies, I shall see you after dinner."

Chapter Thirteen

"*H*ogwash," St. Cloud told his cousin Niles. "The man works for me. If Todd can't look after one little pig for an evening, he's not worth his wages."

The efficient, even-tempered, and elegant gentleman's gentleman was worth a fortune, which was about what it took to convince Todd to play swineherd for a few hours. St. Cloud had no intention of discussing his domestic arrangements with Niles, however, not even to rid the coxcomb of that supercilious grin.

Todd had wrought miracles. The pig was fed, walked, and bedded down in St. Cloud's dressing room, with promises that Pansy would be installed in the stables tomorrow. And St. Cloud was combed, brushed, and polished to a fare-thee-well, from glossy black curls to glossy black footwear. His cheeks were as smooth as a baby's bottom, and the bruise on his face was almost unnoticeable. With his muscle-molding white Persian knee smalls, wide-shouldered black coat of Bath superfine and stark white linen enlivened only by an emerald stickpin the color of his eyes, he made Niles look like a man-milliner and the squire's sturdy sons look like bumpkins.

Most of the guests reassembled in the gold salon

chose to treat the pig incident as a fine joke, reinforcing St. Cloud's belief that an earl with upwards of forty thousand a year had a great deal of social latitude, and that Society was a jackass. It also appeared to St. Cloud that the joke became funnier the more females a man had to marry off. The admiral, with his three platter-faced chits, thought it was hilarious. He joined the squire, with one daughter and two nieces, in proposing toasts to the earl's birthday. Everyone joined in, in high good humor, especially once the lambs' wool punch was served round twice, except Mr. Hilloughby, his mother's current tame cleric, who stuck to tea, and Uncle Harmon, who was in high dudgeon.

Lady Pomeroy sat at the pianoforte, having arranged the candelabrum to best highlight her mature décolletage while shadowing the tiny signs of passing youth. She skillfully picked out carols, seemingly by heart, but purred a request for the earl to turn her pages for her.

Uncle Harmon frowned when St. Cloud acquiesced, taking a seat on the bench so near Sydelle that a draft couldn't have come between them. Lord Wilmott wanted the earl for Elsbeth, Lady Sydelle and her inheritance for the spendthrift Niles. The older man grew perfectly bilious at the thought of his goddaughter and his nephew making a match of it, melding their fortunes while his own expensive progeny got short shrift. Being well aware of his uncle's ambitions, and dyspepsia, the earl moved closer to the alluring widow.

The reverend decided it was time for one last Christmas invocation, for faith, hope, and chastity, and a benediction for the Christ child.

"Speaking of children, St. Cloud, when are you going to provide some for this old pile?" The dowager did not wait for Hilloughby's amen. She couldn't see the blushes of the younger girls, invited for his consideration, St. Cloud made no doubt, and wouldn't have cared anyway. "It's time and past you married and got yourself an heir. I want grandchildren!" She thumped her cane down, hard, on one of the squire's chits' gowns. The girl ran crying from the room, trailing a flounce. "What's that ninnyhammer Fanny crying about now?" the dowager demanded.

St. Cloud removed the cane from her fingers. "You don't need this while you are having tea, and that was not Lady Fanny, Grandmother, but an innocent miss you have embarrassed with your wayward cane and wicked tongue."

"Humph. If all the young gels are such niminy-piminy, milk-and-water chits, it's no wonder you haven't taken leg shackles. But I can't wait forever, you know. This place has been in the Jordan family for centuries, boy, and it's your job to see it stays there."

He sipped slowly from his cup. "I am no longer a boy, Grandmother."

"And I wouldn't ask a boy to do a man's job!"

Lady Fanny tried to play peacemaker again, handing round a plate of sugarplums. "I am sure St. Cloud knows his responsibilities to the name, Mother St. Cloud."

"And to his family," Uncle Harmon put in, as blatant as a battleship. He dragged Elsbeth away from one of the squire's sons and thrust her onto the sofa next to her cousin.

Elsbeth was her usual sulky self, in a pet this evening because she was not the center of male adulation. She and Aunt Fanny had invited the plainest girls in the country for St. Cloud's perusal, knowing Elsbeth would shine in contrast. Now he and every other man in the room, including the squire's gapeseed sons and her own brother, were panting after that fast Sydelle Pomeroy. Even Mr.

Hilloughby's collar got too tight when the widow walked past him, as slow and slinky as sin. Elsbeth bet the widow's skirts were dampened. Red silk, while Elsbeth sat as demure as a debutante in pink chiffon! It wasn't to be borne. Worst of all were the calf's eyes St. Cloud was making at the older woman, when everyone in the room knew he was as good as promised to Elsbeth. Papa said he was only sowing more wild oats, that he'd only offer a lightskirt like Sydelle a slip on the shoulder. Well, Elsbeth was tired of cooling her heels in Berkshire while St. Cloud was kicking his up in London.

"Yes, cousin," she lisped. "Just when are you going to drop the handkerchief?"

He dropped a bombshell, not a handkerchief. "I already have."

The admiral called for another toast. He'd wasted an evening, but the punch was good.

"No, sir, it's not official yet. I haven't had a chance to seek her family's permission, but I expect her here within a few days."

"Oh, dearest, how wonderful! Who are her people? Shall we like her?" The countess's various shawls and draperies dipped in the tea, in her excitement.

"Her name is Juneclaire, and I'm sure you'll love her, Mother. And, no, you do not know the family. They are from Farley's Grange." He pushed the tray back farther.

"Nobody who's anybody lives in Farley's Grange, boy. When do we get to meet her?"

"As soon as I can arrange, Grandmother, and her grandfather was from the *ancien régime*, not that it matters a halfpenny."

"Foreigners," the dowager muttered, secretly delighted he'd chosen anyone but that Pomeroy high flier or Harmon's brat.

"You must give me her address, dearest, so I can extend a formal invitation."

St. Cloud took a deep breath. Thinking it was better to get over rough ground quickly, he flatly announced, "I have no idea where she is."

His mother dropped her vinaigrette bottle. "You aren't bringing one of those independent London bluestockings here, are you? I couldn't bear to live with another pushy fe—" She held her gauze scarf to her mouth and looked away from the dowager.

St. Cloud patted her hand. "No such thing, June-claire's sweet and gentle. You'll see."

"When you find her, cuz?" Niles taunted. He was also delighted, recalculating his odds of winning the Pomeroy's hand. "How did you happen to mislay the bride-to-be?"

"There was a bit of a mix-up with the coaches. That's why I was detained," he said with a bow in his still-speechless uncle's direction. "I am not sure precisely which carriage took her up when the one she was traveling in had a spill." The spill may have been all over Scully, the footman, but St. Cloud was sticking to the truth as closely as possible. He had no idea what he would say if anyone thought to ask how he met the young lady, much less when. "There's nothing improper about it," he lied now, for the squire's wife and the rest of the neighborhood who would have the story by noon tomorrow. "She may have returned home or be staying with the vicar and his wife at Bramley. She might even have gone with her housekeeper on to London. I'll send the footmen out tomorrow to make inquiries, and I'll ride to London myself."

"But you can't send the staff away tomorrow, dearest; it's Boxing Day. All of the servants have the day off for their own feast and celebration. And you have to be here when the tenants come calling for the wassail."

"For their gifts, you mean. Damn."

"Oh, but Mr. Talbot takes care of the staff gifts, and your secretary in London remembered the check for the church alms box. And the bailiff delivers the boxes for most of the Priory tenants. They come just to see you and wish you joy of the season."

"Like feudal times, cuz, you know, lord of the manor and all that. *Noblesse oblige.*"

Lady Fanny thought a moment. "I suppose Harmon could stand in for you."

St. Cloud put his teacup down with a thud. "That's all right, Mother. As you say, they are my people, and I shall be here."

The countess looked toward her brother to make sure Harmon saw what a good boy St. Cloud was. "Besides, dearest, you cannot go up to London, not with our New Year's ball next week. You couldn't have forgotten?"

St. Cloud bit the inside of his mouth. How could he, when she'd written to remind him seven times in the past month? The Priory hadn't made much of Christmas since his father's accident and Uncle George's death, but the dowager insisted that Lady Fanny had to entertain the county somehow over the holiday season, to repay all the invitations she received and to uphold the St. Cloud name. They had settled on a New Year's masquerade ball when they were out of blacks years ago, and the tradition took. Lady Fanny still wore half mourning, and she still piled all of the details for the ball on Talbot, the housekeeper, the bailiff, and her son. He hated the whole affair. "Now there I should appreciate Uncle Harmon's management. It's time Cousin Elsbeth learns how to manage a party, too. I make no promises after tomorrow, Mother."

"But you did promise to see about the ghost, son. haven't slept easy in my bed in weeks, and that cannot be good for my health, on top of all the work for the ball. And then there was the upset about your tardy arrival and now the excitement of your betrothal. I really must have my rest. Of course I cannot be comfortable in my room. . . ."

"Blast it, Fanny, I told you I had the steward go over the whole east wing, and the fellow found nothing. The ghost is all in your head." Lord Wilmott finally found his voice with the realization that there could be no wedding without a bride. Let the boy go haring off to London while Harmon made his own investigation. There was some huggermugger here, and he was determined to get to the bottom of it and get rid of this upstart nobody. Elsbeth still had a chance.

For once in her life Fanny held firm, even against her brother's wrath. "No, Harmon, it's a St. Cloud ghost and perhaps only St. Clouds can see it, although the servants have heard it crying through the chimneys. And there was *no* wind that night so you can take a damper, Harmon."

"Brava, Fanny," the dowager said approvingly "You can't keep the boy tied to you with your me grims or your mutton-headed mismanagement Now you'll try things that go bump in the night!"

Fanny held the cloth to her eyes, and St. Cloud was tempted to take the cane to the dowager and his uncle. Yes, Lady Fanny was vaporish; did any one think she was going to change now? "I though you'd heard noises in the Dower House, too, Grand mother."

"I'm getting old, boy, not senile. You worry abou finding the gel, St. Cloud; Hilloughby can say an extra prayer to get rid of the ghost. That's abou all he's good for anyway." The dowager had almos given up hope that the cleric—or anybody—woul offer for Fanny and get the peagoose and her Wil mott relatives out of the Priory once and for all

The New Year's ball had been her idea at first, to get Fanny socializing again in hopes of marrying the wigeon off. No one wanted her, more's the pity.

With the St. Cloud fireworks seemingly over for the night, the dinner guests took their leave. There was no reason to stay later, with the earl as good as a tenant for life and snow falling. If the snow hadn't been falling, Lady Sydelle might have ordered her carriage and headed for London. As it was, she was in such a snit, she forgot to slink on her way down the hall, after excusing herself to the family still in the gold salon. She stomped down the hall and up the stairs with such determination that she split the back seam of her too-tight dress. There was a crash below in the hallway. Talbot was not made of stone, after all, and neither was the Limoges teapot.

With only family left, Aunt Florrie wanted her Christmas gift, since she wasn't getting to keep the pig and Harmon took the sugarplums away. They all moved to the smaller parlor, where a wooden candle pyramid had been set up on one of the tables and lighted, St. Cloud's gifts on a red cloth beneath. Harmon did not hold with bringing a tree into the house, even if Queen Charlotte was trying to foist her Teutonic notions of *tannenbaum* on the London gentry. Fanny thought a tree with candles, apples, garlands, and cookies sounded lovely. Maybe next year, she thought, when there was a new countess.

She gave her son a pair of slippers with the family crest embroidered on them by her maid. He gave her a pearl-and-diamond brooch selected by his secretary. The dowager gave him her late husband's gold watch, which, besides being mentioned in the entail, was the same watch she gave St. Cloud every year. Every year he had it returned to her bed stand, knowing she hated to be without it. The earl gave her an ebony cane with a carved handle.

"What is it, boy? A snake?"

"No, you old fire breather, it's a dragon."

He gave Aunt Florrie a music box with a bear in a tutu twirling around on top, and she gave him a rock.

Elsbeth presented the earl with some monogrammed handkerchiefs. Her maid did not sew as well as Lady Fanny's. She went into raptures over the gold filigree fan that caught his eye one day as just the kind of gaudy trumpery she might enjoy.

St. Cloud next delighted his other cousin by saying he'd write out the Christmas gift as soon as Niles presented the reckoning, so Niles gave him the snuffbox in his pocket.

He and Uncle Harmon exchanged nods.

"You know, Papa," Elsbeth said, practicing her attitudes over the fan, "now that I am not to marry my cousin, can I finally have a Season in Town? I know Aunt Fanny doesn't go to London, but perhaps St. Cloud's wife can present me. Is she good ton, cousin?"

"Don't be a gudgeon," her brother told her, still in an expansive mood. "If she were a gap-toothed hunchback from the Outer Hebrides, St. Cloud's countess would still be good ton."

"Why? Aunt Fanny isn't."

Chapter Fourteen

$\mathcal{T}$he horses were straining in the traces, hurtling into the night. Foley rode silently beside him. No, it was Todd—No, someone else, watching him try to manage the runaway team. He couldn't do it. They were out of control. Then the carriage shaft started creaking, crunching, cracking under the stress of the wild ride. They'd be thrown, or dashed under the horses' hooves, and the passenger just watched. Then St. Cloud felt the wind and waited. His legs must be broken; he couldn't move them. The horses! Someone, help! The passenger laughed and laughed and—

St. Cloud jerked awake, gasping. He could feel the sweat on his bare chest and hear the echoes of distant laughter. The velvet bed curtains were open—and Pansy was sprawled across his legs. "Damn." There was no way the pig could get up on the huge canopied bed herself. St. Cloud even used the low stool. If this was Todd's revenge for having to nursemaid a pig, St. Cloud would have his head come morning. Boxing Day indeed. He'd give the fellow a box on the ears for this night's work. Then again, this was more like Cousin Niles's style of bobbery, foolish since the check was not yet signed. St. Cloud wouldn't even put such a prank past Sy-

delle, a woman scorned and all that. He sighed.
Either way, he was awake.

"Are you hungry, pig? Silly question, you're always hungry. Let's go." St. Cloud lighted his candle and found his robe and new slippers. He also found where Pansy'd eaten her way out of the wicker basket. "At least that explains the crunching noises I heard."

He piled two plates with leftovers from the kitchen and led the pig into his library, where he restarted the fire and settled back on the worn leather chair. Then he heard the noise, a tapping almost like Grandmother's cane, although more regular. That must be Lady Fanny's specter, he thought, getting up to stand closer to the fireplace, where the sound was loudest. There must be a squirrel in one of the disused chimneys, tapping to open a nut or something. Maybe an owl. The noise would carry through all the grates in the place, echoing eerily enough, he supposed, to spook his susceptible parent. He didn't know why Uncle Harmon or the steward hadn't just sent for the sweeps. He'd do it tomorrow.

No, damn it, tomorrow the servants did not work, and he would be busy shaking hands and listening to speeches. Blast. All he wanted to do was get on his fastest horse and ride to find Juneclaire. He wandered toward the window, a glass of brandy in his hand. The snow was still falling, though lightly. Lord, let her be safe and warm.

He was up at dawn, before most of the household except for Cook, who took one look at her kitchen and started screeching about Priory phantoms and the walking dead. Breakfast was going to be late that morning. St. Cloud and the pig strolled through melting snow toward the stables, where Pansy, at least, could find apples and oats. The earl found his man Foley up and ready to be sent on the hunt. Word had come down from the house last night that the missing female was no less than the future Lady St. Cloud. Foley would ride to hell and back to see his lordship settled, even if he couldn't abide females personally.

"O'course I'm sure I can ride. I had my rest, didn't I? And no, us stable men don't put up with tomfoolery like them at the house, not doing their jobs 'cause it's a holiday. Horses still has to be fed, don't they? And we may as well exercise 'em on the way to somewheres as around a ring. Your message'll be in London by now, my lord, so where else do you want us to look?"

The earl wanted someone to watch the departing coaches at Springdale and at Bramley, but he wanted Foley himself to head toward Farley's Grange by way of Strasmere, making inquiries along the way. "Ask if anyone has seen her, but if not, keep going toward Stanton Hall. Snoop around there if you can, and find out what they're saying about the Stantons' niece. The servants must have some idea of what's going on. I want you there because I know you won't add any more to the gossip than there already is. Try not to use her name when you ask along the way, too. We've got to keep this as quiet as possible."

Sure, then only *half* the county would know the Earl of St. Cloud had misplaced his fiancée.

Little Yorby made Juneclaire wait an hour for the snow to finish melting so her shoes wouldn't get wet and ruined. Then he sent her off with three well-fed kittens, a jar of milk, a loaf of bread he could spare because Aggie was coming home soon, and hope.

There was a family of gentlefolk not a mile down the road, Little Yerby told her, with a sickly little girl. "Mayhap they need someone to teach the young'un her letters, if she lives that long." He took a pull on his pipe, then coughed. "Else Mrs. Langbridge might want another lady round about. There's no family that anyone sees. Mister's a solicitor in Bramley. Tell them Little Yerby sent you."

While St. Cloud prepared to greet his household staff and hand out their vails under Talbot's supervision, Juneclaire prepared for her first interview. She shook Little Yerby's flooring off her cloak, rebraided her hair, and kissed the old man good-bye.

Mrs. Langbridge met her at the door and tried to press a shilling into Juneclaire's hand. "Oh, you're not here for Boxing Day? Of course not. You're not a—Oh, I am sorry. There's just so much to do. Why did you say you had come?"

"Mr. Little Yerby sent me, ma'am, to ask after your little girl and to see if you might need a governess for her."

"My poor Cynthia." Mrs. Langbridge wiped her eyes with an already tear-dampened cloth.

"She hasn't . . . ?"

"Oh, no, she is just distraught over the move." Mrs. Langbridge waved a hand at trunks and bags waiting in the hallway. "She does not want to leave her friends, and her papa, of course, but the doctor thinks a healthier climate might . . . So we are going to Italy tomorrow, Cynthia, Nanny, a maid, and I. Mr. Langbridge cannot travel with us just yet, you see, so things are all at sixes and sevens, with packing and trying to leave the house in order, and Cynthia will fret so, which cannot be at all good for her. Do forgive me, Miss . . . ?"

"Beaumont, ma'am, and you must be wishing me to Jericho. I can see you do not need a governess and you do not need a stranger to keep you from your preparations. Please forgive me for the intrusion and accept my wishes for a safe journey and a swift recovery for your little girl."

"No, Miss Beaumont, please forgive my manners, after you were kind enough to call, and I haven't even offered you tea." She tried to brush away another tear. "I am sorry, my mind is in pieces, what with leaving my Tom and Cynthia so inconsolable."

"Mrs. Langbridge, you seem exhausted. Would you like me to sit with Cynthia for a bit while you catch your breath? It will be no bother, I assure you, for I am in no hurry to go home and only need get as far as Bramley this afternoon."

"Would you, Miss Beaumont? How kind. I should like to spend some time with Tom before he has to go visit a client. Some old hag called him out today, of all days! He is getting ready now and could drive you to Bramley when he leaves."

Juneclaire was removing her cloak. "That would be perfect. And could I make another forward suggestion? Don't you think that Cynthia would be happier about the trip if she could take a friend of her own along?"

"A friend? But we cannot . . ."

Juneclaire reached into her satchel and pulled out a kitten. "Why not?"

"I'll name her Holly," the little girl announced, "so we both remember an English Christmas. Do you think they have holly in Italy, Miss Beaumont?"

"I have no idea, Cynthia. You shall just have to go and see, won't you? Perhaps you shall write and tell me, so I'll know for the future." Juneclaire was pleased to see the hectic flush leave Cynthia's cheeks, although the spots of color remained, betraying her illness. The child was calm now and had taken her medicine without complaint, too rapt in watching the three kittens tumbling on her bed covers. She chose the black kitten "because Papa says everyone in Italy wears black. But, Miss Beaumont, what if Holly isn't a girl? Can a boy cat be called Holly?"

"I don't see why not. Do you know Mr. Little Yerby?"

"Of course, everyone knows Little. He brings the milk twice a week, and sometimes he lets me ride his donkey."

"Well, Mr. Little has one of Holly's brothers or sisters, and he is going to call the kitten David, no matter what."

"Oh, but if Little says his cat's a boy, then that's what it is. The animals always do what he says."

While Juneclaire was spending the morning entertaining a sick child, St. Cloud was standing on the steps of the Priory's porch, drinking wassail toasts with his tenants. By noon he was drunk as a lord, and so was the pig at his side, dressed in a ribbon-and-lace collar Aunt Florrie had stayed up all night sewing. None of his other relatives had made a showing yet, and none of his minions had reported back from the search. Two more hours of this, St. Cloud promised himself, and then he could ride to Bramley, if he could sit a horse.

Juneclaire stayed to watch Cynthia fall asleep for her nap with a smile on her thin face, and then she took luncheon with the Langbridges, at their insistence, although she did not want to intrude on one of their last moments together. They were all praise for her handling of their peevish child. "Oh, no, I cannot take any of the credit." Juneclaire laughed. "Once I showed her the kittens she was a perfect darling."

126

Mr. Thomas Langbridge was a pleasant-looking, sandy-haired gentleman with a worried frown. "I wish a kitten could work such magic on the client I have an appointment with this afternoon. I feel sorry for the old grande dame truly, because she is blind and has lost most of her family, but I wish she would not choose to change her dashed will every time her rackety grandson sneezes."

"And today of all days," his wife complained.

"Not even you, my dear, can accuse Lady St. Cloud of purposely selecting the day before your journey. She had no way of knowing. We must be thankful she waited past Christmas to send for me. And she keeps country hours at the Dower House, at any rate, so dinner will be early if I stay, and you know I must if she invites me, if I wish to retain her as my wealthiest client. I never understood why she did not take her business to any of the solicitors in Ayn-Jerome or even Thackford."

"Most likely she turned them off in her previous tantrums." Mrs. Langbridge was rearranging the food on her plate. Juneclaire had no such loss of appetite and busied herself with the turbot in oyster sauce.

"More likely she trusted my uncle. Try to show a little compassion for the old countess, my dear, even if she is a crusty beldam."

While he enjoyed his mutton, Mr. Langbridge's solicitor's mind was busy chewing a different bone. Somewhere over the vanilla flan he presented his idea: "You know, Miss Beaumont, you might well apply for a position with Lady St. Cloud if you are seeking employment. We would take you on in a minute for Cynthia if the situation were different. You are patient and kind, refined and intelligent. That's just what the old bat—ah, lady needs. I admit to having concerns about her, alone in the Dower House with just her old retainers looking after her. You and your kittens wrought such a miracle with Cynthia, I'd be happy to recommend you for the dowager's companion."

Juneclaire smiled and thanked him. "But I'm afraid you haven't painted a very pretty picture of your employer. I think I should rather face my own family's ill humors than someone else's."

"You can think about it on the way to Bramley. I am stopping by my office there to fetch copies of papers she wants to emend. You could drive out with me, and if you find you don't suit or she is not interested, I shall simply bring you back to town on my return trip."

While Juneclaire once more deliberated over her future on the way to Bramley, the Earl of St. Cloud was riding in the opposite direction, out of the little village. Vicar Broome was aghast to think that Miss Beaumont had not reached Springdale, but he was helpless to provide the earl with any other information. Poor fellow, he thought, the younger man was so smitten, he hadn't even stayed to have a sip of Madeira. Mr. Broome sipped it himself, in celebration of the handsome donation the lovesick earl had made to start up the poor box after the day's distribution. Reverend Broome wiped his spectacles and contemplated his own venality. Should he have reminded the mooncalf of his generous gift just the day before?

He wiped them again, then took them off altogether when the young lady in the rabbit-lined cloak walked into his study. "Miss, ah, Beaumont?" he mumbled, wishing his wife were there. He might know what to do with finances; affairs of the heart were Mrs. Broome's venue. While he was deliberating whether to send a boy after the earl—but who in town could ride at that neck-or-nothing pace?—or after Mrs. Broome, Juneclaire was thrusting a striped kitten into his arms.

"Because you and your wife have been so kind to me," she said, looking so sweet and innocent, he couldn't tell her how cats made him sneeze. And itch. And weep at the eyes.

"How happy I am to see you, Miss Beaumont. There was a gentleman here asking for you. We were all concerned for your welfare."

"A gentleman? Not a portly, middle-aged man who wears a bagwig? That would be my uncle Avery, and I never suspected he would make the least push to find me."

"No, this gentleman was not, ah, portly. He gave his name as Mr. Jordan."

"Oh, Merry!" Then she blushed. Her face was almost as red as the vicar's was becoming from stroking the cat.

"Oh, dear, Mr., ah, Jordan did not insult you in any way, did he? That is, your blushes and . . ." He blew his nose. Oh, how he wished Mrs. Broome did not have to visit the almshouse this afternoon!

"Mr. Jordan? Never! You mustn't think such a thing. He is a true gentleman."

Well, that relieved Mr. Broome's mind, if not his nose. "Have you decided not to go to London, then, Miss Beaumont?" he asked, changing the subject. "Mrs. Broome will be pleased." More pleased than she was going to be about the cat. "May I tell her your, ah, alternate plans, then, so she does not worry."

"Thank her for her concern, sir, but I am not sure what I will do."

The vicar could feel a rash starting on his neck and the check for the poor box itching in his pocket. "My child, have you ever heard of St. Cloud Priory?"

Juneclaire looked startled. "Why, Mr. Langbridge just mentioned it, that I might find a position with the dowager countess there. After what he said about her, though . . ."

"Perfect!" Broome wouldn't even have to consult his conscience about pitchforking this lovely young innocent into the arms of a hardened libertine. The old harridan would make sure nothing untoward took place, and if the young earl was as sincere as he seemed, Vicar Broome would be calling the banns next week, if his throat didn't close right up with cat hair.

Now the minister might believe in the efficacy of prayer, but he also believed in giving his prayers a helping hand, or a shove in the right direction. "I'll write a reference myself. I know the dowager has the reputation of being a holy terror, but I've seen worse reputations proved false, this very afternoon. She's just old and lonely. She needs you. The Lord must have sent you to Langbridge for just that purpose."

He was almost pleading. He was actually crying. Juneclaire was so touched, she said she would reconsider.

Then the reverend clinched her decision. He begged for divine forgiveness and lied through his teeth: "She likes cats."

So while the Earl of St. Cloud was racing past uninformative Springdale and heading for London, where he would knock on back doors himself if need be and haunt the coaching inns, Juneclaire was headed toward his own haunted house to knock on his own grandmother's door.

Chapter Fifteen

No one answered the knock. Juneclaire thought they should leave.

"No, old Pennington must have the gout again. We'll just give him a few minutes to get here. He's Lady St. Cloud's butler, and he's older than dirt. So's her abigail, Nutley, who's too deaf to hear the door anyway. Mrs. Pennington is the cook-housekeeper and she, ah, tipples."

Juneclaire was positive they should leave. She set her carpetbag down on the steps of the gray stone house. "Goodness, no wonder you didn't tell me this before we got here. Why ever doesn't Lady St. Cloud retire them if they are so far beyond their work?"

"I asked the dowager once and almost had my head bitten off. They're like family, it seems, and have nowhere else they'd rather go. Help comes from the main house—you can't see it from here, but the Priory is just beyond those trees. They do the cleaning and such, so Lady St. Cloud's retainers' positions are more nearly pensions."

"Is there no one in the household younger than Methuselah? It cannot be very comfortable or even safe for the old lady."

Mr. Langbridge knocked again, harder. "There's

a young maid, Sally Munch, and a footman. They are walking out, according to the dowager, and I am afraid they are walking out more often than they are working indoors. They're most likely off on holiday this afternoon anyway. But you mustn't think no one cares about the old lady's welfare. The earl has tried to get her to move to the Priory countless times, I understand, but the dowager and the present countess, the earl's mother, have never gotten on. Well, there is no point waiting out here any longer," he said, which Juneclaire was relieved to hear until he concluded, "We may as well go on in. I know the dowager is expecting me."

The solicitor guided Juneclaire to a bench along the wall of the long entry hall. The furnishings were old-fashioned but elegant, obviously expensive and scrupulously clean, from what she could see in the near dark. The dowager might be blind, but surely her staff needed more light than this? And there were no flowers or plants, not a holiday decoration of any kind. If *she* were here, Juneclaire speculated, there would be garlands of fresh-smelling greens, bowls of dried lavender or crushed rose petals, and clove-studded apples. Surely the dowager could smell what she could not see. She'd light all the sconces, too, Juneclaire mused, so the place felt warmer. Yes, she could be useful here.

When Mr. Langbridge came out of a room down the hall, he seemed even more worried than before. "She's agreed to see you," he said. "Alone. I beg you to try to please her, Miss Beaumont, for I'm afraid the dowager grows more addled in her wits every time I see her. She sent for me today because the Angel of Death visited her last night, she claims, so she knows her time is near. I fear for her, indeed I do."

"I heard that, you jobbernoll, you," came an angry voice from down the hall, accented by the pounding of a cane. "Don't you know a person's hearing gets better when they lose their sight? And I ain't dicked in the nob, you paper-skulled paper pusher. Now are you going to send the female in, or are you going to sit in my hallway gossiping about me all day?"

The old lady was still muttering when Juneclaire went into the room and curtsied, even knowing the small, white-haired woman didn't see her. The dowager sat perfectly erect, not the least bit frail or withered. Juneclaire touched her on the hand and said, "How do you do, my lady? I am Miss Beaumont. Thank you for meeting me."

"Humph" was all the response she got back. "Thinks I need a keeper, does he?"

"No, ma'am, just a companion."

"What for? To jaw me dead? Not much else for a companion to do around here. I can't play cards or go for a ride. Can't even do my needlework."

"But I could read to you, and I could drive you about if there's a cart. And I could teach you to knit. Once you get the hang of it, you don't need to watch the needles."

"Humph. Knitting ain't genteel. Ladies do fancy work, miss."

"Yes, but there are many people who need scarves and mittens more than they need another altar cloth in the church. I should think a lady might consider that, too."

"There's some sense in what you say, but you ain't going to be preaching to me about the poor, are you?"

Juneclaire laughed, a pleasing sound to the old lady's ears. "Not if I don't wish to join their ranks, it seems. But I am sure you think just as you ought, my lady."

"You're not one of those Methody Reformers, are you? I don't want any holier-than-thou reverencer sneering behind my back. Frank language ain't going to shock you, is it, Miss Beaumont?"

"My cousins cured me of that ages ago, my lady."

"Ages? How old are you, anyway? Langbridge said you were just a girl. I don't want any shriveled up prunes-and-prisms spinsters around me either. Let me touch your face, girl."

Juneclaire knelt so the old woman could touch her soft cheek, her straight nose, and heavy brows, the thick braids of her hair and the smile on her mouth.

"I am nineteen, my lady, and I haven't put on my caps yet." She laughed again. "In fact, I had a very attractive offer from a gentleman just recently."

Juneclaire jumped aside as Lady St. Cloud thumped her cane down. "What kind of offer, miss? I won't have any hanky-panky around here. It's bad enough with the lower orders sneaking off to the bushes and the pantry and the basement at all hours."

The laughter was gone from Juneclaire's voice. "You insult me, my lady, and also the gentleman. It was a very fine, very proper offer of marriage."

"Pish tosh, miss. If it was such a fine offer, why didn't you take it? You can't tell me you'd rather look after an old crone than have a house and husband of your own. Coming it too brown, my girl."

Juneclaire sighed. "I had to refuse, Lady St. Cloud. He offered out of honor, you see, not out of love. I couldn't hold such a fine gentleman to an empty marriage. It wouldn't be right." She sighed again.

"But you wanted to, didn't you, girl?" the old woman shrewdly interpreted.

"Oh yes, Merry was everything I ever thought a man should be."

Merry? The cane dropped from Lady St. Cloud's

134

hand. "Miss Beaumont, what did you say your first name was?"

"Juneclaire," she answered hesitantly. What new quiz was this?

"And how many gals named Juneclaire do you think are running around Berkshire right now?"

"Why, none others, I should think. I was named after my mother, Claire, and my father, Jules. Why do you ask?"

The old lady didn't answer. She just laughed and laughed. "Turned him down, did you? Oh, how I am going to enjoy this!" She laughed some more, till Juneclaire began to worry about her sanity after all, especially when the dowager recovered and suddenly asked, "You ain't afraid of ghosts, are you?"

So confused was Juneclaire that she blurted out, "They cannot be more frightening than you."

The dowager laughed some more, then reached out to pat Juneclaire's hand. "You'll do, girl, you'll do."

"Does that mean I am hired, my lady?"

"Hired? I suppose it does, for now. Go send in that young solicitor of mine. I want to discuss your, ah, wages with him."

"Thank you, my lady. I'll try to please, I swear it. There's just one other thing, though. Do you really like cats?"

"Cats? Pesky creatures. Can't abide the beasts, always underfoot or carrying around dead things."

"Oh. I'm sorry, truly I am, for I should have liked to stay. But I have this kitten, you see, that no one wanted, and I cannot just abandon it with no home. So I'll have to—"

"I'll learn to love it."

When Mr. Langbridge came back out for her on her bench in the hall, he looked at Juneclaire as if she'd grown another head. Nevertheless, he silently beckoned her back to her ladyship's parlor.

"I have invited Langbridge to take potluck, Miss Beaumont. Are you too tired from your travels, or do you join us?"

"I, um . . . Oh, dear, I know this is not the proper way to start in my new position, my lady, but did you know that Mr. Langbridge's daughter was ill?"

"Of course I did. Asked first thing."

"Yes, but she needs to go to a warmer climate, and Mrs. Langbridge is traveling to Italy with her tomorrow."

"That's well and good, I wish them Godspeed, but what is that to—Oh, I see. We won't keep you then, Langbridge. I expect you to stay next week when you bring those papers back for my signature. I daresay you'll be glad for the company then. And as for you, miss, I suppose you think just as you ought. Just remember, I find it deuced uncomfortable being wrong." The dowager spoke with a smile, though, so Juneclaire went cheerfully off to get ready for her first dinner in her new home.

The three old retainers were in various somnolent stages in the kitchen. Juneclaire introduced herself and explained her new position to Pennington, the only one whose eyes opened at Juneclaire's entry. The butler instantly recognized her for a lady and slowly lowered his bandaged foot to the floor so he could rise and make her a proper bow. Juneclaire had to help him back to his seat. He shouted the news loudly enough to wake his wife from her post-tea, predinner stupor and for Nutley, the abigail, to hear. If Juneclaire worried her ladyship's longtime servants were going to be jealous of an upstart, she was soon dissuaded from that notion. The three were relieved someone else was going to help look after their mistress and thrilled someone else was going to be the butt of her temper. Mrs.

Pennington vowed to fix a special dinner, and Nutley asked if miss needed help with her unpacking. What Juneclaire needed was a hot bath, but none of the servants looked fit enough to walk up the stairs, much less carry a tub and tins of water.

"Never you fear, miss," Mrs. Pennington said, wobbling to the door, "by the time we get a room aired and your things put away, young Sally Munch'll be back with her beau. They never stay away through supper."

Her room adjoining the dowager's was twice as big as the one Juneclaire had slept in most of her life. Did she just leave Stanton Hall a few days ago? It seemed a lifetime. There was a fire in the grate and lavender sachets in the drawers for her few belongings and a thick carpet for her feet. The kitten was being fussed over in the kitchen, and she was being fussed over here. Nutley insisted on brushing out her hair and taking her second-best gown to be pressed. The abigail had not even commented on the meager contents of her carpetbag.

As Nutley remarked to Lady St. Cloud as she helped her mistress change for dinner, "Young miss is Quality, anyone can see that, and if she had deep pockets, she wouldn't be going for a companion, now, would she?" Nutley did not hear the dowager's comments any more than the dowager could see Juneclaire's appearance. Mistress and maid were as one, though, in agreeing that Miss Beaumont was, on first meeting, a jewel.

The jewel was going to look far more brilliant without all the dust. Juneclaire looked at her bath when it came as a starving man looks at a slab of beef. Aunt Marta would call such sybaritic pleasure sinful, so Juneclaire would not think about Aunt Marta now. The morning was time enough to send her aunt a note that she was well. Juneclaire leaned back in the suds. She was very well indeed.

* * *

After dinner Juneclaire read the previous week's mail to the dowager and laughed at her stories about the people mentioned in her friends' *on-dits*. For a woman who did not do the Season, Lady St. Cloud used to keep abreast of the latest gossip with a vast network of correspondence. She was hoping her grandson did not return to steal the girl away before Miss Beaumont got halfway through the letters. Well, he could take the girl, but he wasn't getting the cat.

At first she was worried. "It's not going to trip me up, is it? Wouldn't do to fall at my age, you know."

"Cats are very good about things like that, my lady. And you do have your cane to sweep in front of you. You'll have to be more gentle with it, of course, not knowing the kitten's location. Here, hold it."

Silk and a sandpaper tongue and the rumble of tiny thunder that went on and on. It was love at first touch.

"What does he look like?"

Juneclaire wasn't quite sure what to say. This was the fourth kitten, the one no one wanted. "Well, his eyes were blue, but I think they are going to be yellow. He has a little gold on his chest and a black spot over one eye, and white feet, except for the back right one. That's kind of brownish. And there's a faint gray stripe down his back. He's a bit of this and a patch of that. But he has the sweetest personality!"

"Patches. I like that. Will that do for a name, do you think?"

Juneclaire laughed. "That cat is lucky to have a home; a name is icing on the cake."

"Lucky, then. No, what do the Irish call those

patches of lucky clover? Shamrocks! You did say he had green eyes?"

"Well . . ."

The dowager countess listened while Juneclaire played a few ragged carols. "I'm sorry, my lady. I never had many lessons; my aunt thought them a waste for a female with no prospects. I have no excuses for my poor voice, so I shan't subject you to that. Would you rather I read to you?"

"Perhaps tomorrow. This has already been a most pleasant evening, Miss Beaumont. I don't want to use all my treats in one day, like a child who cries when Christmas is past."

"But there are twelve days of Christmas, my lady," Juneclaire said with a smile in her voice. "What would you like to do now? Do you retire early?"

"What I would *like* to do is play cards." Lady St. Cloud reached for her cane to punctuate her vexation. She remembered the kitten asleep in her lap just in time.

Juneclaire thought a minute, and then her face cleared. "I'll be right back," she told the dowager, then ran off to find Nutley and shout until she had what she wanted. Out of breath but smiling, she came back with her prize, a sewing needle.

"What is it, girl? What are you giggling about?"

"Something else my scapegrace cousins taught me. Here, feel this." She held out a card. "The corner."

"Why, why, you're marking the cards! That's cheating!"

"Not if we both know the marks, it's not. I don't think we'll get so proficient that the dealer will have such an advantage, do you?"

"Miss Beaumont, I think I am going to learn to love you like a daughter. Or a granddaughter."

Chapter Sixteen

$\mathcal{T}$he dowager was having a nightmare. "Don't lie to me, Death. I know who you are and I'm not ready yet, I tell you. I have to make sure St. Cloud is settled before he's ruined for good and all. You'll see, the girl will be the making of the rogue."

Juneclaire heard the old lady's strident voice in the room next door. She had to recall which side held the bed stand before she fumbled for candle and flint in the unfamiliar room.

"You can't take me yet," the dowager was shouting. "He's already made mice feet of the thing. No, I don't want to hear any more of your wicked falsehoods about my sons. Go."

Trust Lady St. Cloud to tell the Devil to go to Hell, Juneclaire thought as she tied a wrapper Nutley had laid out for her over her own flannel nightdress. She hurried to the dowager's room and scratched on the door. When she got no answer, Juneclaire turned the knob and pushed the door open, shielding her candle. The dowager was fast asleep in a large bed. She was snoring gently, and she wore a satisfied smile on her face, having bested the Angel of Death for one more night.

Resisting the urge to peer in the corners or look under the bed, Juneclaire checked to make sure the

140

silver bell was within the dowager's reach in case she needed to call for her companion during the night. Then Juneclaire went back toward her own room. Before she got to the doorway, though, she felt a prickle of sensation at the bottom of her spine. Someone was watching her. She whipped around, almost putting her candle out, but the steady sleep noises were still coming from the dowager's slightly open mouth.

It's just all the talk of death, Juneclaire chided herself, that and Sally Munch's chatter about the Priory ghosts stirring again. The slain monks were walking the ancient halls, Sally had declared as she slid the warming pan between Juneclaire's sheets . . . or something worse.

The young maid's imagination was as overheated as the rest of the little flirt, Juneclaire firmly told herself, blowing out the candle and getting between the long-cold sheets.

Then she heard a tapping noise, like the dowager's cane but not quite. She had that same feeling of being observed. "There are no such things as ghosts," she declared out loud. Then she shouted, "Begone," figuring that if it worked for the dowager, it was worth a try, just in case. She thought she heard a chuckle, but she could not be sure, not with the covers pulled over her head.

The dowager never rose before eleven, but Juneclaire was up with the birds, so she looked around for other occupations to keep her busy. She helped Penny make bread and hid whatever bottles of wine she could find. She fetched the silver tea service, epergne, and sconces for Pennington, where he was polishing at the kitchen table, his leg propped on a stool. And she dragged Sally Munch and the footman out of an unused bedroom where they were checking the bedsprings, to help her gather greens.

The footman cut the holly and pine branches Juneclaire indicated, while she fashioned a wreath out of some vines. Sally, naturally, knew just where they could find some mistletoe. As they worked, Juneclaire tried not to listen to the servants' gossip about the doings at the Priory, some possibly scandalous goings-on between the master, a recognized rake, and his latest flirt. Bets were on in the servants' hall, it seemed, that a betrothal was all a hum, St. Cloud was never going to give up his profligate ways. The stable had it that the master was dead-set on the female, whoever and wherever she was. Juneclaire did not feel she could reprimand the maid for her chatter, but she found the whole conversation distasteful.

"It's worse than that, miss. What did he do yesterday but hare off in the middle of the tenants' visits. Castaway, they say he was. Left in a great rush without saying when he'd be back or nothing. Then what happens but stablemen start walking in the halls at night, with pistols. By hisself's orders, they say. Why, mistress was near swooning, they say. Then comes this morning. Molly, who comes to clean at the Dower House, says a whole herd of workmen arrived at dawn, on Lord St. Cloud's instructions, they say, to check for loose boards and such, banging on the walls. If that weren't bad enough to set the house on its ears, an army of sweeps comes looking for owls and squirrels and bats in the chimneys. So there can't be no fires!"

"And there are guests? I can see where that would upset even the most serene household."

"Which that one's not. Why, that cousin—"

Juneclaire did not wish to hear any more details of life at the Priory. She quickly asked the footman to carry a message to the sweeps to come check the

Dower House flues if they got a chance. "I thought there must be woodpeckers, myself."

"Oh, no, miss. That be the ghost."

Juneclaire read the newspapers to the dowager before luncheon and answered some letters from her dictation. She thought about writing to her relatives. Later.

After luncheon the dowager announced it was time for her nap. "And I want you to go outside and get some exercise. Can't be healthy for a young thing like you to be cooped up inside with a parcel of old biddies, working so hard."

"What work?" Juneclaire laughed. "This has been the easiest day of my life."

"Doesn't say much for the rest of your life, but I'll hold my tongue on that. Can you ride?" Lady St. Cloud asked abruptly.

"Yes, but I did not bring my habit." Juneclaire knew the dowager was well aware of the fact. Nutley must have enumerated Juneclaire's scant wardrobe to her mistress the first day, thus the night robe. Juneclaire had two day dresses, the blue one she had on and the heavier gray one she'd worn on the road. She had the almost fashionable rose muslin castoff from Aunt Marta that she wore to dinner last night and, of course, her unworn white velvet gown. At least the dowager did not have to look at her companion in the same gowns day after day. She wasn't going to get as weary of them as Juneclaire was going to. Juneclaire supposed she could ask her uncle to send on her clothes when she wrote to him, but the gowns she had left behind were all faded and threadbare, and her habit was so thin in the saddle, one more gallop might have her petticoat showing. Perhaps when she got paid, Juneclaire would purchase a dress length or two. But wages had not been discussed, nor a possible day off for her to do any shopping. Since her employer was being almost pleasant, Juneclaire hated to bring up such awkward topics. Instead, she added, "I do like to walk."

"Humph. Walking's for peasants, girl, unless you're on the strut in Hyde Park or such. Nutley can alter one of my old habits for you. Certes, I don't need them anymore."

"If you wanted to ride, we could—"

"No, I'm not going to trot in a circle at the end of a lead line, by Jupiter. It used to be neck-or-nothing with me, and I ain't going to change now."

"Oh, then you weren't always . . . ?"

"Blind. No, I used to see fine; just saw too much, the specialists said. Too many birthdays, mostly. Now I'm too stiff to get on a horse and too old to chance breaking a bone anyway. So those habits are just taking space in the clothespress."

"But I couldn't—"

"Have to. There's no one else who can exercise my mare for me. Flame never held anything but a sidesaddle, don't you know. Prettiest little filly in the whole county, she was. Now go on, get. I need my rest if I'm to learn this knitting of yours tonight. Oh, and don't ride toward the Priory. No reason for you to face those spiteful cats up there without me. My daughter-in-law's relations, they are, and a worse pack of dirty dishes you'll never find."

"You haven't met the Root and the Newt."

"But they're just boys, you said. Fanny's niece is a spoiled hoyden, and that other one is no better than she should be. The nevvy is a basket scrambler. You watch out for him, girl."

Juneclaire laughed. "I thank you, ma'am, but I'm not likely to tempt a man of that ilk. I don't have a fortune and I'm no dasher, as my cousins say."

The dowager had Nutley's opinion that miss would be a real diamond, with some careful dress ing and a new hairstyle, should brunets come back in style. She also had the fact that one of England's premier bachelors had offered for the chit. "You be careful, that's all. When my grandson gets back is soon enough for you to meet the rest of the jackals. Now go."

"Yes, my lady." She curtsied, even though the dowager couldn't see.

"Why, that old—" She bit her lip, even if Nutley couldn't hear. A brown velvet habit was already altered, likely from measurements of her other day dress. The dowager had meant to have her way, no matter Juneclaire's feelings. "Thank you, Nutley," she shouted, giving the abigail a quick hug as she flew down the stairs in her eagerness for her ride. They were used to sending to the Priory for the rare times the dowager went out, Pennington explained while she filled her pockets with apples and sugar cubes (and hid another bottle of cooking sherry that was not destined for dinner). A carriage arrived every Sunday to carry the dowager to chapel at the Priory, he said, and a boy came every day to attend the small stable that served the Dower House.

He wasn't there now, so Juneclaire took down a gleaming ladies' saddle herself and went to lead the mare out of her stall. She did not have the heart to put the saddle on Flame's back. If ever the mare had a flame at all, it had sputtered and gone out before Juneclaire was born. Flame had barely enough teeth to crunch the apple, after Juneclaire found a knife to slice it, and barely enough energy to put one foot in front of the other.

"Still, you cannot be happy in this dark barn all day, and the dowager said we were both to get some exercise, so come along."

So Juneclaire, with the skirts of the most elegant riding habit she had ever worn trailing in the mud and the dust, ambled alongside the geriatric equine on the path where she'd been gathering holly that morning.

When Lady St. Cloud sent Juneclaire out for an airing, she hadn't been thinking of the chaos at the Priory. Lady Fanny was busy having spasms, Lord Wilmott was growing more bilious with each hammer blow, as if the search for defects were a personal affront to his care of the earl's property, and Florrie was in the attics, in the workmen's way, finding pig-size baby clothes. Things were in such a state there that even a ride to the Dower House appealed to the younger members of the house party, since it promised the diversion of investigating the new companion. On being informed by Pennington—after a wait that had Lady Sydelle rapping her crop against her leather boots—that the dowager countess was resting and miss was riding through the holly path, they decided to ride after her. Niles wanted to wager the unfortunate creature wouldn't last a week; neither his sister nor Lady Pomeroy took the bet.

"I bet she is a perfect antidote," Elsbeth declared, "for even the poorest female can find a male to support her if she has any looks and is not fussy. I'd rather be married to a coal heaver than be Lady St. Cloud's galley slave."

"You mightn't have either choice, with that wasp tongue," the Widow Pomeroy snapped at the younger girl, having married a dirty old man whose dirty fortune came from coal mines, although that fact was not well known among the ton.

Leaping to his intended's—his intentions, not hers—aid before Elsbeth could unleash even more venom, Niles taunted, "I don't notice you making any grand match, sister, now that your plans for St. Cloud are scotched."

"Unlike others I could mention, I am waiting for

a love match. Not all females sell themselves for security, you know."

"And not all females are so totty-headed. I bet even the cipherous companion would jump at an offer to escape the drudgery."

"An honorable offer, of course," the widow agreed. "But are you willing to back your wager on another kind of offer? Companions are notoriously virtuous. I'll bet my diamond pendant against—*do* you have anything worth wagering, Niles?—that this Miss Beaumont will accept something less."

"Do you mean you're betting that Miles can seduce the dowager's companion? Why . . . why, that's evil."

"And so entertaining. We have to do something to enliven the days till the New Year's ball, don't we? Niles, do you take me up?"

Niles was reflecting that the woman he wished to make his wife could show a little more interest in his fidelity to her. Not that he intended to remain faithful once the wedding vows were exchanged and the marriage settlements signed, but he hoped for some sign of jealousy, possessiveness even, before the fact. If there was to be a fact. "Sight unseen?" he asked. "I'm afraid I need longer odds, my sweet Sydelle. What say that if I succeed, I also succeed with you, my pet? My honorable offer, naturally."

"Naturally. And if you lose?"

"You can't do this, Niles, not the dowager's own servant. St. Cloud will kill you." Elsbeth was horrified, but not as horrified as Juneclaire, on the other side of the boxwood hedges where Flame was nibbling at the last grasses. And Elsbeth, it seemed, was more concerned with danger to her brother than any damage that might be done to the poor downtrodden companion! Juneclaire could not hear Lady Sydelle's answer as the group rode away.

The dowager was right. These people were scum. They were beautiful, Juneclaire's peeks through the branches told her that, but they were cold and cruel. They were as exquisite as swans, and just as vicious close up. Lady Sydelle wore a scarlet habit with a tiny veiled hat perched coquettishly on her guinea gold locks, and her horse had specks of blood on its flanks from her spur. Juneclaire had never seen a man dressed as elegantly as Mr. Wilmott, or heard one speak so casually of ruining an innocent female. She almost wept to think of Merry and his precious offer. These three did not have enough honor among them to be worthy to shine Merry's boots.

If they were representative of Lord St. Cloud's friends and relatives, Juneclaire wanted even less to do with the Priory than before. She'd had no great esteem for the libertine earl since Mr. Langbridge related the man's scandalous reputation, and that opinion was lowered a notch when she saw his grandmother's condition. He kept her in, if not outright penury, then straightened circumstances, unprotected and locked away where he never had to see her. His very behavior gave the poor woman nightmares; his associates would put even that rough-tongued lady to the blush. The earl did not seem to care what havoc he wreaked on his mother's delicate health either, or on his staff, from what she'd seen. Juneclaire, for one, wished he'd never get back from his latest mad jaunt, undertaken when he was in his cups. She pitied the poor girl he was going to marry and hoped he never found her.

Chapter Seventeen

𝒮t. Cloud returned two days later. Even before his horse was led away, the dowager knew he was home via the servants' grapevine. She calculated how long before Fanny or his man Todd filled St. Cloud's ears with gossip, sending him posthaste to her doorstep demanding an explanation. She sent Juneclaire out early for her ride, saying that her old bones felt snow coming on. Miss Beaumont had better exercise the mare early, she claimed, lest Flame get too rambunctious from standing around all day.

Her grandson arrived not ten minutes later and managed to hold his patience in check for at least five minutes more.

"Grandmother," he said in an affected drawl after the formal greetings, "there seems to be a small creature stalking the tassel of my new Hessians."

Lady St. Cloud was sure he'd have his quizzing glass out, the fribble. "Adorable, ain't he?"

The earl did indeed have his glass out, but he was swinging it on its ribbon to the delight of one of the least prepossessing representatives of the feline species he'd ever seen. "Adorable is not quite the word I would have chosen, my lady. But, pray tell, how does it come about that you have a cat, no, any animal, in the house? You surely never approved of such a thing during my lifetime."

Oh, how the dowager wished she could see his face! "I've changed my mind, St. Cloud, since my new companion insisted."

Aha! The new companion! St. Cloud was on his feet and pacing. His forceful appearance was marred, had the dowager only seen it, by the scrap-cat chasing after him, intent on those dangling tassels. "Insisted, is it? The Dowager Countess St. Cloud taking orders from some encroaching female? They were right: you are not fit to be living alone!"

"I am not living alone, you nodcock. That's what the girl is for. And if any of those sponge-mongers up at the Priory dared to suggest I am missing a few spokes in my wheel, I'll have their guts for garters, see if I won't."

The earl picked up the kitten and dropped it, with his quizzing glass on its ribbon, into the dowager's lap before his boots were irreparably scored with needle claws. He cleared his throat. "We were speaking of the companion, ma'am."

"No, St. Cloud, you were. I was speaking of the hangers-on and dirty dishes you permit to reside under your roof. Your grandfather, the earl, would be spinning in his grave."

"He'd be coming back to haunt me if I left you here with some strange female whose name nobody remembers! They can't tell me where she came from or why. For all I know, she's here to stab you in your bed and steal the silver. You don't understand about unscrupulous people, Grandmother, how they prey on the"—he was going to say old and infirm, thought better of it—"unsuspecting. She could cozen you into changing your will or—"

"Already have."

"What?! I'll see the bitch in gaol first!" He struck his fist on the mantel.

"You'll sit down, boy, and mind your tongue in my parlor. You're giving me a headache."

The earl sat, took a deep breath, and tried again. "My apologies, Grandmother. But I have tried for years to hire you a companion, a respectable female to bear you company and look out for your welfare, since you refuse to move to the Priory. I found women from the best of families, with unimpeachable references. Young women, old women, women I personally knew, by Jupiter! And you refused to meet any of them. Dash it, I would have hired one of the royal ladies-in-waiting if I thought you'd have her. But you, madam, without a word to anyone, take on a perfect stranger. Is it any wonder I am overset?"

The dowager hadn't enjoyed a conversation so much in years. She should have been an inquisitor. "You always were pigheaded, boy. Do you think no one else knows what's best for themselves? You're a fine one to speak, clunch. I have found myself the perfect companion, and we suit to a cow's thumb. Which is a lot more than I can say for you and your misbegotten engagement."

The dowager stroked the cat during the following silence. When St. Cloud finally spoke, she could hear the sorrow in his voice. "There is no engagement, Grandmother. That's the other thing I came to the Dower House to tell you. I haven't said anything to the others yet, but I couldn't find her. I left messages, deuce take it, I left enough bribes to finance Prinny's new pavilion. I found her old housekeeper in London, who didn't know what I was talking about. I promised Mother I'd get back to help with the blasted ball, but my staying in Town wouldn't have made a difference. There's nothing, Grandmother, she's gone."

Not even the dowager could enjoy torturing a broken man, even if he was her only grandson and a cow-handed chawbacon to boot. "About my companion . . ."

"You were right, Grandmother, it's none of my business. If you are pleased, then I am pleased."

"She was not entirely without references, you know. In fact, Langbridge, my man of business, brought her out to me . . . from Bramley."

"From . . . ?"

"With Reverend Broome's commendation. He mentioned something about church pews Mr. Langbridge couldn't quite—"

St. Cloud was gone. Then he was back. "Where the bloody hell is she?"

"Why, I believe she is taking Flame cross-country. There is nothing like a good gallop to put roses in a girl's cheeks."

This time he kissed her hand in farewell but said, "You know, my lady, you are lucky that only the good die young."

If the dowager thought to send him helter-skelter over the Priory's acreage, she sorely misjudged her grandson, and Flame. He left his own horse in the small stable and followed the only path that led away from it. If the old nag could make it farther than the second clearing, he'd eat his hat, which he'd left on the dowager's hall table in his rush out the door.

He did not see them on the path, but then he heard a familiar off-key carol. The angel choir in heaven couldn't have sounded sweeter to his ears. He followed the song through a break in the hedges, and there she was, leading the blasted horse like a dog on a leash. She was wearing the same tatty gray cloak—Juneclaire didn't bother with the long-skirted habit for Flame's daily constitutionals—and her nose was red from the cold. She was beautiful.

"Hallo, Junco," he called.

"Merry!"

Neither knew how the ground was covered, but she was in his arms, or almost, looking up into his face. He was looking as handsome as Juneclaire remembered, certainly neater, in fawn breeches and a bottle green jacket, but his eyes looked tired, and the planes of his face seemed harsher. He'd forgotten how to smile, again. He held her shoulders and said, "Wretched female, I don't know whether to shake you or kiss you."

"Do I get a choice?" was all she could think to say. She felt her face go red at her own ungoverned tongue, but he pulled her closer, then yelped.

"What the deuces?"

"Oh, I am sorry. It's a needle I've taken to carrying around with me." Niles Wilmott had not wasted much time making good on his boasts to Lady Pomeroy. He'd tracked her down yesterday while she was out with Flame. First he plied her with heavy-handed compliments, then barely disguised hints of a financial arrangement. Finally he tried physical enticements, as if she could ever be attracted to a snake in gentleman's clothing. Overdressed clothing at that. Forewarned was forearmed, however, and Niles would not be approaching her again soon. She hoped he died of blood poisoning. Merry raised one eyebrow, meanwhile, waiting for further explanation, so she said, "It's in case I ran into that dastard from the Priory again."

She instantly knew she'd made an error, for the hands on her shoulders tightened till she'd have bruises there. "What dastard? Who insulted you, Juneclaire? I'll—"

"Oh hush, silly. I'm fine. Everyone has been so

nice to me. Well, almost everyone. I have so much to tell you, but you tell me first, instead of glowering at me so. What are you doing here and why are you in such a taking?"

"I am upset, goose, for I have been looking for you for days now, nights, too, in Bramley and Springdale and London and everywhere in between, and you've been right here. If I don't strangle you, it's just because I am too tired. You have led me a fine chase, girl."

"But why, Merry? We are friends, nothing more. I told you you were not responsible for me."

"Nothing more? After a night in a barn? That made you my responsibility, Miss Beaumont." That sounded too severe, even to the earl's ears, and hope made him add, "I cared."

Her hand touched the dent in his chin for an instant, and then she looked away, suddenly shy. "But . . . but how did you find me here?"

"I didn't. I came home to lick my wounds, and there you were."

"Home? You live here, at the Priory?" He nodded. "You're not one of the earl's disreputable friends, are you?"

"Worse," he told her.

Juneclaire felt a hollowness in her stomach. "A relative?"

"Worse still."

She'd known he was an aristocrat. That assurance and, yes, arrogance of his just had to be matched to a title, but the Earl of St. Cloud? If Flame had an ounce of speed left in her, Juneclaire would jump on the mare's back and ride who-knows-where. Merry—the earl—could walk faster than Flame at her quickest, though. Juneclaire did the only thing possible. She kicked him in the shin with her heavy wooden-soled walking shoe. "You liar!"

The earl was wondering why he'd bothered to

save his Hessians from the cat. "I am sorry about being the earl, Junco, sometimes sorrier than you can imagine, but I didn't lie. I am Merritt Jordan."

Juneclaire was limping away, at Flame's speed. "I am sorry, too, my lord, for the earl is not a person I wish to know."

"I did not lie to you about my reputation, Juneclaire, and I shall not lie now and say that it is undeserved. I am no longer that reckless, rebellious boy, however." He took Flame's lead out of Juneclaire's hand and walked beside her. "Besides, you can help me mend it."

Juneclaire ignored that last. "You're not caring about your mother, from all I hear. Aunt Marta says you can judge a man's worth by how he treats his mama."

"That sounds like what a mother of sons would say. My mother has never been comfortable with me, Juneclaire, and I gave up trying years ago. It would take the patience of a saint to put up with her vapors, and I never lied about that. And didn't Aunt Marta tell you not to listen to gossip?"

"Well, you aren't kind to your grandmother either, and that is not hearsay. I can see for myself that you keep her on a tight budget. Those old servants, this one pitiful excuse for a horse. If all this"—she waved one mittened hand around—"is yours, that is unforgivable."

He took that mittened hand in his gloved one and continued walking back to the stable. Juneclaire didn't remove her hand. "Now who told you that faradiddle about my holding the dowager's purse strings? Grandmother is one of the wealthiest women in the county in her own right. She could hire an army and operate a racing stable if she wanted. Have you tried to get her to do anything she *didn't* want? She lives the way she does out of her choice, not mine."

Juneclaire was thinking of some of the other things she'd heard to the earl's disfavor when she remembered another item altogether. She pulled her hand away from his so fast, he was left holding her mitten, the odd, not-quite-finished one. "They say—and it is not gossip, for even Lady St. Cloud mentioned it—that you are engaged."

"Yes."

"Yes? That is all you can say, yes? You can hold my hand"—and make her heart beat faster, although she did not say that—"when everyone is waiting for you to bring your betrothed home as soon as you fi—oh."

"Yes." He kept walking but glanced at her out of the corner of his eye. She was biting on her lower lip and kicking at rocks, and her brows were lowered. He wanted to take her in his arms more than anything, needles and kicks and all. "I told them we were engaged."

She came to a standstill. "Were you disguised then, too? You must have been to say such a thing when you knew it wasn't true."

"I am not a drunkard, Juneclaire. You don't have to worry about that, at least. I said we were betrothed because it's right that we marry after you were so compromised."

"But no one knew that I was compromised at all, and it was my fault for being where I had no business being!"

"They'll find out. And I also said it because I wanted it to be true." There, he'd confessed.

Instead of being won over, Juneclaire stamped her foot. "Well, you're not Little Yerby to make it so because you say it, and I am not Jack!"

"I should hope not, dear heart, whoever Little Yerby and Jack are. Will you come for a walk with me?" They were back at the stable, and he handed Flame's lead to the stable boy.

"But the dowager . . ."

"Knows all about it. Come." He stuffed her unresisting hand back in the mitten and held it firmly, going in the opposite direction. "Are you warm enough?"

She just nodded, lost in her own thoughts. After a bit she said, with not much of a quiver in her voice, that she could not marry an earl.

"Why, my love, are you holding out for a duke? I understand there are few on the marriage market this year, and those are well into their dotage. You'd do much better with a young earl."

"How can you tease? I am a nobody, with no dowry and no connections. And . . . and my parents ran off to France to marry. I know I told you that, but it's worse. They . . . they didn't say their vows until they got to Calais, a week later!"

"Shocking, Junco, shocking. Someday, when I am not trying to convince you to join your name with mine, I shall describe my own parents' marriage. Suffice it to say that Lady Fanny has not been to London in over twenty years for fear of being cut. I have tried to convince her that the past is long forgotten, but Uncle Harmon cautions her otherwise. It is not in his interest to see her remarry, or even move to Town, for then he would have no place here. He knows I will not have him set one foot over the doorsill of Jordan House in London. Juneclaire, if I do not hold you responsible for your parents' sins, can you forgive me mine?"

She nodded, but her mind was only half attending. The other half was gazing in awe at the edifice sprawled across her horizon.

"I promised you a house of your own, remember? I, ah, never said it was small. Do you hate it? It's even worse inside. We don't have to live here, you know. There's London and the stud in Ireland, and I have a hunting box in Leicester. We could buy a

157

cottage somewhere, damn it. Juneclaire, say something."

Something? "I want to go home." The Priory was surely the biggest building Juneclaire had seen since leaving France, where she'd visited some of the cathedrals with her parents. It was possibly the ugliest building she'd ever seen. Gray stone, tan brick, an Elizabethan wing and a modern wing, crenellated towers on one side, Roman columns supporting a two-story porch built right on top of the old Priory itself. One wing ended in the original chapel, another in a vast ballroom built in Henry's times. She could not see the conservatory from here, Merry—Lord St. Cloud—told her, but it formed the central wing.

Juneclaire had to laugh. He was teasing, of course.

"No, Junco, I am not bamming you. I need you."

"The dowager needs me."

"We'll share. I need you to convince her to move up here, where she'll be looked after better. There's a private suite all ready for her. I need you to keep peace between the countesses and referee the cricket matches between the Priory phantoms and the Angel of Death."

"Woodpeckers."

"You heard it, too? See, your calm good sense is just what they need. What I need. Please, Junco, at least consider my proposal. Say you'll come to dinner tonight, you and Grandmother, of course. The relatives mostly grow worse on closer acquaintance, but I swear no one shall insult you."

"I have nothing to wear to such a grand house."

"I believe you are turning craven on me, Junco. Is this the fearless amazon who attacked a bandit with a water bucket? Who fended off an amorous footman with a wine bottle? Who wears a blasted porcupine quill in her lapel? I happen to know you have a beautiful gown, a white velvet gown. I should love to buy you rubies to go with it, or emeralds. I should like to touch the softness of it, against your skin. But I can be patient. Not very, as you know. Come tonight, Junco, come get to know us and give us a chance. Give me a chance."

Chapter Eighteen

$\mathcal{S}$t. Cloud sent over red rosebuds from the hot-houses. Nutley wove them through the wreath of holly Juneclaire wore as a headpiece, with her hair pulled up and back, tiny curls framing her face and a long sweep of brown waves trailing over one shoulder. The abigail pinned another of the roses to the green ribbon that sashed under the high waist, helped Miss Beaumont fasten her mother's pearls around her neck, and declared the young lady a diamond of the first water. The groom, draping the borrowed black velvet mantle with red satin lining over Juneclaire's pale shoulders, stared wide-eyed and open-mouthed. Sally Munch gasped.

"Well, tell me, girl, tell me," the dowager demanded, banging her cane down once she knew Shamrock was tucked in the kitchen with Penny. "Will she do?"

Sally swore she was bang up to the mark, and Pennington, holding the door, added that miss was top of the trees, if my lady excused the cant. Juneclaire wanted to sink with embarrassment. "Really, ma'am, there is no need to make such a fuss."

"There's all the need in the world, miss, and you know it. Facing that pack of barracudas, you'll want all your defenses up, and a gel's best defense is looking her best."

Juneclaire was surely doing that, she acknowledged. She'd never felt so elegant, so pampered, or so unsure of herself. "Will they like me?" she asked, as the footman and Sally helped the dowager into an elegant carriage.

"What's that to the point?" the dowager replied as soon as the coach started moving. "Hell, they all hate me, and I've never lost a night's sleep over it. Besides, if you're worrying about St. Cloud, don't. He likes you enough to chase all over England after you, and he never cared what anyone else thought, especially not that parcel of flats. Oh, Fanny's just a flibbertigibbet, I suppose, afraid of her own shadow and that brother of hers, but the others are—Well, you'll see for yourself."

A very proper butler announced them to those assembled in the gold parlor: "Lady Georgette Jordan, Dowager Countess St. Cloud. Miss Juneclaire Beaumont."

They walked in to a sea of stunned faces. Then St. Cloud came forward and took Juneclaire's trembling hand. He squeezed it and winked. "Oh yes," he addressed the company at large, "I forgot to mention that Grandmother's new companion was my Juneclaire. With all the skimble-skamble over carriages and directions and such, she cleverly came ahead on her own to wait for me here, under the dowager's aegis, of course. Didn't you, my pet?"

His pet was wanting to box his ears, even if he was overwhelmingly attractive in his formal clothes! The devil had very nicely sidestepped awkward questions but also added to the impression that they were affianced. Juneclaire couldn't cause a scene, not when he was leading her to the two women on the sofa. One of them was weeping into her handkerchief. His mother hates me already,

Juneclaire thought in despair. But he was bowing to the other woman.

"I am so glad," Lady Fanny trilled after introductions were made, and Juneclaire thought she meant it.

The other woman was moaning by now, and Juneclaire could not understand how everyone else in the room was ignoring her, even turning their backs.

"Aunt Florrie," St. Cloud was calling, "what's wrong? Aren't you happy I found Juneclaire and she is safe?"

"She'll want her pig back," Florrie wailed.

Juneclaire blinked, then said, "Oh, have you been taking care of Pansy? Isn't she a fine pig? I did give her to Mer—the earl, however, so I shan't be claiming her back. Did you know that we have a new kitten staying at the Dower House? Perhaps the dowager will invite you to tea so you can meet Shamrock."

Florrie was gone, skipping toward the dowager, who sat alone in a high-backed chair. It would be the first conversation between those two unlikely friends. Lady Fanny smiled her thanks and St. Cloud patted her hand, still firmly held on his arm, as he led her away.

"Why haven't you told your mother that we are not engaged?" she hissed at him, trying to maintain her smile.

"What, and cause another *crise de nerfs*? I thought you wanted me to be more careful of her sensibilities?"

They were in front of the other two females in the room, and during the introductions, Juneclaire had to pretend she did not know their identities. Miss Elsbeth Wilmott's gaze was clearly speculative, then superior when she compared her own blond curls, lace overskirt, three tiers of ruffles and rhinestones to Miss Beaumont's rustic simplicity. The country drab would never have a fitting place in society, Elsbeth's curling lip seemed to say. If this sour-faced young woman was the girl Merry might have married, Juneclaire reflected, he was better out of it.

The other woman looked right through Juneclaire, judging her and finding her unworthy of notice. Lady Sydelle Pomeroy directed all of her attention on the earl, having decided that a nonesuch like St. Cloud would tire of the little nobody in weeks. Juneclaire was thinking much the same, observing the older woman's gold locks and nile blue gown, what there was of it. More bosom was showing out of Lady Pomeroy's bodice than Juneclaire had in hers. The woman made her feel like a gauche schoolgirl, and she was happy when someone placed a glass of sherry in her hand.

Then they were facing Niles, the toad. His face was as white as his high shirt collars, and he was tossing back sherries as if they were Blue Ruin. Juneclaire smiled as she held out her hand for his salute, forcing him to extend his own bandaged paw, which he was desperately trying to conceal from the earl. Trying to seduce a paid companion was one thing; attempting to have his way with his cousin's wife-to-be was another. He swallowed audibly. St. Cloud was such a deuced good shot. And had such a deuced short temper. Juneclaire took great satisfaction in letting him squirm a bit, then she inclined her head and said, "How do you do?"

"Magnificent, my lady," St. Cloud whispered in her ear after Niles scuttled away. "And I apologize. That performance was surely worthy of a duchess. I also apologize for my cousin," the earl added, having missed none of the byplay. "He'll never bother you again."

Niles, meanwhile, had attached himself to Lady

Pomeroy's side. He needed a wealthy wife more than ever.

"What about our bet, Niles?" Sydelle asked, not bothering to lower her voice.

"What, are you dicked in the nob? Even if I succeeded, I'd not live long enough to enjoy my winnings. Besides, the fellow just paid all my debts."

The last two people in the room were the live-in curate, who welcomed her kindly, and St. Cloud's uncle Harmon, who uttered his greeting in form. Juneclaire did not have to be a mind reader to sense his disapproval. He wanted his daughter to be countess, she had that from the dowager, and he had an overweening sense of pride. If Juneclaire did not know she was unfit to be Lady St. Cloud, Lord Wilmott's slack-jowled sneer would have told her.

"Don't let Uncle Harmon bother you," the earl told her as they went in to dinner together, forgoing precedence. "He has digestive problems. An overabundance of spleen."

Someone, the earl most likely, had been very careful of the seating arrangements. Juneclaire sat on the earl's left, across from the dowager, with Mr. Hilloughby on her other side. The table was vast enough that she did not have to converse with any of the Wilmotts during the four courses and several removes, although she felt all their eyes upon her, waiting to see if she reached for the wrong fork or spoke with her mouth full. Aunt Marta would have scolded her for less.

Dinner was fairly pleasant, at her end at least, with the dowager quizzing the earl about her London acquaintances. They were quick to include Juneclaire, providing histories and reciting anecdotes that had her laughing. Juneclaire was glad to see the old lady happy and pleased to note how gracefully the earl made sure her food was cut and directions tactfully whispered.

Mr. Hilloughby was pleased to relate the history of the Priory chapel when she turned to him, and begged to show Juneclaire the fine rose window, at her convenience, of course. Then the dowager started recounting bits of her own London Seasons, which had Juneclaire in whoops. She *had* had a bit more wine with dinner than she was used to, on top of the sherry.

She needed it, to get her through the after-dinner gathering in the drawing room, before the men joined the ladies.

The dowager was drowsing near the fire, and Aunt Florrie was counting chair legs, "just to be sure." Countess Fanny had taken up her Bible and seemed to be praying; her lips were moving, at any rate, so Juneclaire did not want to intrude. That left her at the mercy of the two blond beauties.

"Did we hear you were from Strasmere? I suppose you know the baron, then, and his lady. So charming, don't you think?"

"Wherever did you find such a clever seamstress, my dear? So daring to set new styles, isn't it?"

"You are nineteen? Then you must have had your come-out. I do not recall seeing you in London. So many debutantes, you know."

St. Cloud would have seemed like an angel of mercy if he weren't scowling so. He took Juneclaire's arm to lead her away, but not before Lady Pomeroy asked if their newest member couldn't entertain them with a song and some music.

"*All* ladies can play, of course, and I am sure the company is bored with my poor offerings."

They'd be more than bored if Juneclaire sat at the pianoforte, she thought with just a tinge of hysteria, not wanting to shame Merry. She was saved this time by the dowager, who, rousing from her nap, declared that not all who could play well were ladies. "I wish more young gels knew their limits, instead of foisting their meager accomplishments on poor dolts with nothing better to do. Besides, Miss Beaumont has other talents, like teaching a blind woman how to play cards. I'll take you all on at whist, with her help. And my own deck."

Sydelle excused herself with a headache, rather than waste her time talking to Elsbeth or Lady Fanny. The men were all commandeered for the dowager's game, except the curate, who was aiding Fanny at her devotions. He didn't count anyway.

Juneclaire sat behind the dowager, whispering the discards. St. Cloud was partnering his grandmother, straight across from them, and Juneclaire could see his brows lift when he felt the rough edges of the pinpricks. Niles smiled; marked cards were nothing new to him.

Lord Wilmott, however, was furious. He threw his hand down and jumped to his feet. "This is an outrage! These cards have been tampered with." He glared at Juneclaire. "We don't consider cardsharping a drawing-room accomplishment in our circles, miss."

Juneclaire felt the roast pheasant she'd enjoyed at dinner try to take wing. She couldn't look at Merry. It was the dowager who spoke first, though. "Of course the cards are marked, you popinjay. What did you think, I was reading my hands through Miss Beaumont's eye? And where was the advantage, Harmon? If I remember correctly, you had the deal."

Lord Wilmott sat down, red-faced and muttering. Juneclaire released her breath. Then St. Cloud spoke, every inch the earl. "I believe you owe the ladies an apology, sir. Lady St. Cloud has ever been the best whist player of my acquaintance; she has no need to cheat to beat you. And Miss Beaumont is many things, including a guest in this house, may I remind you, but she is not a Captain Sharp. I did not like your comments."

Lord Wilmott mumbled his apologies and took up his hand, ungracefully. His antipathy toward St. Cloud was barely concealed and was magnified when the earl suggested Lord Wilmott apply to Lady Fanny for a physic, if his stomach was in such an uproar it disordered his senses. The dowager cackled and Niles smirked. Lord Wilmott glared most at the outside witness to his humiliation, Juneclaire. Worse, in his eyes, he and Niles were sadly trounced. He excused himself before the tea tray was brought in.

Soon after, Juneclaire noticed that the dowager was looking peaked, exhausted by her triumph. "We should be going, my lord," she told the earl.

He walked with her toward the other side of the room, where the gold drapes were drawn against the night. "I, ah, took the liberty of having the dowager's and your things moved over to the Priory during dinner." He wisely stepped back.

"You what? Why, you arrogant, overbearing—"

"Now don't cut up stiff, Junco; you know it's best for the dowager."

"I know it suits your plans, my lord, and I know you like having your own way."

"Why, there have to be *some* advantages to having a title," he teased.

She was not amused. "I resent being forced to go along with your whims, willy-nilly."

"This, my little bird, is not a whim. I am trying to show you that. Since you are already up in the boughs, I may as well admit to the other decision I took on myself. I had my man Foley tell your people that you were safe here, with me."

Juneclaire had written three letters to her family, then ripped them up, not knowing what to say.

She should be thankful, she supposed, that Merry had undertaken an unpleasant task, but Aunt Marta was not likely to consider her safe, not if she knew the earl's reputation, and not if he kept stroking the inside of Juneclaire's elbow, where her gloves ended. And certainly not if she knew how Juneclaire wanted to succumb to the gleam in Merry's green, green eyes. "Oh, dear."

Chapter Nineteen

*H*e was arrogant and overbearing and quite, quite wonderful! He led her himself to the family wing to a white-and-rose room with Chinese wallpaper. Pansy was waiting there, wearing a baby's bonnet, but clean and shiny and noisily ecstatic to see Juneclaire. Shamrock was curled in a basket by the fireplace, and a freckle-faced young maid sat sewing, ready to help her to bed. The dowager was installed in the suite next door, he explained, with Nutley and Sally Munch each assigned a bedchamber off the dressing room. Nutley was pleased so many more servants would be listening for the dowager's calls, and Sally was thrilled to have all the Priory footmen to practice her wiles upon. The Peningtons, St. Cloud continued, wanted to stay on as caretakers at the Dower House, where they were comfortable, rather than be interlopers in the Priory staff hierarchy. He was sending young Ned and his mother, who was feeling much better with the proper medicine, to help look after the house and the old couple. That should keep everybody out of trouble, the earl said. Then he kissed her hand good night, in view of the new maid, and thanked her for coming, as if she'd had a choice!

He thought of everything, Juneclaire had to admit. Her own three gowns hung in the wardrobe, with the brown habit and two simple gowns she and Sally and Nutley had managed to make over from the dowager's castoffs, and two other new dresses. These, her new maid Parker happily informed her, had been run up by the Priory's own resident seamstress that afternoon, with more to come since miss's trunks had so unfortunately gone astray in the carriage mishap.

There were powders and oils and hot towels, hothouse flowers and a stack of books on the bed stand, a dish of biscuits if she or Pansy got hungry during the night. What more could a poor orphan runaway want? Plenty.

Merry was kind. He cared for her. He wanted her and needed her, he said, and she believed him. He never mentioned love. Juneclaire could barely think in his presence, her blood pounded so loudly in her head. She thought he was the most splendid man in the world, if a trifle imperious and temper-prone. She thought she could make him happy, since the mere thought of him made her smile. She also thought she was halfway in love with him from the night at the barn, and the other half was a heartbeat away. But she was, indeed, a poor orphan runaway, and she would never burden him with such a wife, only to have him regret his good intentions later. Unless he loved her . . .

Merry asked for time to change her mind. Perhaps in time she could change his from just wanting to marry her to not wanting to live without her. It was possible. She thought she'd ask Mrs. Pennington to save her a wishbone when she visited them tomorrow. She went to sleep, smiling.

Tap, tap. Tap, tap. There it was again, Juneclaire thought in a muzzy fog. All those workmen an they never found the woodpeckers. Merry would be angry. She snuggled deeper in the covers.

Tap, crunch. Tap, crunch. Woodpeckers riding on rats? Merry would be very angry. Juneclaire turned over.

Tap, crunch, sigh. On remorseful rats? That was too much. She fumbled for the flint. Someone handed it to her, and she automatically said "Thank you" before lighting her candle.

Either there was a ghost in her room, or Juneclaire'd had too much wine. She opted for the wine. No self-respecting ghost ever looked like this. He had salt-and-pepper hair, a full gray beard and mustache, a brocaded coat from the last century—camphor-scented to prove it—that couldn't button across a wide paunch, and a peg leg.

Oh, good, Juneclaire thought, still half-asleep, that explains the tapping. The empty plate of biscuits by her bed explained the crunching. Well, they were gone, so the ghost could leave and she could go back to sleep. She bent to blow out the candle, and the ghost sighed again, a mournful, graveyard sigh indeed. It occurred to Juneclaire that she should scream. She opened her mouth, but the ghost stopped her by saying, "So you're Merry's bride."

Merry? Only one person ever called him Merry, he'd said. "Uncle George?"

"Aye." He pulled a chair closer to her bed and fed the last biscuit to the pig when Pansy came to investigate. Then he sighed again, scratching behind Pansy's big ears poking through the baby bonnet, as though it were the most natural thing for a pig—or a ghost—to be in a lady's bedchamber at three in the morning. Juneclaire swore she would never take a sip of wine again.

Then she got a whiff of her guest, past the camphor. He'd been partaking of the grape, too, it seemed. "Um, Uncle George, how did you get in here?" Her door was locked; she didn't trust that Niles. The specter waved vaguely at the wardrobe against the far side of the room. Juneclaire nodded. That made sense. Ghosts didn't need to use doors. "Can you tell me why you've come, what it is that you want?" She was thinking in terms of revenge, or a better burial, typical ghostly reasons for haunting their ancestral homes.

"Someone to talk to, I guess." He sighed again. Life, or half life, was hard. "Fanny gets down on her hands and knees and starts praying every time I try to talk to her, when she doesn't swoon. I don't know how many more visits from me Mother's heart can take, what with her sure I'm Death come to carry her off. And Merry nearly ran me through with his sword tonight, thinking I was some nightmare from his French prison days. I tried old Pennington, but he drank down his wife's last bottle of rum and passed out next to her. Now he's taken to wearing garlic around his neck."

"Is that what it is? I noticed something. . . ."

"Don't want to go near the old fellow, and I can't ever rouse Nutley. I swear the woman sleeps like one of the dead."

He should know, but "She's deaf," Juneclaire told him.

"Oh. None of the other servants have been around long enough, so you see, there's no one to talk to. They all think I'm dead."

"Aren't you?"

"I don't think so. Are ghosts hungry?"

"How should I know? You're the first one I've met." Shamrock was now twining himself around the apparition's leg, and Pansy was wearing her idiotic grin of a hog in heaven. Juneclaire shrugged and slipped out of bed. She gingerly reached out her hand and touched his arm with the tips of her fingers. Solid. She poked her own arm to make sure.

172

Solid, and awake. Unless she was dreaming about pinching herself to see if she was dreaming. She sat back down on the bed. "Uncle George? That is, may I call you Uncle George?" He nodded, with another sigh. "Why don't you just come back tomorrow, in the daylight, and have Talbot announce you?"

"I wish it were that easy, lass. I wish it were. I can tell you've a wise head on your shoulders, and I'd explain all about it, if only I weren't so devilishly sharp set. I'd go down to the kitchens, but Merry's got a guard posted there with a pistol. One along the corridor here, too."

"Someone's been stealing food and things and frightening the servants, to say nothing of poor Lady Fanny. You should be ashamed, sir."

"I am, child. Very ashamed. And very hungry."

So Juneclaire went to find the kitchens, with Uncle George's directions tumbling about in her head. She was in the east wing; the kitchens were two stories down, halfway along the central transverse in what was the old Priory's refectory. She went in her bare feet so as not to wake anybody, especially the guard who was asleep at the end of the corridor. A hunting rifle was propped alongside his chair, barrel pointing up. Juneclaire shielded her candle and tiptoed past. So did Pansy.

The kitchen guard was awake, playing patience and sipping an ale. He thought nothing odd about a barefoot houseguest in her white flannel nightgown helping herself to another dinner. Hell, he thought, everyone knew the gentry was peculiar. Once you got over the pig in the baby bonnet, the rest didn't make a halfpenny's difference.

Juneclaire found a hamper to fill, as if she and Pansy were going on a picnic, then covered the whole with a napkin so the guard couldn't tell how much food she was taking, she hoped. She could barely carry the basket as it was, with the candle in her other hand.

"I'd help you, miss, but it'd mean my job, were I to leave my post." The guard was back at his game.

"But you will tell them in the morning that I took the leftovers, won't you? I don't want anyone to think there were burglars or . . . ghosts."

"I'll be sure to mention it, lest they think I was eating more myself than Napoleon's army during the whole Russian campaign."

Juneclaire blushed but held her head high and retraced her steps. She thought she did, anyway. Somehow she found herself in the servants' quarters, built out of the old monks' cells. She turned around quickly and let Pansy lead the way, trusting the pig's unerring nose to get them . . . back to the kitchen. The guard sent her on her way in the other direction, shaking his head.

Her feet were cold, the basket was heavy, and Juneclaire was sure she must have dreamed the whole thing. She tiptoed carefully past the sleeping hall watchman but was not quite as careful about Pansy, who stopped to investigate. Her pink leathery nose whiffled into the watchman's dangling hand to check for crumbs. The guard jumped up and shouted and his chair fell back, crashing. The pig ran away, screaming, and the leaning gun went off, blowing a porcelain bust of Galileo into cosmic dust indeed.

The first door to fly open was Lady Fanny's. Right in front of her was a figure swathed in white cloth, surrounded by swirls of otherworldly clouds. Juneclaire moaned. The countess collapsed onto the floor at her feet, out cold.

The dowager was shouting to know what was going on and demanding to be taken home to the Dower House, where a body wasn't likely to be shot

174

in her bed. Sally Munch poked her head out of the door, fireplace poker in hand.

Then St. Cloud was there, carrying his mother back to her room, calling for her woman, shouting the dowager back to bed, dismissing the guard and the twenty or thirty other servants in various stages of undress who appeared from nowhere. And looking at Juneclaire in sorrow.

She held up the basket and pulled out a roll. "I . . . I wanted it for the pig."

Elsbeth giggled until a glare from St. Cloud had her scurrying away. He jerked his head to be rid of Niles, too. But Uncle Harmon stayed, spluttering about harum-scarum chits and animals who should be in the stable or—with a dark look at Pansy—on the table. The look he gave Juneclaire was no better. "Milkmaids," he huffed, pulling his nightcap back down around his ears and stomping off to the other wing.

St. Cloud clenched his jaw and said he had to check on his grandmother. He would see Miss Beaumont in the morning. He tightened the sash on his paisley robe and bowed.

Juneclaire didn't doubt he was wishing the sash was around her neck. She fled to her own room and threw herself on the bed. Uncle George was gone, naturally. No one would believe her anyway, and now she had lost Merry's esteem.

His family hated her. They thought her a gapeseed, an unmannered bumpkin born in a cabbage patch. And they were right. She *had* been a milkmaid, just that one time for Little Yerby, true, but she was no fine lady like Sydelle and Elsbeth. She couldn't play or sing or flirt or fill a gown so well. Her friends were farmers and servants and barnyard animals, not lords and ladies and London luminaries.

And Merry was disappointed. She could see it in

his angry face. He did not need another hysterical female in his household, or one who caused more ruckus and row than all the others combined—and on her first night there! Juneclaire sobbed into her pillow; the cat and the pig were already damp with her tears. She did not belong here, she thought, and she would have to leave before she disgraced Merry further. There was no way he could learn to love a milkmaid, and there was no way she could make a proper countess. You couldn't make a silk purse out of a sow's ear.

Chapter Twenty

The food was gone in the morning. Juneclaire had put it on the desk, out of Pansy's reach, and the maids had not been in yet to light the fire, so Uncle George must have come back. Juneclaire wished he'd woken her up for a chat, for if he thought being dead was hard, he should try being Miss Beaumont. She was not *really* Merry's fiancée, she no longer had duties as the dowager's companion, and everyone, snooty relatives and well-trained servants, was treating her with polite condescension. They hated her. There was a hideous sculpture of some martyr being devoured by a lion in the niche where Galileo used to be. Lady Fanny most likely directed the maids to find the ugliest piece in the house, in hopes Juneclaire would relieve them of it next.

Breakfast was a disaster. Juneclaire and Aunt Florrie were the only women there. That court card Niles made oinking noises at her, while eating rasher after rasher of bacon. Lord Harmon barely concealed his disgust behind the newspapers, and Mr. Hilloughby kept his eyes firmly on his kippers. Merry pretended nothing had happened.

With his black curls damp from combing and his cravat loosely tied, Merry looked so handsome,

Juneclaire had a hard time swallowing her toast past the lump in her throat. His brows seemed permanently puckered and his lips never turned up, but he was courteous, caring—and cold. He was too busy to show her around this morning, he apologized, what with the New Year's Eve ball just tomorrow night, and no, thank you, he said, there was nothing she could do to help; she was a guest. The weather was too inclement, at any rate, for her to accompany him on his rounds. He had arranged for Mr. Hilloughby to show her the chapel this morning and for Aunt Florrie to take Juneclaire to the attics to pick a costume in the afternoon. This was from the man who wanted her to spend time getting to know him, to see if they would suit. He had obviously decided.

Juneclaire was set to ask the dowager for a carriage ride back to Stanton Hall as soon as Lady St. Cloud awoke. That way Merry could have no worries about her safety, no embarrassing responsibilities toward her. Before she left, though, she was curious about one thing: "My lord, what happened to Uncle George?"

Niles dropped his coffee cup, and Mr. Hilloughby took a coughing fit. The footmen's eyes were all on the carved ceiling. Juneclaire barely registered all this. She was pinned in St. Cloud's stare like a mounted butterfly. She'd never seen him so angry, not even last night, when he walked barefoot over Galileo's remains, not even when Charlie Parrett had him in a death grip. Still, she would not look away. Let him think she was an unschooled hobbledehoyden. Let him think there was a breeze in her cockloft. He would *not* think she was a coward, unless he heard her knees knocking together.

He finally broke the silence by pronouncing, "We do not speak of George Jordan in this house," in the same tones he might have used to intone the eleventh commandment.

Then Aunt Florrie chirped, "We don't mention making water either."

Juneclaire would not stoop to questioning the servants, who were so in dread of the master's temper that they'd take the turnspit dog's place sooner than go against his wishes. She could not chance upsetting the dowager or Lady Fanny with her queries, and she was not about to ask Mr. Hilloughby, not after St. Cloud's edict.

She did, however, manage to check the family Bible in the old chapel, after dutifully admiring the age and architecture of the place. The stained-glass windows did not glow, not on such a dreary day outside, and the stone floors kept the sanctuary bitterly cold. Worse, Mr. Hilloughby was a historical scholar. While he described the life and last days of the original St. Jerome of the Clouds in excruciating detail, Juneclaire read through generations of Jordans. Uncle George was crossed out.

The dowager refused to hear of Juneclaire's leaving.

"That's a shabby return for my taking you on, girl, leaving me alone with the hyenas. No, I won't hear of it." She stabbed her cane halfway through the Turkey runner in her sitting room. "You will be happy here, and that's final."

The earl had inherited more than a title and wealth, it seemed.

Juneclaire was surprised at how well Florrie knew her way around the vast attics. She understood the earl's aunt was frequently lost in the Priory's warren of corridors, chambers, and alcoves. Aunt Florrie knew just what she wanted for

Juneclaire, too, and knew right where it was, give or take a trunk or three or four. The St. Clouds must never have thrown anything out.

"Here, this will be perfect for you, dearie," Aunt Florrie said, holding up a wide-skirted shepherdess dress, complete with apron, crooked staff, and stuffed, fleece-covered lamb. "It's the best of all the costumes."

Juneclaire's heart was not in preparing for a masquerade. It was downstairs, brooding. She didn't care what she wore. She didn't care if she attended, even if she'd never been to a real ball in her life, much less a masked one. Aunt Marta would convert to Hindi before she let such wickedness occur under her roof. Nonetheless, the outfit seemed to mean a great deal to the older woman, so Juneclaire said, "Perhaps you should be the shepherdess, Aunt Florrie, and I could be something else." She looked around. "Queen Elizabeth, maybe, or Anne Boleyn." She felt like Anne Boleyn, after all.

"Oh, no, you have to be the shepherdess. It will be wonderful, you'll see." She was cutting apart the stuffed lamb with embroidery scissors from her pocket. "Besides, I am going to be Yellow. Last year I was Rain, but Harmon became angry when the floors got wet."

The dowager decided to have dinner on a tray in her room. Juneclaire suspected the old lady was feigning weariness for her sake, so she did not have to face the company again, but she leaped at the excuse.

"It's no such thing, missy. I saw them Christmas and last night, and I'll have to do the pretty for the ball tomorrow. That's three times in one week, and with that bunch of counter jumpers, three times a year is enough. Of course, you're free to go down if you want."

"Oh, no, I promised to teach you to knit cables, and you promised to teach me vingt-et-un. And Lord St. Cloud sent up Miss Austen's new novel and Scott's ballads. I need to try on my costume for to-morrow and—"

"Cut line, girl. I'm glad for the company."

The dowager approved the theme of Juneclaire's costume. "Innocent and sweet, in case there's any talk. But pretty and feminine, too, if I remember correctly. Just the ticket. My costume? I'm going as a crotchety old lady, what else? No one'll recognize me, and that's only fair, for I sure as Harry won't recognize them!"

Juneclaire kept back all the uneaten food from dinner and asked for more to be sent up, for the pig. She let Parker help her into her night rail and brush out her long hair, and then she dismissed the maid for the night. She got into bed with a Gothic tale from the Minerva Press and waited for Uncle George.

The heroine was locked in a deserted tower. The steps were crumbly, the candle was low, small things chittered nearby. Everywhere she turned, spiderwebs stuck in her hair. Drafts blew through the cracked windows, and the door . . . slowly . . . creaked . . . open.

And there was Uncle George, stepping out of Juneclaire's wardrobe. Tonight he wore doublet and hose.

While he was eating, she told him her troubles. "They all think I'm a clodpoll, except for Merry. He thinks I'm a nightmare. The dowager won't let me go, and the rest of them will make fun of me if I stay. Tomorrow night at the ball they'll have all their friends to laugh and sneer at poor St. Cloud's goat girl. Elsbeth and Lady Pomeroy will be gor-

geous, and I'll forget the dance steps. I've only practiced with my cousins, you know."

George waved a chicken leg. "Your problem,
puss, is lack of confidence. Don't worry, I'll take
care of it."

"You? How can you take care of it when you don't
even exist?"

He sighed, feeding Pansy the cooked carrots.
"Never could abide cooked carrots. Do you think a
ghost cares what it eats? As a matter of fact, why
would a ghost eat at all? I thought we settled that
last night."

"Yes, but they won't talk about you, and they've
struck your name out of the records. If you're not
dead, why don't you just come back?"

"I promised I'd explain, but it's hard. You see, if
I'm not dead, then I'm a murderer."

"A murderer?" she shrieked, louder than she intended, and suddenly there was a pounding at her
door.

"Juneclaire, are you all right? Open the door."

St. Cloud would kick it open if he had to, she
knew. She looked helplessly toward Uncle George,
who shrugged and picked up another chicken leg.
She unlocked the door and opened it a crack. "I am
fine, my lord."

He was glaring at her again. "I thought I heard
voices." He thought he heard a man's voice. He
tried to look past her into the room.

She did not think this was a good time to mention
Uncle George again. "I was, ah, reading."

"Out loud?"

"I was practicing, you know, for when I read to
the dowager."

"And you are all right? Not frightened by those
silly stories of the Priory ghosts?"

"Oh, no. Not at all. Are you?"

He snorted. "Hardly. I'll just be going, then. Good night, Miss Beaumont."

"Good night, Lord St. Cloud."

Juneclaire was almost as unhappy as the night before, until she started to hear screams and screeches from the far corridor, where the Wilmotts were installed. She tied on her robe and found her slippers and ran with St. Cloud and some of the servants to the east wing. Niles and Harmon Wilmott were already in the hall, trying to comfort Elsbeth, who was sobbing, and Lady Sydelle, who was raving hysterically about goblins, ghosts, and going home. Elsbeth had her hair tied in papers, and Lady Pomeroy had some yellow concoction spread all over her face. Juneclaire smiled. Uncle George was taking care of things for her.

The Earl of St. Cloud sat in his library, his head in his hands. Half a bottle of cognac hadn't helped. He was still in a deuce of a coil. He was fond of his Aunt Florrie, but he did not want his children to be like her. Juneclaire was touched, dicked in the nob, attics to let. Or else she was playing some deep game he did not know about. How could she look like such an angel and be so jingle-brained, if not downright evil? Nothing she said rang true anymore. He did not know what to think, except that she was turning his life and his household upside down.

And yet he was so attracted to her that just the memory of the chit in her virginal white nightgown, with her brown hair tumbling around her shoulders, set his juices flowing. Then he remembered how he was ready to commit mayhem at the thought of someone in the room with her. He was jealous of the blasted ghost! Botheration, he was jealous of the damn pig that got to spend the night with her. Life with Juneclaire would be hell.

But how could he cry off the engagement? A gentleman did not. And he was the one who had insisted, who had announced their betrothal to his family. He was obliged to marry her now, aside from the night in the barn. Blast her and the dashed pig. They had him by the shoat hairs.

Chapter Twenty-one

$\mathcal{J}$uneclaire was walking the pig before breakfast when she heard the commotion. She followed the noise around the ballroom wing to find St. Cloud and a group of servants with axes, ladders, and hammers. They were searching for ways an intruder could have entered the house, Sally Munch explained to her, from her place at the fringes of the workers. Lord St. Cloud was directing the removal of climbing vines and overhanging branches. He walked ahead of the group, checking the loose ground under the windows for signs of recent disturbance. He paused to study an area under a balcony where a great many footsteps showed in the dirt. The workers gathered round, wondering if the master was going to order them to chop down the balcony.

Sally Munch was hanging back, so Juneclaire had a fairly good idea to whom at least half the prints belonged. Pansy snuffled around, then went straight to the new footman, the one with the shoulders of a prize fighter. Sally blushed, but the earl merely requested that Miss Beaumont kindly remove the pig from the field of investigation.

Juneclaire stepped closer and looked down. Thinking out loud, she said, "Those can't be his

footprints anyway. Uncle George has a peg leg."
She clapped her hand over her mouth. "Oh."

With one frigid glance the earl sent the workers
off. Juneclaire shivered. Her words would be spread
throughout the mansion along with the coffee cups
and chocolate. She had to go explain to the dowager
before Lady St. Cloud heard from that prattlebox
Sally. Before she took one step, a steel-gripped hand
clasped her wrist like a manacle, and she was silently pulled away from the house. That is, St.
Cloud was silent, frowning fiercely down at the
ground. Juneclaire protested, struggled, and ran to
keep up lest he drag her face-down in the dirt if she
fell.

He did not stop until they reached a high stone
wall and a gate. St. Cloud released her hand, with
a look daring Juneclaire to try to escape. She was
too busy catching her breath and wondering where
they were. He found the key under a loose stone
and unlatched the gate, then pulled her through.
They were in a small cemetery, and Juneclaire had
a moment's fright that he meant to murder her and
leave her body there. How awful to think her last
sight of him was to be that terrible scowl. He wasn't
even looking at her, though, continuing his long,
angry strides toward the far corner.

"There," he said, stopping finally in front of a
small grave site. "Uncle George."

Pansy was happily rooting in the leaves and stuff
that had fallen on Uncle George's marker. Juneclaire pushed her aside and read the dates.

"He has been dead these four and twenty years,"
St. Cloud said. "My fifth birthday."

"There must have been a mistake."

A muscle flexed in the earl's jaw. "The only
mistake, madam, was in my thinking you a sane,
sensible type of female. You are upsetting my

household with these idiotic ravings, and you will cease at once."

Juneclaire stood up. "I see. Uncle George is dead; therefore I am seeing ghosts, talking to spirits, feeding phantoms."

"There are no such things as ghosts. You are either hallucinating or else you are the victim of some unscrupulous charlatan, preying on your weakness."

"Unless, of course, I am in league with this fiendish scheme to . . . what? To send your mother into a decline, to rout your houseguests, and terrorize your servants. Thank you, my lord."

He watched the pig. "I never said that."

"No, but you thought it. Did it never occur to you, my lord, that you could be wrong for once? That someone, dead or alive, could act contrary to your wishes?"

"I saw him, dash it! I saw his body when they brought him in!"

"Tell me," she said quietly, holding out her hand.

St. Cloud took it, thinking he would air the dirty linen and then she would be gone. That was best for all. He looked around till he spotted a bench under a stand of bare-branched lilacs. "Come. It is not a short story." He did not sit down next to her but propped one Hessian-clad leg on the stone seat. He stared into the distance, into the past.

"The Wilmotts lived on the neighboring estate, Motthaven; they were minor gentry but, then as now, perpetually overextended. Uncle George and Mother were childhood sweethearts. The second son of an earl should have been a good enough match for his daughter, but Lord Wilmott wanted more, and Robert, the oldest son and heir, seemed interested. George was reckless, drinking, gambling, all the usual vices, so Wilmott had an excuse. He refused his permission. The two tried to elope but were brought back by Wilmott, his son Harmon, and Robert. Uncle George was shipped out to the army, more dead than alive, I understand. And Mother . . . Mother married Robert Jordan, the heir to St. Cloud and soon to be the earl.

"They were happy enough, I suppose. I seldom saw them, for they spent most of their time in London or traveling. Uncle George never visited." St. Cloud started pacing, kicking up leaves.

"Then he was gravely injured, and the army sent him home to St. Cloud. He was here over eight months, recuperating, and I got to know him well. He was full of stories and games to delight a little boy, when he felt well enough. We were nearly inseparable, they say. He was bored and I was . . . lonely. Then came Christmas and my birthday. My parents came here, with a large house party. And . . . something happened between the brothers."

Juneclaire knew he was not telling the whole story, but she did not interrupt.

"There was a confrontation, in view of the entire company, where Uncle George threatened to kill his brother. The two of them stormed out of the house, and Uncle George was never seen alive again."

"What happened? Did he kill your father?"

"My . . . father? No, but not from lack of trying, I fear. When neither came back that night, search parties were sent out in the morning. They found my father at the old quarry, grievously wounded and at death's door. They found George's body the next day, at the bottom of the quarry. I saw them bring him home. No one intended a small boy to be there, of course, but I was. It was a sight I shall never forget." He cleared his throat and went on: "The earl had a ball lodged against his spine, pneumonia, and severe loss of blood. They feared for his life. Still, he managed to declare the disaster an

188

accident. Lord Wilmott was magistrate and so proclaimed it, rather than let the county know the brothers had been fighting over his daughter, my mother. As if that could stop the gossip," he added bitterly.

"The earl partially recovered. He never walked again and was angry and pain-racked for two more years until he finally succumbed to an inflammation of the lungs. He never permitted George's name to be mentioned. Mother never recovered her spirits and never dared face the ton, beyond the narrow Berkshire society."

"Then George isn't a murderer at all?"

"Wasn't. Legally, no, for his shot did not actually kill my father. Morally? He is dead and better so for what he did to my parents' lives. Leave him rest, Juneclaire, let my family's skeleton stay in the closet. Stop upsetting my mother."

But Juneclaire was not listening. She was wondering how to get word to Uncle George.

First she had to explain to the dowager.

"It really is George with a peg leg and not someone hammering nails in my coffin? That's a relief. You're sure it's George and not some other spook come back to life? I wouldn't want to see my late husband anytime soon."

"He won't eat cooked carrots."

"That's George. He tried to tell me, but I was too foolish to listen, I suppose. The boy never had a particle of sense anyway, always falling into one scrape or another. You tell him to stop playing off his tricks and get back here. Now go on, girl, I need to be alone to think about this."

Juneclaire locked her door so the servants would not think her more addled than ever, and then she tried calling Uncle George. She whispered his name in all the corners of her room and under her bed. She tried her best to find a secret door in the back of her wardrobe, dislodging everything and pounding on the bare wood. If there was a false wall, like in the Minerva Press books, it must catch from the other side. Finally she took to calling, "Uncle George" up the chimney and down the floor grates, unaware, of course, that the sound echoed throughout the family wing.

Countess Fanny was prostrate, too unnerved to attend her own pre-ball dinner. Her frightened abigail let Juneclaire talk to her for a minute.

"No," the countess cried, "he has to be dead, or he'd have forgiven me by now. I said I would wait, and I did not. Now he's come back to haunt me."

Juneclaire wanted to kill the wretch herself, if he wasn't already dead, of course. She was no more kindly disposed to George's nephew either, especially when St. Cloud directed the footmen not to serve Juneclaire anymore wine with dinner. Her only satisfaction was seeing Elsbeth's pasty face and the black shadows under Sydelle's eyes.

Juneclaire was a success at her first ball. So was Pansy. The shepherdess costume was becoming, with the apron tied at her narrow waist, the short, ruffled petticoats allowing the merest glimpse of well-turned ankle, and the low bodice not as innocent as her flower-decked hair. Pansy, a ham in sheep's clothing, trotted alongside, to the delight of the company.

Since the ball was a masquerade, none of the sixty or so guests was announced, but everyone knew who she was. They had all come to inspect the female who rumor claimed had snabbled St. Cloud. The men were quick to sign the pretty gal's dance card, and the ladies were pleased to find her a well-behaved chit. With the dowager's approval, Miss Beaumont could be no less.

Precedence also went by the wayside. St. Cloud asked her to stand up for the first dance, instead of partnering the highest-ranking lady. He was dressed as Sir Philippe d'Guerdon, the sword-for-hire knight who first won the Priory of St. Jerome of the Clouds for the Crown. The Frenchman was wily enough not to wreck the place during the siege and wise enough to ask for it as his reward. He anglicized his name to Jordan and founded his own dynasty. His ancestors stayed wise and wily, increasing their holdings, filling their coffers, staying on the right side of whatever war or rebellion occurred. They prospered until this night, when the last Jordan stood in the guise of the first, bowing to the lady who would continue the line, God and Juneclaire willing. And if St. Cloud could get his heart and his head to come to the sticking point.

She was so damned beautiful, innocent and appealing at the same time, how could he doubt her? She greeted his neighbors as if she were truly glad to meet the stuffy old matrons, the giggly young girls, the spotted youths, and the snuff-covered squires. He was proud to lead her into the dance, he told himself, proud they all thought she was his.

His bow was as courtly as only a knight wearing a chain mesh tunic and scarlet tights could make it, and the broadsword at his side threatened only once to trip him up in the dance. Juneclaire thought this moment might be worth the rest of her lifetime listening to Aunt Marta's scolds. She smiled, and the sideline watchers shook their heads that another green girl had fallen for the elusive earl. Then he smiled, and they all sighed. St. Cloud was cotched at last.

Aware of their recent awkwardness, St. Cloud tried to reestablish some of the closeness he had felt with Juneclaire at first. "I suppose you have a New Year's wish all picked out, Junco. Does it have to be a secret?"

"New Year's is for resolutions, sir knight, not wishes, didn't you know? Instead of depending on luck and happenstance, resolutions depend on oneself."

"May a humble knight not wish for a favor from a pretty maid?"

She showed her dimples. "A man may wish all he wants, but a man resolved to have a thing works to make his own wishes come true. And a lady's favor is a paltry thing for a whole year's resolution."

"I believe that depends on the lady. But what is your resolve, Miss Beaumont?"

Juneclaire knew better than to interpret his words as a desire to win her heart; he was just a practiced rake. She also knew better than to admit her real resolution, which was to reunite Uncle George with his family. Instead she said, "I think I shall try not to be so impetuous. I've been in too many hobbles as is."

He gave her another of those rare smiles, so she impetuously went on: "And you, sir, should resolve to laugh more. Uncle George says you were a cheerful little imp of a lad."

Juneclaire found herself by the dowager's side before the music had quite finished. She excused herself to check on Pansy in the refreshment room with Aunt Florrie, who had changed her persona, not her costume, to Sunshine.

When she returned to the ballroom, St. Cloud was dancing with Sydelle Pomeroy, Cleopatra in a black wig and a cloth-of-gold gown held up by little more than asp venom. She had a bracelet on her upper arm and half of Egypt's kohl supply on her eyelids. And a crocodile smile on her lips. Niles was glaring from the sidelines, an unhappily togaed Marc Antony, the cost of persuading Sydelle to stay for the ball. His bare shoulders and hairy shins were sorely missing their buckram wadding and sawdust pads, all Juneclaire's fault, naturally.

"Dash it, puss, if you keep setting his back up like that, it's no wonder he turns to that high flier."

Juneclaire turned. Father Time was standing beside her, long beard, flowing robes, scythe in one hand, hourglass in the other. "Uncle George, I've been looking all over for you! Where have you been?"

"Hush, missy. Not now."

Her next partner was approaching, Sir Walter Raleigh with spindle-shanked legs. "But when? I have news."

"The library. Twelve o'clock. They'll all be busy with the unmasking. Sh."

Juneclaire had to let him go off to the refreshment room.

"Deuced fine costume, that," Sir Walter commented. "Even has the ancient's shuffle down perfect."

She danced with a cowled monk, Robin Hood, Henry the Eighth, and a Red Indian in face paint, feathers, and satin knee breeches. She watched the French knight dance with Elsbeth's wood nymph, a Columbine, and Diana the Huntress, complete with arrows that fell out of her quiver during the Roger de Coverly.

She also watched Father Time say a few words to the dowager, but mostly he stood near the windows, watching Lady Fanny where she held court on a divan. St. Cloud strolled over in his direction once, chain mail being devilishly warm to dance in, and Juneclaire held her breath.

St. Cloud thought it was too bad that the rules of a masquerade didn't permit him to quiz the guests,

193

for he'd dearly like to know the identity of the fat joker in the fake beard. St. Cloud had first noticed Father Time because of Juneclaire's intense interest in him, but then the fellow kept eyeing the St. Cloud ladies. St. Cloud included Juneclaire in that small group, for he was determined to announce the engagement at the unmasking if she was willing. Everyone was expecting it, from the sly looks and innuendos he was receiving, and Juneclaire's name would be bandied about if there was no public notice. In the meantime, Father Time was as close as a clam, and St. Cloud had to partner the admiral's youngest daughter. He didn't know what she was supposed to be, but she looked like a lamp shade. No one else had asked her to dance this evening and, as host in his own home, swearing to be a reformed character, he knew his duty.

He knew his duty at twelve o'clock, too, when Juneclaire was not in the ballroom for the unmasking. He couldn't very well make the announcement without her, and he could not even kiss her happy New Year, damn it, when the infuriating chit had shabbed off on him. Again. Plainly his duty was to find her and hold a pillow over that beautiful face. He started looking for her as quietly as he could, considering he clanked with every step.

Juneclaire was in the library, explaining to Uncle George that he wasn't a murderer at all, but he was buried in the family cemetery.

"Must have been my man Hawkins. He was supposed to ride for the doctor. I never could figure what happened to him." Uncle George was sitting at the earl's desk, eating lobster patties and drinking champagne.

"But aren't you happy? You can come back now. Vicar Broome over at Bramley remembers you; he said so when he was sending me here. He can help you reestablish your identity if Lady Fanny won't. You can come home!"

Uncle George took another bite. "Old Boomer Broome still wears the collar, eh? Well, he can help with my soul, but that's not enough, I'm thinking, to keep my body from getting to hell via a hempen ladder. You see, I wasn't quite honest with you, poppet. Not that I didn't think I'd killed Robert. When Hawkins didn't send me word, I was sure I had, and I fled the country. And after that, nothing seemed to matter, so . . ."

Juneclaire's heart sank. "How bad?"

"Bad, puss. Did you ever hear of Captain Cleft, the pirate?"

"No."

"Good."

"Surely there's something we can do. Merry would know who to—"

"No, I won't hand the boy any more shame." He was up and using the scythe as a cane to limp toward the door. "Come on now, you're missing the ball. All those young fellows will be looking for the second-prettiest girl here."

"Who is the first?" she asked, dreading lest he name Sydelle.

"Why, Fanny, of course. I wonder if there are any macaroons?"

They were nearly to the supper room when Juneclaire begged him to consider consulting a lawyer. "Lady St. Cloud's man Langbridge is very kind. I'm sure he'd help. Please say you'll try. Otherwise I'll—"

She never got to say what she'd do, for just then St. Cloud spotted them. He was furious that Juneclaire had deserted him, and for a pillow-stuffed humbug at that! He was even more furious when Father Time limped into the refreshment room and his flowing robe billowed up to reveal a peg leg.

This was the bastard who was haunting St. Cloud's house!

With a mighty bellow St. Cloud drew the broadsword from its sheath at his side. The bloody thing was so heavy, he needed both hands to hold the point up. Guests scattered, women screamed. Father Time saw Nemesis coming and reached out with his scythe. He swept the punch bowl to the floor, then the tub of raspberry ices, shipped out from Gunther's specially. Then he fled back to the library, while the French knight picked his way through the sticky mess past one happy pig in sherbet. When St. Cloud reached the library, followed by half the company, the old man was gone. Disappeared, vanished.

"Good show, St. Cloud," the admiral called out. "Out with the old year, eh? Happy New Year!"

Chapter Twenty-two

"*It*'s not Uncle George, I tell you!" The tea-
cups were rattling again. St. Cloud wondered if he'd
ever know another peaceful breakfast, with coffee
and kippers—and no conversation. Why couldn't
Juneclaire be like other women and sleep till noon?
Why did she have to look so delicious in peach muslin, with a Kashmir shawl over her shoulders?

"He likes macaroons and hates carrots, just like
the dowager said he would," she insisted.

"Juneclaire, *I* like macaroons and hate carrots.
That does not make me Uncle George any more
than it makes your impostor."

"But he knows the secret passages and the
priests' holes. Not even you know them."

"I told you, my father died before he passed on
the information. He was afraid Niles and I would
get lost in the tunnels."

"He knew you'd bedevil the housemaids, more
likely," Lord Wilmott interrupted. "You were an
undisciplined cub even then. I say this is outrageous. George Jordan, indeed! The fellow is gone
and good riddance."

Juneclaire stuck doggedly to her argument. "But
he would know the trick to getting into the hidden

compartments. His father would have told him, my lord."

"Any number of servants could have known, even this Hawkins person he mentioned. Maybe that's who he is, some old employee come to blackmail the family or something. It won't wash; the dirty linen's been hung in public so long and so often, it's not worth a brass farthing. I told you I would have my man in London look into the matter of Hawkins."

"You won't find him; he's in the graveyard."

"Damn it, Juneclaire, you only have some actor's word for that!"

"But I wasn't seeing ghosts, was I? There really was a man with a peg leg?" He had to agree. "Then why can I not be right now? I'm not crazy, Merry. Why do you have to be right always, just because you are St. Cloud?"

Uncle Harmon's gorge was rising. "Why are you even listening to this rag-mannered fishwife, St. Cloud? George Jordan disgraced this family, miss, and it has taken over twenty years to rebuild our standing. Twenty years before *you* got here to stir things up."

Now St. Cloud pushed his plate away. "You forget yourself, Uncle," he said quietly. "Miss Beaumont is entitled to her opinions, and I respect her for expressing them. She and I may or may not quarrel over the coffee cups for the next twenty years. That is our decision. Where you break your fast is yours . . . for now."

Juneclaire was not sure if he meant they may or may not be married, or they may or may not argue, but she was content. He had stood up to his family for her.

Harmon Wilmott was not content. He knew better than to disparage the drab female who was ruining all his plans, but the thought of another uncle coming back from the beyond, this one with a more valid claim to St. Cloud's largess, stuck in his craw. Drooping jowls quivering in outrage, he declared, "George Jordan is better off dead. The man was a coward and a ne'er-do-well."

Before Juneclaire could say that Uncle George seemed to have done well enough on the high seas, St. Cloud stood up and tossed his napkin on the table. He may as well have thrown the gauntlet. "Uncle George was a soldier, a decorated hero. No one shall say else. If you are finished crumbling your muffin, Miss Beaumont, perhaps you would accompany me this morning."

He took her to the attics again, leading her gently this time, pointing out various ancestors' portraits along the way, telling her some of the history of the place. What he wanted her to see was in the lumber room with the broken bed frames and rickety tables. The earl pulled a gilt chair with only one armrest over toward the window and wiped the seat with his handkerchief for her. Then he pulled a painting out from behind a warped chest of drawers and turned it so Juneclaire could see.

Two young men looked back at her. Boys, really, they were cut from the same cloth as Merry. Both had black hair, worn long and tied in back as was the style, and both had green eyes. The seated one had Merry's serious look, as if he already knew the weight of his duties. The other, younger lad was smiling. He had Merry's chin. Captain Cleft.

"This is not the man I chased last night," St. Cloud said. "I knew Uncle George. I knew him well."

"But that was over twenty years ago, you clunch, and you were just a child. People change, especially when they lead hard lives. You said yourself the body they brought back was mangled. It could have been Hawkins, Merry. It could."

He sat on a stool next to her chair and looked out the window. "I said I will send to London, have my man-at-law look into the matter. But—"

"But you are not happy at the possibility. You'd prefer to think that I am a gullible nodcock and some plump old graybeard has fallen down your chimney and into the wainscoting by accident."

He took her hand. "I am sorry for thinking you were foxed or purposely trying to cause trouble. And I swear I'll try to keep an open mind." He laughed at himself, bringing her fingers to his lips. "How is that for a resolution? Is it too late? I've already admitted I was wrong about you. But, Junco, there is more to the story than you know. My mother is weak, you know that. And she went through hell for the man, not once but twice. I cannot ask her to face him again."

"It has to be her decision, doesn't it?" She returned the pressure of his fingers, trying to give him strength and comfort.

"Then where is he? If he is George, why doesn't he walk through the front door and shake my hand like an honorable man? Why didn't he come forth and say what happened that night at the quarry? You said you convinced him he wasn't a murderer."

This was not the time to tell Merry his uncle was a pirate. Then again, she thought more cheerfully, if he could accept that, he could accept a penniless nobody in the family, too. "I, ah . . . believe he's working on that now. You St. Cloud men seem to have a surfeit of pride, you know. He has his own sense of honor."

St. Cloud stood and drew her up beside him, still holding her hand. "Speaking of honor, Miss Beaumont," he started.

She pulled her hand back. "No, my lord, I know what you are going to say and I don't want to hear it. I do not want your words of honor and duty and making things right."

He brushed a curl away from her cheek, but his hand stayed to touch the soft skin there. "No? I thought marriage proposals were supposed to start that way. I am supposed to ask for the honor of your hand, and you are supposed to thank me for the honor of the offer. That's what I've always heard, anyway. I only did it that once before, you know, in the barn. But here, I've turned over a new leaf for the new year. I'll admit I could be wrong again. What words should I say instead?"

Words of love, you cloth-head, she wanted to shout. But she only whispered, "If I have to tell you, I do not want to hear them."

He was staring into her deep brown eyes as if the answers to the universe were hidden there. His fingers stroked her knitted brows, her chin, her lips, sending tremors where she did not know tremors could go. "Ah, my sweet, perhaps we do not need words after all." He bent his head. She raised hers and closed her eyes. His breath was warm on her lips. His hands had moved to her back, pulling her closer till their bodies were touching, the lean strength of his against the soft curves of hers. His breath came faster as their lips came to—

"Pardon, my lord, but there are two young persons come to see you and Miss Beaumont."

"Good grief," Juneclaire said, "what are you two doing here?"

Rupert and Newton Stanton were staring around his lordship's library as though they'd never seen so many books in one place. For all the attention they spent to their schooling, likely they had not. Root was wearing a spotted Belcher neck cloth in imitation of the Four-Horse Club, and Newt was dressed in the height of absurdity in yellow pantaloons and shirt collars so high and so starched, his ears were in danger.

After Juneclaire's introduction St. Cloud surveyed them through his quizzing glass like particularly unappealing specimens of insects suddenly come among his books. "Indeed, to what do we owe the unexpected pleasure?" he drawled.

Root squirmed and Newt felt his collar shrink. They knew Satan St. Cloud's reputation. Then again, it was his reputation that sent them here.

"Actually, Mama sent us," Root confessed. He was the eldest. He knew his duty. Hadn't Mama spent two days drumming it into him? "She got your note, saying Clarry was here under your protection."

Newt giggled nervously. "There's protection and there's protection," he continued, trying to sound worldly. Compared to St. Cloud he was as urbane as a newly hatched chick. "So Mama sent us to check."

Juneclaire was embarrassed for her family. "You gudgeons, you are insulting the earl," she hissed.

Root stood firm. "Reputation, you know. His. Yours."

"Well, of all the—"

"Excuse me, Miss Beaumont, I am not quite clear on the purpose of our guests."

Juneclaire knew from that sardonic tone that St. Cloud was very angry. "It's my fault, my lord. I should have written to Aunt Marta myself, to reassure her of my well-being. I'll just take my cousins to the kitchens, shall I, and get them a bite to eat for their return trip and send them—"

"I say, Clarry, we just got here!"

"Mama's not going to be happy, 'less she knows for sure there's nothing—"

"Miss Beaumont," the earl interrupted, in a

202

quiet, smooth voice, "prefers to be called June-claire."

The boys nodded. "Yes, sir" and "Yes, my lord." Their tutors would have been shocked to see such instant obedience. Even Juneclaire was impressed.

"Now, Master Newton, Master Rupert, you shall answer me this: Did your esteemed parent really send two unlicked cubs to ask my intentions toward her niece?"

Juneclaire giggled, thinking of his intentions not ten minutes past. He sent her a quelling look. Both boys found the design in the carpet fascinating. Put like that, Mama'd sent them to their doom. And the earl was not finished. "Did she treat her responsibilities so negligently that she did not inquire into Miss Beaumont's health, how she came to be here, or her future plans, but only the state of her virtue? Did she think so ill of Miss Beaumont to think that she might consider *carte blanche*? That does not speak well of her upbringing at your mother's hands. Finally, did you, men-about-town that you are, think that I would bring my *chérie amour* here to my ancestral home to meet my mother and grandmother?"

"That's enough, my lord. Let them be. They're only boys; they meant no insult."

"No? I wonder what they were supposed to do if they found you dishonored, call me out?"

Newt was quick to pipe up, "Oh, no, my lord, we were only supposed to tell Cla—Juneclaire not to come home again, ever. But if things were all right and tight, we were to invite you back to Stanton Hall."

"Hell will freeze over before I—" Then he noticed Juneclaire's scarlet mortification. "I am sorry, my dear, that you had to be witness to this." To the boys, he said, "You may tell your parents that Miss Beaumont is respectably established."

Root did not think such a bang-up Corinthian would shoot a fellow for doing his duty. He knew his mother would have his hide for not. "Don't see no chaperon," he stated. "Don't see no ring."

"If you want to see your next birthday, you'll—"

"With your permission, my lord, I'll introduce my cousins to Lady Fanny and the others in the morning room. Perhaps Mr. Hilloughby, the *curate*, will be there, Root."

The boys were in love, Root with St. Cloud's pastry chef and Newt with Niles Wilmott's hummingbird-embroidered waistcoat. Add to that heady mix tales of ghosts, secret passages, and lurking strangers, to say nothing of being able to tell their friends they were on intimate terms with Satan St. Cloud himself, and the Stanton boys would have sold their mother for a chance to stay at the Priory. Then Elsbeth walked in.

Miss Wilmott had been feeling sorely used, neglected, put upon, and cast in the shade. Her cousin was not going to marry her, and her father was not going to take her to London. Ordinarily two rustics barely her own age would not hold the young beauty's interest, but the Stantons treated Miss Beaumont with the greatest indifference and called Sydelle Pomeroy "ma'am," the same as Aunt Fanny! Elsbeth's Cupid's bow lips smiled at the brothers, and anyone in the room could hear two hearts fall at her feet.

"Please, Clarry—Juneclaire, ask him if we can stay. Worried about you, really, no matter what Mama said."

"And it's snowing. You don't want us to have to ride out there in that, back to dreary old Stanton Hall, not while there's such jolly times here. Please ask him, and we will give Mama any story you want about how you got here."

His brother kicked him. "Not blackmail, cuz. Stick by you anyway."

Juneclaire had taken her cousins apart from the others. Aunt Florrie wanted to count their teeth. Now she had to laugh at their earnest entreaties. "Why don't you ask him yourself?"

Newt stammered, "He's not an . . . ah . . . easy man, Juneclaire. One look from him and I feel like checking my buttons. And his reputation ain't one to let a fellow rest easy if St. Cloud imagines some insult. Aren't you afraid of him?"

She smiled. "No, he's just a bear with a sore foot sometimes, especially when it comes to things like honor and family." And me, she thought fondly.

Root looked at her with respect for the first time in her memory. "Brave for a girl, Juneclaire. Proud to be kin."

So she walked the earl over to the window to note the heavy snowfall. "I know they're not much," she admitted, "but they are mine. And perhaps you'll be a good influence on them."

"Heaven help them." St. Cloud looked over to where the others sat, the two halflings vying with each other to bring a giddy Elsbeth the choicest tidbits. He smiled. "On the other hand, perhaps Uncle Harmon will have an apoplexy."

It snowed for two days and nights. There were no visits from neighbors, no mail in or out, and no Uncle George. St. Cloud put the Stanton sprigs to work in the library, looking for a hidden latch to the trick door. The proximity to so much learning might have had an effect if Elsbeth hadn't insisted on helping, for lack of anything better to do. Her father suddenly insisted Elsbeth get some fresh air, so all of the young people went on sleigh rides and indulged in snowball fights, even St. Cloud. Then Harmon thought Elsbeth should practice her needlework more, so the mooncalves sat at her feet, sorting yarns and making up absurd poems to her lips, her ears, her flaxen curls. Uncle Harmon was tearing his hair out, and it looked as if Elsbeth was getting to London after all, anything to get her out of the reach of the nimwit brothers.

At night there were card games with the dowager, charades, children's games of jackstraws and lotteries that turned into hilarious shouting matches, caroling round the piano. St. Cloud was enjoying every minute of his uncle's distress and every moment of the lighthearted games. Even if he did not participate, or when he made up a table for the dowager's whist, he watched Juneclaire and listened for her laughter. He imagined other holidays, real children playing at jackstraws and hide-and-seek in the mazelike Priory—their children. He smiled.

The third night he suggested dancing. He wanted to hold her in his arms. Between Root and Newt, the dowager and his own mother, the earl was finding it deuced hard to be alone with Juneclaire. The dowager, Harmon, and Mr. Hilloughby were at the deal table with Talbot, the butler, who had been drafted to make a fourth. Lady Fanny sat with her needlework behind her mother-in-law to call out the shown cards for Lady St. Cloud. This was the closest the two women had sat to each other since the former earl's funeral.

Aunt Florrie was playing the pianoforte, erratically but energetically. Niles danced with Sydelle, St. Cloud finally got to hold Juneclaire, and the Stantons took turns with Miss Wilmott. The other brother turned Aunt Florrie's pages, although she never seemed to be playing the same song as in front of her. Elsbeth begged for a waltz, and Root the odd man that set, picked up Pansy, who was dressed for the occasion in diamond ear bobs and pearl choker. Everyone was laughing and gay, even Lady Pomeroy, for once, when a shrill scream rent the air.

"What is the meaning of this?" A sharp-featured woman pushed into the room, dragging a portly gentleman in a bagwig behind her past the inexperienced footman who'd been left holding the door. Rupert said, "Mama," and Juneclaire's face lost its pretty flush. Aunt Florrie kept playing.

Aunt Marta took a better look around, dripping snow on the carpet. There was a blind woman playing cards, one of her sons was dancing with a tousled hoyden, the other with a pig wearing jewels. Her niece was in the arms of the worst rake in England—with no ring on her finger! "I demand to know," she screeched, "just what is going on!"

St. Cloud bowed. He pulled Juneclaire closer to him with one hand and used the other to encompass the room. "Obviously an orgy, ma'am," he drawled. "You know, swine, women, and song."

Chapter Twenty-three

"*F*or your information, Lady Stanton, I have never seduced a female in my care, be she houseguest or housemaid." The earl chose not to recall that was before what almost happened in the attics. He had also never struck a female, but that was before meeting Aunt Marta. This was the outside of enough, being taken to task by an evil-minded old skinflint who never prized her niece in the first place and likely only wanted to wrest a healthy marriage settlement out of him. First she'd sent her husband, Avery, for a "man-to-man" talk. Avery got as far as "Nice gal, my niece. Want the best for her," before St. Cloud's frosty stare had him switching to a discussion of crop rotation. Lady Stanton was not so easily intimidated.

"We'll stay till Twelfth Night since the countess invited us; then I am taking Claire home."

"Miss Juneclaire stays as long as she wishes, with the dowager's blessings."

"Humph. We'll see about that. What future does the gal have here, I'd like to know?"

"What future did she have at Stanton Hall? Mother to someone else's brats, or your unpaid servant? She is a valued guest here, better dressed, in more congenial company, and with far fewer demands on her time, Lady Stanton. Is her happiness worth nothing?"

"Not as much as the banns being called, and I don't care who you are! Lord Stanton is still her legal guardian, and *we'll* see where Claire goes and with whom."

St. Cloud was not worried about the harpy's threats as much as the idea that she might stay past Twelfth Night, three very long days away. No, Avery Stanton was not going to challenge St. Cloud. Not even that mouse of a man was so foolish. What concerned the earl more was Juneclaire's feelings.

After luncheon he asked her to visit Lady St. Cloud with him, knowing full well his grandmother was napping. Nutley made the perfect chaperon, sewing in the dowager's sitting room; she was busy and she was deaf.

Juneclaire sat on a brocade divan near the fireplace with the kitten on her lap playing with—Drat, so there's where his tassel had disappeared to. She looked the picture of innocence in a high-waisted sprigged muslin, a soft glow on her cheeks from the fire's warmth. He knew she was also a woman of great spirit and caring. He thought she was even coming to care for him. He did not want to hurt her, ever.

"Miss Beaumont, Junco, I, ah . . ." She looked up at him with those doe eyes, her dark brows raised in expectation. "Blasted expectations!" he muttered, pacing the width of the room.

"Oh, dear. I suppose Aunt Marta's been filling your head with her flummery, my lord. Believe me, I do not expect—"

"Well, you should, and it's not flummery! I should have offered for you in form days ago. I should have asked your uncle's permission the minute they stepped through the door."

"But you did offer. You were everything honorable, and so I told Aunt Marta. There was no need—"

"There was every need, and more every day you spend under my roof even if you are too green to see it. Now it's too late."

"Too late?" Her heart must have stopped because suddenly she could not breathe. Now that he'd seen her family, he realized how impossible an alliance was. Now that she was convinced she had to marry him for whatever reasons he chose to give if she was to be a whole person ever again, he had changed his mind. He was withdrawing his offer.

"Yes, and it's all that dastard George's fault! How can I offer you my name when it may not be an honorable one? How can I discuss marriage settlements when I don't know if I'll have a roof over my head?"

"I don't understand, but none of that matters." She was perilously close to tears. He hated vaporish women.

"Of course it doesn't matter to you, Junco. You'd live in a cow byre with your goats and pigs and sheep—only you'd starve to death because you'd never eat any of them! It matters to me that I can provide for you, that you can take your place in society with your head high, not stay hidden away like my mother."

She swallowed past the lump in her throat. "Uncle George?"

"Uncle George. I didn't tell you the whole, that day in the cemetery. You'll find out soon enough, if the cad has come back. I'm just surprised your aunt hasn't filled your ears with the tale; it's common knowledge." He kept pacing, not looking at her. "George came home from the wars injured, remember? My parents stayed away the whole time, until the holidays. I don't recall if they spoke then. I was in the nursery most of the time, of course, and there

210

were other houseguests. I was brought down for luncheon that day. It was Christmas, you know, and my birthday. You have to realize that I was small for my age, and Uncle George had never been around children before. He said 'Merry Christmas, Merry. Happy fourth birthday.' And everyone laughed, because it was my fifth birthday. And then he must have counted back—I remember him mumbling while I waited for my cake. Suddenly he shouted, 'If he's five, he's mine!' and he lunged at my father, knocking him down. In front of forty *belle monde* busybodies. I have carried a certain unsavory stigma throughout my life, as you can imagine."

"But your—the earl acknowledged you."

"Who knows what he would have done if there had been another son? But he was paralyzed that day, and George was dead. I was the last Jordan. Until now. You, at least, are convinced that I am not. If George is alive, *he* is the earl."

"No," Juneclaire insisted. "You were baptized as Robert's son and reared as Robert's son. And Uncle George would never make that kind of trouble, I know he wouldn't."

"How do you know what he will and will not do? He left my father there to die, Juneclaire."

"No! Hawkins was to have gone for help. Uncle George has as much honor as you do! That's why he hasn't come back, Merry, because his past isn't quite ... suitable."

Merry stopped pacing. "Pray tell, Miss Beaumont," he drawled in that slow, deadly tone he used to frighten lesser mortals, "precisely how ... unsuitable is Uncle George's past? Where has he been all these years?"

"At sea."

"It could be worse. Other Jordans have gone into

the navy, although I suppose he signed on as a common seaman."

"Not the navy," Juneclaire croaked.

"Then a merchant marine. Better still. Perhaps he joined the East India company and made his fortune."

"I believe he made his fortune," she said, barely above a whisper. "Have you ever heard of . . . Captain Cleft?"

"Oh, God, we're all ruined. You'll go home with your aunt. Uncle Harmon will have to find Elsbeth a husband before . . . and Mother. Hell and damnation, Mother."

Now it was even more important that they find Uncle George.

Luckily the company made a short evening of it so they could look. The dowager refused to join "those toadeaters" downstairs, and Lady Fanny had taken to her bed under Aunt Marta's aspersions that the countess was not a proper chaperon for a young girl. Uncle Harmon was closeted with vinegar water and digestive biscuits, and Aunt Florrie was busy writing a letter to her dear friend Richard. The Lion-Hearted.

Sydelle had excused herself after dinner. She was leaving in the morning, despite Niles Wilmott's fervent, nay, desperate, pleas. Lady Pomeroy saw no reason to stay. With that battle-ax of an aunt in the house, St. Cloud could never wriggle out of an engagement, and Lady Pomeroy was not cooling her heels until Twelfth Night, just to see a parcel of peasant urchins dress up as Magi and go around begging gifts. She'd had enough of those bucolic entertainments, thank you, and was anxious to get back to London, even if it was thin of company. So *la belle* Pomeroy used her packing as an excuse to avoid the gathering of puerile Stantons and lost-cause St. Clouds.

Root and Newt had escaped their mother's eye to the billiard room, forsaking even Elsbeth, who quickly claimed a headache. Niles took himself off to drown his sorrows with his cousin's excellent brandy, for lack of a better idea, and Mr. Hilloughby declared he had to work on his sermon.

All of which left Juneclaire and St. Cloud all alone in the gold parlor, except for Aunt Marta and Uncle Avery. Aunt Marta did not believe in gambling, so cards were out. Juneclaire did not play well enough to entertain with music. They had no mutual friends and no common interests, and the earl and Aunt Marta each represented what the other most despised. It was not a comfortable gathering, especially in contrast to the past few nights. St. Cloud as host could not retire before his guests, and Aunt Marta would have dyed her hair red and gone on the stage before leaving her niece alone with the earl. Therefore Juneclaire yawned, and yawned again until Lady Stanton decided they would all do better with an early night. She walked Juneclaire right to her door and would have locked her in if she weren't sure that the libertine had copies of all the keys to the house anyway.

Juneclaire would just have to do her hunting without Merry. Under the heavy eyes of Pansy—Aunt Florrie had tried darkening the pig's lashes with bootblack to match Sydelle's—and with the assistance of a curious kitten, Juneclaire removed every single item from her wardrobe. When the closet was absolutely bare, she pulled and twisted, pushed and poked at every shelf, hinge, and hook. There had to be a way to get into the secret passage from her room. Uncle George had done it, at least twice. There were seams in the wood panels on the sides and back, but she could not get any of them to move. Nothing.

She rested her hands on the closet rod that held the hangers while she thought—and the bar turned under her hands. Then she rolled it the other way, away from her, and one of the panels slid back. She found it! Juneclaire poked her head through, hoping to see Uncle George on the other side, but she saw nothing, only darkness past the little circle of her own light. She thought she'd better go get Merry.

As Juneclaire backed out of the opening, though, the cat came to investigate and kept on going. "Oh, no, Shamrock. Here, kitty. Come back, kitty, kitty." Kitty did not come back. Shamrock would be lost forever, and the dowager would be heartbroken. There was nothing for it; Juneclaire had to go after the foolish furball.

She was *not* being impetuous. She made sure she had a fresh candle in her holder and another in her pocket, along with a flint. She put a hatbox in the opening to make sure it did not shut and checked the mechanism on the other side, a kick-wheel device, so she could get back in, in case.

Someone had swept the floor in the secret passage, but not well, and she could see footprints and, yes, the mark of Uncle George's peg leg going in both directions. Shamrock's went in only one. Juneclaire followed, trying to keep count of the doors, the turns, the side passages. She couldn't. She turned to check and no longer saw the light from her own room. For one awful minute she thought she'd be lost forever; maybe curiosity was going to kill more than the cat this night. Maybe Merry would be heartbroken. No, he would be relieved. Then reason reasserted itself: Merry would come after her in the morning and give her one of those dire looks and sarcastic comments. She'd better find Uncle George to lead her back.

She found the cat instead, sitting next to one of the wheel devices, licking its feet. Juneclaire picked the kitten up, hugging it more for her comfort than its. Now she had two choices: she could wander around these corridors looking for her own room for the next eight hours or so, or she could turn this wheel and pray. "Please let the room be unoccupied."

Her prayer was answered. Unfortunately, the answer was no. She found herself and the kitten in her hands in a closet so full of silks and satins and shoes and hats that there was hardly room for her to stand. A light shone through the crack in the door facing into the room, and she could hear voices. She took a deep breath. Hungary water . . . Niles. She decided to assay the dark passage again, with rats and bats and spiders, rather than come face-to-face with that slug in his bedroom.

As she was backing out of the narrow opening in the back of the closet, however, Pansy was coming in. The lonely pig's sharp nose had no trouble finding her mistress in the maze and no trouble detecting the wine and biscuits Niles had in his room. She pushed past Juneclaire, who lost her footing. Juneclaire reached up to save herself and the cat and the fop's expensive wardrobe from a fall, and grabbed onto the hanging bar, which turned, nearly shutting the rear panel on Pansy's curled tail. Pansy went flying forward, pushing open the doors.

Juneclaire followed. What else could she do? If a woman, a pig, and a cat flying out of an armoire astounded Niles and his companion, the sight that met Juneclaire's eyes was only slightly less shocking.

Somewhere in the middle of his second bottle downstairs, Niles had finally had a better idea. Instead of letting the Widow Pomeroy and her voluptuous charms—not the least of which was her ample checkbook—hie off to London in the morning, Niles had one last card up his sleeve. And a cinder in his eye.

Juneclaire's garbled account of the cat, the secret passage, and "I'll just be going now" was lost as the elegant widow, *en dé shabillé*, explained how poor Niles needed her assistance. What Niles needed was more time. The wine stood ready on the low table, the bed stood ready, and his flea-brained sister had dashed well better stand ready to burst in on them at the right moment. This wasn't it, so Niles shoved the damned interfering wench out the door.

Juneclaire leaned against the wall, breathing hard, her eyes closed.

"My, my, what do we have here?"

Her breathing stopped altogether, and her eyes snapped open. Merry, with his abominable quizzing glass, was surveying her disarranged hair, her heaving chest, her flaming cheeks. "Do you know what a good influence you have been, Miss Beaumont? I am still maintaining my New Year's resolution to keep an open mind. I find my affianced bride coming out of my loose screw cousin's bedroom, looking, ah, shall we say, hot and bothered, and I haven't even skinned him alive yet. Aren't you pleased?"

Juneclaire was happy there was a wall holding her up; for sure her trembling knees were not. "We . . . we're not engaged," she quavered.

"True. Then I'll skin him after I murder him."

"No, he didn't . . . I wasn't . . . Don't go in there!"

"Why, did you already do him in with your darning needle? And here I thought you were going to be less impetuous."

"Stop it, you gudgeon, he's not—"

"Juneclaire Beaumont, what are you doing out of your room?" Aunt Marta yelled loudly enough that Uncle Avery peered out of his room across the hall. "And you, St. Cloud, how dare you carry on in this abandoned fashion right under my very nose? I'll—"

They were never to find out what Aunt Marta was going to do because a shriek came from inside Niles's room. The earl pushed past Juneclaire and flung the door open.

When Niles tossed Juneclaire out of his room, he forgot about the pig. Pansy didn't mind, as long as the biscuits were in reach. When they were gone, she went snuffling around, looking for Juneclaire or another friend. Her wanderings took her closer to the fire, where Sydelle was leaning over Niles, dabbing at his eye with a scrap of handkerchief. Pansy whiffled closer, right up Lady Pomeroy's skirt. Hence the shriek. Sydelle fell forward, and Niles, simply doing what came naturally to an immoral, licentious lecher, pulled her down on top of him.

"Congratulations, cousin," St. Cloud said from the doorway. "May I be the first to offer my felicitations."

And Elsbeth, tripping down the hall, said, "For heaven's sake, Niles, if you changed your plan, you should have told me."

Aunt Marta declared, "Well, I never," to which Uncle Avery sadly replied, "Twice, my dear, twice."

Chapter Twenty-four

𝒯he dowager was so pleased with the match that she decided to go downstairs to see Niles and Sydelle off to London. Lady Pomeroy wanted to see the last of St. Cloud Priory, and Niles wanted to see the notice in the papers before Sydelle changed her mind. Juneclaire was walking the dowager down the long hall.

"Tell Talbot to serve champagne," Lady St. Cloud ordered. "That ought to ruffle your aunt's fur, the old hellcat. Maybe she'll take those scamps of hers and leave early."

Aunt Marta disapproved of the couple, among other things. She would not come down. Juneclaire was afraid St. Cloud really was going to send her off with the Stantons, though, so she tried to divert the old woman. "Do you actually think Niles and Sydelle will suit?"

"Like hand in glove. He'll have his glove in her pocket, and she'll have her hand on his—Well, she'll keep him under her thumb. They're both decorative, expensive fribbles, with less morality than alley cats. He'll have his gaming and clubs, she'll have her respectability and a title when Harmon sticks his spoon in the wall, and they'll both go their own ways. Perfect marriage, my dear, perfect."

"I think it sounds perfectly horrible, cold and mercenary."

"Wouldn't do for just everybody, mind, but those two? Besides, it'll get them out of my grandson's house. Now, if I can just remind Harmon that the older Stanton twit will inherit a tidy pig farm one day, and won't he and Elsbeth be happy in Farley's Grange, I might get them out of here also. What are you giggling about, girl? You don't think Harmon's already figuring that Sydelle has that London town house and the right connections to fire Elsbeth off? Trust me, the man's liver mightn't be up to snuff, but his wits ain't gone begging."

She was right. Lord Wilmott had decided that Sydelle needed his chaperonage on the journey to London and Elsbeth's help with the wedding plans. Root's and Newt's hearts were breaking as they stood on the steps waving farewell to their first love, until the earl invited them to help exercise his bloodstock. Lady Fanny waved her handkerchief to the departing coaches, and Aunt Florrie waved a dead halibut.

Juneclaire helped the dowager back inside and made her comfortable in the morning room with the rest of the champagne. "Fine day's work, my girl," the dowager said, lifting her glass to Juneclaire. "Now if we can just see the dust of your relatives, the place will be near livable again."

Juneclaire rearranged some figurines on the mantel. "I . . . I'm afraid I'll be leaving with them, my lady."

"Gammon, you're engaged to my grandson. You belong here."

"No, my lady. I am not really engaged. He just offered because he had to."

"Nonsense, girl. Satan St. Cloud hasn't done anything he hasn't wanted to since he was in short

219

pants. You're good for him, miss. I could hear him laugh when you were dancing and such."

"But Uncle George . . ."

"Faugh, you haven't got your eyes on a man old enough to be your father, have you, girl? He's Fanny's. Always was and always will be, though heaven knows what he or his brother ever saw in the widgeon. Robert wanted her, too, you know. Always jealous, even if he had the title and estate. For the life of me I don't know how I raised two such bobbing-blocks. If you tell me my lobcock of a grandson is making mice feet of his future now, too, I'll take my cane to the both of you, I swear I will. But don't worry, girl, George'll bring him round."

"Then Uncle George is here, and he can tell Merry about—?"

"He said he'd make it right. Soon. Word of a Jordan."

Juneclaire couldn't wait, not if Aunt Marta was going to carry her away after tomorrow night's celebration marking the end of the holy season. It may as well be the end of Juneclaire's life, she thought dismally. Aunt Marta was already guarding her like a rabid sheepdog, not allowing her two minutes alone with Merry, following her to her bedroom and coming back an hour later to make sure Juneclaire was in bed, alone, with her door locked and bolted.

Locks and bolts on the bedroom door meant nothing to Juneclaire, of course, but no one had thought to ask how she came to be in or out of Niles Wilmott's bedroom last night. She had no chance to explain to Merry about the trick of the secret passage until now. It was his house; he should know.

Juneclaire wrapped a warm shawl over her shoulders and turned the bar. It was much harder, with the hangers all back in place, but the back panel finally slid aside. She counted doors until she was behind the master suite, she hoped. She turned the wheel and the door opened, revealing . . . nothing. She was in an empty closet. She mentally recounted doors and rooms, until she realized she must be in the mistress's chamber. The unused bedroom reserved for the countess, Merry's wife. Good. At least now she—and Pansy, of course—wouldn't have to burst out of my lord's closet like blackbirds from a pie. She nudged the wardrobe door open, waiting for protests from unused hinges, but rust must be another one of those things unacceptable in an earl's residence. Edging her way out of the closet, she tiptoed toward the right, where light showed under a connecting door. Juneclaire listened for a minute, in case Merry's valet should be with him. Should she knock? Maybe this wasn't a good idea after all.

As usual, Pansy took matters into her own . . . knuckles. She knew a friend was on the other side of the door, and she knew her friend had something to eat. She grunted, loudly.

"What the bloody—"

Pansy trotted through the now open doorway, but Juneclaire stood where she was. She never thought he'd be naked! Or half-naked, for he did have britches on, but his chest was bare except for dark curls that spread to where his hard muscles tapered into a lean vee that disappeared to where he *did* have britches on. She didn't trust that gleam in his green eyes, and why the rogue picked now to smile she never knew, but when she lowered her own, they saw—Oh, dear, this wasn't a good idea at all.

"It's not what you think, Merry," she hurried to say. "I am not here to compromise you like Niles. Not that *I* meant to compromise Niles, of course, for you know I did not."

His smile broadened. "If you are not here to cry

foul on me, my dear, I am completely and devotedly at your service."

"I am not here for *that* either, you gamecock." If her cheeks were any warmer, they'd surely burst into flame.

He pressed his hand to his heart, reminding her that he had no shirt on, as if she needed a reminder, and said, "You wound me, Junco. I thought my last Christmas wish was coming true."

"Why . . . why you are foxed, my lord!"

"Either that or I must be fast asleep and dreaming, for the oh-so-proper niece of the redoubtable Lady Stanton could not be standing in my bedroom in her night rail. No, I must be jug-bitten because in my dreams you aren't wearing any heavy flannel wrapper. In fact, you aren't wearing—"

"Merry! I came to tell you about the secret passageway. I found the trick to opening the doors in the wardrobes."

"Did you? I always knew you were a clever girl." He had her hand and was leading her toward an enormous canopied bed in the center of the room.

"Merry, you don't understand. We have to go find Uncle George." She tugged to get her hand back.

"Oh yes, Uncle George." The name seemed to sober him, for he released her, but he sank down on the bench at the foot of the bed. He did not seem eager to go search for his missing relative. "Good old Uncle George, the pride of the Jordans."

Juneclaire sat beside him. "Merry, maybe the situation isn't so bad. Lady St. Cloud thinks he can fix things. He promised her."

"And Aunt Florrie thinks King George is going through a stage, like teething." He brushed her long braid back off her shoulder and put his arm there. "I'm sorry, Junco, truly I am. I wish things were different. I wish I could have made your wishes come true. You almost made mine, you

222

know. You helped get the Wilmotts off my hands, and you showed me how happy this old pile could be." He pulled her closer.

"And I felt welcome here, as if I truly did belong, so my wish almost came true, too."

They were quiet for a moment, thinking of what might have been. Then they both started to say, "I wish . . ." at the same time. "You first," Juneclaire told him, nestling at his side.

"I wish there was a way, that's all, without dragging you through a scandalbroth. You?"

"I wish you weren't quite so honorable, my lord, because none of it matters to me." She turned her face up for his kiss, and not even the earl was noble enough to turn down what she was so sweetly offering. He did groan once, but that may not have been his conscience complaining.

Some while later, Juneclaire was half out of her nightgown and more than half out of her mind with wonder at the strange new feelings throbbing through her. Somehow she and Merry were no longer on the bench but were in the middle of his wide, soft mattress. If Merry was whispering her name and nonsense in her ear—and he was, for she could feel the tickle of his breath—then someone else was in the room with them.

"Well, Pansy girl, looks like history repeats itself, all right. If this isn't the way the whole argle-bargle started, my name ain't Giorgio Giordanelli."

Juneclaire looked up. There was a Romany Gypsy at the foot of the bed, complete with flowing shirt, scarlet sash, and colorful scarf tied at his neck. He also had a thick gray beard, a fat belly, and a peg leg. She giggled. "It isn't."

He tossed her a blanket. "But it has been, puss, it has been."

The earl had been struggling to regain his composure if not his buttons. He sat up and made sure

Juneclaire was decently covered before turning to the apparition. "Uncle George, I presume?"

"In the flesh. Or should I say in the nick of time?" He met the earl's hard, green-eyed stare with one of his own. "Are you going to make an honest woman out of her, or am I going to have to run you through?"

"That depends, *Uncle*. Do I have any honor? Are you going to leave me with a name I'd be proud to offer a woman?"

Uncle George sat on the bench and lifted the pig up next to him. "Are you proud of Satan St. Cloud?" he asked, and Juneclaire was astonished to see Merry flush. She was also amazed to see where the color started. Catching her glance, Uncle George snorted and threw the earl his paisley robe from the bottom of the bed. Merry's muffled curses did nothing to ease Juneclaire's embarrassment.

"Don't tease, Uncle George," she begged. "Just tell him what happened."

The earl crossed his arms over his chest and sat back against his pillow, like a pasha holding court. "Hold, Junco. I am not even convinced this . . . Gypsy is my uncle. He could be a horse thief or a fortune-teller."

George shook his head. "You know, Merry, I think I liked you a lot better when you were a curly-haired tyke."

"And I think I liked you a lot better when you were dead. Do you have papers? Proof?"

"I have friends working on the paper stuff. But proof?" He scratched the pig's ears while he thought. "You were just a wee lad; I'm not sure how much you remember. Then again, you weren't as young as I thought. Let's see. I found my lead knights for you in the nursery and we repainted them, but there was no red paint, so we stole one of your grandmother's rouge pots. Your pony's name was Thimble, but any of the old grooms would know that. They wouldn't know about the day you tried taking him over a hurdle without a saddle, a groom, or permission, because I promised I wouldn't tell, after I found you, picked you up, and brushed you off. Fanny'd have kept you off a horse till you were twenty if she knew you'd been thrown."

"And you brushed off the back of my pants a trifle more vigorously than necessary, if my memory holds."

"You didn't try that stunt again, did you?"

"No, Uncle George, I didn't. Do you still have the crescent scar from the wound that sent you home that time?"

"Still testing? You know it was shaped like a seven. Lucky seven, we called it. Want to see?" He reached for his sash.

Juneclaire hid her face against St. Cloud's robe. He laughed and she could hear the rumble in his chest. Then St. Cloud sighed.

"God, how I missed you when you died. No one would say why, just that you were too evil to talk about. What the hell happened?"

George got up and poured himself a glass from the decanter on an end table. "Two hotheaded fools, that's what happened. You know about the party?" They both nodded. "I was beside myself and dragged Robbie outside until he agreed to meet me at the old quarry. We went, with no surgeon, no seconds, no witnesses, only my man Hawkins to hold the horses. I cooled down along the way. He always loved Fanny, too, you know, and I hadn't been there when she needed me. He was. So I was going to delope, I swear it. But he shot first, got me in the leg. As I fell, my gun discharged and the shot hit Robbie. It looked bad. He begged me to take what money he had and run away so I wasn't charged with murder, because all of the guests heard me threaten to kill him, and only Hawkins, my own batman, could say nay. I was scared, I was bleeding, I didn't know what to do. So we decided that Hawkins would ride for help and I'd head for Portsmouth and wait for Hawkins to come for me with news." He poured another drink and downed it in a swallow. "He never came. I was in no frame to do anything, delirious, sick, my leg turning uglier and uglier until some butcher amputated the thing and saved my life, I suppose. I cursed him enough at the time. I knew Robbie was dead or he'd have sent for me, even if something had happened to Hawkins. I couldn't face Fanny or my mother, not with one leg and a murder charge against me, so I signed on as junior purser with a cargo ship bound for Bermuda. After that I never wanted to ask about the St. Clouds because I never wanted to hurt more. We went aground, but that's another story. Just know I never meant to kill your father, Merry."

"I believe you, but why did you come home now, after all these years?"

"Not to steal your inheritance, boy, or cause trouble. Robbie called you his son, and you're the earl. I never wanted the title or the Priory either. I'm getting on, Merry, and I just wanted to see Fanny one more time. But she ain't happy, and it fair breaks my heart all over again. I mean to have her this time, if she'll forgive me and if I can straighten up a few loose ends."

"Like a price on your head?"

"I have some friends working on that." He poured another glass but let Pansy slurp this one.

St. Cloud raised his brows. "What are you going to do, if you clear the minor detail of being a criminal, set Mother up in London for the gabblegrinders to picnic on, or take her on the high seas?"

"I'll take her to Town if she wants to go; there's

226

nothing to be ashamed of. And I'm retired, boy, so you don't have to fear seeing her face on a reward poster. I thought she'd be happiest on my island in the Caribbean. You know, flowers and warm weather, beaches."

"You have your own island?" Juneclaire asked.

"I was a *very* good pirate, puss. As I see it, if I get those confounded papers, then I can try convincing Fanny. I daresay I've changed in the twenty years." He ignored Merry's rude noise and Juneclaire's giggle. "I should know by tomorrow. That ought to answer your questions about the family honor, Merry." He nodded toward Juneclaire. "You mind answering mine?"

Juneclaire blushed again, but Merry threw his uncle's words back at him: "I should know by tomorrow."

George laughed hard enough to shake the bed. "None of my business, right? In that case I think I better escort Miss Beaumont back to her room, Merry, since *you* ain't so clear about your intentions." He ignored the earl's furious scowl and turned to Juneclaire. "I'd wager you were the clever one to find the trick panels. This mutton-head must have looked for years. But you were lucky. There's another mechanism in the passageways, a trapdoor that drops trespassers right down to the cellars, unless you know the key." He winked at her. "I'll tell the bacon-brain *that* secret on your wedding night."

Chapter Twenty-five

$\mathcal{J}$uneclaire went to bed without worrying she'd have nightmares about falling through trapdoors. She had no more fear of being dragged back to Stanton Hall in disgrace; she'd stay here in disgrace if she had to. But she was not really worried. Juneclaire was not going to let Merry's pride, or hers, come between them, and no pitfalls either, no matter what Uncle George said.

She woke up smiling and eager. Today was Three Kings Day, Epiphany, Twelfth Night, when Christmas wishes came true. She crossed her fingers, rolled over in bed three times, and said, "Rabbit, rabbit, rabbit," before her feet touched the ground, although that was supposed to be for May Day. She hugged Shamrock for luck and Pansy for good measure.

St. Cloud was showing Uncle Avery the home farm, and the boys were in the stables, most likely losing their allowances to Foley and the other grooms in dice games. The dowager and Lady Fanny were still abed, and Aunt Florrie was helping in the kitchen. Juneclaire took Pansy to visit the Penningtons and Ned rather than sit with Aunt Marta in the morning room listening to lectures. She still had too much bridled excitement after her visit, so she took Flame out for a walk to burn up some energy and minutes.

For dessert after lunch Talbot carried in the traditional Twelfth Night cake, which was supposed to have a pea and a bean hidden in the middle, denoting the king and queen for the day's festivities. Aunt Marta declared it a pagan ritual from pre-Christian days and refused to have anything to do with such rigmarole. Aunt Florrie looked near to crying, so St. Cloud ordered the footman to cut the cake quickly and pass the servings around. Florrie had been toiling all morning, helping make the batter, she told them in a reedy voice. She worked very hard, she said, making sure no one would be left out when the cake was cut. Why, she'd put in a cherry pit saved from last summer and a bit of a colored egg from Easter. A button, a pencil stub, a pussy willow catkin, one of her dear nephew's baby teeth, one of those pretty red mushrooms . . . Eight forks hit eight plates at once.

Late that afternoon they traveled in two carriages to the village of Ayn-Jerome for the local celebration. Aunt Marta went, she said, sniffing in Mr. Hilloughby's direction, only to see a proper church. In truth she did not like being alone in the hulking Priory with no one but servants.

There was a candlelight parade down the main street, headed by three boys dressed in loose robes and paper crowns, followed by the other local children, some dressed as shepherds. They led the adults into St. Jerome's Church for the service and a reenactment of the arrival of the three kings bearing gifts for the Holy Child. Afterward, there were trinkets and pennies, sweets and fruits given to all the children, and mummers, acrobats, and jugglers performing in the torch-lit street. Food stalls were set up, ale was passed round with servings of roast venison or beef, St. Cloud's contribution. The villagers toasted him, his house, and one another.

Root and Newt got a trifle above par, Lady Stanton sat rigid as a rail in her carriage, Juneclaire searched every face for Uncle George, and Aunt Florrie brought home some holy water, since Pansy had never been baptized.

The evening lasted forever, it seemed to Juneclaire, sitting on tenterhooks next to the dowager in the gold parlor. Lady St. Cloud obviously knew something was in the offing, too, for she patted Juneclaire's hand and urged her to keep reading, when Juneclaire's eyes kept straying to the door. The earl was as stone-faced and serious as ever, except for the dancing light in his eyes when he glanced Miss Beaumont's way.

Finally Talbot walked into the room with his stately tread, his head held high. "My lord, my ladies," he pronounced, "there are callers." He paused and gulped audibly. "Lords Caspar, Melchior, and Balthasar." Then he turned and fled.

Aunt Marta's jaw hung open and Aunt Florrie clapped. The three wise men had indeed come, not in rough costumes, but in velvet and ermine and satin, with gold crowns and jewel-laden pendants, each bearing a silver casket on a pillow.

The youngest, Caspar, coughed and stepped forward. "We come from Lon—ah, the East, where, ah, great tidings are heard."

The oldest, Melchior, adjusted his spectacles and pulled down his fake beard so he could speak his piece. "We come bearing gifts."

Balthasar, his clean-shaven face blackened with cork, opened the chest he held to reveal a king's ransom in jewels and gold. Juneclaire squeezed the dowager's hand, quietly describing the scene. Then Balthasar hopped forward on his peg leg and laid the casket in the younger countess's lap. "For you, Fanny, all for you. And don't you dare swoon, because it took me long enough to coach my players and you have to pay attention."

Lady Fanny's lip trembled and she was shredding her handkerchief, but she did not go off in a faint. St. Cloud came to stand behind her, his hand on her shoulder.

Uncle George peered at her, then nodded. "Always knew you were stronger than you let on. Anyway, didn't know what you'd do with frankincense or myrrh. Buy you all you want, if you say so, of course. Thought you'd be happier with this." He directed Caspar forward.

Mr. Langbridge, the solicitor, bowed at Fanny's feet and lifted the lid of his chest. "A royal pardon, my lady."

"And a pretty penny it cost me too, Fanny. Half my island, the sugar plantations, and two of my ships. Don't worry, though, puss, there's plenty left. Oh, and Prinny might throw in a knighthood if I pay a few more of his debts." He beckoned to Melchior.

Melchior stepped forward with twinkling eyes and opened his offering. Then he started to sneeze so hard from the cat in the room that Uncle George had to take over Vicar Broome's lines.

"It's a special license, Fanny. Will you do it? Will you marry me at last?" He wasn't fool enough to get down on one knee, not when the other was a piece of ivory, but he sat next to her, reaching for her hand.

Tears were falling from Lady Fanny's eyes—and a few others in the room—but she raised her handkerchief to wipe the blackening from George's face, leaving him an older, heavier, gray-haired, and sunweathered version of the boy in the portrait, but with the same straight nose and cleft chin, and the same love for her shining in laughing eyes. "Can you forgive me for not waiting, George? I tried, but I did not know where you were, and the baby . . ."

"Can you forgive me for doubting you? For staying away so long?" He suddenly recalled the avid audience, family, guests, servants crowded in the entry, and pulled Fanny to her feet. When they were near the door, he turned back and took another paper from one of the silver chests. George tossed it to the earl, saying, "I brought you a gift, too, my lord. It's another special license. Merry Christmas, Merry."

St. Cloud took two glasses, one of the champagne bottles opened in celebration, and Juneclaire's hand. "Come, my love." He frowned down Lady Stanton's incipient protests and smiled to Aunt Florrie, decking Pansy with the pirate's treasure like a porcine Christmas tree.

When they reached the library, he quickly looked around. "We never did find the secret panel for this door. I can only hope Mother keeps the old scoundrel busy for a while." He poured the wine and held a filled glass to Juneclaire. He raised his and toasted: "To happiness and laughter, and joy ever after, and you by my side. I cannot be as dramatic as Uncle George, but will you be my wife, Juneclaire? Will you make me the happiest of men?"

"To satisfy your sense of honor?" Juneclaire knew the answer, but she wanted to hear him say it.

"Honor be damned."

That was not good enough. "Because Uncle George gave you no choice?"

"Because my heart gave me no choice, Juneclaire."

He put the glass down and reached into his coat for a small box. "A gift for you."

Juneclaire waited while he opened the box. A ring rested on a satin bed, a square diamond crowned with an emerald, a ruby, and a sapphire. "It's the St. Cloud engagement ring. Will you accept it, my love?" He was putting it on her finger before she could answer. That was good enough.

"But I have no gift for you," Juneclaire protested.

"You have already given me so much, my family, my home. That's more than any man deserves. Yet I ask for the greatest gift of all. Will you give me your love, too, Juneclaire?"

"You don't have to ask, Merry. It's already yours and always has been."

He lifted his glass again but brought it to her lips. "To us." After she sipped, he turned the glass so his lips touched where hers had been. "Now all my wishes have come true." Then he shook his head, put the glass down, and went to lock the library door. He came back and took her in his arms. "On second thought, I still have one wish. . . ."

He was, regrettably, poor. Having inherited nothing but a pile of debts, an impoverished estate, and an improvident young stepmama along with his title, Aubrey, Viscount Wellstone, was a few pounds and a diamond stickpin away from debtors' prison. He had few practical skills, no calling to the church, and no affinity for the army. He did have a gentleman's education, of course, which meant he was equally as useless in Latin and Greek. So Stony, as he was called by his many friends, turned to the gaming tables.

He was, even more regrettably, a poor gambler.

He lost as often as he won, never getting ahead of his father's debts enough to make the ancestral lands more profitable, or to make sounder investments. Before he turned twenty-six, the diamond stickpin was long gone, following his mother's jewels, his grandfather's art collection, and every bit of property or possession that was not entailed. The Wellstone fortunes were at low ebb, nearly foundering on the shoals of bad speculations, bad management, and sheer bad luck.

Then one night the tide turned. No hidden cache of gold was found behind the walls of Wellstone House in Mayfair, none of his stepmama's suitors was suddenly found suitable, nor had Stony finally resigned himself to that age-old cure for poverty: finding an heiress to wed. Neither had the viscount's skill with the pasteboards miraculously improved. In fact, he lost heavily to Lord Parkhurst that evening at the Middlethorpe ball.

"One more hand," Stony requested as politely as he could without begging, as that middle-aged gentleman rose stiffly to his feet, gathering his winnings. "One more hand to recoup my losses."

Lord Parkhurst shook his head. "I'd like to stay, my boy. Lud knows I'd play all night. But I promised my wife I'd look after her youngest sister. It's the squinty one, but the last of the bunch, thank heaven. I swore I'd make sure the girl has a partner for dinner and all that, so she doesn't look like a wallflower, you know. Not that dancing with her own brother-in-law will make her look like a belle, I swear, but my wife seems to think she'll show to better advantage on a gentleman's arm than perched on one of those spindly gilt chairs."

Everyone knew Parkhurst danced to whatever tune his pretty young wife was calling, so Stony wasted no more time trying to convince the man to stay. He scrawled his initials on an IOU and handed it over. He'd be handing his fob watch to the cents-per-centers in the morning, right before he started packing for Wellstone Park in Norfolk. He shuddered at the thought of his stepmama's tears when he informed her they would have to put the London town house up for rent. He was sincerely fond of Gwen, who was barely ten years his senior, but Lord, her tears would make the leaks in the Park's roofs seem like a trickle. He shuddered again at the thought of Gwen never finding a gentleman to wed, not among the turnip growers and sheepherders in the shires. He took a long swallow of brandy. At least the Middlethorpes wine was free. Maybe he'd ought to go fill his pockets with their chef's lobster patties. Heaven knew his pockets were empty of everything else.

"Damn if I wouldn't rather have you take my place," Parkhurst was saying, holding up the voucher, "than take your money."

Stony set down his glass and brushed back from his forehead a blond curl that needed trimming. "My lord?"

Parkhurst cast a longing look at the fresh decks of cards on the green baize-covered tables, the gray, smoke-shrouded room filled with like-minded gentlemen, the maroon-uniformed footmen with their decanters of brandy. Then he looked at the white scrap of paper he held. Stony held his breath.

"Why not?" Parkhurst said, a smile breaking across his lined face as he took his seat again. "My wife did not say I had to do the pretty with the girl myself, just that the chit wasn't to be left sitting alone all night. A handsome young buck like you, Wellstone, could do a lot more for her popularity. Why, if such a top of the trees beau pays her court, the other chaps are bound to sit up and take notice. At least they'll ask for a dance, just to see what had you so interested." He picked up the pack of cards and started shuffling. "The more I think about it, the better the idea sounds."

It sounded too easy to Stony. "I won't marry her, you know."

"Humph. If I thought you had intentions of sniffing after her dowry, I'd have to call you out. What, let the chit run off with a pockets-to-let gamester with nothing but his pretty smile to recommend him? She might have a squint, but the gal's still my sister-in-law."

Stony was not smiling now. He stood to his full six-foot height and looked down his slightly prominent nose at the older man. "If I had wished to repair my fortunes with a wealthy bride, sir, I could have done so any time these past few years."

"Aye, and you'd have picked a female with a bigger dowry and better looks, I am sure. That's why I made you the offer. Everyone knows you ain't shopping at the Marriage Mart. I'm not saying that trying to repair your fortunes at the tables is any nobler than marrying a girl for her money, but at least you've got principles. And you've never been known as a womanizer, like so many other wastrels, trading one bit of muslin for another as fast as you change your waistcoat."

Stony had never been able to afford to keep a mistress, much less a closet full of waistcoats. The occasional willing widow, now, that was another story, one he deemed irrelevant to the current conversation.

"By George," Parkhurst was going on, "my wife would have my head if I handed the girl over to a rake. But you're not one to ruin a gal's reputation, I'd swear, not when you know you'd have to pay the preacher's price. No, you're a gentleman born and bred, one who can show an innocent girl a good time and keep the fortune hunters and reprobates away without breaking her heart—or my wife's." He took the slip of paper again and raised his brow in inquiry.

Stony fixed his blue eyes on that debt he could not pay. "One night?"

"That's it. One ball that's almost half over already and you'll escort the ladies home so I don't have to leave the game in the middle. Agreed?"

Stony nodded. "Agreed."

Parkhurst ripped up the voucher.

Viscount Wellstone turned the female's squint to a sparkle.

A career was born.